HOPE'S PROMISE

a Novel

a Novel

TAMMY BARLEY

WHITAKER
HOUSE

HOPE'S PROMISE
Book Two in The Sierra Chronicles

Tammy Barley
www.tammybarley.com

ISBN: 978-1-60374-109-5
Printed in the United States of America
© 2010 by Tammy Barley

Whitaker House
1030 Hunt Valley Circle
New Kensington, PA 15068
www.whitakerhouse.com

Library of Congress Cataloging-in-Publication Data

Barley, Tammy, 1969–
  Hope's promise / by Tammy Barley.
    p. cm. — (The Sierra chronicles ; bk. 2)
  Summary: "In the rugged Civil War-era Nevada Territory, newlyweds Jake and Jessica Bennett find their faith tested by severe drought, cattle stampedes, and the betrayal of a trusted friend"—Provided by publisher.
  ISBN 978-1-60374-109-5 (trade pbk. : alk. paper) 1. Newlyweds—Fiction. 2. United States—History—Civil War, 1861–1865—Fiction. I. Title.
  PS3602.A77557H67 2010
  813'.6—dc22
                        2010010591

2 3 4 5 6 7 8 9 10 11 UJ 16 15 14 13 12 11 10

Dedication

To the enduring memory of Uncle Hank Gosselin and to all who bring happiness and hope to others.

Acknowledgments

My deep appreciation goes to...

Terry Burns, literary agent extraordinaire,
and to my "brother" in China, Chen Likai, for his valued friendship and gracious assistance.

You will be secure, because there is hope;
you will look about you and take your rest in safety.
—Job 11:18 (NIV)

Chapter One

May 1864
Western Nevada Territory

W ould you care to rest awhile, Jess?"

Suppressing a smile, Jess leaned forward in the saddle as her horse clambered up beside Jake's to the top of the rocky bank. When the ground leveled out, she glanced at the progress of the small herd of Thoroughbred stallions close behind, then tossed a lightly accusing gaze at her husband.

"Rest awhile? Are you coddling me, Bennett?"

In the shadow of his hat brim, Jake's whisky-brown eyes sparkled at her as he grinned the crooked grin she loved. "No, ma'am, I wouldn't dare." He nodded sagely to Taggart and Diaz, the hired men, who wore bandanas pulled up over their faces against the rising dust as they wrangled on the opposite side of the herd. "But the boys haven't stood on their own feet twice since sunup, and they're looking peaked."

"Peaked?" Jess looked at the burly, orange-haired Irishman and the sinewy, born-in-the-saddle Spaniard and burst out laughing. "Those two wouldn't walk to their dinner plates if they could ride!"

Whistled on by the two cattlemen, the sleek, long-limbed Thoroughbreds continued toward the mountains, their heads bobbing. From her position riding flank, Jess took in the beauty of white noses and ankles flashing amid the bays, chestnuts, and blacks, all framed by the red earth and green pines of the Sierra Nevadas.

They were going home.

Jess quieted, but her smile remained. "I couldn't stop now, Jake. We have only ten miles to go before we reach the ranch."

Ten out of seventeen hundred, she mused, *and eight months since I've seen this part of the country.* When they had left the ranch, they hadn't been married and she hadn't been certain she'd ever come back. Even so, she hadn't forgotten the beauty of the mountains, her love of the ranch in Honey Lake Valley, and her dream to raise horses with the good man beside her.

Jess's horse stumbled, then recovered. Amid the scattered rocks and fragrant clusters of gray-green sagebrush around them, desert flowers added brilliant splashes of purple, red, and orange to the landscape. When they had left the ranch, the land had been brown, dry from a year of heat and drought. Clearly, the winter snows and spring rains had come, for, now, life bloomed everywhere.

Well, almost everywhere. With a twinge of sadness, Jess pressed a gloved hand to the flatness of her stomach.

She and Jake had married in the fall, on one of the most beautiful autumn days God had ever created, at his father's farm. As a wedding gift, Jake had given her the herd of Thoroughbreds, which had been grazing in the paddock while the pastor had stood with them beneath an arch of trees and joined them as husband and wife.

All she had wanted had been to give Jake a child in return. And now, it seemed she was barren.

"What do you suppose they're thinking, your horses?"

Jess dropped her hand and smiled. "*Our* horses," she corrected him. "They're probably wishing they had taken a train, instead."

Jake chuckled, his broad shoulders threatening the seams

of his white cotton shirt. "Is that what you wish, Jess? That the Pacific Railroad was nearly finished instead of only beginning?"

"No, I wouldn't want to be packed into a noisy passenger car any more than you would. I'd rather see the land, be a part of it."

"Well, this land looks as though it's seen some rain this year."

"I was just thinking the same."

"What else were you thinking?"

Jess glanced at him. Since the day they'd met in Carson City more than a year before, she'd often been startled by how closely he paid attention, how he seemed to know her thoughts. "Mostly, I'm looking forward to seeing everyone at the ranch," she answered evasively. "Ho Chen, Doyle, all the Paiute women, and Two Hands…. I wonder how many of the mustangs Lone Wolf was able to breed."

The Bennett Mountain Ranch. Our ranch. Tickled by the thought, Jess laughed out loud in pure joy.

"Jess?" The curiosity in Jake's voice pulled her gaze to his.

"We're going home," she said, a pleasant tightness in her chest. "I feel…." She lifted a hand, uncertain how to describe it. "I feel like a young falcon about to soar into the wind for the first time."

He smiled with understanding, then suddenly turned tense, alert. He drew his Remington. An instant later, Taggart and Diaz did the same.

"What—?"

Suddenly, a rock burst on the ground beside Jess. The sharp report of rifle fire echoed across the desert. All at once shots exploded, pelting the road around them with shattered stones and dust plumes. Drawing her own revolver, Jess whipped her mare around and looked past Jake to an outcropping of rocks, where rifles barked as gun smoke curled away.

The mare abruptly jerked, then reared high, spilling Jess's hat and causing her long braid of hair to tumble free. The horse teetered on its hind legs, then fell over backward.

Pain exploded through Jess's back and lungs.

Then, darkness.

An image flashed through her mind—the ranch, only not as they'd left it. Where the workshop, supply shed, and stable had once been, large, black smudges marred the ground. Eerie dread filled her at seeing the vision and at realizing that, though she could see the ranch compound, she could hear no wind, no movement, no sound at all.

There was a flash of daylight, then Jess felt the sharp rocks beneath her back and smelled the pungent tang of gun smoke. Pain seared through her right arm. Beside her, she saw her horse—its neck spattered with blood and bearing a bullet hole—thrash once more, then lie still.

"Jess?!"

Her gaze shifted to the back of Jake's boots, which stood rooted a few feet away, his long legs and broad shoulders tense. He had positioned himself and his horse between her and the outcropping of rocks. The gunfire had stopped. "I'm all right, Jake. You?"

His hat shifted with his answering nod, but his attention remained fixed on the distant rocks. Finally, he turned and went down on one knee at her side. "The gunmen are gone."

"And the Thoroughbreds?"

"Taggart and Diaz just rode after them. They'll bring them back." With great care, he leaned over her and felt her ribs, but pain ripped through her side, and she winced and caught her breath. "Anything feel broken, Jess?" he asked as she winced again.

"I don't believe so, but my ribs hurt when I inhale."

He pressed gently on her left side where she pointed, shifting his big hand before pressing down again. "I can't feel any movement through your corset. I suspect that contraption just saved you from anything worse than bruising. Your ribs will likely hurt for a few weeks, especially when you breathe in, but they should heal fine." He glanced at the cut on her arm that had begun to burn like fire, then stood and retrieved a bottle of whiskey and a clean bandana from his saddlebag.

With her good arm, Jess carefully pushed herself up, forcing herself not to groan from the pain in her side. Ranchmen never complained, even when shot. She had become one of them, and she wasn't about to fuss over a little bruising and a simple cut.

Jake walked a few paces to where her hat had fallen on the other side of the dead horse, then hesitantly returned it to her. She pulled it on, sensing his concern for her with the simple gesture, and felt overwhelming relief that he hadn't been injured in the attack. "Jake, those men couldn't have been outlaws. They must have been Paiutes."

He looped his horse's reins around his arm and handed her the folded bandana. "Those were my thoughts, as well. If they'd been outlaws, they would have gone after the horses."

He'd known, Jess realized. That was why she'd seen him fire only warning shots into the ground. She and Jake had friends among the Paiutes, and several Indian families worked at their ranch.

"Bands of Paiutes have been trying to warn off immigrants for the last few years," he said, "shooting from the hills along the Lassen Trail and north of Pyramid Lake. Apparently, things have gotten worse, and the Paiutes have gotten bolder. You're wearing britches, and your braid was up under your hat. When your hat fell and your braid came free, they took off, so apparently they're just warning folks away. None of the Paiutes I've met have ever killed innocent settlers."

"But why attack this far south? You're not the only rancher around here who employs them."

"I agree, it doesn't make sense." Jake looked toward Taggart and Diaz, who had regained control of the Thoroughbreds less than a mile away. One man rode on either side of the herd, heading toward Jake and her at an easy pace to calm the skittish horses. "Let's see your arm."

Blood had soaked into the blue flannel shirtsleeve along her forearm, and from the throbbing pain, she knew it was more than just a simple cut.

Something flickered in Jake's eyes. "You were shot?"

"No, I wasn't. I must have hit it on a rock when I fell. Come to think of it, I lost my gun." She briefly scanned the ground for it, but he eased the sleeve up her arm and she looked away, certain that if she saw the wound, it would hurt more. "How bad is it?"

Jake held her forearm in his hand and gently rotated it. "It's a gash, but I won't have to stitch it."

The cork made a dull *thunk* as he pulled it from the whiskey bottle. The bottle glugged, and then searing liquid ran over her arm with the piercing sting of a branding iron. She drew in her breath. Her ribs screamed.

"Bennett!"

"Do you know you call me Bennett only when you're put out with me?" He poured more whiskey.

Jess hissed through her teeth, then smiled a little at the tease in his deep, mellow voice. "I think it's a habit."

"To be put out with me?"

For the sake of her ribs, she fought against a chuckle. "No, to call you Bennett in front of the men." Jess knew he was keeping their conversation light on purpose. "If the men hear me call you Jake, it might change your status in their eyes. They don't need to see you as my husband; they need to see you as their boss."

"Only on the range, Jess. When the doors close at night, there will only be you and me."

Jess stiffened as though she'd been struck. He'd wanted to reassure her with his words, she knew, yet it was a painful reminder that she still wasn't expecting after nearly seven months of marriage. *But,* she told herself, *what matters most right now is the ranch, and building it with Jake.* A quarter of a mile away, Taggart and Diaz had dismounted and now stood, talking, keeping a casual watch on the desert while the horses grazed. Their horses, hers and Jake's. Horses that would enable them to be less dependent on cattle for their income, and to be one of the first ranches in the northern Sierras to raise horses to sell. If only…. Now that they were out of danger, she allowed herself to ponder the odd vision she'd seen. The cold fear returned, and her knees and legs began to tremble.

"Jake, when I fell, I saw something…in my mind."

In the shadow of his hat brim, his sun-bronzed face turned thoughtful. Jake corked the whiskey bottle and set it aside, took the cloth from her hand, and began to bind the wound. "What was it that you saw?"

"The ranch compound, except some of the buildings were gone, as were two of the corrals," she recalled. "Only one corral remained. Where they had stood, the ground was black, as though barrels of gunpowder had been spilled. Seeing it scared me, Jake. I saw it for only a second or two, but in that instant, it felt as real as if I were actually there. Then I opened my eyes and saw the horse beside me, and then you. I think something bad is going to happen."

Rather than wave her off or make excuses for what she had

described to him, he remained beside her, an elbow on his knee, looking pensive. She loved him for always listening to her.

"Has this ever happened before?"

"No. I have felt strongly about the outcome of various events, though, so strongly that I knew what would or wouldn't happen. A year ago, when Ambrose was listed as missing in the war, I knew my brother wasn't dead. I *knew* it."

"I remember. You also told me last autumn that you believed outlaws would attack the ranch, and then they did."

"So, you believe me?"

"I don't doubt that you saw what you say you did. Yes, I believe you." He briefly scanned the foothills, and she followed his gaze; there was no unusual movement among the rocks and sagebrush. "Do you remember my pa's neighbor, the older lady who walked with two canes?"

"I met her just once, but I remember her."

"When I was a boy—no more than nine or ten—she hurried over one night in a fluster and told my pa a tornado was coming, no more than an hour out. Almost exactly an hour later, the tornado struck and took out half our corn before it dissipated. Later, she told my pa that she occasionally had feelings about such things and even saw a number of events before they happened. Premonitions, I reckon. I've heard about other women with similar foresight, whether or not their husbands have the good sense to listen to them. No, I won't discount what you've told me."

"But you don't believe it."

"I won't lie to you, Jess. I'm not sure if I believe it or if I don't." He reached over and lightly squeezed her good arm. "Let's just take things as they come."

Jess struggled not to feel disappointed, but she was glad Jake had listened to her. Within hours, they would learn firsthand if what she'd envisioned had, in fact, happened.

As Jake helped her to her feet, she dearly hoped they would find the ranch to be just as they'd left it, but she didn't believe it would be so.

At Jess's insistence that she would no sooner ride double due to her injuries than Jake would have in her position, Jake had pulled the saddle, bridle, and gear from the dead horse and saddled the Thoroughbred stallion he would ride so that Jess could ride his calmer quarter horse. That was the only thing she'd concede to.

Jess was more willful and determined than a Chicago storm.

Lord above, he loved that about her.

Unfortunately, it also made his gut churn in agony.

When her horse had fallen over and crushed her beneath it, his heart had nearly exploded. He'd held his breath as the gelding, struggling to rise, had rolled over her again, thrashed, and then finally lain still beside her. Years ago, about twenty miles south of where they were now, his first wife, Olivia, and their baby daughter, Sadie, had been on their way to visit family when a band of outlaws had attacked and killed them both. Jake had nearly died himself when he'd discovered their bodies. He couldn't endure losing Jess or seeing her harmed again.

The premonition Jess had described sat like a passel of thorns in his mind. He could work through whatever came, but what about Jess? She had been raised the daughter of a horse breeder in Lexington, Kentucky, and when her family had moved west, she had kept the books for her father's business, Hale Imports. She had not been raised for this life. She was strong and determined now, but what if years of the hardships of living and working on a ranch in the wilderness became too much for her, as they did for many ranchers' wives? The fear had entered his mind weeks ago, when he'd lost several of their Thoroughbreds to Plains Indians, and the gunmen's attack—and what she'd suffered as a result—had solidified that fear. Would he eventually lose her?

"Bennett?" came Jess's voice, pulling him out of his musings. "Your face has turned as stiff as iron. I can tell you're worried about something. What's on your mind?"

Rimmed with long, sooty lashes, Jess's sage-green eyes bore into his as she brushed several loose strands of her brown hair from her face. Her soft, rose-red lips revealed she was all woman, even though she rode with the ease of a man, albeit having a care for her injured side. He hadn't been alone with her for a single moment in weeks, even after nightfall, and now her ribs were injured. Though he'd waited with great patience all this time to be alone with her in the ranch house, what he'd had in mind would have to wait until she'd healed. All that mattered was that he keep her safe and give her a horse ranch to replace the one in Kentucky she'd loved and left behind four years ago.

He eyed her revolver, which was holstered once again in the gun belt at her narrow waist. Seeing to it that she was safe and happy was no small task. Trouble seemed to follow her—that is, when she wasn't out looking for it.

One of the Thoroughbreds started to break from the herd. Jake changed its mind with a quick wave of the coiled rope in his hand, then forced a new thought into his own head so he could answer her without dishonesty. "Well, Mrs. Bennett, I was just hoping there'd been enough rain to make the river run high again. I plan to sink right into it, boots and all."

Jess's rosy lips curved into a smile. "You'll rust your spurs."

"Hardly. After riding for weeks behind this herd in all the

dust they've been raising, my spurs'll need a good soaking just as much as I will."

"Perhaps," she agreed, "but that's not what turned your jaw to iron. Plus, a muscle in your neck stood out when you glanced at my gun."

Jake sighed. A dozen or so yards ahead of him and Jess, Taggart and Diaz were riding in comfortable silence, their attention on the herd. There was little chance they would overhear. Even so, Jake discreetly lowered his voice. "What's on my mind is that, for years, you held your family together, despite the war's efforts to pull you apart, and you were strong for your ma before she died. You didn't have anyone to depend on but yourself for a long time, and I respect all you did for them. But—"

"But I'm impulsive."

"No. Courageous."

Jess blinked.

"You weren't born for this life, Jess, and the Almighty must have known you'd need plenty of courage, because He surely gave you a barrelful." He grinned, then more soberly looked at the bandana he'd knotted on her forearm as a makeshift bandage. "I'd just like you to tell me if this life ever becomes... hard for you. I'll do whatever I can to keep that from happening, even if we have to give up the ranch and move on."

Her eyes flashed green fire. "Not born for this life? Bennett, do you think I'd rather be dungeoned up in the dank corner of a store, tallying rows of numbers, than be here with you? And what about Olivia? You married her and 'subjected' her to ranch life, too."

"Times weren't hard for Olivia and me. Besides, she *was* born for this."

"I grew up in the South, amid political upheaval, secession, and the knowledge that, during my lifetime, war would come and possibly destroy all I held dear. How would you have replied if I had said that to you?"

Jake lifted a shoulder, acknowledging her point. "I probably would have said that trials build character. But I was brought up this way. You and I are different."

"Look again." Jess huffed indignantly. "I thought I was the one who fell off a horse and had the sense knocked out of—"

"I don't want to lose you."

At his confession, her angry expression abruptly vanished, and her face held only understanding and love. "Then I'll be careful not to get 'lost.'"

Jake returned his attention to their herd. Her words sounded nearly as soothing to his mind as the smooth, Southern accent with which she had spoken them.

Lord above, he loved that about her, too.

"Hey, boss," Diaz called over his shoulder to Jake. "Those *vacas* are on your ranch, but they don' carry your brand."

Jess peered at the herd of eighteen or twenty cows grazing about an acre's length away. Diaz was right. Instead of Jake's sideways B brand with the flat side down, each red-and-white hide bore a circle with an M in the center. The cows leisurely enjoyed the Bennett Ranch's bunchgrass as if they'd always called the place home.

The nearest ranch was located so far from their own that Jess had never seen another brand within a mile of the compound. That uncomfortable realization, coupled with the fact that none of their ranchmen, mustangs, or cattle were in sight, fueled her apprehension.

Something was very wrong.

The men whistled the Thoroughbreds on, and, finally, over the tops of the sagebrush, the ranch buildings came into view.

The massive stable should have been the first building they saw. It was gone, and none of the smaller structures that had once huddled beside it remained to block the view of the barn.

Jess felt rather than saw Jake tense beside her.

The Paiute village that had stretched along the riverbank lay dismantled and scattered, as if the wigwams had been forcibly torn apart and the branches dragged beyond the outskirts of the camp.

Taggart and Diaz exchanged troubled glances but drove the horses the final distance into the compound.

Where the workshop, supply shed, and stable had once sat, large, black smudges marred the ground. Only one of the three corrals Jake had built remained.

In silence, Jake, Taggart, and Diaz guided the stallions into the sole corral, and Jess gingerly closed and latched the gate, her sore ribs reminding her not to move too quickly.

The men stepped to the ground, then tied their reins over the top rail of the corral. While Taggart and Diaz began to unload and unsaddle their horses, Jake gently lifted her down.

Jess also untied her saddlebags and set them aside, then loosened the cinch strap. Though the buildings that had stood on the east end of the compound had been destroyed, the barn to the north and the smithy and cookhouse to the immediate west of it seemed to be in good condition, although no inviting, fragrant smoke rose from the cookhouse chimney. Southwest of the cookhouse, the bunkhouse lay low and long as it always had, and south of that—between Jess and the initial slope that led up into the Sierra Nevada Mountains that she loved—rose the pine logs that formed the two-story ranch house. Its wide, front window, brown with dust, would benefit from cleaning, and the porch and the two steps leading up to it looked weathered and in need of repair.

By all appearances, the ranch had been deserted, except

that to the west, beyond the bunkhouse, the garden had been planted, and, beyond it, on their property, someone had built a new house.

The silence was shattered by the loud, metallic cock of a shotgun. All of them spun to face the ranch house.

Chapter Two

The front door opened slightly, making a gap less than a hand's breadth, and a long, steel gun barrel pointed out at them, supported by a sturdy, black-skinned fist and forearm. "State your business!"

Jake sighed and rested his gloved hands on his hips. "Doyle, it's Jake," he called out.

"Boss?" The end of the barrel slanted down toward the porch. "That you?" Cautiously, the tall cattleman eased the front door open and ducked his head under the lintel as he stepped out, his shotgun butt still tucked against his shoulder.

Jess pushed her hat back on its strings and let her braid fall into view. She'd really have to quit wearing men's britches.

Recognizing them, Doyle relaxed and approached with a grin, and they all met halfway between the porch and the corral for firm handshakes. He smiled down at Jess. "It sure is good to see you again, ma'am."

"Doyle, please call me Jess, as you always have. Where are the other cattlemen? The Paiutes? Ho Chen?"

The cookhouse door creaked open to reveal a round, yellow-brown face atop a short, trim frame. "Miss Jessie?"

"Ho Chen!" Jess hurried to him as quickly as her side would allow, happy tears threatening, stinging her nose. The ranch cook, her longtime confidant, bowed neatly, as was his way, revealing the long, black braid that trailed down his back. He smiled broadly and, having witnessed the careful way she walked, patted her gently on her shoulder.

"What has happened, Miss Jessie?" He looked over at the four horses they'd arrived on. "Where is Mr. Ambrose?"

Jake and the others joined them at the cookhouse, and the men exchanged greetings. With the exception of Ho Chen, all the men stood heads, shoulders, and chests above Jess. She was tall for a woman, but she'd almost forgotten that Jake had hired only giant cattlemen. Or, perhaps, God just didn't make short ones. She lifted her chin to meet their eyes, glad to be reminded of this amusing aspect of home.

Jake answered Ho Chen. "I image we all have questions, but first we need to feed and water the horses."

Ho Chen smiled and pushed the cookhouse door wide. "By time you are finished, supper will be ready. Come, Miss Jessie. You sit; I fix."

Jess's boot heels echoed on the wooden floor, and she paused to take in the spacious, whitewashed room she remembered so well. The wall nearest the door was studded with a row of coat pegs, and the simple yet solid plank tables stood end to end, six tables in two rows, bordered on each side by long, serviceable benches, their legs heavily dinged from spur rowels, just like nearly every inch of the floor.

To the right, an enormous, custom-made sideboard divided the kitchen from the mess hall. Beneath it, open-fronted shelves were divided into cubbyholes that stored boxes of teas, spices, discarded ammunition boxes full of forks and spoons—she always laughed at that—and a hand mill covered with a layer of coffee-colored dust. Opposite the sideboard, Ho Chen lifted an empty cauldron from the hearth of the wide, stone fireplace and arranged logs to start a fire. To the left of the fireplace, in the corner, Ho Chen's bunk was neatly made; to the right, a narrow door led out to the pigpen.

Jess knew that the lidded barrels that lined the floor between the sideboard and fireplace contained flour, oats, sugar, salt pork, beans, salt, and coffee. She looked inside a few to check the supply. They were nearly empty.

The long table piled with tin plates, crockery mugs, and iron skillets had previously held baskets of dried fruits, nutmeats, and jerky, but Jess didn't see any baskets at all. Above her, only a few remaining braids of chili peppers and onions dangled from nails hammered long ago into the low beams. Now, dozens of bare nails protruded from them.

Ho Chen's fire had begun to crackle cheerfully, but Jess felt as hollow as a dried reed in a cold, December wind. How could so much have changed?

When Jess, Jake, Taggart, Diaz, Doyle, and Ho Chen were gathered around one of the tables for a supper of stew and biscuits, Jess addressed Ho Chen's earlier question about Ambrose. "My brother rejoined the war," she explained. "I'd wanted to bring Ambrose back here, but Kentucky is his home, and the war goes on and on. He felt he needed to stay."

Beside her, Jake broke open a biscuit and glanced up at Ho Chen. "Reese—remember, the thin, young ranch hand who rode east with us?—he's the one who snuck into the prison camp to get Ambrose out. After he saw the cruelty the Federals inflicted on the prisoners, he left us at my pa's farm and headed south to enlist." Jake's voice held the sincere tone of apology Reese would have wanted to convey to Doyle.

Across the table, Doyle's dark face showed a private battle between the pain of betrayal and the acceptance of Reese's choice. Jess squeezed his hand. "You know Ambrose and Reese don't believe in slavery any more than I do."

"I know, Jess. Every man in that war is fighting for his own reason." He pointed a thumb to the thin, silver wedding ring on her finger, apparently ready to change the discussion. "I knew

23

the first time the boss slapped eyes on you he'd be giving you one of those."

"Ha-ha!" Taggart had said little during the past few days, but now his round belly shook as he elbowed Doyle and winked a blue, Irish eye at Jess. "The first time the boss saw ye, a Unionist mob was draggin' ye out of a telegraph office, and ye were howling like a banshee. Ye were what he needed, all right." With mock solemnity, he nodded his head of bright-orange hair. "The boss here was a kind soul to save those boys from ye."

The men chuckled, but the moment of levity quickly faded. Jake nudged his plate to one side. "What happened here, Doyle?"

Doyle took a deep breath. "Last autumn, about a month after you rode out, a gang o' white men come, their horses packing near as much weight in lead as they did men. Said the Paiutes had no business taking pay that rightly belonged to white men, and that they come into the valley to 'clean out' ranch Indians." Doyle wiped his face with his hand, as if trying to rub out the memory. "Those men done run them off. Lone Wolf and some of the others came back a week or two after, though they left the women and children with relatives in Idaho Territory."

Stunned, Jess abruptly set down her spoon. "Lone Wolf's son, Two Hands, the Paiute women…they're all gone?"

"Yes, ma'am. They was good folk. I was sorry to see them go. All stayed quiet around here for a while. Then, this spring, a few more Paiutes showed up with a couple of their women."

On Jess's right, Ho Chen bowed his head and quietly laid his hands in his lap but said nothing.

"About a fortnight ago, a sorry-looking group of those white men showed up again, drunk and mean as jackals. They shot up the place and tore apart the Paiute village, and then one of them threw a lit cigar onto the dry hay in the stable." Doyle shook his head. "The flames took over quick. We got the horses out, but the stable came down, and those two sheds caught fire. Hank—he's the new neighbor—he come lickety-split out of his house, barrel first, and let his shotgun do the talkin'. I guess those men was sober enough to get the message, because they took off like the devil himself was a-shootin' hellfire."

Taggart's hairy, orange eyebrows lifted. "So, *that's* why ye came out of the house ready to spit lead."

"That's right. Mostly, folks hereabouts are decent, but some come intending trouble. You can't be too careful." Jess clenched her hands, her attention rapt as Doyle continued. "After they left, we know we couldn't do anything to stop the fire, so we just let it burn out."

Jake looked at Doyle and Ho Chen. "I would have done the same," he assured them.

"I appreciate that, boss," Doyle said. "The next mornin', Will and Ho Chen and me saw to it that the Indian folks got to their reservation at Pyramid Lake, and Lone Wolf and some of the others left to fight with the Paiutes in the north against the white men who attack them. Seth and Hank took the horses— yours and Hank's—to your captain friend at Fort Churchill. Seth is staying there, watchin' them so none of them gets run off again."

Self-loathing cut through Jess. She knew that if she hadn't allowed Jake and the others to take her east, if she had gone alone, they would have been able to stop all this.

Diaz pulled a knife from its sheath on his belt and took a small hunk of wood from his vest pocket. He leaned his elbows on the table and, with the blade, started carving away delicate peels of wood. The calmness of the activity was belied by the tight lines in his brow and the alertness in his gaze. "The line camps are gone? And how did this *hombre*, Hank, build a house on the boss's land?"

Ho Chen answered. "Mr. Hank come right after first men attack. We take Paiutes to reservation, help them settle, then come home one week later. Many men build for Mr. Hank; house already half complete. Other Bennett ranch land sold, and another man buy land past the new house. He has not yet built, but Mr. Hank say the man took down winter line camp houses right after he buy land."

"Boss, Hank is a good man," Doyle said. "I didn't figure you'd want us to run him out after he bought his property from the government land office. He didn't know they'd parceled up your ranch."

"You figured right," Jake said. "The government land sale wasn't his doing."

"That's it?" Jess fumed. "The government simply sold off portions of land ranchers like you bought and paid for under previous laws and walked away with the money? You filed preemptively to prevent this!"

"That's where Hank and Will are now," Doyle said. "Hank realized what the land office had done, and he's gone to see to it that you keep the rest of what's yours."

Jess shared a look of reluctant forbearance with Jake. "Well, bless Hank for that," she said.

Jake took a drink of coffee, and Jess saw the gesture as it the much-needed respite it was—a chance to absorb all that Doyle and Ho Chen had told him. "Are those cattle with the circle-M brand Hank's?" he asked Doyle.

"Yeah, they are," the big man answered. "The other ranch hands who worked for you last year left before winter. You saw that the river's low? Well, only a little snow fell, and even less rain this spring, just enough to grow a little grass. Before long, it'll dry out. They saw this coming and went to find work someplace far from here."

Jess stepped up onto the bottom rail of the corral and rubbed the silky, chestnut nose of the horse that had nudged her for attention. Evening had set in. To the west, the last glimmer of sun disappeared behind the silhouetted peaks and smooth slopes of the Sierra Nevadas.

As her hand shifted to the stallion's cheek, Jake's hand caressed her back. "The horse looks contented," he murmured against her ear. "You have a special touch."

"So do you." Jess yearned to turn her head and kiss him, but the three ranchmen filing from the barn hefting bundles of hay for the Thoroughbreds made her hesitate. Jake dropped his hand and discreetly moved a few steps away. Jess fought her annoyance that, though they were home, she and Jake still were not alone. "It was good to enjoy beef and potatoes and vegetables again after going for so long without."

"Ho Chen said the supplies are low," Jake said. "We'll have to replenish them soon. Would you go over the books in the morning and count what's left to see how much currency we have available?"

She smiled over her shoulder at him and allowed her voice to flow with sultry, Southern charm. "If you ask real nice."

"Jess...." He half grunted, half groaned. "Your ribs are bruised," he said quietly.

Doyle and Taggart dropped their bales into the corral and headed back to the barn, but Diaz entered through the gate to feed the horses—the "little beauties"—by hand.

"We'll talk about it later, Bennett," Jess promised as she and Jake left the corral and strolled in the direction of the ranch house. Suddenly, she shivered and halted.

Beyond the house, thick, night shadows overlaid the foothills. Sagebrush dotted the rocky base of the Sierras, giving way to the occasional juniper tree, and, even higher up, pines lined the first of countless summits. Jess's gaze darted to every branch that trembled, every patch of darkness that appeared to shift its shape. Her cheeks burned with awareness.

Jake stopped beside her. "What are you looking for?"

"It feels like we're being watched," she murmured.

Jake's own sharp eyes probed the dark mountainside. "You saw someone?"

"No, I just—" She sighed. She couldn't see anyone. "I just know."

"I don't see anything."

"Neither do I. But I feel someone there."

"Jess, we were exposed to danger for a long time while we were crossing the Plains and the Rockies, and we lost eight of the Thoroughbreds to Indians. It may take a while for you to realize that you're safe."

Jess forced herself to remain reasonable as they continued toward the house. "I know, but I was right about the premonition. The ranch turned out to be just as I saw it."

Jake's look of concern turned to one of understanding. "I'll have a look around in the morning."

Gratitude filled her. That was as much as she could hope for. "Thank you."

They stepped onto the porch, where an orange cat lay, sphinxlike, in front of the door, the end of its tail twitching in curiosity as its unblinking eyes studied them.

"Are you still here?" Jess crouched down to scratch its ears. It leaned its head into her hand, purring in contentment. "Did you and Olivia ever name her?"

Jake crouched beside her and rubbed the cat from neck to tail. "No, we just referred to her as 'cat.' I don't see the point in naming an animal that won't come when it's called."

Jess smiled and allowed Jake to help her up. He pushed

open the door, invited her to precede him inside, then closed it behind him.

"It's dark as a mine shaft," she said.

"If you wait there, I'll light a lamp." Jake moved past her to the right, his heavy footfalls stopping in the vicinity of the fireplace. The glass chimney squeaked against the brass brackets of its collar, and when a match was struck, a wide flame danced and crackled atop the wick. Jake replaced the glass and turned the wick higher.

He stood at the mantel of the fireplace, a duplicate of the one in the cookhouse. On the sloped, pine ceiling two full stories above, its uppermost chimney stones edged the elongated, dancing circle of lantern light. Beyond the chimney, plank stairs ascended to an upper hall no bigger than a small rug. Three doors stood beyond the rustic, homey, stick-and-branch railing.

Jake returned to Jess's side and took her hat in a silent offer, hanging hers and his own on two pegs near the front door.

Jess surveyed the main room, furnished simply with a leather sofa, two matching chairs, and a low table, all arranged around the hearth. At the back of the room, near the bottom of the stairs, Jake's desk sat in the shadowy corner, buried in envelopes and papers. "Everything looks in order," she commented. In truth, it looked perfect. The last time she had stood here, this house had been Jake's, and she had stayed as a temporary guest. Now, this house was hers, too, and she could stay forever.

Jake entered the short hallway between the fireplace and the stairs, glancing into the small kitchen on the right, then the dining room on the left, which they had never used. "Yep, everything's just as we left it." As he turned around and reached for Jess's hand, his gaze darted to the large window facing the compound, and he pulled it back. "Shall we go to bed? I put our saddlebags in the bedroom."

He led the way upstairs, carrying the oil lamp, but instead of following him into his room on the left, Jess entered the room a few steps away to the right—the room she'd stayed in the year before. The window in the far wall admitted meager starlight, which illuminated the high, sloped ceiling. She could see that the bunk was there, as was the tiny mirror nailed to the wall beside it, but the other furnishings were missing.

"Jake?" She moved back into the hallway and paused at his doorway. The lady's dressing table and her old trunk sat across the room on either side of the window that she knew faced the mountain, and her saddlebags perched on the brightly colored Indian blanket that covered his bed to her right. Standing on the other side of the bed, Jake took off his shirt and tossed it onto the floor beside the tall chest of drawers. Atop the wooden surface sat the oil lamp, casting warm, golden light over his skin.

He set his hands on his hips, a casual stance that rather nicely emphasized his chest and the arm muscles fully capable of lifting a yearling calf.

Jess wanted to touch him, to feel him against her. She could hardly breathe. "Do you have any idea what that does to me?"

He gave a slow, crooked grin as he rounded the bed and approached her. "My throwing my shirt on the floor? Apparently, it makes you sway on your feet in appreciation. I'll have to do that more often."

Jess lifted her face and matched his smirk. "Only if you're fond of picking it up again."

With soft laughter, Jake sat on the bed and began to remove his boots. Jess took advantage of the moment to move her saddlebags to the floor and open the top drawer of the dressing table. Within it was nestled the jewelry box Jake had crafted for her last summer. Through its beveled glass lid, she could see the diamond and sapphire earrings that had belonged to her mother, an inlaid rose-and-vine-patterned comb, and the emerald pendant Ambrose had given her for her birthday, just as she had left them.

She lifted the box out, raised the lid, and fingered the shimmering mementos. Next, she opened the bottom drawer of the dressing table. The letters Ambrose had sent her several years ago from the war—his handwriting, his thoughts— remained securely bundled there.

These items were all that she possessed to remind her of her late mother and her brother. During every day of the eight months they'd been away, though drunks had invaded the ranch and burned the stable, the cattlemen had kept these secure. Her heart felt lighter than it had since they had arrived home.

Jess tucked her treasures back into the drawers and slid them shut, then lifted her gaze to the window—and felt the unsettling sensation she had experienced earlier return. "Jake, would you mind if I turned down the lamp?"

Jake's bare feet sounded on the floor, then his hands gently pressed her arms in understanding. "I'll blow out the flame."

A moment later, the room was dark, and Jess, invisible now to anyone who might be out there, shook off her concern for the night. She could just make out Jake's form. Six foot one without his cowboy boots and hat, and he belonged to her. She silently thanked God for His gracious favor.

Jess wasn't sure if one of them moved, or if both of them did. All she knew was that he was unbuttoning her shirt, and she was reaching up to kiss him. Suddenly, she gasped in pain as her ribs protested what they had in mind.

"Jess." His movements had stilled.

"I'll know you'll have a care for my ribs, Bennett, and I can't go much longer without touching you. Please...."

He lowered his mouth to her cheek, and she turned her face into the kiss, loving the taste of his lips as they warmly caressed hers, the feel of his arms as they closed around her and carefully pulled her against the solid chest she admired. He smelled of all things wonderful—horses, leather, and man. He deepened the kiss, and suddenly her fingers were in his hair, clenching, wanting, needing.

Finally, his mouth drew back, and his whiskers rasped her cheek. "You mentioned that if I'd like you to look over the books, I'd have to ask you real nice."

"Definitely." Her fingers slid down his sides and then up his back, trailing along the sickle-shaped scar that stretched from his ribs to his shoulder blade, the scar brought about by falling timbers when he'd tried to save her parents and baby sister from the fire that had destroyed their house.

Jake's hands tilted her face to his, and his dark eyes searched hers with concern. "Does my back bring you bad memories?"

"Not anymore. Now I see your scar as the mark of a man who risked his life to save my family."

Jake didn't say anything more, nor did she. They both had lost people they loved, but then they had found each other, and a new love. And Jess knew that they both would cherish every moment God gave them. Beginning now.

Jake leaned up on a bare elbow and began to untie the bandage on Jess's arm by the light of the moon, which had finally risen.

Jess turned her head on her pillow to watch his ministrations. "Has it stopped bleeding?"

"Well, let's have a look." He removed the last of the bandage. "No more bleeding. Looks like it'll heal well." After pulling on his trousers, Jake dampened a towel in the water basin beside her dressing table, then eased onto the bed beside her. "If you'll just sit there and be gorgeous, I'll clean what I can away from the cut."

Jess smiled at the unexpected compliment, then thought about their return to the ranch hours before. "I was so disappointed at what had happened while we were away," she said.

The damp towel stilled. "You mean, you wish you hadn't come back?"

"No, I mean I wish I had never let you leave with me. If you and the others had stayed here, none of this would have happened."

The towel resumed. "Maybe not and maybe so. Nothing has happened that can't be fixed. I built the first stable, and we can build another one. I was more concerned about you, that another loss would be hard on you, and that you might not want to stay."

"Just where do you think I'd want to go, Bennett?"

"You've mentioned Greenbriar."

Both the comment and his tone chafed her. "I grew up there, and I loved it, but my father left Greenbriar to Ambrose. Besides, it's in Kentucky. Do you think I'd rather be ducking Yankee bullets than the kind they're firing in the West? This is our home. This ranch is our Greenbriar. You're letting me help you turn it into a horse ranch. Yes, we have obstacles to face, but that would be true anywhere. We might as well face them in the land we love." She lifted her hand and traced his jaw with her fingers, then tried to speak more calmly. "I once told you that I refuse to lose anyone else I love. Do you think I'd ever find happiness again without you? The ranch will survive; we'll both see to that. Other than the ranchmen, I don't know what kind of people you're accustomed to, Bennett, but I don't look at circumstances and see what can't be done; I see only what I can do. You're right—we can rebuild the stable, and anything else that unravels. But I have to tell you, I didn't marry you for the ranch. I married you for yourself, a man of honor." With her thumb, she softly caressed his bristly cheek. "If we lost the ranch, you'd never be less than the man you are. You'd never give in; you'd never allow circumstances to beat you. I'm not with you to share the good times, Bennett. I'm with you to share the journey."

In reply, Jake leaned down and kissed her tenderly, then eased away, shaking his head in wonderment. "I can't imagine any man who saw you not asking your pa permission to marry you."

"Three men did ask my father, Bennett, before we moved here from Kentucky. All were handsome and successful, and they offered elegant homes and a place in society. But that wasn't enough for me, so I didn't marry them. I was waiting to find you."

Silver moonlight gilded the side of Jake's handsome face as he smiled. "Do you always get what you want?" he teased.

Jess's heart plummeted. Beneath the Indian blanket, her stomach remained flat. Barren. "No, I don't get everything I want." *Oh, Lord,* she prayed, *why can't I give this wonderful man a child?*

"Jess, what's making you so sad?" He lay close beside her, freely giving his attention and comfort. "I've seen that expression on your beautiful face now and again since winter. Is it your brother?"

"It isn't Ambrose. It's just a matter I have to settle for myself."

Rather than press her, which, as he certainly knew by now, would result in nothing more than time squandered, Jake patiently eased under the covers, enclosed her hand in his own, and held it on his pillow between them.

Jess drifted in and out of sleep, exhausted from weeks of riding but tormented by sore ribs and her body's inability to conceive. The latter issue weighed heavily on her thoughts and intruded into her dreams. Finally, she awoke to the sound of Jake's deep, even breathing. *How will I survive all our years ahead with this terrible longing?* she wondered.

In his sleep, Jake stirred, and she felt a tug along her arm. Between them, still clasped within his hand, lay hers, her pale skin against his bronze, their fingers endlessly entwined.

Chapter Three

Y ou're up early, Jess."

Seeing Jake stride toward her, tall, bronze, and manly, loosed a swarm of delighted butterfly wings somewhere in the region of her heart. She'd known Jake for more than a year, yet he still triggered the same strong attraction each time he unexpectedly appeared. It always took a moment for the wonder to fade into the realization that he was truly hers.

He leaned a brawny forearm on the desktop beside her, bringing his handsome face and whiskey-brown eyes level with hers. "I'd have thought you would have slept longer. None of us got much rest during the journey."

Beneath the brim of his brown hat, his eyebrows formed a steady ridge that could gather into a fierce scowl when some injustice was done, lower in deep contemplation, or soften in teasing, in gentle regard, and even love—when he would permit it to show, as he currently was doing. The creases at the outer corners of his eyes always followed the subtle shifts of his brow, and the angular lines of his nose and mouth, as well as the hard muscles of his habitually unshaven jaw, added to his virile, roguish bearing.

The inner butterflies reached tornado strength. Her hands ached to reach out and—

Jess grabbed two fistfuls of the dark-blue flannel that stretched over his solid chest and pulled his mouth to hers. Without hesitation, he kissed her back, and her thumbs searched beneath his bandana, trailing the warm skin along his neck. His fingers wove through her hair, holding her just as intently as she held him.

Reason gradually returned, and, with it, the sounds of men moving about the compound and a low fire crackling in the hearth. Early...he'd said something about her waking early.

Reluctantly, they released each other, but his forearm remained beside her, his hand doing delightful, distracting things down her side.

"You were up even earlier than I was," she said. Then, "Bennett, if you wish to have a conversation with me, you'd best put a little distance between us."

When he searched her face, she was certain her cheeks were flushed, because he grinned as he stood to his full height and leaned against the wall.

"Ho Chen left a pot of coffee and a mug by the fireplace for you," Jess told him, trying to change the subject. "Did you search the foothills?"

Jake moved toward the fireplace. "For more than two hours, every place where a man can stand, sit, or lie and still see the ranch. There are no strangers out there, Jess. No reason at all to fear."

"Are you sure?"

"Certain." He poured himself a mug of coffee, then pulled one of the leather chairs around and settled into it. "What have you learned from the numbers and receipts?"

Jess gestured to the account book and the two neat stacks of papers on the desk. *Good tidings first*, she cautioned herself. "Well, from what I learned from Doyle this morning, the government land sale has created a bit of a land rush, and a lot of folks have been immigrating into northern California—the land survey revealed that the ranch is in California and not Nevada Territory, as a matter of record—and Lone Wolf was able to get a decent price on the cattle he sold last autumn.

Ho Chen purchased all the food they needed for the winter and spring, and there are enough coins left from the sale to resupply for the summer and fall, buy wood to build another large corral, and hire several men to help out for the season."

Jake took a sip of coffee, then rested the mug on his knee, his eyes never leaving her face. "And the unpleasant points?"

"Buying the Thoroughbreds and then wintering at Fort Laramie cost dearly." She sighed. "I'm so sorry your father's neighbors couldn't abide my accent."

"Because we spent the winter there, we were able to get home sooner. I don't regret it at all, Jess."

"I'm glad we're home, too, but we spent nearly all we took east with us. We have enough from the cattle sales to keep *us* until winter, but with half the ranch land sold, the remaining one hundred cattle and the horses have half the available forage. The lack of rainfall means that the little grass we do have will soon die, and since there was even less rainfall than snow, the lakes and rivers didn't fill from snowmelt this spring. The acres of land our neighbors bought was where we grew the grains we needed to feed the cattle through the winter and to sell for additional income, so we won't have that, and we have no stable to house the horses if next winter brings a decent snowfall. If this summer is as dry as the past three have been...I don't know how we'll survive another year."

Jake set his coffee mug on the table, then rested his elbows on his thighs as he weighed what she'd told him. Seeing his broad, roughened hands, which hung between his knees, relax—the same hands that had built a sound, thriving ranch from a desert wilderness—inspired confidence that swelled up from Jess's middle until her mind began to fill with possibilities. Individually, each of them had overcome terrible hardships; together, they could move mountains.

"We have three hundred twenty acres left," Jake said.

"With good rains, that would feed one horse per acre."

"As it is, we'll need two or three acres for each cow. That'll leave no room for the horses."

Guilt bit her hard, and she tucked the papers, account book, and pencil into the desk drawer. Jake was converting his cattle ranch into one for horses to please her. Firmly, she tamped down the debilitating guilt and reasoned that cattle in northern California and Nevada Territory were plentiful and no longer in high demand. Converting to a horse operation had been the right choice. If the animals survived the summer heat, if steady rains came, and if heavy snows fell throughout the coming winter, they would do more than survive. They would flourish, all the while doing what they both loved. All those *if*s currently appeared most unlikely to favor them, but, somehow, she and Jake would find a way. "So, do we sell the cattle?" she finally asked.

"We'll sell all but thirty. We'll keep ten for meat and twenty for breeding and milk."

"That leaves two hundred thirty acres for the horses. At three acres each," Jess swiftly calculated, "we can have as many as seventy-six horses now, and can sustain more than two hundred during years with good rainfall. Counting our mustangs and the ranch horses, which Seth is looking after, and the Thoroughbreds, we probably have close to seventy in all."

"Some of the mares were expecting when we left and should have foaled by now," Jake pointed out. "That number may be closer to eighty."

Jess laughed. "Diaz is going to love that. Doyle said he and Seth and Will bred the Morgan stallions with the mustangs a few months back, so we have until next spring to ready this place for about forty new colts and fillies." Jess rocked back in her chair, envisioning the young horses frolicking through the sagebrush. "With the harsh summers and winters we've had, wolves and bears will come down out of the mountains to hunt. If we don't want to contend with stampedes, we'll have to fence off the land," Jess thought out loud. "Wood fencing would be too expensive, but we could use wood posts strung with rope."

"Rope won't be much of a deterrent if they stampede," Jake said. He stood and pushed the chair back where it belonged.

"At Fort Laramie, I heard one stockman say he knew of a ranch where they tied nails to the roping. We can do the same with thorn branches. Where are you going?"

Jake lifted an eyebrow conspiratorially. "To bring our workers home."

"You're going to get the Paiutes now?" Jess hurried up the stairs behind him, her sprightly steps echoing her enthusiasm. "I'll need only a moment to change!"

Inside their bedroom, Jake laid a hand over her fingers, stilling the swift movements with which they had begun to disengage her buttons. "No, Jess. You can't come. I need you to stay here." Jake entered the bathing alcove to the left and lifted one of his Henry repeating rifles by its octagonal barrel. He checked the loading, then deftly added cartridges to the gun belt slung around his hips.

The curtain was flung aside. "What do you mean, no?" She tossed her long, brown braid over her shoulder. Her chest rapidly rose and fell where she'd left the buttons undone, and her eyes kindled bright, green sparks. "The Paiutes are my friends. I'm going with you."

"Jess, I have to get to the reservation and back before sunset. I don't have time to discuss this with you."

"Excellent." She grabbed the barrel of the other Henry rifle and verified that the magazine tubes were filled with cartridges.

"That'll save us both loads of time." She laid the brass frame over her arm and rapidly rebuttoned her red wool gown.

Something between a groan and a growl rumbled up from his throat as he followed her back into the bedroom, where she knotted a bandana at her neck. She pulled her gun belt down from its peg on the wall and buckled it on, sliding the Remington revolver into its holster.

Apparently, he needed to make the time to reason with her.

"Your side is paining you. I see it when you bend."

She glanced at him. "It's only slight discomfort, Bennett. The ribs are neither cracked nor broken. You said so yourself. And before you say it, I wrapped my arm in a clean bandage this morning." She kicked off her low-topped moccasins and pulled on the high, deerskin boots she wore whenever she rode, stubbornly clamping her teeth against her bottom lip, probably to force back the pain in her side.

"Jess, I admit that I love your tenacity and the friendship you carry in your heart for the Paiute people. They've certainly seen too little of it. But a lot of white men are none too anxious to see a cattleman escorting Indians to his ranch. I don't want to have to worry about you if there's trouble."

With a quick, decisive jerk, Jess finished tying her laces and stood to her full height to glare up at him. "I can look after myself, and you know it."

Setting the butt of his rifle on the floor, Jake reached out a hand and brushed several loose tendrils back from her eyes, first on one side, then on the other. Her cheeks were red and her forehead damp from exerting herself. He had fallen in love with that Hale tenacity of hers, and now....

"You want me to stay so you don't have to fear for me, but if I stay, I'll be the one passing the hours wondering if something has happened to you. We were already shot at scant miles from here, and in the past two years, everyone we both loved was taken from us. I think we'll eventually leave behind this unease we both feel, but for now, let's get through what we have to get through together. We cover each other's backs, and neither one stays behind suffering uncertainty. Agreed?"

Just for once, couldn't she give him a chance to point out an error in her logic?

Her green eyes softened, and her rose-red lips curved into a mischievous smile. "Are you going to comment next on my impetuous nature, or my courage?"

Her startlingly beautiful, upturned face was a perfection of earthen hues only God could have achieved, and she possessed the heart of a scamp. "Let's settle midway between and call it tenacity."

"I can live with that. What about you?"

"Though your fervor may gray me before my time, I'm just going to keep loving you and be forever thankful that you're on my side."

Jess rode out alongside Jake, Taggart, and Diaz, pistols at their hips and rifles strapped to their saddles. Behind them, Ho Chen drove the wagon at his own insistence. In all the years Jess had known the quiet man, to her recollection, he had never insisted on anything.

As the miles passed, and the orange rock peaks above Pyramid Lake took definitive shape, Jess and the ranchmen grew increasingly alert, searching far and near for aggressors, whether they be Indian or white. Ho Chen sat equally alert, rocking stiffly atop the wagon seat, his brown-skinned hands tight on the lines; however, his eyes scanned only ahead, solidifying Jess's silent conjecture that he was looking forward to seeing someone in particular at the reservation. Almost certainly, it was a Paiute woman who had snagged his heart.

Jess resumed her scrutiny of the mountains around them. Caution flashed like quicksilver through her veins as she watched notches and fissures for discolorations and movements and listened for shifting stones and the almost inaudible fluttering of desert plants and brush. Fortunately, she felt none of the burning awareness she'd had at the ranch when she'd sensed she was being watched.

Jake had been to the reservation a time or two before, and he took a path Jess couldn't discern but with which he was clearly familiar. Finally, the snaking, green-blue Truckee River appeared, and Jess smiled to see people scattered along its banks, some wearing deerskin dresses, others wearing calico, and a few in trousers wielding fishing nets. Several round, dark-brown faces watched as they approached, their manner quiet and still as they assessed the motives of the intruders.

Then, Ho Chen called out a greeting—nothing could have shocked Jess more—and one of the brown faces, the face of a woman in a calico dress, formed a smile as her hand waved at him.

Jake called out a greeting in Paiute, and several faces Jess recognized, men who had worked at the ranch the year before, laid down their nets and hurried over, their smiles welcoming and friendly.

Jess dismounted with the others, and about fifteen Paiutes immediately swarmed around them, calling them "brother," "sister," and other endearing terms. Nettle, a Paiute woman Jess had befriended before leaving the ranch, wiggled through the crowd and seized Jess's hand. Her black hair was bobbed short as a sign of mourning.

"I am so glad to see you, my sister!" she said. "Doyle and Seth told us you married Many Horses!"

"Nettle! It is so good to see *you*!" Jess hugged her petite but solid friend, smiling to hear the Paiute people's name for Jake. Many Horses. He certainly had many now.

Nettle wore the same deerskin dress with long fringe that Jess remembered, and the same plain, Indian blanket around her shoulders, but now, both showed signs of age and mends. Her dark-brown eyes reflected her enthusiasm at their arrival, but the lines that drew away from her slightly flared nose and thin mouth—lines carved by years of hardship and resentment shared by nearly all the Paiute people—had deepened in the months Jess and Jake had been away.

"What has happened, Nettle? Why are you all wary on your own reservation?"

Nettle's husband, Black-Eye, whose quick humor had always been blessedly infectious, answered from where he was standing with Jake and Diaz. "Come, we will all sit together and talk."

Nettle and the other women hurried ahead and spread animal skin robes on the grass for them to sit on while Jake and the cattlemen tied their horses to trees near the river. Since the Paiute women always kept stew cooking so that their families could help themselves whenever they were hungry, the meal was ready. From their wigwams, they brought forth horn spoons and simple wooden bowls, into which they ladled stew from kettles hung over small fires. Even when food was scarce, the Paiutes always fed their guests, even if doing so meant they would have little or nothing to eat in the days following. To them, good friends were family, and they cared dearly for family.

They all sat together on the robes and began to eat the antelope stew. Jess's curiosity about Ho Chen was appeased when she allowed her gaze to linger on him and the short, pleasantly round Paiute woman who had handed him a bowl of stew and was now sitting down on a robe beside him. They stole tender but darting glances.

"Doyle and Ho Chen told us that men made you leave the ranch," Jake said to the group. He included the women in the discussion, as was the Paiute custom.

"They were coyote!" a woman interjected. "Very bad men!"

Jake said something in their language, his tone one of agreement with her assessment, then spoke in English. "When Jess and I returned to the ranch, we brought twelve more horses to breed with the others, so we have about seventy horses, and we'll keep some of the cattle." He spoke openly and directly, in the way of the People. "I need to hire men to help with the horses, cattle, and repairs, and I need help taking care of the garden and attending to many chores. I came today to ask if I could hire you again."

In the circle of brown faces, Jess saw assorted reactions to Jake's words. There was one expression of cautious hope—that from the woman beside Ho Chen—and the others reflected varying degrees of wariness and sober judgment. *What has happened to them since they've been here?*

"What's happened here, Black-Eye?" Jake asked the question Jess had held back.

"The Great White Father in Washington gave us this land. He said if we stay here, he will give us clothes, seeds to plant, and food to eat. We received clothes only once, years ago, and no clothes since and no food." Black-Eye leaned his long, thin arms on his equally thin legs, his mouth hardened at the offense.

Despite the heat of the sun, unpleasantly cold nausea swam through Jess. The suffering of these people had been caused by her nation's leaders—self-serving leaders who never left their elegant homes or their elegant parties with their elegant friends to see the despair and desolation they wreaked with the indifferent flourish of a pen. Never had she felt a greater guilt that was not her responsibility to endure. Never had she been more pleased to live in the West, away from the States and the individuals who determined Indian policy, and to live among people faithful to and protective of one another, who honored what was right.

"The coyote men came to the ranch, so we left," Black-Eye said, "and this land that was to be ours is not."

Jake frowned. "White men came here, too?"

"Other men," the woman beside Ho Chen said. "They graze their cattle on reservation land, they shoot and eat our rabbits, and they take our fish from the river. They also dig on our land, looking for gold. We ask the Indian agent for his help, but he does nothing."

"At times, they harm our women and steal our daughters," said another man Jess hadn't met before. His long, black hair lifted on the warm breeze, unbound, like the people longed to be. "The soldier fathers do not allow us to get our daughters. Sometimes, the soldiers bring our daughters back, but many of our daughters have been treated very bad and hurt as though their souls have been taken from them, and the guilty men are not punished."

Beside Jess, Diaz's glare darkened. "Why are they not punished?"

"Some are," Ho Chen answered, "but so many girls are taken that soldiers cannot find them all or punish the men."

To Jess's other side, Taggart snorted, his face nearly as red with anger as with whiskers. "That's why Indians shot at us near Smoke Creek. They're trying to bring some level of justice."

Black-Eye sat silently as if listening to the chant and flow of the river that slipped past them. "If we work at your ranch," he told Jake, "more bad men will certainly try to make us go. We are not the only ranch Indians who have been made to leave."

"If we stay here," Nettle told her friends, "we are no safer, but no harm will come to Many Horses or Jessica or our brothers at the ranch."

Jess kept her seat. Just barely. "Most of you know us," she spoke up. "For those of you who do not, neither Jake nor I are able to value our own comfort or safety if that same comfort and safety is denied to others. When we arrived today, we greeted one another as brothers and sisters, as if we shared the same father and mother. Permit us, then, to be true brothers and sisters to you."

Jake sent Jess a look of pride, one that said he was honored to call her his wife, then faced the Paiute people again. "A year ago, the ranch was attacked because people wanted to harm Jess and take our horses," he said, "and many of you fought beside us to protect the ranch. The ranch isn't safe, and neither is the reservation. Bad men could attack, whether we all stay here or return to Honey Lake Valley. But the valley and the northern Sierra Nevada Mountains have belonged to your families for generations, since long before I came, since long before any white men came. The land is more yours than it is mine, and you have the right to live there and to profit from it. I need to hire people I can trust with my wife and horses, and I trust you, but know that if you come, sooner or later, we may be fighting side by side again. Many bad men are strolling around free, and the lack of lawmen in these parts makes that a near certainty."

Without intending to, Jess sat taller, brimming over with respect for the code of honor Jake and the cattlemen held. Her husband had spoken with honesty, and she knew he would willingly defend a people whom cruel whites starved and raped and killed. Cattlemen were a rare breed, and she felt something noble and good stirring in her, knowing she had become one of them.

Black-Eye's gaze darted to the hills and the small plain

beyond the river; he remained alert to any trouble, as did the others. "We have always spoken together about a matter for five days before deciding what we will do," he said to his people. "We have listened to each other's wisdom and have let emotions settle so that we decide well. But we cannot decide this as a people. Your families must choose for yourselves whether to go to the ranch of Many Horses or stay on the reservation or go north to be with the clans. At no place will we be free from harm, but I think that at the ranch of Many Horses, our white brothers will protect us, and we will protect them."

"Truckee, Truckee," many of the Paiutes murmured, nodding as if in agreement.

"That means 'Very well, very well,'" Diaz explained to Jess. "They agree with Black-Eye."

"My daughters and I will go to the ranch," said the woman seated beside Ho Chen. "Thank you, Many Horses."

"I'm grateful to you," Jake told her. "But my name is Jake, and all of you are welcome to call me that."

"Nettle and I will go, and our son, Natchez," Black-Eye said. Nettle rose with the woman beside Ho Chen, and both went to ready their belongings.

The man with long hair reached out and clasped wrists with Jake. "My wife, Spruzy, and I will go. I am called Lee." Lee's gaze held steady, and Jess knew by his calm nature that he'd be a good man to work with the horses. He spoke to the woman beside him—Spruzy, no doubt—and Spruzy stood, her broad, fleshy cheeks showing tension. Whether the tension was the result of Lee's decision or of anger at bad white people, Jess didn't know. What she did know was that these people needed to experience peace without having it snatched away.

Two men who had worked at the ranch the previous summer spoke to Jake in Paiute, and the three of them laughed over some shared recollection while everyone else left to pack or to say good-bye to their friends. Jake's wide grin and the crinkles in the corners of his eyes revealing his delight told Jess these men would be coming, too.

As the men strode toward their camp, Taggart, Diaz, and Ho Chen readied the horses and wagon, and Jess began to roll up the robes they had sat on. Jake knelt beside her and lent a hand. "How are you feeling, Jess?"

"Like we're really about to go into the horse business." She knew he was asking after her arm and side, but if she didn't complain, then he'd have no reason to exclude her from moments like these. She sat back on her heels. "Where is Pyramid Lake from here?"

"To the north. I wish you could see it."

"I wish I could, too, but we need to get these people to the ranch before we lose daylight. I understand. We'll probably visit here again. When we do, you can show me the lake."

Jake helped her to her feet, and the look he shared with her brought sweet memories of the closeness and passion they had shared the night before.

The sunshine and mountains wrapped around Jess like a promise. The horse ranch she had dreamed of for years was finally getting its start with the help of their friends, and before her stood a man whose bold gaze sent her heart skipping absurdly with joy, who loved her with all that he was.

At twenty-one, Jess had experienced enough of life to know that such moments of bliss inevitably gave way to trials. She hoped this moment would last a good, long while, but something inside told her it was about to turn bad.

As Jake left to help the Paiute men bridle their horses, Jess looked over to see Ho Chen helping the smiling, animated woman, who had sat with him while they'd eaten, and two young girls in dingy, ill-fitting calico dresses load baskets, rugs, and dishes into his wagon.

Jess felt prepared for whatever might come, but she also felt a protective, maternal instinct rising in her. These people were coming to help at the ranch because she and Jake had asked them to. She loved their kindness and their ways, and she wasn't about to let any more harm come to them.

When Jess approached the wagon, Ho Chen gave her a respectful bow, then moved to one side. "Miss Jessie, this is Lily"—hovering at his elbow was the short, slightly plump Paiute woman who had sat with him while they'd eaten—"and her daughters, Mattie and Grace." Behind her stood two girls in dingy, ill-fitting calico dresses. The older girl, with a piercing, hardened gaze, looked to be about ten years old; the younger, about six years old, held on to Ho Chen's hand. She appeared uncertain but still bore a trace of hope in her eyes that better things would come. Jess recognized them as the girls who had helped load the wagon, and she dropped to her knees beside them without being aware that she meant to.

Had Jess's baby sister, Emma, survived the house fire, she would have been two years and two months old, and she wouldn't have known a single moment of the uncertainty and brutality Mattie and Grace must have witnessed nearly every day of their lives. Their soft, black hair was cut short like the hair of most of the others, meaning these girls knew someone who had died or been killed. The caring and warmth between Lily and Ho Chen indicated it must have been Lily's husband. Their father.

Jess ached to hold them close, to undo or erase everything that had turned Mattie's face to stone and Grace's to near despair. "You two remind me of my little sister," Jess finally said, bringing out a gentle smile, even though she felt the heat of indignation rising in her cheeks and eyes, accompanied by the urge to grieve out loud for the good they had never known.

Grace released Ho Chen's hand and cautiously stepped closer to Jess, stopping about an arm's length away. "Where is she?"

"My sister is in heaven. The Spirit-Land," Jess clarified.

"Then her soul is happy," Grace said.

Jess's breathing quickened, and her gaze turned misty, but she let out her emotions in a brief spurt of laughter rather than tears. "Yes, her soul is happy in the Spirit-Land."

Grace stepped closer until her shin rested against Jess's knee, her wary expression giving way to childlike curiosity. "Were her eyes the color of sage? Like yours?"

At this, Mattie moved closer, too, though she remained behind Grace. Peering over her sister's shoulder, Mattie's stony face did not change, but her mouth relaxed into the barest hint of wonder. "Your eyes are green," she said. Her voice sounded quiet, breathless, as if she did not speak often.

"My sister's eyes were blue, like the sky," Jess answered.

Both girls' faces tipped up to the cloudless expanse miles above, Grace's brown eyelids crinkling lightly, as if she were trying to envision what blue eyes must be like.

"Taggart," Jess called.

The Irishman looked over from his position beside the wagon, to which he was affixing an iron kettle. "Ye need somethin', Jess?"

"If you have a moment, these two young ladies are curious to see blue eyes."

Taggart smiled good-naturedly and huffed his way over with the swagger of a man who rode horseback far more often than he walked. Well aware of the distrust most Paiute children felt toward white men, he slowed as he neared and removed his hat—to lessen his appearance of height, perhaps—then went down on one knee near Jess and the girls.

"You have hair like fire," Grace said.

"Grace," her mother warned gently, her look stern but also kind.

From the twelve Paiute children who had lived at the ranch the year before, Jess had learned that one of the first courtesies their parents strictly teach them is never to laugh at or insult someone because of his appearance. The Great Spirit Father made every person special.

"Or like a sunset," Grace amended.

"That I do," Taggart agreed, his belly shaking and his pale cheeks and temples creased in mirth, "and rarely does it see a brush or a comb. When I was a wee lad, my mother braided my hair and bound it with a blue ribbon to go with my eyes. But I didn't much care for it, and before I'd arrived at school, my hair looked like this."

By his conspiratorial tone, Jess suspected he'd tried to replait it after school while walking home so as to hoodwink his mother, but any mother of a son like Taggart would have been instantly wise to him.

Mesmerized by his unusual, fiery-orange hair and beard, Mattie and Grace had to force their attention politely to his comparatively unremarkable, pale, cornflower-blue eyes.

"I believe the people are ready to go, Miss Jessie," Ho Chen said. Then, after exchanging question-and-answer gazes with Lily, he smiled warmly at the girls. "Would you like to ride with me in wagon to ranch?"

Mattie and Grace looked to their mother, and she nodded. Grace took Ho Chen's hand as before and walked sedately with him and her mother toward the wagon, not laughing or bouncing like other children might do—*white children*, Jess mentally corrected herself. She and Taggart stood up and watched Mattie follow obediently behind her mother.

"Thank you, Taggart," Jess murmured.

"Now, don't ye worry yerself about those girls," he said. "Ye know better than anyone that the ranch is a good place for lettin' go o' sorrows and findin' peace."

His bold comment stunned her. None of the other cattlemen had ever before said a word to her about her personal matters or past. As a breed that spoke only when necessary and only what was relevant, they held fast to the code that prohibited interference in anyone else's business, figuring rightly that some people had events in their pasts they'd just as soon leave there and never resurrect again.

Undaunted by her mute gawk, he pulled his battered, brown hat over his orange head and tugged his britches and gun belt higher up on his paunch. "The boss, the lads, and I saw to it that ye healed from yer grief, Jess. We'll all see to it those girls'll be healed, too."

Chapter Four

"Jake...?" Jess couldn't keep the apprehension out of her voice.

"Just keep riding, Jess. It's best to try not to face aggressors squarely. If you keep going, they figure you're afraid and often won't waste the effort on a confrontation. If you stop and face them, they see that as a challenge, and it stirs up their need to best you."

Jess lowered her shoulders in an attempt to lessen the tension in her neck and back. It didn't help, but then, she hadn't truly believed it would.

She saw Jake send casual glances to Taggart, Diaz, and Ho Chen. Each of the men nodded in turn, aware of the gang of eight or nine men riding up behind them from less than a quarter of a mile away. Ho Chen took the lines back from Mattie, whom he had been teaching to drive the wagon.

Mentally, Jess counted up their own group. Nine men, four women, and two girls—fifteen in all, ten of them Paiute. A few of the Paiutes were carrying sidearms or shotguns, and others carried bows and arrows, but they could be hung for using them against a white man. Ho Chen didn't carry a firearm, though things wouldn't go much better for him, a Chinaman, if he did.

That left Jake, Taggart, Diaz, and her to protect them all.

Pulling in the reins with her left hand, Jess surreptitiously lowered her right hand to tuck the excess fabric of her flowing, red wool skirt between the saddle fender and her leg, clamping the mass of it in place with her knee. Just below the pommel, her Henry rifle stock jutted out from its sheath, now with unobstructed access.

Jess slanted her gaze to Jake, Taggart, and Diaz. Likewise, they shifted furtively, tightening a leather glove or nudging aside the coil of rope they habitually carried over their pommels.

The expressions on the faces of the Paiutes had hardened. They'd been unjustly attacked by settlers before, and they'd almost certainly seen friends and relatives killed. They clearly thirsted for fair treatment but knew it would never be granted.

On the other side of the wagon, Diaz tapped a spur to his horse, nudging it into a brief trot, then slowed it again when he was positioned abreast of Ho Chen, Mattie, and Grace. Jess had been riding point with Jake. Now, she drew back the reins, slowing her mare until she was alongside the wagon seat opposite Diaz. The girls' mother, Lily, came up close behind Diaz on a black mustang, clutching her blanket with her free hand. She was unarmed.

Suddenly, one of their pursuers whistled sharply, and the gang broke apart and surrounded them, forcing them to stop, drawing their sidearms as they closed in.

Instantly, Jess and Diaz had their rifles in position, ready to fire. She heard the double click of Taggart's revolver.

In a steady gesture, Jake lowered a gloved hand, indicating to Jess and the others to hold their fire. He turned in his saddle to assess the situation, then faced the fat, grizzled man who had taken position partway between him and Jess. He appeared to be the gang's leader.

Beneath what looked to be an expensive, black hat, the leader's greasy black-and-gray hair stuck out like porcupine quills on either side of his head. His round cheeks were clean-shaven, and he had no mustache under his upturned nose. His slow, confident smirk became a leer as he shifted his gaze to

Jess. Swollen, pustulant gums held several rotting teeth. Jess swiftly redirected her focus to his tobacco-juice-stained shirt and coat so as not to gag. She felt his leer pass over her again, an obvious attempt to provoke some response from Jake since their appearance and their guns had failed to do so.

Jake sat with his gloved fist resting atop his thigh, scant inches from his holster, quietly considering the man.

Jess's teeth ground in tension as she watched the three men closest to her. *Why doesn't Jake ask what they want and end this stalemate?* she thought with frustration.

Several moments passed, but nobody moved. With his piggish face reddening in anger, the leader tried his leer once more.

"Henry, in case you're wondering," Jake finally said.

The man frowned in confusion, looking now at Jess's inarguably feminine shape.

Her ribs began to burn in pain from the effort of holding the rifle level, and the cut in her right arm was throbbing as though it had been struck repeatedly with a hammer. Knowing anger would serve her better than fear or self-pity, Jess forced her quick breaths to deepen as she willed a rage to rise within.

"Her name is Henry?" the fat man asked, pointing with his head to Jess. He scowled in disbelief before moving his gaze to Mattie and Grace, and his leer became real.

So did Jess's rage.

"Accuracy within four inches at three hundred paces," Jake continued. "Twenty-four inches at a thousand paces." Jake looked the man up and down. "You appear to be more than four feet tall and at least twenty-four inches wide. If she aims at your gut, she'll do no worse than lift off your head, and here it'll lie for the coyotes to find."

At the mental image, the red faded from the man's cheeks. "She's g-got a Henry repeating r-rifle?" he stammered.

Jess sensed a growing wariness among his companions. Whether they wanted to steal supplies, intended to prevent the Paiutes from working on a white man's ranch, or had some other motive, it seemed they were beginning to lose interest.

"Sixteen shots without reloading," Jake said, as if he were delivering a Sunday sermon. "About forty shots per minute."

"Breechloader," Taggart added helpfully.

Jake glanced over his shoulder at Jess, then pointedly shook his head. "If you knew just how accurately that woman can shoot, you wouldn't still be sitting there with that gun in your hand."

Saddle leather creaked and horses pawed at the ground as the man's companions shifted uneasily. The two in Jess's line of vision eased their revolvers into their holsters.

Their leader began to do the same, then suddenly turned and shot at a rabbit-sized hunk of quartz ten paces distant. Virtually simultaneous with his bullet's *ping*, the *boom* of Jess's rifle discharge pounded their ears, and the quartz rained down in fragments and dust around the small, smooth stone his bullet had struck instead.

Immediately after, Jess swung the bore of her rifle to take aim at the man's heart.

He raised his hands to his shoulders, palms out, the butt of his revolver held gingerly between a thumb and forefinger. His mouth hardening over his defeat, he nevertheless lowered the gun into its holster.

His men had already begun riding in the direction they had come from. Throwing Jake a look of disgust, he grabbed up his reins, then looked over Jess, the wagon, and the Paiutes once more. "Fine. Keep whatever whiskey your redskins brought. We'll find more someplace else!"

He thrust his spurs into his horse's sides and rode out at a run, swiftly overtaking his men and leading them out of sight.

Jess let out her breath and lowered her gun to relieve her arm and ribs. Around her, the others also lowered their guns, and Jake reined his horse around to check on everyone and make sure each of them was all right. Lily checked on Mattie and Grace. They were clinging stiffly to Ho Chen, who patted their hands and spoke softly to them, then gave Lily a reassuring nod.

As Jess sheathed her rifle, Jake rode up beside her. "Jess?"

"I'm fine." She'd tell him the truth later—that, underneath her skirt and petticoats, her legs were trembling violently. "So, they were after the whiskey?"

Near the front of the wagon, the corked necks of several brown bottles protruded from the white, woven blanket they were wrapped in. Jake asked Lily to hand him the blanket she was wearing, and he draped it over the bottles. Jess knew the Paiutes used the alcohol to treat cuts and injuries, as the cattlemen did, but the men who had surrounded them had been pursuing it for a more gratifying use.

Jake gave her a long look, his handsome features revealing thoughts and emotions faster than she could discern them, then gave the signal for everyone to continue on.

Fading twilight and emerging stars overhead lit the ranch compound as the group dismounted and started to unload the horses and the wagon. They had encountered no further mishaps, and that was reason enough to celebrate, but the buoyant mood that had captured them all in the past hour insisted upon celebration on an even grander scale—an hour ago, they had begun to see cows branded with the Bennett Mountain Ranch mark, and the horses and riders alike had thrilled to know they were nearly home.

Doyle appeared beside Jess just as she was about to lift the saddle and blanket from her mare's back, and he lifted them himself. "Someone here has been pacing a hole in the earth waitin' for your return," he said.

Jess glanced around but couldn't see much beyond Doyle and the saddle. "Who—"

"Will!" Jake's voice called in greeting.

"Will?" Jess beamed up at Doyle, then ducked under her mare's neck and followed the sound of the ranchmen's hearty greetings.

Jake, Taggart, and Diaz grinned and thwacked the spindly young man's back as if he was the prodigal brother who'd finally returned, and they nearly jarred the tan hat from his equally tan head. The bland color continued down his soiled, white shirt and light-brown trousers and boots, then up again to his bony face and the hazel eyes he turned upon Jess. Below the whisker-studded knob of his Adam's apple, his red bandana gave the only hint of color on his entire person. He smiled at her, revealing perfect, white teeth that one would expect to see on an actor strutting the stage at Piper's Opera House.

The youth might be plain-looking, Jess knew, but his smile had always been jaunty enough to draw the same kind from others. "It's good to see you again, Will."

"Miss Jess...uh, I mean, Mrs. Bennett...." He spoke slowly, as always, as if the words were out for a stroll in the sunshine and were in no hurry to get anywhere.

"Don't fret over formalities, Will; I'm still Jess."

"Uh, yes, ma'am. I missed seeing you around here, Miss Jess. You sure liven the place up."

Jess tossed an impish smile at Jake. "I'm delighted somebody appreciates that aspect of my nature."

Diaz gave a debonair bow, his inky, black mustache lifting at the corners like a raven's wings. "The boss appreciates you, *Mariposa*, as do I."

"*Mariposa?*"

Taggart was about to deliver some sarcastic remark, Jess was certain, but little Grace's approach stayed his lips.

"*Sí*," Diaz answered. "She is *la Mariposa*—'Butterfly.' It is the special name I give her."

Grace looked up at Jess, wagging the stem of a wildflower she had picked, absently caressing her cheek with the petals. "Why Butterfly?" she asked Diaz.

"Because she is like the sunbeam that has burst into colors and dances on the wind, like the butterfly."

Jake sent Jess a look of warm agreement over Grace's head, and Jess felt a small hand touching her own. Grace pressed the wildflower into it, lifting her gaze now to Jess and Jake. "Mother said you kept those coyotes from harming us today. Now I will call you Mother and Father."

Overwhelmed by the warmth and love woven throughout Paiute customs, Jess was still trying to find the words to respond when Grace turned again to Diaz.

"May I have a special name?"

"Well, le's see." Diaz pensively smoothed his mustache with the edge of his finger. "You are young lady who likes flowers, sí?"

Grace's nod had her bobbed hair skimming her tiny shoulders.

"Then, I think I call you *la Mariquita*. That means 'Ladybug.'"

Grace's lips folded in, and the corners of her mouth turned up in the ghost of a smile—the first Jess had seen from her. "Thank you. Will you give a special name to Mattie, too?"

Diaz squatted down beside Grace and tenderly regarded Mattie, who stood by her mother but peered stonily back at her sister, Jess, and the group of cattlemen. "If Mattie would like a special name, *Mariquita*, then she must ask for one."

"I will tell her."

Grace walked back toward her mother and sister, still not running or skipping, as other little girls did, but Jess did detect a small bounce in her step.

Jake winked at Jess as he clapped a broad hand on Will's shoulder. "The rest of us feel like celebrating. How about you?"

"That sounds mighty fine, boss. I'd like nothing better, and Doyle and I have already seen to the horses."

"Then let's help the Paiutes get settled for the night," Jake said. "After that, we'll clear out the cookhouse and get some music playing."

"I'll help Ho Chen with supper," Jess announced. She turned toward the cookhouse, but Jake caught hold of her sleeve.

As Taggart, Diaz, and Will strode away to join their Paiute friends, Jess heard Taggart mutter, "How do ye do it? Women and horses, it's all the same. Pulled to ye like dust to the land. I'm thinking I should have a mustache black as a Spaniard's."

"Believe me, *amigo*," came Diaz's voice, "it won' help."

Will guffawed; in retaliation, Taggart pulled off his hat and, with it, amiably thwacked the youth.

Jake dropped his hand from Jess's sleeve, and his respectful distance from her in front of his men didn't trouble her as it had the previous evening. She knew now that they'd share plenty of closeness when they were alone. "What was it you wanted?"

"I just wanted you to myself, to enjoy a minute with you."

He faced the open desert to the east, and she shifted to take it in beside him. Pale, gold starlight glittered above the scattered, lone mountains, which resembled the hulls of ships made from clay, and the bristly sagebrush plains spread out like blankets between them. A warm breeze ruffled Jess's sleeves and teased the hairs around her face that had come loose from her braid.

The year before, she had found God here, during moments

like these, and even now she knew He was close, filling the land, waiting to give help to anyone who needed it and asked Him.

"Thank you, Jake."

"Hmm? For what?"

Her gaze encompassed him, the ranch, and the people and horses who would share it with them. "Everything."

"It'll take a lot of work building it and keeping it."

Jess stretched her arms wide in the pose of a most willing volunteer. "You picked the right person to help, 'from this day forward.'"

"Yes, ma'am," he agreed, his admiration momentarily unfettered. "I did."

As they were setting up a table outside the cookhouse in preparation for dinner, Jess looked out at the recently constructed plank house nearby and saw a nearly bald man of fifty or so years set what appeared to be a heavy crate outside his front door, then turn to pull the door closed. He hefted the crate again and, holding it above his slightly rounded middle, began heading in their direction.

Will helped Jess lower the legs of their end of the table to the ground near a pair of burning torches they had set up as Jake set down the other end at the edge of the flickering light. "Hey, boss," Will said, pointing to the cheery-faced man whose grin widened as he approached, "come on. Let me introduce you two to our neighbor."

Will took the crate from the man, which was filled with plump, red apples, and set it on the table. "Hank Beesley, meet Jake and Jessica Bennett, owners of the B Creek Ranch." At Hank's look of momentary confusion, Will said, "That's what folks call the Bennett Mountain Ranch for short."

"Hank," Jake said as he gave the neighbor a hearty handshake.

Hank cordially tipped his hat to Jess. "Mrs. Bennett."

"We're rather informal here, Mr. Beesley," Jess said. "Everyone calls me Jess."

"Well, Jess, then I'm Hank," he said, the exuberant pink of his face apparent even in the dim torchlight. "I sure am sorry I purchased land that belonged to you. When I heard that the government was selling this land and for such a good deal, I bought right away."

"Mr. Hank is the one who took me to the land office so we could save the rest of your land," Will explained.

Jake raised an eyebrow. "How did you manage that?"

"Well," Will lowered his chin slightly and rubbed his nose, "Mr. Hank here apparently knows about land and paperwork and such. All I had to do was practice writing your signature some before we left, and act stampeding-bull-mad when we got there."

"He was quite convincing," Hank avowed. "I can safely say there is little chance the men at the land office will risk a repeat encounter by selling any more of your property. The acres to the north and east will remain yours."

Despite her worries over what the loss of half their land would mean, Jess felt a smile growing at what the two men had done to save the remaining half of their land.

Jake patted Hank on the back. "A man can never have too many good neighbors," he said.

Hank nodded. "I apologize again that I didn't know what those land agents were up to when I bought mine. Back east, in the States, the government has decreed that freedom must endure at all costs, and good men are dying in a war to advance that cause. Meanwhile, here in the West, that same government is taking freedom away so the men who work for them can line their pockets." Though his words revealed his frustration at the events, Jess saw that the ruddiness in his cheeks and an underlying smile remained, as if his cheerfulness never disappeared entirely.

Hank hooked his thumbs in his suspenders. "A lot of folks have been moving into the valley, many of them from the South," he said with a polite nod to Jess, his ever-present grin back in place and brighter than the torches. Jess felt her heart growing lighter just by being near him. "Word is, there'll be six school districts in Honey Lake before the end of this year."

"The government land sale has caused a land rush," Jake observed. He glanced at Jess, then waved a hand to invite Hank to sit at the table with them. "Have there been tensions between Unionists and secessionists around here?" he asked him.

They brought over a bench and sat, and Hank moved the apple crate to the bench beside him. "A lot of Southerners have settled along the marshy land on the far side of Honey Lake, though it's drying up in the heat," Hank said. "Some folks are calling the place the Confederate tules, and, yes, some folks are causing tensions, but most just look to their own business and leave each other alone."

Black-Eye and Lee approached the table, and Hank stood up to greet them. "Good to see you back!" he said.

Jess scooted closer to Jake to make room for the two Paiute men. Fragrant aromas of meat and biscuits began to drift over from the cookhouse, and, from the sound of things, Taggart was warming up his fiddle for their welcome-home celebration.

"Jake, Hank is the man who ran off the bad men who attacked us and made us go to the reservation," said Black-Eye, who smiled nearly as much as Hank. "His gun barks like a hungry wolf."

They chuckled at that, and Jess continued to laugh softly at the mental image of a rosy-cheeked Hank pleasantly emptying his shotgun at several drunks—who hadn't expected opposition to their assault—as they rode away, tails between their legs, their eyes wide.

Jake lifted his hat and combed his fingers through his brim-dented hair. "Hank, I'm also grateful to you for helping Seth take the horses to Fort Churchill. I'll be leaving in the morning to bring them back and to get supplies for the ranch."

"*We*," Jess corrected him. "*We'll* be leaving in the morning."

Jake sent Jess a look that said, "We'll discuss it later."

"I'd be happy to come along," Hank said.

Jess thought the kind man would likely "be happy" to do just about anything. She liked him immensely.

"We can take my wagon, as well as yours," Hank offered. "That way, we'll be able to bring back most anything either of us needs." His cattle lowed peacefully in the darkening night. "My cows seem to like your land over there, and yours seem to like the grass on my land. I'll get them back in their proper places in the morning. I didn't take time to do it today since I was planting trees."

Jake shrugged. "It's a simple enough matter. We'll leave the boys to do that after we leave."

"Were you planting apple trees?" Jess asked.

"Yes. It looked like you were getting ready to have a celebration, so I brought over some from last season for you to enjoy."

"How very kind," Jess said, rising. "I'll cut them and cook them down with some sugar. They'll be wonderful over biscuits. You'll stay, of course, and enjoy the festivities?"

"I'll stay just to taste the apples over biscuits!" he declared, and, while the other men expressed an eagerness to do the same, Jess looked to Jake and raised her eyebrows in a silent request for assistance.

Jake readily stood and rounded the table to lift the crate and spare her ribs the effort.

In the cookhouse kitchen, Lily and Ho Chen bustled about, preparing as much of a feast as their supplies could provide, while Mattie and Grace arranged plates and eating utensils on the sideboard.

After plunking the crate atop a barrel, Jake tipped his hat to the two girls, leisurely pulled out his knife, and began peeling an apple while they looked on. Once the fruit was peeled, he peeled another; then, he cut them into large, neat wedges, which he deposited on a clean plate. After wiping the knife on a towel and sliding it back into its sheath on his belt, he opened another barrel and spooned up a little sugar from the bottom, which he sprinkled leisurely and liberally over the apple slices. The girls stopped stacking plates and watched him prepare the ripe, juicy apples as if he were Santa Claus just come down the chimney. Jake set the plate on the sideboard, reached for a jar from one of its shelves, and removed the cork stopper, shaking a fine, brown spice on top of the apples.

Jess stepped back into the shadows and observed her husband as he wordlessly gained a measure of Mattie and Grace's trust and admiration. The apples now sparkling with sugar and decorated with cinnamon, Jake brought the slender cinnamon jar to his nose and made a show of delighting in the spice's scent, then set down the open jar on the edge of the sideboard, by which the two sisters were standing. This drew two sets of dark-brown eyes to the jar and its contents. When neither of them moved or reached for the jar, Jake picked it up again and tilted it toward them, inviting them to sniff. Grace was the first to bring her tiny nose near, and her eyes widened as a huge grin split her face. She bounced a little on her toes, and her reaction was apparently enough to encourage Mattie to lean forward and inhale the cinnamon scent for herself.

However, the stony expression never left Mattie's face, and she didn't respond in any way, except to watch Jake's hand as he replaced the jar's cork stopper, returned the jar to its shelf, and lifted an apple slice from the plate. Her gaze continued to follow the apple as he bit into it with a juicy crunch that ended with his eyes closed in bliss and a hip leaned against the sideboard, as if his enjoyment of the flavor had sapped his strength.

Next, Jake lifted the plate and offered the apple slices to Mattie and Grace. With a little giggle, Grace took a slice and shoved the whole of it into her mouth, then pressed both hands over her smiling mouth and chewed industriously. Likewise, Jess pressed the back of her hand over her own mouth to keep from laughing aloud at the child's delighted expression.

Mattie watched her sister with hard eyes, and Jess felt the sudden urge to teach the ten-year-old how to play poker. Grace reached for a second apple slice, and Mattie glanced warily at Jake before selecting a slice for herself. She looked it over carefully, eyed Jake once again as he took another piece, and finally bit a fraction off one end. Her only reaction was to blink a few times before quickly nibbling some more. Jake did not react visibly to her initial reticence, nor to her eventual acquiescence. He simply turned to lean his elbows on the sideboard as he took another slice of apple. Soon, Grace leaned against him, and Mattie even inched a little closer, as the three companionably enjoyed the plate of apple slices.

Jess noticed that Lily had already hung an iron pot of water over the fire to heat. After watching her carry the crate of apples to the cutting table to peel and slice, Jess selected a knife and joined her at the task while Ho Chen dumped steaming, golden-brown biscuits from a pan onto a serving platter, then covered them with a clean towel.

As she peeled apples, Jess stole an occasional glimpse of her husband with Mattie and Grace, thinking how wonderful a father he must have been to his own little daughter before she died. He was a man meant to have a family.

At the thought, her heart swelled in painful regret, which intensified as the dull ache in her lower back told her that her monthly was, as always, right on schedule.

In the eating area, which had been cleared of all tables and benches, Taggart's fiddle sang to a lively beat, and Will joined him on his harmonica. Hank and the ranch hands strode in, clapping to the beat, and Diaz grabbed Nettle, who was laughing, and began to swing her around the makeshift dance floor.

How good to be home, Jess thought, trying to take her mind off the disappointment that haunted her.

Chapter Five

Despite the private debate Jess had had with Jake the night before over whether she would accompany him to Fort Churchill, she enjoyed the long day's ride toward the fort, anxious to see Seth and help bring their horses back to the ranch.

She knew that Jake's determination to keep her safe battled his determination to let her be who she was—a horsewoman who needed to ride, to work with the horses, and to feel the wind as desperately as he did. Near the end of the previous night's disagreement, Jake had admitted that he knew always forcing her to stay behind at the ranch would make her feel like a cougar that wanted to run but was caught in a snare, and that her feelings toward him and their life would cool, then grow cold, until she couldn't bear him or their life together any longer. He'd finally capitulated, saying that if no legitimate reason arose to keep her at the ranch, she would be free to ride with him, and he would work out his own concerns as best he could.

Summoning greater tactfulness than she'd known she possessed, Jess had gently reminded him that she had proven on more than one occasion to be an asset in difficult situations, and that she, too, still harbored fears of losing him, just as he did about losing her.

Hank drove his wagon, while Ho Chen drove the one belonging to the ranch, and, unlike cattlemen, who rarely disturbed a good silence with dialogue, Hank was an avid conversationalist. He was talkative even when relating the recent loss of his wife and the town where they'd lived, and that he was in the middle of transplanting apple and cherry saplings, intending to grow a larger orchard than his previous one. He also kept bees and sold the honey, describing for Jess the fascinating process of gathering and cleaning the substance.

The four of them had ridden southeast along the foot of the Sierra Nevadas until daybreak, then passed from what they now knew to be California into Nevada Territory and continued southeast at a brisk pace past Lake's Crossing. Now, as they followed the winding Carson River east, the evening sun behind them turned golden, laying long, bold shadows at the feet of thousands of sagebrush and occasional junipers like sewing pins spilled all over the desert floor. Jess let her thoughts wander to pass the time, losing herself in the fluid movements of human, horse, and wagon shadows as they stretched out like flowing ink before them. She was mesmerized by the distortion of Jake's and her shadows as they curved like diving porpoises over rocks and sagebrush, by the crisscross of the horses' legs as they trotted, by the flashes of daylight between the long spokes of the wagon wheels as they turned beneath their loads. These were calming sights, the likes of which she had not given a thought to in years, it seemed. And, perhaps, that was how long it had been since her mind or her circumstances had allowed her more than merely brief moments of peace.

Less than a mile in the distance, a group of square, white buildings gradually materialized out of the desert, pleasantly set before a canopy of tall, whispering cottonwoods that stretched over the Carson River.

Having anticipated a fort similar to Laramie's handsome, well-built structures within their high, stockade fencing, Jess was stunned to discover that Fort Churchill seemed to be a fort in name only. It wasn't at all what she'd expected. The bustling place looked more like a growing town than a young military post. It was unwalled, sprawling, and open to the desert dotted with lone mountains.

In the center lay a huge, square parade ground on which a hundred or more men drilled around a dizzyingly high flagpole flying the federal stars and stripes. Around the quadrangle stood buildings of whitewashed adobe brick. As they made their approach along a relatively smooth road, Jake pointed out officers' and enlisted men's quarters to the north and west; fort headquarters, quartermaster's quarters, commissary, and hospital to the east; and a guardhouse with a jail and the powder magazine to the south. Beyond all these adobe buildings, many of them fronted with eight-foot-wide porticos, were outlying structures of board—the bakery (which Jake said the cattlemen tended to frequent), a sutler's general store, a laundry house, a telegraph office, a blacksmith shop, and a group of single tents for enlisted men. The stables were to the south, near the river.

"I expect we'll find Seth and the horses to the south and east, near Buckland's Station," Jake said. "There's likely to be plenty of grazing land there near the river."

Jess pushed dancing brown hair back from her face. "Might we go see them before we meet Captain Rawlins?"

Jake threw back his head and laughed. "Since you won't settle down until you do, I think we'd better." His mouth curled up in the crooked grin that she loved, and he called out their intentions to Hank and Ho Chen. The two waved in acknowledgement, then turned their wagons in the direction of the sutler's store.

Within minutes, the fort had passed beyond Jess's consideration, and she had to remind herself several times to walk, not trot, her horse so it could cool down before being stabled. She had to remind herself just as often not to stand in the stirrups as she searched for the herd of sleek, gleaming mustangs that Jake and the men had captured the previous summer.

When she finally caught sight of them, her heart tripped in happy relief, and she felt warm tears trickle down her cheeks to see young Seth Griffin lift his tan hat from his mud-brown thatch of uncombed hair and wag it in greeting. After her family had died and Jess had been brought to the ranch, Seth had been the first cattleman to make her laugh. Her laughter had been like the very first raindrop of a much-needed storm, and, after that, the ranch had begun to feel like home.

Among the mustangs and Morgans—and four or five spindly-legged, knobby-kneed foals—were Meg, her own graceful, Appaloosa mare, whom she'd owned for four years; Cielos, Jake's big, black stallion; and Luina, the little palomino mare who adored Diaz.

Reunited at last with their horses, they would soon bring the rest of the herd back to Honey Lake Valley, where each person at the ranch would forge a new beginning and, she hoped, gain the peace that he or she dearly longed for.

As Tom Rawlins knelt, feeding split logs into the parlor hearth until the flames drove back the last of the encroaching chill, Jess observed him over her cup of tea and saw a man of interesting contrasts. His movements were neither hurried nor restive, yet the thoughtfully frowning mouth beneath his blond mustache told of the many concerns that invariably fell to men of his rank. In his gray eyes was the knowledge that difficult tasks must be done, but in his face was the patience to bring them about. Recently having come off duty, he still wore his crisp uniform of federal-blue trousers and shell jacket, the shoulders of which bore the gold, double-bar insignias of captain. When the room was sufficiently warm, he stood and unfastened a pair of brass buttons at his throat.

Opposite the hearth, Jake settled into the settee beside Jess, his face content after a full supper. His brown felt hat was on his head, where it belonged, and Jess smiled to herself, realizing she had rarely seen him without it, except for when he was sleeping. He was a rancher, and he wore it as a matter of course, whether indoors or out. It never occurred to anyone who knew him to take offense, including Tom.

"I'm grateful to you for allowing Seth to remain here with the horses," Jake told him.

"As am I, Tom," Hank added, his hands folded contentedly over his rounded stomach. "When those drunks ran the Paiutes off the ranch, Seth told me you were the one Jake would have him turn to."

"Where is Seth?" Jess asked.

"He didn't want to leave the horses," Jake told her. "Hank and I will take shifts and watch them through the night, spelling each other so we all can sleep."

Tom took the empty chair near Jake. "I have two spare bedrooms, and you're welcome to them for the night. I offered one to Seth when he came, but he's refused to leave the horses."

"Much obliged," Jake said. "We were attacked when we returned to the ranch with the Thoroughbreds, and Jess's horse was shot and fell on her, bruising her ribs." He smiled warmly at her. "I expect she'd be grateful for a bed rather than a bedroll on the hard ground."

"Where were you attacked?" Tom asked.

"Between Pyramid Lake and the ranch, near Smoke Creek." Jake shifted beside Jess, as if a memory troubled him, but then it passed. "I think those Paiutes simply meant to scare off more settlers. As soon as they realized that Jess was a woman, they left."

Jess recalled the startling vision she'd had during the attack of the blackened rings on the ground and the missing buildings, but since Seth had certainly told Tom about the event itself, she said nothing.

"I'll speak to the general about setting up a guard station near Smoke Creek," Tom said. "The Paiutes have tried to scare away other travelers, as well. Honey Lake Valley is starting to teem with immigrants escaping the war in the States, and those people don't know the differences between the Plains warring tribes and the Paiutes, so many of them respond violently. This spring's financial crash on the Comstock—you two haven't heard about that? Well, the crash sent undesirable elements from Virginia City into new directions, so the Paiutes have a lot to contend with."

Jess sat up straighter, wondering how the market crash might have affected her father's best friend, Edmund Van Dorn, and the import store Edmund and her father had owned together. "What exactly happened to the market, Captain?"

"The stocks of the big silver mines dropped from far above their real value to as much below," Tom said, "and the wildcats collapsed."

"Ophir stock, once held at more than four thousand dollars per foot of mine, is now valued at around four hundred," Hank put in. "Gould & Curry, only months ago valued at over six thousand dollars per foot, now sells for less than fifteen hundred, and nearly all other mining operations are the same. Thousands of people have been ruined, work has stopped on the wildcat operations, and good mine owners and managers realize they must move forward in a sounder manner."

"I'm concerned for my father's import store in Carson City,"

Jess admitted. "His best friend and business partner owns it now."

"Edmund is a shrewd businessman," Jake assured her. "He would have known this would eventually happen and prepared for it."

"Edmund...." Tom said, looking thoughtful. "He and I worked with the sheriff to find those men who attacked you, Jess."

At Hank's baffled smile, Jake told him about the nine men who had attacked Jess in a street in Carson City the year before, under the belief that, since she had a Southern accent, she must have been a Confederate sympathizer, a traitor. Jess picked up the story from there and briefly explained how her family's house had been doused with kerosene and set afire a few days after the assault, resulting in the deaths of her parents and baby sister.

"They left a Confederate flag in the yard," Jess added, unable to keep a note of bitterness from her voice. "Then, last fall, two of the arsonists were part of a group that raided our ranch to steal the mustangs. The other seven men who attacked me in the street were never found, but at least those two were brought here and imprisoned. One of the men's reactions at seeing me alive was effectively an admission of guilt that he was the man—or one of the men—who killed my family and also meant for me to die in the fire. But I had been walking with Jake some distance from the house when the fire had started, so I escaped."

The room went deathly still, but Jess realized that only Tom had stiffened at her words. The captain silently set down his coffee cup. "Jake, Jess, I thought you knew. Those two men... they weren't the ones who murdered the Hales."

In an instant, Jake was no longer relaxed but sharply alert. "How do you know?"

Tom sat forward on the edge of his chair, his gray eyes showing concern. His blond hair, straw-colored mustache, and brass buttons blazed golden in the firelight, as if he was an angel sent by God to warn them. "After that mob raided the ranch, your men brought the men here to the jail and pointed out the two who had attacked Jess in Carson City. When I told them they were being charged with murdering the Hales, they readily gave their names and said they'd recently been released from jail. Disorderly conduct," Tom added. "Both of them had been jailed for shooting up a saloon the night your family died. The warden confirmed all that they said. Also, they both had money in their pockets when they were brought here—a lot of money, and money they hadn't had while in jail, or else it would have been recorded as unusual. It was only after they'd served time for being disorderly that they were paid to do some deed, perhaps to attack your ranch."

"Or maybe they just needed the horses," Jake said. "Any idea who hired them?"

"They refused to tell where the money had come from, even though they were made to carry heavy bags of sand here for days."

An idea sparked in Jess's mind, and she latched onto it like a drowning man clutching a lone branch. The thought that someone had hired them to attack the ranch and perhaps harm Jake or her was unbearable. "Perhaps they stole the money?"

Tom shook his head. "No. There had been no report of stagecoaches or wealthy people being robbed to come close to explaining that amount of money any other way. I'm sorry."

As tension ran like hot iron through her veins, Jess curled her fingers around fistfuls of her skirt. "Can't you question them again? Perhaps with a greater threat to their well-beings than the burden of sandbags?"

Jake laid his hand over Jess's. "Tom's an experienced officer, Jess. I'm confident he conducted a detailed investigation."

"I did," Tom affirmed, "and I would have, whether or not it had been a good friend who had asked me, though I was particularly intent upon finding answers in your case. Unfortunately, the men cannot be questioned further."

Jess felt as if a frigid, otherworldly ghost had just passed through her. "Why not?"

"They're dead," Tom said. "While my men were transferring them to the territorial prison, they wrestled a gun from a lieutenant and tried to escape. Both prisoners were shot and killed."

Jess's fingers began to tremble. "Whoever murdered my parents in the house fire, who also meant to kill me...he's still out there?" Her voice sounded to her like that of a frightened child in a dream—distant, unfamiliar.

"There's no way of knowing who hired them," she heard Tom say, as though he was calling from across a chasm. "Before the financial crash, plenty of people had that much money."

Near her, Jake's voice rumbled. "A band of outlaws set fire to other houses after the Hales' house burned down."

"The Hale fire was the first," Tom said. "I believe it may have given someone a notion of a way to drive Southerners out of the territory."

"You believe an individual or a private group is financing a private war against Southerners," Jake said, processing Tom's comment.

At this, Jess pushed through the haze of shock and drew her own conclusion about the death of her family. "Then, the murder of my family wasn't motivated only by politics." She met Jake's steady gaze, then shifted her eyes to meet Tom's. "The attack against my family was personal. Who could possibly have hated us that much?"

Jake asked the next logical question. "Are they still in the territory, or California?"

Tom held up his hands. "We've begun assuming the facts and inferring the conclusion of those assumptions. I said that I *believe*; I did not say that my belief has been proven."

"It's the only answer that makes sense, given everything we do know," Jake said. "Are Southerners still being attacked?"

Tom rubbed his thumbs together. "For some months, we, along with other federal authorities in the region, have been watching certain people whom we suspect to be members of the Knights of the Golden Circle."

"The secret secessionist organization," Jess murmured. "I've heard rumors of them."

"This seems to be a Northern counterpart to that group. We believe their Western headquarters to be in San Francisco," Tom said with a nod, "though their operations and plans appear to include the entire Pacific Coast, or at least the states and territories they believe they can induce to join them. We watch their movements closely and take precautions accordingly. They operate on several levels, from terrorizing transplanted Southerners—such as hiring outlaws to set houses afire— to placing their leaders in local offices of high governing authority."

"Oh, my," Hank said, speaking for the first time in several minutes. He appeared to be reviewing all that had been said, and then he leaned closer to Jess. "What caused you to think that the two men who attacked you on the street in Carson and later raided the ranch were the same men who killed your family?"

Jess thought back to that moment after the battle at the ranch. She had been on horseback, and the burly man had stood on the ground, staring up at her. "The one man said, 'I never expected to see you again.'"

"So, he didn't say, 'I never expected that you'd be alive,' or 'I never expected that you'd survived'?" Hank asked.

"No," Jess confirmed. "He was just surprised to see me at the ranch." She dropped her face into her hands and spoke into her palms. "I believed he'd tried to kill me along with my family, and that his shock at seeing me was an admission of his guilt." Her fingers curled fiercely in her hair. "He merely hadn't expected to meet me again after the attack in the street! All this time, I thought I had closure. I thought that justice had been served, and that my parents and sister had been vindicated!" She dropped her hands and looked up at the three men with an angry scowl. "Did you know that my sister's nursemaid also died in the fire? Her name was Elsie, and she was my close friend. Now, my parents, my sister, Emma, and Elsie are gone, and you're telling me that we still don't know who is responsible? You're telling me that a secret Unionist group, a mirror organization to the Southern Knights of the Golden Circle, may be responsible for depredations that continue?" In her fury, Jess stood up, her voice rising to a near shriek. "Are you telling me that a personal attack against my family is what killed them, and that I may yet be seen as a threat to the people responsible if they discover I'm still alive?"

Jake stood up and came around behind her, clamping his strong hands on her arms as a means to still her as much as a means to calm her. "If someone paid Union loyalists to wage a private war against Southerners in the West," Jake said to Tom, "isn't it possible that one or two men were paid to kill Jess's family, that the Hale fire just happened to be the first? No one was seen running from the house after the fire was lit, so it's almost certain that the arsonist was only one man."

"It's possible," Tom said. "But that fire and the events surrounding it diverged completely from the other instances that followed, all of which had notable similarities. For instance, a Confederate flag was left at the Hale fire, but not at any of the others. It was also the only fire set in the center of a town. The rest were set at houses on the outskirts of towns, or in distant, outlying areas. And at none of the other sites was an empty tin of kerosene found. That was only at the Hale house."

"Kerosene?" Hank frowned. "How large of a tin? Could it have been one that Jess's family used in their home? Perhaps it was merely misplaced before the fire."

"No, it had been emptied," Jake said, "and the tin wasn't the size used in homes. It was one of the larger types used by mining companies to light the deep shafts they dig." Jake's hands gently squeezed Jess's shoulders, easing their pressure now, letting her know she was not alone. "The fire spread lightning-quick," he added.

Hank's ever-present smile showed deep concern. "I sure am sorry, Jess. It sounds as if the man responsible for your loss may never be found."

"What was odd about it," Jess said, "was that my father was out of the house walking when the fire started. He had a very distinctive appearance, so the arsonist must have seen him, but I was some distance away, so I wouldn't have been seen. Whoever struck the match intended for my father to survive… perhaps to constantly suffer the loss of his family." She felt the strength leaching out of her as dormant feelings of dread and regret resurfaced, torturing her thoughts and exhausting her spirit. Jake must have felt it, because his chest was suddenly at her back, his arms supporting her. "How can anyone harbor so much hate?"

"*'Because iniquity shall abound, the love of many shall wax cold,'*" Jake said softly. Jess recognized the words Jesus spoke in the gospel of Matthew. Jake lowered his cheek to her temple, apparently not caring who saw the intimate gesture. "That's why we make close friends of good people who still love and care for each other." She felt his head brush against hers in a nod toward Tom and Hank. "Good people aren't hard to find if you look for them."

Outside, perhaps in the quadrangle, a bugle sounded tattoo. Tom stood, his blond hair and buttons still gleaming, his eyes kind as he gazed down at Jess. "It's been a long evening. I'll show you to your room so you can rest."

Jess leaned her head back against Jake's shoulder and looked up at his friend. "Is there any way you can find out who might be involved in the Union conspirators' organization?"

"We've been looking into it," Tom said. "So far, we have no leads, though we will continue to investigate and search, just as we'll keep following the movements of the Knights of the Golden Circle." He glanced at Jake, then looked back at her. "But after all this time, I'm afraid we have to accept the possibility that we may never know who killed your family...or why. That will be hard to live with, I know."

Jess's back stiffened, and she stood to her full height. "You don't know me well yet, Captain, so I'll tell you plainly: I won't accept that. I will always listen; I will always watch. The person who killed my family is walking about a free man—free to harm someone else, free to harm me if he learns I survived the fire. One day, he'll make a mistake, and I'll be there to see justice done."

Chapter Six

Jake whistled and waved the mustangs and Morgans into the livery stable corral on the outskirts of Carson City, then followed the last of them in, latching the gate behind him. Inside the corral, on the far side, Jess stepped to the ground, rigid with determination, and began to unsaddle her horse. She'd fought her fears with anger a number of times before, and he was pleased to see that she was boldly determined to prevail against the unexpected threat against her rather than cowering like a frightened rabbit.

He watched her pluck the saddle from the horse and lay it atop the corral fence. She was slender, but healthy and strong, and that was part of what drove his passion for her; as the wife of a rancher, she needed that strength to survive. Her headstrong ways were also part of what prompted his concern for her—he wouldn't call it worry—and his caution. Despite what they'd discovered from Tom Rawlins, Jake didn't expect a vindictive acquaintance of Jess's father to recognize her, much less attempt to harm her, with a crowd looking on in broad daylight. He would never permit her to be harmed, and he would watch out for her, though not so blatantly as to make her feel trapped. And he'd keep her safe.

Near Jess, Seth shouldered his saddle, then lifted Jess's saddle with his free arm. She followed him in Jake's direction. Jake had purchases to make for the ranch, and Jess wanted to visit a dress shop to buy fabric scraps so she could make new dresses for Mattie and Grace. She also wanted to visit Edmund Van Dorn at Hale Imports. To accomplish all their tasks and get the much-needed supplies and horses back to the ranch as soon as possible, they would need to split up. As Jess and Seth approached, Jake stepped down from his saddle and explained his thoughts. "And, Jess?" he added, opening his saddlebag. "I'd like Seth to go with you."

"I don't need a watchdog, Bennett. No offense intended, Seth."

Jake paused from searching his saddlebag and pinned her with an unwavering gaze. "If Seth doesn't go, you don't go."

As her face reddened and her mouth pressed shut, Jess appeared to battle several irascible comments but finally jerked her head in what he took as a nod of agreement.

Looking more than a little pleased with Jess's watchdog comment, Seth stood a little taller, a young but confident man, with a bearing that conveyed the fact that he could make accurate use of the gun at his hip, if necessary. To give them a moment alone, Seth slipped out through the gate with the saddles to leave them in the care of the man working inside the livery barn.

Jake took a coin pouch out of his saddlebag and gave it to Jess. She accepted it and slipped it into the pocket of the yellow calico dress she'd sewn the summer before from fabric and white edging lace that he'd bought her. He loved how the sunny color accentuated the long, golden highlights among her long, chestnut-brown hair, as well as her eyes, green like sage leaves. "Yellow looks beautiful on you, Jess," he said, unable to tell her his feelings any other way. He pointed a gloved thumb in Seth's direction. "I just want you safe."

A softened expression made her mouth relax, and he was tempted to kiss it, but dozens of people bustled past the corral, and Ho Chen and Hank were waiting for him in two wagons a few steps away. Jess sighed, lifted a hand toward his cheek as if to touch it, then lowered it again to her side. Her mouth curved up in a smile, assuring him that she understood his concern. "I know, Bennett."

Seth ducked his head beneath the low storefront awning as he stepped with Jess from the boardwalk into the street. "How many Thoroughbreds did you bring from the East, Miss Jess?"

"Twenty, but we lost eight to the Plains Indians on our way to winter at Fort Laramie." She beamed up at him. "Just wait until you see them, Seth. Long, sleek lines, and their coats shine like onyx and topaz."

Jess envisioned their foals—nearly the height of a Morgan, with the muscles and fortitude of a mustang and the pure speed of a Thoroughbred. The Bennetts' ranch might be the only one within two thousand miles to possess such a breed. Their horses would bring a good price, and they would be beautiful to look at. Perhaps a few of them might even race.

Just then, she and Seth rounded a corner and walked straight into pandemonium. Two gangs of men—miners, judging by the black dust covering them—thrust soot-smeared fists and blackened trouser knees into adversaries' stomachs, jaws, and noses. The words they hurled at one another indicated they were employed by rival mines. Several bystanders who tried to stop the fracas found themselves embroiled in it.

For an instant, Jess felt again her alarm from the year before, when a group of men had attacked her on a similar street. But this time, Seth was in front of her, backing up to push her away from the fight.

Suddenly Seth was slammed against her, and her head struck a hard wall, Seth's weight abruptly driving the breath from her. He muttered something in anger, then pushed away from her, and she saw him go after the man who had shoved him.

Through a black haze of pain, she heard a murmur pass among the crowd of bystanders, as if they were uncertain of their ability to remain passive and uninvolved. Jess crumpled, hearing commotion around Seth. She reached blindly toward the wall for support.

As she blinked away the darkness, she saw three or four of the enraged miners at the far side of the conflict hurl themselves at a new target. Beside her, Seth had gained momentum and was holding his own against two of the roughnecks.

Then, one of the men spun Seth around, and the other shifted to gain advantage over the youth from behind. Struggling for breath but enraged herself, Jess grabbed onto the belt of the man who had lunged toward Seth. Jolted off balance by the unexpected weight, he started to fall, pulling Jess down with him. As he landed, his wrist gave a sharp, crunching *snap*.

Howling in agony, the man struggled free of her grip and regained his feet, his eyebrows arched in pain—and, apparently, in surprise that a woman had taken him down. With barely a glance at his comrades, he ran off, clutching his unnaturally twisted hand as he shouldered his way through the crowd.

Gravel kicked up as the three or four thugs across the road struggled to overpower their latest target, but the big man fought with quick evasions and hard punches, swiftly dropping the attackers one by one.

One man lay at Seth's feet. As Jess looked up, the second man ruthlessly hurled the youth against the wall. Seth slid to the dust, momentarily stunned.

"Seth!"

The miner crouched over him, grabbed the remnants of Seth's vest, and tried to drag him to his feet for more.

"Let go of him!" Jess screamed. She pushed herself to her knees. Four men lay around the big man, who suddenly stood alone in the street. He spun around to face the other insurgents, but Jess's view of her apparent rescuer was blocked by a row of beefy knuckles, which reached down and hauled her up by her bodice. No sooner did she hear fabric ripping than she was thrust aside into the sharp, plank corner of the building beside Seth. Pain exploded in her shoulder and head, and she collapsed near him in a darkening stupor.

There was a sudden breeze, and a large body struck the building full-length beside her. She did not see the man who had thrown the miner, and as the rogue toppled facedown in the dust, she lost her grasp on consciousness.

She came to a dim awareness of the crowd breaking up and could hear someone giving an order to move the inert forms of the miners out of the street.

"Miss Jess? Miss Jess!" Though she was relieved to hear Seth's gasping voice, nothing within her could compel her to answer.

"It's all right. I'll get her."

Jess knew that voice—the deep tone, the quiet strength of it. Jake. As his sturdy arms lifted her up, her cheek fell against his soft, flannel shirt, and she inhaled the scents of leather and horses. Her fears bled away, and she let the darkness take her.

Two male voices mingled somewhere in the distance, their words a jumble. Jess was content to be left to rest and simply listen to the calm, steady beating of the heart beneath her ear.

A jingle of tiny bells sounded, and then the noises of town diminished. It seemed she was inside an expansive stillness, and she felt a flutter of disappointment as she was lowered from the warm flannel to a cool couch, worn rough.

Tapping heels rapidly approached, bringing with them a rustling of silk.

"Ma'am," Jake's voice said, "I apologize for the—"

"Great Scot and all of England!" a woman exclaimed. "J-Jessica, m'dear, I thought ye died! What—what's happened to ye?"

A slim, cool hand touched Jess's forehead, shaking slightly, and Jess flinched in pain when it passed over the tenderness on the side of her head that had hit the wall. Almost absently, she realized that her face felt sweaty and cold, and that an odd sound in her ears like crackling champagne bubbles was drowning out the voices around her.

"Do you know her, ma'am?" came Seth's voice.

"That I do. And ye, young sir, look as though ye've caught a bit of what's ailing my dear friend here." Swiftly, the woman's voice changed to a commanding tone. "Ye just sit yerself right down there on that chair—no, never you mind about dirtying the upholstery...well, now that I think on it, perhaps one of the wooden stools would serve ye better. Wherever did ye collect all that dust ye're wearin'?" Her voice faded. Jess heard water splashing into a basin.

"We had a scuffle with some fellows in the street," Seth said, his voice sounding clearer to Jess. The sound of champagne bubbles was diminishing.

A big, warm hand now lay against Jess's cool cheek, and a scent like earth and leather reached her nostrils. "You're one tough woman, Jessica Bennett," Jake said.

Her heavy eyelids finally parted, and she saw Jake squatting close beside her. A faint bruise discolored his whiskered jaw, his dark eyes had that sober, scrutinizing look, and his brown hat sat squarely on top his head. Lovely—she'd gotten him into yet another scrape.

"Bennett, what are you doing here?" she murmured as her head rolled back on the sofa pillow.

"Seeing that you stay out of trouble. Again."

She frowned at the teasing glint in his eyes. "I didn't have any troubles until you came along."

"It seems to me you've had plenty." Jake expertly felt her ribs, his hands warm through her dress and corset. The relief in his face told her he detected no additional injuries. "I was a couple of blocks down the street when I overheard the trouble. Somehow, I knew you'd be in the middle of it." The corner of his mouth lifted, and he plucked at her sleeve, now in tatters. "How does your side feel, and your arm?"

"No worse than before." She propped herself up on an elbow to search the room, pressing a hand to the knifelike pain in her head. "Where is Seth?"

Jake moved aside so she could see him seated across the room. "Is the headache bad?" Gently he pulled her hand away and inspected the injury with the same patient tenderness she'd seen him use to soothe a newborn calf.

Determined not to complain, she gingerly shook her head no. "A cool compress would be nice, though," she said softly.

"Now, Jess, m'dear," the woman said, "try and sit up if ye can...there now, that's better. Ooh, I best get ye a shawl. Ye seem to have lost a bit o' coverin'."

As Jess leaned back against a sofa pillow, she looked down at the jagged tear in her bodice and another at her hip, then dazedly accepted the wrap being draped around her shoulders. She had cuts on her arm where her sleeve had torn, and her skirt was ruined.

The room spun and then stilled. Jess finally recognized the comfortably filled space as the dressmaker's shop she and her mother had frequented when they'd lived in Carson City. There were new bolts of cloth, many in pinks and yellows and greens, spools of ribbon, shelves of laces. In their usual places were the long mirrors, jars of buttons, and an assortment of other feminine trappings.

Jess summoned a smile as the shopkeeper set the basin on the couch beside her. "Thank you for taking us in, Gusty. I imagine we've caused you quite a stir."

"Not a bit." Augusta Scott—Gusty, to all who knew her—waved away her words of gratitude as only a friend can. "I'm thinking it'll be good for business." She wet a cloth in the basin and handed it to Jess. "Ye'll be needing a new gown now, after all."

Jess smiled dutifully but regretted ruining the yellow calico. Jake had liked it on her; he'd even complimented her on it less than an hour before. Feeling well enough to recall her social graces, Jess introduced everyone as she pressed the cooling cloth to her head.

Gusty cleansed and bandaged her wounds, then Seth's, with the efficiency of a battlefield nurse. Every part Irish, except for her late husband's surname, she was perhaps in her mid-forties, pleasantly round with lively, attentive eyes as blue as Taggart's and copper-and-silver hair, which was pulled back loosely in a twist.

Jake stood and politely declined being fussed over. The only real injuries seemed to be to his knuckles, and those he soaped and washed in the basin. "I'm grateful for your help, Mrs. Scott. Would you mind my leaving Jess here while I purchase some supplies? Seth will know where to find me if there's a need."

"Now, don't ye be worrying none about Jessica here, Mr. Bennett. She can rest herself awhile, and when she's feeling up to it, I'll find her a ready-made dress to replace the one she's wearin'." With a warm smile, she bustled away with the basin to refresh the water.

Seth rose to his feet and faced his boss. "I'm sorry, Jake, that I didn't keep Jess from harm."

Jess yearned to reassure the youth, but she knew he first needed absolution from Jake.

"It's a good man," Jake told him, "who doesn't concern himself with the odds. I've rarely met a man with greater courage, or one I trusted more."

Jake didn't apologize for Seth's injuries, and neither would Jess. None of them had caused the brawl, none of them could have prevented it, and Seth, a cattleman from skin to soul, wouldn't have appreciated anyone pointing out a weakness in him.

Seth nodded, then left them alone to trail after Gusty, asking if she would consider sewing a few stitches in his vest.

Jake watched Jess for a moment as she bathed her face and neck with the damp cloth. "It seems that every time you and I are in Carson City together, you end up covered in dirt and left in rags."

Jess knew him well, well enough to realize that his attempt at levity was for both their benefits. She laid a hand on his bronzed wrist, careful to avoid his bruised knuckles. "I'm not always in rags, Bennett," she murmured. "But, in all fairness, neither am I someone who is likely to fret over a scuff on my boot."

Jake's smile was genuine. "No," he agreed, "you're not."

The tiny bells above the door jingled, and Hank politely swept off his hat and closed the door behind him, huffing slightly. His ever-present smile brightened as his eyes darted about the room, then rested on Jake and Jess. "I left my wagon up the street with Ho Chen," he said, pulling a folded bandana from his pocket and wiping a trickle of sweat from his forehead. "I pushed through the crowd just in time to help move the men who were too stunned to peel themselves off the road. Heavy lifting, even for a farmer." He grinned, pocketed the bandana, and lifted his hat to replace it atop his head. "Now that I see that everyone looks well attended to, I'll go back and—"

Gusty's brisk footsteps clicked on the wooden floor, and the

Irish woman emerged with a basin of fresh water. Her blue eyes landed on Hank like a forty-niner's hand on a solid gold nugget, but she quickly recovered and gave him a bright nod of greeting, which appeared brighter still as sunlight streaming through the window turned her hair the hue of a new copper kettle.

Hank's gaze followed her effervescent shadow, which bustled along behind her, as he lowered his hat again and tried to recover his line of thought. "Uh, I'll go back—to the back, of the shop here—and try to find some material for...curtains. For my house." After his clearly improvised explanation, he hurried with apparently some presence of mind toward the calicos filling the shelves at the bottom of the staircase.

Jake rose to his feet as Gusty placed the basin of fresh water beside Jess. "Well, then," Gusty said with a tone of amusement as she surveyed the three burly men standing amid the pinks and yellows, ribbons and laces. "I don't know that I've ever set eyes upon a more handsome clothier's shop." Her voice trembled with the final few words, words that, though pleasant, seemed to Jess like they'd been calculated to make the men aware of their surroundings, as if part of Gusty suddenly hoped they'd leave.

Rather than dampen her cloth with clean water, Jess laid the cloth aside and lowered her feet to the floor, her headache tolerable. A moment ago, Gusty had seemed pleased, even eager, to see Hank walk through her door, but now that he was standing at the bottom of the stairs that led to her upper-level apartment, her cheerfulness suddenly seemed artificial, as if she was attempting to hide some uncertainty. Jess realized that Gusty must have been quite startled to discover that she had survived the Hale house fire after a year of believing she had died.

Jake thanked Gusty for her assistance, told Jess he'd meet

her at the corral in a few hours, and left to see to his errands, shrewdly leaving Hank behind.

So, men do things like that, too, Jess thought, chuckling softly. Did Jake intentionally seek out reasons to be near her? As he strode past the window, he gave her a wink. *Apparently so.* Perhaps that was why he'd gotten to her so soon after she and Seth had been pulled into the fight on the street. Jake loved her, and he couldn't help staying attuned to her whereabouts with his eyes and ears, just as she couldn't help but search him out when she knew he was nearby.

Jess turned toward the selection of ready-made dresses with a new goal in mind—to select a dress that would be worthy of Jake's admiration.

"One of the secrets to a happy marriage," her mother had once told her, *"is to stay beautiful, so that he keeps falling in love with you."*

She must have been right, Jess mused, for her father had loved her mother right up until the moment they both had died.

Jess abandoned her melancholy for an appreciation of the love they'd shared as she set out to find a dress Jake would love on her.

Gusty helped Hank to select some fabric for his curtains, and, at his tentative request, warmly agreed to sew them to the measurements he specified. She invited Seth to leave his vest with her, saying they could return for the items before they left town that evening.

Just as pleased at the way Hank and Gusty were getting along as she was at her anticipation of Jake's delight once he saw her, Jess twirled slowly in front of a tall mirror in her federal-blue calico dress dotted with tiny red roses. Small, white buttons trailed from the square neckline down the bodice to the top of the hoop skirt, and the waist was cinched with the leather belt Jake had braided with his own hands. The sleeves, huge and puffy at her shoulders and fitted along her forearms, accentuated her tiny waist. Underneath the dress and layers of crinoline, petticoat, and pantalettes, her deerskin moccasins, though not visible, were blessedly comfortable. Jess buckled her gun belt just below her waist, knotted her bandana behind her neck, and, after brushing back loose strands of hair, set her hat on her head.

"And how are ye comin' along, m'dear?" Gusty asked as she approached Jess with her characteristically clicking heels. After a quick assessment of Jess's appearance, Gusty nodded and smiled. "Lovely as a gun-totin' faerie, ye are, Jess...and married to a handsome man such as that! I think your mother would be...p-proud." The older woman's voice caught.

"Is it that difficult to accept that I'm alive?"

"No, though it was quite a jolt seeing ye, and no denying it. I—" She glanced toward the stairs that led to her apartment, then faced Jess again, her blue eyes wide, as though she'd recently watched a ghost emerge through the closed lid of a coffin and was apprehensive of its return. "I thought I was seein' your mother at first," she said, lowering her voice. "Then I saw ye hadn't the lines by yer eyes, and ye hadn't her pallor. Jess...I was there that night." Gusty gripped her hands together, visibly shaken.

Jess immediately understood. "You saw the fire."

"I'd just delivered a finished gown to your neighbor, Mrs. Nolan, for her final fitting. When I rounded the corner and saw your parents' house blazin', I thought hell had risen right up through the streets of Carson." She rapidly crossed herself.

Jess grasped Gusty's hands, desperate to know what had happened after Jake had signaled Lone Wolf and the other mounted cattlemen to whisk her safely away. "Did you see my mother inside? She was upstairs. And Emma—my baby sister? What about a stranger outside who might have started the fire? Did you see anyone running away from the house, or watching it?" she added, knowing that an arsonist may have done just that.

"Everyone worked to put out the fire; no one stood about," Gusty answered, still talking quickly, as though she'd left water boiling on the stove and felt pressed to go. "I—" She closed her eyes briefly, perhaps reliving that night. "For a moment, I was alone at the side of the house, near the back, and fire was slitherin' up the walls like evil snakes had come for me. No, I saw no strangers," she said again. "Then...then I was running; all the way home I ran, seeing the horror, over and again." She finally opened her eyes and refocused on the present, on Jess. "I thought ye'd died," she said, almost imploring. "I thought that all of ye had died."

"But I'm here now," Jess said, having relived the fire often enough herself to know the horror of Gusty's resurrected nightmare.

The older woman's eyes welled up with tears, and Jess hugged her in mutual consolation. Apparently, Jess wasn't the only one feeling like the emotional equivalent of a spinning top that day.

Seth and Hank must have overheard their conversation, for Seth now laid a hand on Jess's shoulder, partly to comfort, she suspected, and partly to remind her that they were planning to meet Jake at the livery corral. In an equally wordless response, Jess nodded her thanks at Seth's kindness and looked to the door to acknowledge their imminent departure.

Gusty was still wiping at her tears when Jess, Seth, and Hank paid her for the goods and her sewing work. When she shooed them out the door with a courteous reminder to return later for Jess's fabric remnants, Seth's vest, and Hank's curtains, her shopkeeper's smile was nearly back in place; she'd begun to regain control over her features.

Plainly smitten, Hank didn't seem to notice anything indecorous about Gusty's behavior, perhaps because he empathized with the terrible sting of loss. His expression warm and sincere, he finally placed his hat back on his head, only to tip it to Gusty once again as he followed Jess and Seth out the door.

Between the two men, Jess began the walk toward the import store, but as they passed Gusty's store window, she turned back, looking through the window as Jake had done, in time to see Gusty's petticoat lace and shoes disappear lightning-quick up the stairs. A door slammed, rattling the glass in its pane.

Jess continued walking with Hank and Seth. She hoped that whenever she was reunited with Miriam Van Dorn, her mother's cherished friend would react with fewer hysterics to Jess's "resurrection." Thinking realistically, Jess rolled her eyes at the likelihood of such an outcome. Gusty was, as a rule, as solid as the rocks at Stonehenge. If discovering that Jess was alive had shaken *her*, then, in all likelihood, Miriam Van Dorn would faint dead away.

Chapter Seven

Jess pulled back from Edmund Van Dorn's warm embrace, not wanting to let go. His sparse but frantic mud-gray hair had receded since the autumn before, and he had thinned considerably beneath his tweed waistcoat and trousers—although, even in her earliest memories of him, his tall frame had never carried excess weight. Now, he stood slightly hunched and as limp as day-old celery, as if life had ridden him hard, but his plain, clean-shaven face beamed in a genuine, almost fatherly welcome.

"It's good to see you, Jake," Edmund said, shaking the brawnier hand, then indicated the thin, silver band on Jess's left ring finger. "I knew you were smart enough to marry her."

Jake chuckled. To Jess, her husband looked like a handsome, sturdy chunk of granite amid the import store's fragile crystal hollowware, dainty crystal figurines, and prim crystal chandeliers. Jess smiled at the thought...and longed to be close to Jake, and alone.

"We hope you don't mind our stopping by uninvited," Jake said. "This is the first we've been in town since last year."

"That's just fine," Edmund assured him. "I was about to close up, anyway." He flipped the sign on the front window from OPEN to CLOSED, locked the door, and led them toward a grouping of gleaming parlor furniture that smelled of fresh lemon oil. "How long have you two been back?"

In response to Jess's inquiring look, Jake flicked a warm gaze over her new gown as he held out an arm for her to precede him into the sitting area.

"We rode in to the ranch on Thursday," Jake said, taking a seat beside her. Trusting Edmund as much as her father always had, Jake told Edmund plainly about Ambrose's rejoining the Confederate army, about wintering at Fort Laramie, and about the events at the ranch since their return. Edmund discussed the slowed business at Hale Imports, the store he had co-owned with Jess's father.

They sat amid dining sets, table linens, bedsteads, dressing tables, paintings, and gilt-framed mirrors, all spotless and shining in the afternoon sun. Her father and Edmund had built this store, and she and Ambrose had helped to paint the walls and varnish the luminous wood floor. She could still hear the brisk, rolling gait of her father's boots, even now.

"Your father's shares in the store are yours now, Jess," Edmund reminded her, "and Jake's, of course. I'm sorry to say that after expenses, there has been very little profit this spring. Actually, it cost a portion of the business's savings and a bit of restructuring to keep it afloat; you've already noticed that we have fewer luxury goods and, instead, offer more choices for middle-class citizens, though I believe we'll always carry champagne and tinned oysters. The market will eventually come around, and I've set aside your share of earnings in the safe. They're minimal just now, but they're yours."

Jake briefly met Jess's eyes with a tender, knowing gaze and gave a slight nod. Jess's heart swelled with love for him, understanding him perfectly and agreeing with him completely. Jake lifted the cup of coffee Edmund had poured him to his lips, allowing Jess to answer.

"I no longer keep books at Hale Imports, Edmund," Jess began. "I no longer order or uncrate goods; I don't assist the customers or contribute in any way to the earnings. You have no reason to keep the name Hale Imports, except out of remembrance; no Hales work here anymore. This is your store, and I help keep a ranch now. I cannot and will not accept income I didn't earn."

The grooves around Edmund's muddy, gray-brown eyes deepened as he frowned. "But, Jess, Isaac wanted you to have his share of the store."

"He assumed I'd still be working here. Edmund, would you take money you didn't earn?"

Edmund leaned back in his chair and shifted his shoulders slightly, casting his gaze about as if the plaster ceiling and painted walls held answers. He uncrossed and recrossed his legs, then finally faced Jess again, his wrinkles softening with a reluctant smile. "Your sweet mother was the only Hale I ever met who escaped the family trait of obstinacy."

Jake chuckled. "That's because Georgeanne wasn't born a Hale. She only married one."

Jess slanted an impish glare at Jake but didn't bother to deny the Hale stubbornness that, on most occasions, served her well. She decided to address one of the reasons they had come. "Edmund, my father had other investments that I know little about. I need to settle any outstanding accounts. That income rightfully belongs to Ambrose as the only son." She looked to Jake for confirmation, and he nodded. Turning back to Edmund, she asked, "Did my father leave his will with you?"

"His will? No, but he left me the name of his lawyer in San Francisco…though I'll have to recall where I placed it. When I find it, I'll contact him for you and learn everything I can." He leaned closer, his face earnest. "What I do know is that your father gave Greenbriar to Ambrose, and he specifically told me that he wanted the income from his investments to be used to provide for you."

"Thank you, Edmund." Feeling both hopeful that any remaining money could be used for the ranch and, conversely, reluctant to accept what may otherwise have gone to Ambrose,

Jess set aside her mixed emotions to recall the ride she and Jake had taken through Carson City before coming to the store. "We went to the cemetery earlier, and then rode by to see the lot where our house had stood. A new house has already been built." She didn't mention how seeing the unfamiliar house perched between the two neighboring houses she knew so well had stunned her, as had spying the woman who had thrown open a window upstairs, near where her own room had been, to shake the dust out of a rug before snapping the window shut again.

"...built as soon as the ashes had cooled and had been raked away," Edmund was saying. "Jake, Jess...." The tone of his voice had turned to one of quiet warning, drawing Jess's complete attention to his words. "You realize that Miriam still doesn't know that Jess survived the fire."

This time, Jess relied on Jake and his calm, easy diplomacy to reply. Miriam had been her mother's dearest friend, but Jess had seen a side to Miriam that her mother, with her gentle heart, had overlooked—that of a gossipy, flirtatious society matron, blithely unaware of just how good a man she had married. Jess didn't trust herself to answer Edmund with any quality of tact.

"Do you think it safe to tell her now?" Jake asked calmly but with an undertone of urgency. "From what Tom Rawlins said, the arsonist was never caught."

"She still tends to gossip," Edmund said, "and if the truth makes it to the wrong ears, Jess could be harmed. Perhaps it's best to leave matters as they are. If enough time passes or if the perpetrator is caught, then I can tell Miriam that you survived—and that Ambrose is alive. Which reminds me...." His hands on his knees, Edmund pushed himself to his feet. "Ambrose sent a letter here for you." He disappeared into the storeroom and emerged to hand Jess an envelope. She eagerly snatched it from him, and he chuckled.

"I haven't received word from him since we left Illinois," Jess explained, barely glancing at the envelope before breaking open the seal. *My dearest Jessica,* Ambrose had begun the letter, as always. She smiled and read on. "Ambrose writes that he's going to send a painting of mother from Greenbriar in Lexington here to your import store by way of an ocean steamer."

"It's *Hale* Imports, Jess," Edmund clarified gently, "and it will always remain so."

Warm tears gathered in her eyes at Edmund's altruism and his loyalty to his friends, to her family. Jess searched for words that would sufficiently convey her gratitude, but he was already speaking again.

"The painting of Georgeanne...I remember when your father commissioned the artist. That must have been twenty-five, thirty years ago. It was shortly before Isaac and Georgeanne were married," Edmund told Jake. "As I recall, Georgeanne looked then much like Jessica looks now."

"That beautiful, was she?" Jake murmured, more to her than to Edmund.

"That she was," Edmund said. "At the time, Isaac had just started raising Saddlebreds."

"I don't remember a time when he didn't," Jess said. Even in her earliest memories, her father's Thoroughbreds and Saddlebreds had always graced the paddocks of Greenbriar.

Painfully missing her brother now, Jess finished the letter and returned it to its envelope to reread it with greater leisure back at the ranch. "Even now, while he's fighting in a war, Ambrose is looking out for me. He's sending the painting so that I 'won't feel so greatly the loss of Mother,' as he words it." She formed her mouth into a smile and searched the glimmering depths of Jake's whiskey-hued eyes, knowing he alone would fully understand the love overwhelming her, as well as the joy that she would soon have a visible reminder of her mother. Jake had neither paintings nor photographs of his first wife, Olivia, or their daughter, Sadie. He knew what it would mean to possess more than vague recollections of someone dear who had entered—and left—one's life.

Jake held her gaze a brief moment, then nodded toward the sun, which was beginning its slow descent across the western sky. "Jess and I wanted to see you while we were in town, Edmund."

"Say no more, say no more," Edmund said amiably, standing with them. "Jess may resemble her mother, but she's always resembled her father and brother in her love for horses. I'm sure you both want to get them home."

Jake pulled his small notebook and pencil from the pocket of his vest and wrote down a few lines in large, bold strokes. "I also need to post a notice of hire at the livery stable," he said. "Not all the Paiutes were willing to return to the ranch." He added the name and location of the ranch, plainly visible.

"Is that safe?" Edmund asked.

Jake tore out the small page and put the notebook and pencil back in his pocket. "According to Tom Rawlins," he explained, "the financial crash has cleared out a lot of drifters, and men around here need work. If they don't, they won't bother to ride all the way to Honey Lake looking for a job. No one knows her as Jessica Bennett, and the only two who knew she survived, and knew where she lived, were killed trying to escape their prison guards."

Jake kept his voice calm, and Edmund didn't know Jake well enough to recognize the tension Jess noticed in his cheeks. For her benefit, Jake had stayed and talked with Edmund, but she could tell he was anxious to get her out of Carson City.

"I'm more concerned about Jess's being here in Carson," he said, confirming her thoughts. "After what Tom said about the arsonist's not having been found, I'm beginning to think Jess was safer at my pa's farm in Illinois in the midst of Northerners than she is two thousand miles away from the war, but we won't be staying in town long enough for anyone to recognize her. She's spent most of the day in a clothier's shop, and we'll be riding out shortly." He glanced at Jess. "You asked Mrs. Scott to not tell anyone about you?"

"Yes. She promised, and I believe her."

Edmund rubbed a knuckle under his chin and voiced another concern. "Won't it be possible that the new cattlemen you hire will have difficulties working alongside the Paiutes? You said there's already been some trouble once."

Jake grinned the crooked grin Jess loved. "If a man wants a job bad enough to leave Carson for the desert to work horses and cattle, he won't care who he's working with. And anyone who doesn't want to work alongside Paiutes is free to leave."

At the sound of porcelain and glass shattering on the floor behind them, all three spun around to see Miriam Van Dorn staring gape-mouthed at Jess from the doorway of the storeroom. After a moment, she collected herself and closed her lips. A year and half had passed since Jess had seen her mother's friend, but she couldn't help the uncharitable observations that lanced through her thoughts. Miriam was two inches shorter than Jess; her long, stringy hair, dyed the unnatural black of a coal scuttle, was frazzled, fluffed, and stacked atop her head like layer after layer of prairie pie. Remarkably pretty, gray eyes gave way to a slender nose and a pinched mouth that looked like it had been sucking on pickled lemons. Viewed straight on, she boasted no definitive figure, aside from a general bulkiness swathed in stylish black and white taffeta, but as she turned to drop her gloves onto Edmund's desk, her profile revealed a degenerated bosom pushed up and out from her body, no doubt an attempt to convince onlookers that she had not, in fact, lost the firmness of youth. A swayback trunk consisting of mostly congealed fat ended appropriately with a built-in bustle of the same substance.

There was no doubt about it. She looked like an S.

Immediately, Jess's conscience condemned her as Miriam hesitantly moved in her direction, crying, then laughing, then crying again, her expression seeming to show a battle between great relief and equally immense disbelief. She swayed, and Edmund curled an arm around her waist to support her. Laughing again, Miriam blinked to clear her owlish eyes of tears, then spread her arms open wide. "J-Jessica?"

Whatever Miriam's words and actions of the past, Jess decided, she was plainly happy to see her. With choked laughter of her own, Jess hugged Miriam as close as their hoop skirts would allow.

"You remember Jake Bennett, don't you, Miriam?" Edmund asked, and Jess carefully moved away. "He stayed with us for a night after...after we lost Isaac and Georgeanne. He and Jess are married now."

Miriam seemed to be noticing Jake for the first time, and she swiftly dried her cheeks. "Yes, certainly. It's good to see you again, Mr. Bennett."

Jake politely touched his hat.

"Well, Jessica," Miriam said breezily, apparently starting to regain her bearings, "you certainly chose well. He was so dedicated to making sure that your mother and father received a proper burial, and little Emma, too, of course. But how did you escape? Where have you been all this time?" She giggled and fanned her face with her hand. "Oh my, I'm afraid I'm in a dither. I just came here to walk home with Edmund for supper; I never expected such a surprise. You both must join us. We'll have to use the old china plates, though; I just shattered the new ones I bought." She giggled again, waving away any concern at the mishap. "Oh, we have so much to talk about. I'm so excited to see you, Jessica; I can't *wait* to tell Agnes Peat!"

Jake, Jess, and Edmund all spoke at once, intent to impress upon Miriam how critical it was to safeguard the fact that Jess had survived the fire. Just as quickly, they ceased, and only Jake spoke. "Edmund, we'll leave it to you to explain to Miriam everything that's happened. Ma'am, we thank you for your kind supper invitation, but Jess and I have to gather our horses and wagons and head back to the ranch. Some folks there need the supplies."

Miriam's hands trembled as she reached out, grasping empty air. "But when will we see you again?"

"You and Edmund are welcome anytime you'd like to visit," Jess said warmly, meaning it. "Edmund, you know where the ranch is?"

"From Lake's Crossing, northwest toward Honey Lake, on Long Valley Creek," Edmund recited and grinned. "The old mind hasn't left me yet."

Jake and Edmund shook hands, and Miriam and Jess hugged again. At Edmund's suggestion, Jake and Jess exited out the rear door through which Miriam had entered, away from the bustling street.

As they walked toward the livery corral to meet Hank, Seth, and Ho Chen, Jess looked up at Jake, loving the whiskers that roughened his jaw, loving the pensive glimmer in his eyes, which gazed at her from the shade of his hat brim. "It was so good to see Edmund again."

"Edmund's a good man."

"I was glad to see Miriam, too," she added, surprising herself.

They walked several paces without saying anything more,

and Jess's conscience stung again at how critical she had been of Miriam. She said as much to Jake. "The Paiute people would never belittle a person for her appearance."

Jake glanced at her again. "Neither would you. Everyone occasionally has unkind thoughts, Jess. You know that a person's consistent character is what really matters."

"I haven't always thought highly of her character, either."

Jake stopped walking, and Jess stopped beside him. "Some cattlemen become cattlemen because they want to leave their less-than-admirable pasts behind," he said. "They know that cowboys don't judge, and they don't ask personal questions that aren't their business. Everyone's done or said something—perhaps lots of things—that he later wishes he hadn't. Holding those words or those deeds against a person continues to hurt him for something he may already regret. What good does that do him? What good does that do the person who won't forgive, for that matter? The resentment and anger only simmer in his mind, and he ends up spoiling his own happiness." Jake lifted his big, rough hand to Jess's cheek. "Is that what you're trying to say? That you feel bad for holding something against Miriam?"

"You're saying you think she's changed?"

Jake shook his head. "No, I'm saying that if you don't forgive, you're hurting yourself, as well as others. Try to let the anger go. If a person continues to do wrong to you, you're wise to forgive the other person—and to acknowledge that he'll wrong you again." He placed his hand on her back. "God gives people plenty of second chances. The Paiutes and the cattlemen do the same, because that's what they want from everybody else."

Jake was usually a man of so few words that Jess was always in awe when he revealed the depths of his thoughts. Occasionally, knowing the way he thought made her feel like a wretch. Like now.

"I think I sometimes resented Miriam because I felt that my mother deserved a better friend than her."

"Wasn't your ma sickly, preferring to stay in your house?"

"Yes."

"Seems to me that your ma still could have found another friend if she'd wanted one. It also seems that Miriam remained loyal to your ma, even though she didn't get out much."

They started walking again, Jess mulling over his words. Perhaps her protectiveness toward her mother had made her unreasonable where Miriam was concerned, at least to some extent. She'd learn to look at matters with more forbearance, as Jake did.

She frowned, another of the day's events still troubling her. "I regret that the yellow gown was ruined, Bennett. I know you liked the color."

He smiled down at her, the corners of his eyes crinkling in a way that made her want to touch them. "If the other one hadn't been ruined, I wouldn't have gotten to see how beautiful you look in blue."

Chapter Eight

J ess stepped out onto the ranch house porch and into a wave of early morning heat, already rolling back her sleeves to cool her arms. She saw their neighbor, Hank, carry a shovel around behind his house on his way to the orchard he had begun to plant. He stopped to pick up the remaining apple tree saplings, which leaned against his shed, their roots wrapped in burlap. In front of his house, a newly planted, lone sapling stood between his porch and the creek, lending a welcoming look to his home, as did the blue curtains that now hung in his windows. Jess had initially thought that his purchasing the curtains had been little more than an excuse for him to talk with Gusty, but now she realized their practical value—they blocked out the hot rays of the sun.

Seeing her, Hank lifted a hand and waved, his pink face and cheery smile visible even from a distance, and Jess returned the wave. Turning his back to the last tree he'd planted the day before, Hank walked four paces, carefully checked his alignment with the other trees in the row, and then began digging a new hole. Beyond him, his cows were grazing, and Spruzy, one of the Paiute women, whom he'd hired to perform light chores, was churning butter on his porch, her broad face bent over her task.

Jess descended the porch steps, surveying the work Jake and the men had completed in the week since their return from Carson City. A straight line of fence posts dotted the perimeter of their land far to the north and along two-thirds of the eastern side, approaching the rebuilt Paiute village, which sat huddled in the shade of cottonwood trees. There sat a wagon, stacked with fence posts, and a crew of six ranch hands, already digging the first successive, pre-marked holes of the day. Kneeling at the edge of the long, morning shadow between the barn and the smithy, Jake and Doyle, their shirtsleeves rolled back and their powerful arms glistening—Doyle's, the color of black coffee; Jake's, of tanned leather—steadily worked with hand drills, boring holes through wooden posts, which had yet to be set into the ground. In the grassy valley beyond the northern border, Jess saw four ranch hands on horseback on either side of their two herds, watching over their seventy-nine Morgans, mustangs, and Thoroughbreds—eight mares had foaled—and one hundred cows, plus twenty-seven tiny calves.

For the past week, she had been one of the four on horseback, and she'd loved watching the colts and fillies bounding about on their knobby-kneed, spindly legs, startling the stumpy calves, which would run from them, wide-eyed and bawling, to their mothers. But the previous evening, after supper, Ho Chen had privately asked Jake if he could be part of the fence crew until the work was complete, explaining that he would be "happy to dig." His request had surprised Jess as much as it had Jake when he'd told her about it later at the ranch house. As Jess had turned down the oil lamps that night, she'd recalled seeing the way Ho Chen had cast cautious glances at Lily as they'd worked together in the kitchen, and remembered that he'd baked several tiny, sweet treats specially for Mattie and Grace.

Upstairs, as Jess had stood in the bedroom doorway watching Jake remove his boots, she'd announced, "Ho Chen is in love with Lily."

Jake had paused with a boot in midair, considering what she'd said, then had lowered the empty boot to the floor.

"Last year, when you wanted me to think about whether

I wanted to marry you and stay here on the ranch, you kept your distance so that my decision would come from the mind, as well as the heart," she'd said, pushing several long, loose strands of hair off her face. "I think Ho Chen wants to do the same for Lily, and for himself."

"Will you help Lily in the kitchen in his place?" Jake had said simply.

She had smiled and answered, "I'd be glad to."

Now, there was a bounce in Jess's step as she passed the bunkhouse and continued toward the cookhouse. Early this morning, Jake had told Ho Chen that he could join the fence crew, and as Jess looked over, she glimpsed the side of his round, yellow-brown face and the long, black braid down his back as he lifted a post from the wagon. Already, she looked forward to preparing breakfast with Lily. Ho Chen had worked as cook for Jess's family for four years before they'd both come to the ranch, and he had never shown evidence of any romantic interests before—nor did he much now, as Jess thought about it. Jake was a man who noticed everything, but he hadn't picked up on the subtle differences in Ho Chen's mannerisms. Jess knew Ho Chen extremely well, and she couldn't help but notice his occasional glances toward Lily, his uncharacteristic humming, and his soft, genuine smiles at Lily's two daughters.

Jess swung through the cookhouse door and hung her hat on a peg. Respecting the code of the cattlemen, she couldn't pry into Ho Chen and Lily's fledging relationship—at least, not outright. But, as a woman who was hopelessly in love with a wonderful man, and who had been brought up amid the chivalry of the South, she was fascinated with matters of the heart, and she determined to be a good friend—and a good listener—should Lily choose to confide in her.

Ho Chen and Lily were perfect for each other, she knew. Both were alone and had been for some time, perhaps too long.

Both shared cultural similarities and were well suited for life in the Western territories. They both possessed great love for their families and friends, and they could stand together during hard times and against the harmful persecution of ignorant settlers.

Jess rounded the sideboard and tied an apron around her slender waist. "Good morning, Lily," she greeted the woman standing over the counter.

The bob of black hair lifted to reveal a smiling face—but not Lily's.

"Good morning, Nettle," Jess swiftly corrected herself.

Nettle put an arm around Jess and welcomed her into the work area. "Good morning, my sister! Ho Chen said that Lily should weave larger hats for Mattie and Grace, like his, so she took them to gather reeds."

"Then you and I will cook breakfast together," Jess said, easily matching the other woman's enthusiasm. Ho Chen's conical hat was remarkably similar to those worn by the Paiutes, though with a wider brim that provided added shade. To Jess, Ho Chen's suggestion was more than a kindly tip, and even more than a glimpse of the caring father and husband he could be. It was one of many tumblers falling in place to unlock the dreams and contributions of many that would turn their ranch into a productive and peaceful home for them all.

Together, Jess and Nettle prepared a hearty breakfast, and after the men had eaten and returned to work, they washed the dishes, then gathered clean buckets to go milk the cows.

Outside, Nettle stretched up on her toes—her head almost reaching Jess's shoulder—and peered out toward the valley nearly a mile away. Jess could barely distinguish the tall, thin figure of Nettle's husband, Black-Eye, walking his horse—the pair of them were no bigger than a gnat at this distance—near the herd of grazing beeves. Across the herd from Black-Eye, a slender speck, their teenage son, Natchez, likewise kept watch.

"The grass is already drying," Jess commented. "Jake wanted the fence built so that the herds won't overrun the neighbors' properties, but in this heat, the forage won't last long. We may have to use whatever free range we can."

"He still makes my heart dance," Nettle said, her gaze focused on her husband. The lines around her flared nose and thin but smiling mouth reminded Jess that Nettle had lived through severe droughts before, and that she trusted she would endure this one, as evidenced by the fact that she found Black-Eye of more immediate interest than the lack of rain.

Thinking again of Ho Chen and Lily, Jess saw a way to discreetly broach the matter of their relationship and discuss the courting differences of the two cultures—through Black-Eye and Nettle. Jess smoothed a hand over one of the two cows the men had tied behind the cookhouse, then pulled a short stool partway beneath it. Sitting down, she placed the bucket under the cow's distended udder and braced one foot before the vessel to prevent it from spilling over. "How did you meet Black-Eye, Nettle?" she asked, leaning her temple against the coarse hair of the bovine's belly as Nettle did under the second cow standing behind her.

"I saw him at a festival dance of many clans. Such gatherings are the only time our young women are permitted to talk to young men who are not our cousins."

Jess watched Nettle's shoulders rock rhythmically back and forth as she squeezed milk from the cow's udder.

"He was dressed in his best clothes, adorned with many feathers," Nettle said, fond remembrance in her voice. "When I see the fringes of his blanket lift like feathers in the wind, I am reminded of his appearance that night. My mother made a long, deerskin dress for me that had nearly one hundred fringes and shells," she added.

"So, Paiute women meet men at dances?"

"Often, yes."

Jess doubted that the lively Fourth of July shindigs they put on at the ranch would be quite what Lily or Ho Chen would choose as a preferred setting for a courtship. "How else do Paiute couples meet?"

"Meeting is not always simple; we do not marry our relations, and our eighth cousin is as close to us as our first. We may see each other while hunting or gathering with other clans. We may winter together and see each other in a nearby camp, or attend the festivals of our people. A young woman's parents may be friends with the parents of the young man, much like the white settlers."

Jess checked her milking progress; the bucket was perhaps a quarter full. "What happens after a man sees a woman he likes? Does he bring her gifts?"

"Oh, no. He never speaks to her or visits her family. Instead, he tries to draw the young woman's attention by showing his riding abilities or other skills."

Jess had seen Ho Chen continually show his own abilities and skills to Lily's daughters, and she had also seen both Ho Chen and Lily subtly reveal interest in each other. Yet both seemed reluctant to advance their courtship. Jess contemplated what she knew of each of them. Perhaps they simply wanted time— Lily, especially. The Paiute people considered most decisions for many days and consulted their wise people extensively before making a choice. And, perhaps, the problem was simply the differences in the way their cultures courted.

"Nettle, how did Black-Eye—"

Across the compound, a shout went up. Jess ducked away from the cow and set her bucket to the side as she stood up.

One of the ranchmen near the wagon of fence posts signaled to Jake and pointed. Jess quickly scanned the open sage plains to the east but saw nothing. Apparently, though, Jake had, because he returned the signal, then searched the compound until his eyes found her.

Nettle came to stand beside her. "Horsemen coming," she said.

"Horsemen?" The moment Jess saw the slender column of dust rising near the southwestern foothills, apprehension crawled up her neck on sharp, cold little mouse claws. In the year that she'd lived at the ranch before marrying Jake, riders had occasionally passed by on their way to Susanville, as well as the occasional immigrant family, but in the days since they had visited Tom Rawlins at Fort Churchill, the sense that told Jess trouble was coming had awakened more intensely within her. This time, with these riders, the sharp claws of fear didn't stop.

Two men appeared over the ridge, riding at a leisurely pace, though headed straight toward Ho Chen and the fence crew. Jake laid aside his drill and went to meet them.

Following her instincts, Jess hurried to join him.

"Charles Shane. Most everybody calls me Charlie." Glimpsing Jess, the man plucked his hat from his head of golden hair and cordially tipped his head to the side. "Ma'am." With his tan skin, flaxen hair, and very blond, very thick mustache, he reminded Jess of a spirited palomino.

"Jake Bennett." Jake firmly shook his hand, then shook that of the hollow-cheeked, bearded man, who stood half a hat taller than Charlie. That man touched a dirty knuckle to his hat brim in deference to Jess.

"I'm Eli Payton. I saw your notice in the livery stable in

Carson City that you're looking for a ranch hand." Jess could scarcely detect a mouth moving beneath his black, untrimmed mustache and matching beard, which hid part of his ears and nearly all of his neck. "I've been working the mines in Virginia Town, but I was let go when all the trouble started with the investors."

"Have you done ranch work?" Jake asked him.

Eli nodded toward the distant herds. "I know horses and cattle both. Worked them all my life, until the mines on the Comstock started paying. I met up with Charlie about a day ago. Says he knows this territory from one end to the other."

Raising his eyebrows with interest, Jake shifted his weight to face the other man. "Is that right?"

"Yep. I came West in '49 and worked at the Bar W outside of Grass Valley for about four years. Then I spent about ten years leading folks over the Oregon Trail, across Nevada Territory, and scouting new routes over the Sierra Nevadas. For the past year, I've been hauling freight on the Placerville Road. I was on my way back from doing just that when I met up with Payton here and he told me a rancher near Honey Lake was looking to hire. I'd surely like to settle into one place for a spell and quit running around like a prairie hen."

They're just men looking for work, Jess told herself. *You can't keep worrying over every rider who happens by.*

Jake paused to reflect, then nodded. "You can turn your horses loose in the corral; the bunkhouse is over there. I could use two more sets of hands putting this fence in. This is my wife, Jess," Jake added, almost as an afterthought, keeping his eyes fixed on the men's faces.

Jess watched their expressions just as closely, noting nothing more than polite curiosity in either of them, and her discomfort eased a trifle.

"I'm obliged." Payton turned his bearded face toward Jess once more, then led his gelding to the corral.

Charlie paused to shake hands with Jake, then pulled his white hat over his blond mane, giving it a gentlemanly tug in Jess's direction.

"Well?" Jess asked Jake once the men had passed beyond the range of hearing.

Jake's stance would have appeared reserved to anyone looking on, but Jess saw the warmth he felt for her in his gold-flecked eyes and the hint of a smile on his lips.

"What do you think, Jess?"

"I felt uneasy when I first saw them coming, like they were a threat approaching," she admitted.

Jake listened, as he always did, with keen alertness, as if he perceived every inflection in her voice and watched for even the finest indication of restraint in her face. "And now?" he asked.

For an instant, Jess felt absurdly shy before his regard, like a schoolgirl enamored of an attractive doctor who had just bandaged the scrape on her knee. "I feel better now that I've met them," she said, *and now that I know just how closely you're watching over me*, she thought, but was too abashed to speak it aloud. "But I still feel some distrust."

In the corral, Charlie and Payton pulled saddles and gear from their horses and laid their belongings over the top fence rail. They each carried a rifle and wore a gun, but so did most other men who worked in the desert or the Sierra Nevadas.

"Does one of them trouble you more than the other?" Jake asked.

Jess wanted to kiss him just for asking. That question alone assured her that he took stock in her intuition; he wouldn't have asked it otherwise. She felt tension like hot rivulets of mercury drain from her shoulders and arms. "No, I don't perceive a difference, and, as I said, the uneasiness isn't as strong as it was at first. Perhaps I let my emotions run wild with the mustangs."

His gaze remained steady. "I don't want you to doubt your instincts, Jess. You're wise to weigh them against other factors going on within you and around you, but don't disregard them." He leaned his head a fraction closer and winked. "They've served you well this far, right?"

Jess grinned. Now she wanted to kiss him just because she could.

Jake lifted an eyebrow; he hadn't missed the change in her expression. He rarely did. "Something else on your mind, Mrs. Bennett?"

She returned his gaze boldly. "I want to kiss you."

"Hmm."

His breathing seemed to have deepened.

"You know, my ribs feel much better. I feel almost no discomfort at all."

"Hmm."

His breathing had definitely deepened.

For a moment, Jess fell silent as Charlie and Payton walked past, carrying their gear in the direction of the bunkhouse. Now she understood how Nettle had felt watching Black-Eye a short while ago. Watching one's husband handle a horse or work with his hands did things to a woman.

She drew out her smooth, sultry, Southern drawl to hit him with both barrels. "There are only ten hours left until sundown...."

"Hmm."

"Why are we going into the barn?" Jess asked softly.

Jake's broad, white cotton-clad back moved like a shadow in the starlight as he pulled open the barn door and left it wide.

"Diaz said one of the mares will foal in the next few days," he said, keeping his voice as quiet as hers so they wouldn't waken the cattlemen who were scattered about the compound, snoring in the cool, open air. "Since we're here, I want to take a minute and ready a stall so Diaz can bring her up when he thinks she's ready."

A quick glance around assured Jess that they were the only ones moving about the compound. In the valley, nearly a mile away, four ranch hands on horseback were watching the horses and cattle, the herds resembling a pair of dark lakes amid the plains of sage and bunchgrass.

Breathing a sigh of relief that they were finally alone, Jess caught Jake around his middle before he could step inside, pressing her cheek to his back. She let her fingers enjoy the cottony softness of his shirt, the hard, flat expanse of his stomach, the expansion and contraction of his ribs, and the warmth he emitted, a faint breeze having swept away the day's heat.

He pressed his hand against her forearm, where the cut he had tended had healed. His hand shifted to grasp her fingers, and then he pulled her into the shadows within the barn, where no one would see them if he awakened.

The sweet, musty scent of hay mingled with that of the rich aroma of the leather saddles and bridles hanging on the wall somewhere in the darkness. She heard a bristly swishing sound from one of the stalls, the tail of a restful mare that had foaled a few days before.

Jake didn't wait for Jess's eyes to adjust to the heavier darkness. His hands, firm of purpose, caressed the contours of her waist, rising to her ribs, then slid around her to pull her against him.

She rose up on the toes of her moccasins, gripping his shirtfront, and sensed his head lowering toward hers. His lips found her jaw, then slipped down to the curve of her neck just under her ear, and nuzzled her there, warm, so very warm.

With one of her hands, she released her grasp on his shirt and reached up to touch his sandpaper-rough chin, urging his lips to touch hers.

Jake stepped back and briefly enfolded her fingers in his before letting go. Jess realized that she could see him fairly well now as he nodded meaningfully to the door, then bent to pick up an armload of hay.

Somewhere beyond the barn, out of the still night, came the faint *ching, ching* of jinglebobs that the ranchmen loved to affix to their spurs. The repetitive, birdlike twitter neared, and, following Jake's lead, Jess grabbed a pitchfork to spread the hay he'd deposited in the stall, though she was tempted to use the tool to oust whoever had spoiled her quiet moment with Jake.

A slender cattleman backed into the barn, gently pulling a newborn calf on a rope. The calf gave a low wail as its front knees buckled and it collapsed against the doorframe.

"Diaz!" Jess thrust the pitchfork into the pile of hay and ran to take the rope from his hand.

Diaz narrowed his eyes, trying to see into the darkness, as he moved to lift the calf in his arms. "How did you know it was me, *Mariposa*?"

"The sombrero," Jess said, suddenly breathless.

Diaz stepped past her into the barn with his burden, the calf's head hanging over his elbow as if the newborn animal was unable to hold it up any longer. Behind her, she heard the glassy *clink* of a chimney lantern and the scratch and flare of a match being lit. Jake replaced the chimney and adjusted the wick as she and Diaz shuffled into an empty stall.

"What's the trouble?" Jake asked.

"Only little *problema*," Diaz said, going down on one knee and laying the calf on the ground. "Her mother will not feed her. Taggart is bringing another *vaca*." Beneath his glossy, black mustache, his white teeth flashed at Jess in a reassuring grin. "Do not worry, *señora*. She will be all right."

Apparently, Jake agreed; he was already returning to the stall where he'd begun spreading hay. "I'm readying a stall for your mare, Diaz," he said. "Bring her up whenever you think she's ready."

"Okay, boss."

Just then, Taggart entered, huffing through his flame-orange beard and towing the surrogate cow. "If God meant for man to walk all the way across a ranch," he grumbled with his usual, dry humor, "then He wouldn't have made horses, now, would He?" With one blue eye squinting, he peered accusingly at Diaz and stabbed a stubby finger toward the shamelessly grinning man. "There I lay, sleepin' dead as a stone, and he prods me with a brandin' iron or some such—"

"It was my boot, *hombre*."

Taggart pushed the cow into the stall with the calf, still muttering. "'No time to saddle a horse,' says he. 'Fetch a milk cow quick and bring it to the barn.'" Taggart leaned a plump arm on the gate of the stall, still breathing hard, and waggled his hairy eyebrows at Jess. "*He* rode, of course, carryin' the wee beastie over his saddle—no effort on his part, no effort at all." He loudly dramatized the last few words to be sure Diaz overheard.

"Go inflict your complaints on other ears, *hombre*," came the reply, as if spoken by the cow, but Jess could see the glimmer of Diaz's spurs through its legs. "The calf fell at the door, and I carried it here."

Jess chewed the inside of her cheek as Taggart wiped sweat from his forehead and sized up the distance from the barn door to the stall. "In truth, it's a pleasant night for a walk. Can I bring ye anything, lad?"

Unable to hold back her laughter, Jess retrieved the pitchfork, still giggling when she entered the empty stall to assist Jake. He grinned at her and took the tool from her hand, spreading the hay himself.

Not willing to stand about while the others worked, Jess brought over more armloads of hay. Jake pushed it evenly to the corners and across the middle of the stall, until the hay was nearly a foot deep.

He moved past her to put the pitchfork away, and Jess leaned against the stall to watch Taggart cut slices of apple for the cow and Diaz support the calf while it fed, already looking more alert as it gulped voraciously from a teat.

Jake came up along the far side of the stall, maintaining a casual distance from Jess. "You boys all right?"

"I'll take care of it, boss," Diaz said.

"Aye, I'll be here, as well," Taggart said, "in the event Diaz needs me to do any more of his work for him."

"Good night," Jess called, and preceded Jake out into the fresh night air.

They walked along the stream, heading east, away from the compound. A light wind caressed her cheek. Aching to feel more of the breeze, Jess untied the thread of deer sinew that bound her braid and unwound her thick rope of hair, then yanked her hat off and hung it by its cords over the butt of her revolver. She drew her fingers through her locks, lifting them, letting the breeze cool her scalp and the back of her neck.

"I love it out here," she said, "away from the noise and crowds of the city. It's simpler here; there's only the land and the animals and what you can accomplish with them." She spun to face Jake and walked backward as he studied her face. "You were right to bring me here like you did. I don't believe I've ever told you that."

"It's beginning to feel like a horse ranch," he observed,

indirectly acknowledging her comment. "The man who owns the general store in Carson said that the increase in business and travel by Overland Stage has compelled the company to add new stations and increase the number of coaches and horses, from Virginia City all the way to Salt Lake. He said the Overland is looking for good horses, and they're willing to pay two hundred dollars for an average horse, and more for a good one."

Stunned, Jess stopped—or meant to. Her moccasin caught on a rock, and she sat down hard. Jake quickly reached out a hand to her, but she laughed and pulled him down beside her. "Two hundred dollars?"

Jake chuckled with her. "In gold."

"I almost can't believe it!"

"It seems that your idea of a horse ranch was a good one."

Jess gleefully hugged her knees and leaned back, her hair swirling pleasantly around her. "They'll want a steady supplier," she said, already thinking ahead. "Someone who can provide large quantities each year." She grunted. "If only the land office hadn't sold half of the ranch acreage! We could be supplying them with feed for the stock, as well."

"Remember, Jess, we'll need to build up our numbers first. That means any decent sales and profits are still two years out." With a thoughtful expression, Jake removed his hat and rested his elbow on his thigh. "It's right now I'm concerned about. That bunchgrass is going to hold out for only a few more weeks, and then I'll have to sell some of the cattle to buy feed to get us through. And unless it rains, which I don't expect it to, we're going to have a bigger problem staring us down."

Jess stilled and saw the stars reflected in the low, nearly stagnant stream. During the summer before, the water had been nearly waist high and had moved like a fleet-footed lizard along its banks. Now it was no more than boot deep. The larger rocks on the bottom were bared; one could step across without getting wet feet.

"Honey Lake?" she asked.

"It's little more than mud now," he said. "Soon, it'll be dry as sun-baked bones, and we're going to have to pump from the well to water the horses and cattle."

"We can't do that," Jess murmured. "We need the water for ourselves."

"And so does Hank," he agreed.

Jess looked out over the desert. She'd heard it called a cold desert, meaning that although it became parched and barren during dry spells, it also saw snows, sometimes deep drifts, when the winters obliged, bringing an abundance of grass come summer.

When she'd first moved to Nevada Territory with her family and had kept books in her father's import store, a customer had mentioned the Honey Lake region to her father, saying that grass and food grew so easily there that the people in that area were known as Never Sweats—they never had to work to make grains, crops, or anything else grow. *This is not one of those times*, Jess thought in frustration; matters were even worse than she had believed. Once again, factors beyond her control were thwarting her dream, and threatening the lives God had placed in their care.

Jake gently tugged her hair. "Jess—"

"What have you done in the past?" she demanded. "What have you done before when the conditions became this inclement?"

Rather than answer, Jake lifted his eyebrows, as if searching his mind for a gentle answer.

"Conditions have never been this bad, have they?" She grunted again and dropped her forehead to her folded knees, thinking. Suddenly, she threw her hair back. "Then we'll have to take the herds somewhere else until the rains come. Fort Churchill, perhaps. We can't go to Pyramid Lake—I refuse to be one of those whites who take resources away from the Paiutes—and Eagle Lake can't be much better off than Honey Lake."

"Sam Buckland uses the Carson River by Fort Churchill to water his herd, and the river's likely low, as well," Jake said. "There would be little natural forage."

"What about Lake Tahoe?"

"Much of the land around it is owned by hotels and private investors."

Jess shoved a few hairs out of her face. "Bennett, we're not going to save our herds and make everyone happy at the same time."

"I'm not going to trespass, Jess," he answered quietly but definitively.

Jess sighed in frustration, but she knew he was right, and her heart gave a tiny flutter of admiration for the man of honor he was, and the code he and others like him adhered to. "You're right," she said, then leaned forward and gave him a quick kiss. "But we are running out of options. Unless you know of another lake or water source…?"

"The only other lake I know of is Shasta."

"Lake Shasta…is it big?"

"Yes, and it has plenty of coastline."

Jess saw his hesitation. "Then, what's the problem?"

"It's about a hundred and fifty miles from here, with little water in between."

Wanting to scream, wanting to cry, Jess pushed to her feet and strode along the dry bank of the stream, walking faster and faster, determined to wear herself out so that she could no longer feel anything. No more worry. No more fear. No more wanting and working for something that would only be taken away.

"Jess!" Jake caught up with her and grasped her arm, trying to slow her; she shook it free. She rapidly passed the Paiute village, where five brave men, three kind women, and two precious little girls were sleeping peacefully, believing that this life in this place would be better than what they'd left at Pyramid Lake. At least, there, they'd had water—a lake full of it!—and fish they could eat. Sure, Honey Lake Valley was the land of the Never Sweats—at least, it was whenever the skies decided to rain. A lot of validity the nickname had now.

Jess heard Jake keeping pace behind her. He had lost so much—his wife, his daughter—and now, all he had left was this land in which they were buried, this land that could no longer support the ranch he'd built with his hands, which drifters and outlaws seemed determined to tear down. And she couldn't even give him a child....

Finally she stopped, winded, breathing hard—not from exertion, but from anger and despair and the single-minded Hale stubbornness that refused to let her cry.

Jake spun her around and tugged her gently against him.

She burrowed.

"I don't want to leave the ranch," she said, her forehead pressed to his chest. "Not even for a few months; not even for a few weeks."

"I know."

"We don't have a place to go."

Jake pressed his cheek to the top of her head. "We have a little time. We'll figure something out. And maybe rain will come. God once sent a flood to a desert, you know."

"I wouldn't mind building an ark," she said, "if it meant we'd have rain."

"I wouldn't mind having challenges," Jake murmured huskily, "as long as I could kiss you under the stars."

His hands touched her cheeks and lifted her face. Jess felt the heat in his stare only an instant before he settled his mouth on hers and rocked her in his arms, comforting…beguiling… taking her away.

Chapter Nine

W hy do you hug your horses, Mother?"

Jess smiled down at Grace, delighted with the Paiute children's custom of calling women they respected "Mother" and good men "Father." Jess was accustomed to the women calling her "sister," but she still felt a thrill and sense of belonging each time she heard it. The term meant that she was not alone, that others cared deeply about her and would help if she had a need, that they knew she was devoted to them. Hearing Grace call her "Mother," however, sent a powerful happiness surging through her soul, and she felt immense love for the girl and her sister in return.

She slid her hands along the warm, satiny fur beneath Meg's mane, the side of her face resting against the horse's neck. A hug it surely was, and more. To Jess, this fur beneath her fingers was the best contact a ranch woman's hands could have. Had she never owned a ball gown of airy, almost liquid, silk, she might have regretted not knowing the smoothness of that cool caress against her skin; but, had she never felt the glossy vitality that overlaid the horse and seemed to emanate from the animal with its every heartbeat, then she never would have touched true life.

"Such a touch, *Mariquita*," Diaz answered before Jess could find words to explain, "feels like touching all life at once."

Diaz lifted Grace to his left hip, his right being unavailable due to the Remington holstered there, and beckoned the small palomino, Luina, toward where they were standing near the center of the corral. A special bond existed between the horse and the man, Jess knew—a rare connection that a person would find with only one horse, as if God had made each one to be part of the other, then gave them a lifetime to find each other. Only a true horseman or woman, like Diaz and Jess, fully understood that connection. As Jess rubbed Meg's neck and watched Luina approach Diaz without hesitation, she believed with everything she was that Meg and Luina felt those shared bonds just as strongly with her and Diaz.

"Touch her neck here, *Mariquita*," Diaz said, placing his dark, earth-brown hand against the mare's neck, and Grace did the same with her tiny, delicate hand of nearly the same color. "Little Luina is very soft here, no?"

Grace nodded with sufficient enthusiasm to send her short, black hair swinging, and spontaneously wrapped her unoccupied arm, still plump with babyhood, behind the red bandana tied at his neck. "Luina," she repeated.

In the space between Diaz and Jess, Mattie stood quietly, her face hard, but her eyes were fixed on Luina's tan neck and butter-yellow mane. Jess took hold of Meg's headstall and gently brought her chestnut nose down as she knelt beside Mattie. The Paiute girl's young face and old eyes shifted to Jess.

"Her name is Meg," Jess said.

Mattie's gaze returned to the mare, her hands still hanging at her sides.

Jess pulled some loose oats from her pocket and held them out to Mattie, pouring them into the girl's upturned palm. Immediately Meg turned her head toward the treat, and her lips moved to claim it.

Mattie dusted her hand on her rugged, calico dress, then let it fall at her side again.

Her treat enjoyed, Meg evidently decided that what she needed now was a scratching post. Jess dug the balls of her feet into the ground to resist being pushed over as Meg rubbed her forehead on Jess's available shoulder.

A giggle erupted from Mattie, apparently at the horse's need to scratch an itch and at Jess's patiently bland expression as the animal did so, until Meg ceased her assault on Jess's shoulder, blew out a breath, and stood restfully still. Then, Mattie quieted and finally touched Meg's mane and neck, not tentatively and not eagerly. Her movement was wooden, but the tension in her face gradually eased, and she studied the horse's side with apparent interest. "She has white spots," Mattie said.

"She's an Appaloosa," Jess explained. "Her coloring is chestnut—that means most of her is brown—but Appaloosas also have a large, white patch on their rumps, and other white spots around the patch."

"What color is Luina?" she asked.

"Luina's coloring is called palomino," Jess said, relieved to find a thread of conversation she could possibly use to draw the child out of her shell. "Palominos have light-colored hides and even lighter manes and tails. When she's not expecting a foal, Luina loves to run; she'll run for days if you let her."

Grace turned her face to Diaz, brushing her forehead against the brim of his sombrero. "Can I ride her?"

"*Sí, Mariquita*; Luina was sad, thinking you were not going to ask!" His grin of gleaming, white teeth beneath his smooth, black mustache evoked an equally bright smile from Grace, and he set her on the horse's broad back, just behind the withers.

Once she foaled, Luina would be as slender and sleek as before, but now, her belly bulged like a ripe lemon on a stick, and Jess wondered if the mare might be expecting twins.

Mattie continued petting Meg but watched Diaz lead Grace around the corral on Luina's back, her sister's hands clutching the pale, yellow mane.

After Diaz had walked Luina twice around, Grace's toes

were wiggling in delight, and her eyes gleamed like onyx. The Spaniard stopped near Mattie. "Do you want to ride, *señorita?*"

Mattie met his patient gaze as if determining whether she could trust him. "I will ride," she said.

Rather than lift her, Diaz wisely offered a knee for her to step on, leaving her in control of her person and not subject to a "white" man's whim. Mattie stepped onto his knee and pulled herself over Luina's back, then protectively held on to her younger sister.

Jess gave Meg a last pat, then slipped out of the corral through the gate to watch Diaz lead his horse and her riders. He spoke to them warmly and performed a few silly antics— like looking over his shoulder at Luina, wide-eyed and anxious, and asking her, "Why are you following me?"—making Grace giggle and Mattie give in to a smile.

Jess's concerns of the night before had dissipated with the new day, and the interaction between the people of the ranch as they helped one another and worked with the animals kindled new hope and fanned her fervent conviction that they would somehow provide water for the horses and cattle—and a good life for all who lived here.

At the sound of hoofbeats, Jess turned to see Seth step down from his horse and loop the reins over the topmost rail of the corral fence. He politely nodded his tan, bony head at her, then strolled with an uneven gait toward the bunkhouse, a bandana knotted around his thigh seeping blood, his trouser leg torn in a neat, curved line. When he disappeared inside, Jess cast Diaz a curious look.

"Gored," Diaz said helpfully.

A good life, Jess thought, recalling her previous musing, *but not without its ups and downs.*

Grace looked up at Jess. "What is 'gored,' Mother?"

"It means a cow's horn cut him," Jess said.

"Why?" Mattie asked.

"Perhaps she thought Seth meant to harm her calf."

"Now he will suffer?"

Jess glanced at Mattie, surprised at her choice of words. Yes, in her decade of life, the girl must have witnessed much injustice done, even to young children, perhaps even to herself—Jess swallowed the horror of that possibility. Almost certainly, Mattie had reason to feel that those who hurt others deserved, in turn, to feel pain.

Seth was a gentle young man, and Jess knew that Mattie wasn't angry at him but at injustice. "Yes," Jess said, hoping she wasn't wrong to feed Mattie's need for retribution, "now he will suffer."

"What was that about?" Jake asked quietly, coming up beside Jess. He'd heard the exchange but was more concerned with the defiant tilt of her chin and the uncertainty yet swimming in her eyes.

Just as quietly as he had spoken, she told him what he'd already heard; she didn't, however, reveal what she was thinking. He leaned a booted foot on the bottom rail of the corral fence, watching a loose lock of hair whip across her face, unheeded, and the mental gears that were turning behind it. "The Paiutes are starved, hunted, and killed," he said, keeping his voice low. "Anyone in their place would want to see those wrongs righted somehow."

"Their parents teach them to forgive," Jess said, choosing her words carefully, "no matter what anyone does to them. Neither their parents nor God want the Paiute children to seek vengeance. What if I answered her wrongly?"

"This is a land without laws, Jess," he gently explained.

"People bring about justice as best they can. If one man intentionally harms another, is it wrong to prevent him from harming someone else?"

At this, Jess finally looked up at him; the emotions that churned in her heart and reflected on her face reminded him of waters swirling beneath the surface of a hot spring.

"Justice and vengeance are not the same, Jess, though on occasion the two seem to serve the same purpose. Mattie doesn't want to see her people hurt; she wants people protected who cannot protect themselves. A sheriff will hang a man for stealing a horse; that's the kind of justice done here, and Mattie likely knows about that. So, if a white man takes a horse but doesn't kill it, and is hung merely for stealing the animal, then why is the white man who killed her father walking around free?"

Jess's green eyes hardened. Apparently she hadn't known.

"You let her know that justice will be done, love," he said. "I expect that was what she needed to hear more than anything."

Jess turned her face away so that all he could see was the top of her hat and the curve of her cheek. "I want more than justice done to whoever murdered my family," she admitted, "and I know it's wrong to say so. I want the man who burned my family's home to suffer."

"The Almighty doesn't want us seeking vengeance, because He knows that once you harm someone as he's harmed you, you become comfortable with your actions, and then, when another person harms you worse, you retaliate even more forcefully— and become comfortable with that, too. Soon, you've turned into what it was you wanted to destroy, and you're the one causing all the hurt. You're also so full of anger and bitterness that you've destroyed your own chances of finding peace." Jess watched the girls ride, freely giving them the attention all children crave. "I've seen men destroyed by their own thirst for vengeance," he said. "The best we can do is try to forgive, so that another person's past actions don't continue to drag us down. We can also trust that the Almighty made hell unpleasant enough to punish those who go on hurting others, and that He made heaven happy enough so that the rest of us can forget the wrongs done to us on earth."

"God wants to forgive everybody," Jess murmured. "I heard that a hundred times in church."

"Yes, but not everybody wants to stop doing wrong and be forgiven."

"So they will suffer."

Jake nodded and joined Jess in watching the girls. He saw Mattie actually smile at Diaz, though it was here and gone, like a deer darting into a thicket.

Beside him, Jess's chin had lowered, and she absently shook her head. "Their father was murdered by a white man? No wonder they're so slow to trust."

Because Jess now realized that, and because she had lost her own father, Jake knew that she would watch out for them all the more. He also knew exactly what she felt. "We can't see justice done to the entire West," he said, "but we can bring justice to three hundred and twenty acres of it."

The brim of her hat dipped once. "That we can," she said.

"If one man intentionally harms another, is it wrong to prevent him from harming someone else?" Jess heard Jake's question in her mind long after he rejoined Doyle near the barn and resumed drilling holes in the fence posts. Uncertain how she felt about his words, she tethered the subject to a distant part of her mind, where she could return to it another time.

Right now, in the corral, Grace lay gently on Luina's neck, rubbing under her mane with splayed fingers. Mattie still held responsibly to Grace's waist, but her expression revealed a modicum of wonder.

Diaz smiled to see it, but he was also keeping watch over the palomino. "Le's give Luina a rest, little *señoritas*," he said. "I wanted to walk her to help the foal to come, but I do not want to tire her."

Grace gave Luina another pat, then held out her arms, and Diaz lifted her down. Mattie began to climb down herself, but Diaz, having a concern for Luina's enormous sides, set Mattie to the ground and quickly stepped away. Whistling, he led Luina through the open gate, then latched it and started toward the barn.

"May I have a special name?" Mattie called after him.

Diaz turned, the invisible smile beneath the curve of his mustache apparent. He thought for a long moment. "I will call you *Valentía*," he said softly. "*Valentía, señorita,* means 'Courage.'"

As Diaz and Luina disappeared into the barn, Mattie still stood staring after them, a genuine smile on her face.

A minute later, Diaz returned, just in time to see Taggart jouncing toward them astride a rattletrap buckskin with so rough a gait that Jess had to bite her lower lip to keep from laughing. The horse stopped suddenly, nearly flinging the Irishman over its head. Taggart pushed himself upright, muttered something uncomplimentary to the horse, then gazed between Diaz and Jess. "I'm cursed," he announced.

Mattie studied the animal's coloring; it had a tan hide and a black mane and tail. "What do you call it?"

"An earthquake," Taggart assured her. To Jess, he said, "Do ye suppose when God drew the plans for this one, He said, 'Why not make its legs all different lengths?'"

"It's called a buckskin," Jess told Mattie. "The cattlemen named it Broom."

Taggart ran his bandana over one half of his face, then the other, each visible blue eye searching the compound. Then, he pointedly noted the empty saddle on Seth's horse. "Hasn't Seth bandaged himself yet?" A strangled yowl erupted from the direction of the bunkhouse. "Aye, he's to the whiskey, then. Bites like a dentist's drill, it does."

Jess thought that a rather accurate assessment, having felt the blistering sting of whiskey more than once herself. Still, she knew enough not to pay any obvious notice to the boy. Though young, he was a cattleman, a breed that would downplay an injury with subtle humor, that would even die from a wound before admitting to pain. They were bitten, stepped on, kicked, and thrown as a matter of course; not one of them would permit themselves to be perceived as weak.

All eyes rolled with empathy to Seth's empty saddle. Grace apparently saw an item that drew her interest, because she climbed two slats of the corral fence to better see the rope of tightly braided rawhide coiled over the saddle horn.

"It's a lariat," Jess explained.

"Not just a lariat, *Mariposa*," Diaz corrected her gently. "It is a lasso; it has a knot that holds a circle—a running noose," he explained to the girls. "The Spanish word for a simple rope is *la reata*, but for years, the American *vaqueros* have called it 'lariat.' When it is made to hold a loop, it is a lasso, though the *vaqueros* say both lariat and lasso."

Jess felt her cheeks flush with warmth. Since she'd arrived at the ranch, she'd heard the cattlemen use both words interchangeably, and she hadn't noticed the subtle difference. It seemed that though she knew horses, she had a thing or two yet to learn about the tools of the cattlemen's trade.

"Let me show you, *señoritas*," Diaz offered as he uncoiled the lasso and moved several paces from Seth's horse. "See? The lasso always has a loop, like the O in *lasso*."

Diaz let the straight end trail on the ground beside him and gripped the braided rawhide near his left hip. With his right hand, he swung the loop over his head, adding slack, expanding the loop, as he took careful aim at Taggart. "Don' move none, *amigo,*" Diaz instructed him.

Mattie and Grace both giggled, and Jess pressed her knuckles over her mouth to suppress her own laughter.

Taggart propped a fist on his knee. "Ye think I'll sit by while I'm roped by the likes of ye? Ye'd sooner find me riding Broom with a horseshoe in my britches—"

The rope fell neatly around him, not even brushing the brim of his hat.

Grace climbed over the corral fence and hurried over to Diaz. "Can I rope Taggart next?"

Jess used her bandana to wipe the tears of mirth running from her eyes.

Taggart lifted off the lasso, his mouth twitching, but masked it and slanted an accusing gaze at Diaz and Jess. "Am I the only one who does work around here?"

"No, *amigo,*" Diaz assured him, coiling the lasso. "I am looking after Luina until her foal comes, and *la Mariposa* here is teaching the little *señoritas* how to hug a horse. *Very* important work, *amigo.*"

"I had a little time available before I needed to make dinner," Jess said, smiling at the girls. "What better way to spend it than by showing two young ladies some of the joys we receive from the work we do?"

"Well, now, who can argue with that?" Taggart gathered his reins and, after the silent plea for deliverance that he cast skyward, prepared himself to ride Broom back to the herds. "If Seth survives the whiskey, remind him that cows don't watch themselves."

Jess pocketed her bandana, now damp, and her laughter

faded as the reason for Taggart's presence became clear. "You came to see to his welfare."

"I came to see if I'd be talkin' to myself the rest of the day," he avowed, nattily smoothing his riotous, orange beard with his hand, but as he circled the horse, he glanced over his shoulder at Jess and the Paiute girls, and one blue eye winked at them.

When the midday meal was complete, Jess sat with Nettle, Lily, Mattie, and Grace in the shade of a coppice of cottonwoods, surrounded by Paiute dwellings—dome-shaped wigwams of interwoven branches.

The two girls sat obediently near their mother as she wove reeds she had gathered into a hat, but their eyes stayed on Jess as she opened the saddlebag she had brought and drew out the two calico dresses she had been working on every night after supper.

"Mattie?"

Her face wooden, as usual, Mattie looked to her mother for permission, then came to stand beside Jess as she unrolled the larger dress and held it up.

Lily and Nettle ceased their friendly chatter, and Lily laid aside her weaving and stood up. "Mattie, look how beautiful it is!" she exclaimed.

When Mattie hesitated, Lily took it from Jess, her round face beaming with thankfulness, and held it up to her oldest daughter.

Dark-blue roses stood out from a tan background. The dress hung straight down from the slightly scooped neck, which was gathered with a hidden ribbon, to the long flounce ringing the bottom of the wide skirt. Ivory machined lace, which Jess had found in the middle bedroom of the ranch house, encircled the neck, the bottom flounce, and the lower edge of the puffed, three-quarter-length sleeves.

"There's also a tie belt that matches the calico," Jess said as she unrolled Grace's dress. The style was identical, but with a deep, tan background speckled with dark-green roses. Grace's eyes welled with tears as she stood and Jess held it up to her. "It'll be lovely on you," she said.

"Thank you, Mother!" Grace exclaimed, and Mattie echoed her words, albeit with her customary, quiet stiffness.

Jess ached to erase their sadness, especially Mattie's. She wished their sorrows could be gone *immediately*, just as she wished the ranch could get past its problems immediately and the arsonist who'd killed her family would be found immediately. Mentally, she sighed. Success took time, she had learned from her father, and to achieve what she wanted, she would have to face challenges, both external and internal, that she did not want to face. But she was, by blood, a Hale. Through time and determination, she would overcome every challenge she encountered.

Delighted to see their enthusiasm, Jess waited until a momentary lull before speaking. "If you girls will try them on, I will hem the bottoms, and then the dresses will be finished."

Lily looked at her with patience in her pleasant, hazel eyes. "My sister, it is our custom to bless a gift of clothing before it is worn. We will wait until we all stop work and come together at supper, then we will bless the clothes. I am sorry that we must wait; I know that you have much you must do, and that you wished to finish the sewing now."

"I apologize to you," Jess said. "I am not yet familiar with many of your traditions. I can hold the shoulder seams of the dresses to the girls' shoulders and measure the length that way, if that's all right, and then I can still finish the sewing now."

Lily and her daughters looked pleased with this suggestion,

and Jess stood, tugging two pins from her pincushion. Grace was closest, so Jess turned her around and slipped one pin through the shoulder of the new dress, securing it to the shoulder of the one she wore, then did the same above her other shoulder. Jess pulled the fabric toward Grace's ankles, then sat down before her. As she pinned up the hem, parallel to the ground, Mattie hugged her own dress against her and waited quietly for her turn. Jess glanced over at Lily and Nettle, who had resumed weaving conical hats out of reeds. As she stuck another pin into the tan and green fabric, she caught a glimpse out of the corner of her eye of Lily glancing over at the corral, where Ho Chen and Charlie were tamping dirt around the base of another fence post. Jess lowered her face to hide a smile.

"Nettle," she said casually, "you never told me how Black-Eye courted you."

Lily seemed to hesitate for an instant, but Jess couldn't be certain; the woman's broad hands—the color of creamed coffee—deftly manipulated twenty or more dried reeds that stretched like spokes of a wagon wheel far beyond her lap while she strung long, dry grasses through the last circlet of cross-reed to secure it to the slowly expanding hat.

Nettle pulled a large needle threaded with a long, dry piece of grass through the last cross-reed of the hat she was weaving, and the short, black hair around her dark face swung as she looked up with a smile, evidently pleased to talk about her husband.

Grace looked over at Nettle. "You are going to tell a story, Auntie?"

"Auntie?" The startled question was out before Jess could halt it. "I'm sorry; it isn't my place to meddle." She could try to help bring two people together who showed tangible interest in each other, but she would not intrude into sensitive matters that were not her business. If Lily and Nettle were sisters, then the stark difference in their skin and eye colors almost certainly meant that a white man had fathered Lily—and had probably molested her mother in the process.

"Do not be concerned, my sister," Lily said, her manner warm and motherly, though she was only a few years older than Jess. "My people are very direct; we see this as honesty, and we respect this. When our mother was young, she married a German trapper, and I was born."

Jess breathed a quiet sigh of relief, glad to know she had been wrong about the circumstances surrounding Lily's birth. She folded up another section of hem and slipped in another pin to hold it.

"After my father died," Lily continued, "my mother married a Paiute man, then Nettle was born. We both grew up among the Paiutes and our mother's family, and Nettle's father was father to us both. I was named after a lily flower because my skin was very pale and my hair light, like mud."

"Is Spruzy your sister?" Jess asked, relishing the freedom to speak directly without the risk of being seen as a gossip.

"Spruzy is a distant cousin," Lily said, "but to us, she is our sister."

Nettle playfully nudged Lily with a big, broad elbow. "Enough about you; let us talk about Black-Eye."

Lily sent her a patient, older-sister smile, but Jess saw Lily's gaze dart again to Ho Chen and the other men, who now were moving the wagon into the shade of the cottonwoods downstream to continue their labors.

"Grandmothers have the special care of their granddaughters when they are of age to marry," Nettle explained. "After Lily had married and moved into a dwelling with her husband, I came to womanhood."

Lily laughed good-humoredly. "Then why are you such a child?" she asked, and Grace giggled.

Nettle ignored her sister. "A girl cannot marry until she has come to womanhood," Nettle continued, steadily weaving, the excited inflections in her voice revealing her enthusiasm to share about the customs of the Paiutes with Jess. "To our people, this time in our lives is sacred, and we all participate in a festival. Then the young woman and two of her friends—they are both older—go apart from the People and live for twenty-five days in a small wigwam that is made just for the three of them.

"Three times each day, the young woman must gather much wood and make five stacks, as tall as she is able—fifteen stacks every day. She does this to gain strength and to show unmarried young men that she is able-bodied. She also fasts from all meat during these twenty-five days. This made me weak, but my two friends greatly encouraged me."

"We also fast from meat five days every month all our lives," Lily added, instructing her daughters, as well as Jess. "By doing so, we prove we will sacrifice to make certain that our families have enough food and that we will remain strong."

Jess unpinned the tan and green calico dress from Grace's shoulders, laid it over her saddlebags, and pinned Mattie's dress to her shoulders with a smile.

Nettle knotted a new strand of grass to the end of the last. "At the end of the twenty-five days," she said, her voice still ebullient, "her attendants take her to the river to bathe, and then she returns to her family's lodge. To pay the attendants for providing food and encouragement and friendship, she gives them all of her clothing. Sometimes she gives away many dresses," Nettle added.

"When she begins to live with her family again," Lily said, "everyone knows that she is now a marriageable woman, and any man who is interested in her may court her."

"But how does he do that," Jess asked, removing then resetting a pin, "if he does not speak to her or her family?"

"As I mentioned, grandmothers have the special care of their granddaughters," Nettle said, her face aglow with reminiscences of courtship. "When a young woman returns to her family's lodge, she sleeps away from the others, beside her grandmother. After the family goes to sleep for the night, the young man who wishes to court her—he will have worked to draw her attention, as I explained when we were milking cows yesterday—enters the dwelling in full dress and sits down at her feet."

"If she is not awake," Lily put in, "then her grandmother wakes her to let her know a suitor is calling."

"He does not speak to her or her grandmother," Nettle continued. "But he stays with her, tirelessly, sometimes for hours, to show that he will always be there to care for her." She giggled. "Black-Eye stayed many long nights. I never wanted him to leave."

Jess had wanted to learn their people's courting customs so she could discover if there was a way she could help bring Lily and Ho Chen together, but she was becoming caught up in the foreign but endearing way Paiute men wooed young women. The images Nettle evoked stirred something pleasant deep within her heart; all the people in a Paiute village celebrated together and cherished each person as rare and special. If people in the States did the same, she reflected, perhaps the North and the South would have found a way to avoid the war.

"If neither the young woman nor her grandmother speaks to the young man," Jess asked, "how does she let him know when she wants him to leave?"

"She throws the previous day's porridge at him," Nettle said, and burst out laughing.

Jess laughed, too, as surprised at the Paiutes' unpredictable sense of humor as she was at the comment itself. Standing before her, Mattie didn't quite smile, but she pulled her lips in, and Grace giggled beside her mother.

"Behave yourself, Nettle," Lily pretended to scold her. "What manners you will teach my daughters!"

Neither of the girls appeared to mind in the least.

"How does she really let the man know she wants him to leave?" Jess asked.

"She rises and then lies down beside her mother," Lily said. "Sometimes, the man is not the one she wants to marry, and other times, she grows tired and must sleep. Then he leaves as quietly as when he arrived and sat down."

As Jess had gotten to know Lily, she had begun to see that she seemed to mother not just her daughters with her cheerful words and expressions, but everyone else, as well. Perhaps that tendency had come about because she was the oldest child, and, perhaps, it had come about from having to raise two daughters without a husband, and her efforts to make up for the hardships her girls—and others—had to endure. Whatever the reason, Jess enjoyed being near Lily as much as she enjoyed Nettle. Both women had special ways of enlivening and engaging those around them.

Jess braced her hand against a tree and stood, letting sensation return to her feet. "How many times will the man sit at the feet of the woman?" she asked.

"For months," Nettle answered. "Even a year or longer, if the woman has not decided."

"Our parents never force us to marry, or choose a husband for us," Lily said. "Our children learn at a young age to listen to the way others discuss matters and make decisions. Our women are respected as much as our men for their knowledge and wisdom, and others ask for and consider our advice when the People must make an important choice. When the time comes for young women to choose husbands, they have the knowledge and experience to choose for themselves."

"It's very different from how I was raised," Jess said, "but I think it's a better way." She unpinned Mattie's shoulder seams and invited the girl to sit with her, delighted when she did. Jess took thread, a needle, and a pair of scissors from the sewing kit she'd brought along—the same kit Jake had used the year before to put stitches in her leg. She remembered the way he had looked as he'd taken her ankle in his hand to remove the stitches, his head bent so close beside her hand that she'd longed to touch him.

"How long did Black-Eye visit before you decided to marry him?" Jess asked Nettle.

"I decided before he came to visit," Nettle said, giggling while Lily eyed her with mock censure. "It is true! I made him come for months after his first visit"—she giggled again—"but I knew before the first time he entered our lodge." She leaned toward Jess, Mattie, and Grace, her warm, onyx eyes drawing them further into her story. "I was awake when he entered the doorway, and his shoulders nearly blocked all the moonlight. He sat so close that my feet felt the warmth coming from him, and I could see him smile. At first, I pulled my blanket over my face, but then I let him see that I was smiling, too. He always wore the same blanket every night he came, and when we married, he gave it to me. Then I made him a new one."

Jess began sewing Mattie's hem with tiny, even stitches, folding the excess fabric inside the hem so the dress could be lengthened as Mattie grew. Seeing Mattie's quiet interest, Jess transferred the dress to her lap, passed her the threaded needle, and demonstrated a few stitches. "How did you finally let him know that you wanted to marry him, Nettle?"

"I told my grandmother, and she told my parents. Then my father sent for Black-Eye and asked him in front of me if he loved me. It is much the same with all Paiute women. Black-Eye said yes—"

"He must have known about the morning porridge," Jess said, sotto voce, to Lily, who joined her laughter.

"Black-Eye said yes," Nettle continued with a grin of her own, "and then my father reminded each of us of our duties as a married couple. Black-Eye was to provide my food and necessities, help raise our children, and protect me and our family—with his own life, should that be necessary. I was to gather firewood, dress the game, prepare our food, make his moccasins, clean his buckskins, dress his hair, weave mats for the floor of our dwelling...to do all the work to care for the home, much as white women do." Her voice turned dreamy. "I promised to be himself, and to fulfill that promise."

"I don't understand 'be himself,'" Jess said, gathering Grace's dress into her lap and then threading another needle. Lily didn't seek out Ho Chen, Jess saw, though she did look up at the mountains above where the men were settling yet another post in the ground.

"When a woman promises to 'be' her husband," Lily said, her gaze still averted, "she says she will live for him instead of living for herself, and will work always to bring him happiness. She loves him, so she wishes to do this. A good husband will do the same; he will be kind and give of himself, and both will be happy."

Jess recalled what she had told her brother, Ambrose, the day he had left Nevada Territory to return home to Kentucky. "For most of my life, I didn't want to marry," she said, "though women in the South—in the southern part of the States—have always married. There, it is almost unthinkable not to. Here, most women must marry, as they have no other means to provide for themselves, especially if their fathers die. Among my people," Jess said, privately amused that she had spoken like one of the Paiute women, "a woman's father often chooses her husband for her, and I have seen many young married women treated badly, like chattel—slaves—because their fathers gave a dowry of money and possessions to their husbands when they married. Bad husbands use their wives' dowries for their own gains, and selfishly ignore their wives' needs. I once told my brother that I would never marry because I did not want to spend my life with such a man."

"But you married Many Horses," Nettle said.

"You knew before Black-Eye came to your lodge that he was the man you wanted to marry," Jess said. "White men are not like Paiute men. Many are bad, as you have seen. It takes time to find a good one, sometimes years. White men don't always allow you to see who they really are. I had to work here with Jake for months before I knew for certain that he was a good man. You both know as well as I do that when you have witnessed many people cause pain to yourself and others, trust comes slowly."

Nettle had nearly finished weaving the hat. Now, she used a knife to cut off the excess length of the reed closest to her last stitch. That completed, she folded over the remaining end and began to loop the grass strand around it, neatly hiding it within the outer edge of the hat.

Jess checked on Mattie's progress; her stitches weren't as straight or as evenly spaced as her own, but she was doing well, and when the girl looked up, Jess smiled and gave her a spontaneous hug with her free arm.

Mattie responded with neither a smile nor a frown but met Jess's eyes for a moment before she bent her head again to her sewing. *Patience*, Jess reminded herself. With patience, she would help Mattie to trust her, and, she prayed, let her sadness go.

Jess leaned back on her hands and looked over at Jake,

who was laboriously drilling fence posts beside Doyle. With patience, she would move mountains, she and Jake together.

Chapter Ten

Jess wiped her nose on her yellow calico sleeve, absently wishing this old gown had been ruined in Carson City instead of the one with the lace—made from the first dress fabric and lace Jake had ever bought for her. Still, this one was serviceable enough, and the blue one with red roses was too fine to wear while working.

She paused from chopping onions to turn up the wick of the oil lamp, glancing as she did at the growing fire that snapped beside Ho Chen's empty bunk. She was thankful he had begun to sleep in the cool air of the compound with the cattlemen. It had been a long time since she had needed to work off grief.

Jess set her fists on the cutting table, and the half-chopped onion swam out of focus. Luina's colt had been born fourteen hours earlier—scant minutes after Jess had returned from hemming Mattie and Grace's dresses at the Paiute village. Diaz had called Jake over, and together the three of them had helped Luina deliver the colt. Jess had sat near Luina's head, soothing the palomino with soft words and steady caresses as she labored to give birth, and Jake, his arms being longer than Diaz's, had patiently pulled the colt from its mother. Diaz, more experienced with deliveries, had provided advice. Yet, after all their effort, the colt, shiny and as black as his father, Cielos, had slid into Jake's lap, stillborn.

Jess wiped her nose again, telling herself that the stinging inside her nostrils was the result of the onion, and grabbed up the knife. When the onion was diced, she directed her attention to the rest of the meal and quickly set herself to peeling and chopping potatoes, measuring flour, kneading dough, dicing ham, and slicing apples amid sips of bitter coffee.

She kept seeing the vision of the death in her mind—the motionless foal; Luina sitting up and nudging its lifeless body. Jake and a few of the other men had buried it behind the stable while Diaz had stayed with Luina. Afterward, Jess had prepared dinner, the ranch people had eaten, the girls' new dresses had been blessed, and then Jess had gone through the motions of cleaning and sweeping out the cookhouse, all the while seeing the lifeless colt as if it overshadowed everything she'd seen. She had gone to bed with Jake, but even after his breathing had deepened, she had still lain awake, sickened, angry, miserable. To Jess, Luina's pregnancy had been a sign of hope, a sign that the dreams she and Jake shared for the ranch were moving forward. During the previous year, both she and Jake had attended every birthing and had shared a smile over the heads of the others who had come to witness the miracles. But, since they had returned, every time their dreams had taken an exciting leap forward, adversity of some sort had risen up like an opposing, runaway locomotive to derail and smash them.

Rather forcefully, Jess balled the biscuit dough on the counter, then wiped her hands with a towel. After a brief search, she found the pot she needed and hung it over the flames. Into it she poured the dried apples she had chopped. She added water and sugar, then let the fruit and syrup boil and thicken. To the large kettle of chicken broth she'd brought to a boil, she added the chopped potatoes, onions, and ham.

Finding a way to bake the biscuits rapidly became a frustration. Until now, she'd had the use of a proper baking pan that fit nicely into the "oven"—the low, wide opening built into the side of the fireplace for the purpose of baking, which produced perfect, golden biscuits—but she had sent the baking pan over to Hank filled with cinnamon apple crisp in gratitude for the apples he'd given them. With images of the dead colt emblazoned on her mind, the normally small challenge of finding a way to bake biscuits felt overwhelming.

Jess stirred the bubbling apples with a wooden spoon to keep them from burning, then searched anxiously through the stacks of clean pots and skillets to find something she could use to bake the biscuits—"sourdough bullets," the men called them. She wasn't about to waste the four quarts of flour she had used, especially since money was limited and they had to make their supplies last, but she couldn't find a way to bake them. If she used an iron skillet, the bottoms would burn before the tops and insides were done; if she used a kettle, they would clump together and be doughy.

Pushing back tangles of hair that had wriggled loose from her braid, Jess hitched up her skirt and knelt beneath the cooking table to dig behind barrels and crates of foodstuffs in an attempt to find some vessel that would suffice. She succeeded only in losing her temper.

"Need a hand, Jess?"

Startled, she bolted upright and banged her head on the underside of the table. "Ow! Bennett! What are you doing here?" Careful to avoid the edge of the table, she backed out and sat on her heels, rubbing her head. Jake was standing close beside her in bare feet, trousers, and a blue cotton shirt he'd left casually unbuttoned. For once, he wasn't wearing his hat.

Rather than help her up, he squatted down beside her, his brown eyes alert as he searched her face, as though it were the beginning of his day instead of the middle of the night.

"Actually," he said, his voice gentle and deep, "I was wondering why you were here."

Jess pushed herself to her feet, dusted herself off, and gave the apples a stir, in no mood to be in anyone's company, even his.

Jake joined her in front of the fire and peered into the pot, inhaling deeply. "I figured you'd be here trying to work out the things on your mind, love," he said softly, "but why are you cooking so much?"

Why couldn't he leave her alone? "I have to wash the laundry tomorrow," she said shortly, then grabbed another wooden spoon and stirred the potato soup. "I won't have time to cook dinner."

"Lily or Nettle could do that, Jess."

"I'll need their help with the laundry!"

Jake leaned a shoulder against the mantel, watching her frenzied movements. "Jess, your pa raised horses most of your life; you must have witnessed the death of a foal before. What's really troubling you?"

Jess slammed the spoon on the mantel and glared up at him. The stillbirth of the colt had snapped the final strand of her emotional rope. Because of her, Jake had lost half of his ranch, and they had invested funds that would have helped them now into Thoroughbreds they couldn't afford to feed. Because of the dry weather, the water they needed was nearly gone. Drifters intended to drive off the Paiutes, who depended on her and Jake, and whoever had murdered her family had not been caught—and probably still wanted her dead. Jess had depended on the birth of Luina's foal to encourage her that they would overcome all this, and yet it had died instead, reminding her of her own inability to conceive a child.

How could she possibly tell Jake what she was feeling? He stood there, calm as could be, as if no circumstance could ruffle his composure, though she knew full well that when he'd lost his wife and daughter, he'd thrown himself into his work, just as she was doing. It was the only thing she could do at this hour of the night that would allow her to see the fruits of her efforts, and now she couldn't even find a stupid baking pan.

Jess spun and started shoving aside the pots she had recently searched through. She'd use that big skillet and just burn the biscuits.

Behind her, she heard Jake stirring one of the pots. "Are you making the biscuits to eat with these apples?"

"Yes, if I can find a way to bake the dough."

Jake immediately strode over to her and pulled down a wide, flat-bottomed pot with three stubby legs from where it hung above her head. His shirt grazed her arm where her sleeve was rolled back; he had washed before turning in, and now smelled of soap and of the fragrant cedar that lined his chest of drawers and clung to his clean clothes. Holding the pot in one hand, Jake lifted down a perfectly flat lid that fit it with the other hand. "Here, this'll do." He set both the pot and the lid on the cutting table, where the round balls of dough were waiting. Reluctant curiosity drew Jess to his side.

"This is a Dutch oven," he said. "Ho Chen uses it mostly on roundups or other days when he travels with us and cooks for the men. It works pretty well."

Jess said nothing as he moved close behind her, slid his arms between her elbows and waist, and lowered his lips to her right temple for a gentle kiss. Feeling inanely as if she had four arms—two peach-toned and slender, and two powerful and sun-browned with dark hair—she followed his movements and placed the clumps of dough around the bottom of the Dutch oven, until the bottom was fully lined and half the dough had been removed from the table.

With the anger drained out of her by her mental release of steam, as well as Jake's quiet self-composure, Jess let her flour-covered arms hang still and leaned her head back against Jake's shoulder.

Across the cookhouse, the dining area was dark and silent, and the partly open door ushered in cool drifts of air from

151

outside. The long tables and benches rested quietly, that part of the room otherwise barren, except for the twelve unlit candles and their holders set high in the three walls surrounding the tables. Had it already been almost a year since Jess had placed them there? One year since her animosity toward Jake for keeping her at the ranch had turned into something warmer? It had been July 3, and everyone at the ranch had excitedly prepared for their Fourth of July celebration.

"How is this?" Jess asked while standing on a chair, bright sunshine streaming through the door, holding one of the iron candleholders Doyle had expertly fashioned for her high against the wall. The holder looked like a long, iron nail, its shaft square and twisted lengthwise to form a simple yet attractive design, with a flat loop at the end to hold the base of a candle.

Jess's Paiute friend, Red Deer, looked up from her place by the fire, where she was boiling pine nuts, and dusted her hands as she came around the giant sideboard, her face showing kind appraisal. With the tables and benches outdoors, the floor had been cleanly swept, and Nettle and two other Paiute women chatted happily while they slipped colorful glass beads onto long strings.

"I think it needs to be higher, Jessica," Red Deer said, "so the candles will give more light."

Jess stood up on tiptoe and reached, trying to keep her balance on the chair. The ceiling was higher than she'd thought, and she still had three feet of whitewashed wall above her in which she could place the candles before their flames would pose a threat to the ceiling above. If she could...only... reach....

Jess heard booted heels behind her on the plank floor.

"Allow me."

At the sound of Jake's deep voice, Jess started, nearly dropping the candleholder, but she caught it against the wall. Her head dropped back in mild exasperation. "Bennett! You scared—aagh!"

Abruptly, Jess found herself seated on his shoulder, grasping the wall for balance as he straightened to his full, dizzying height. A strong arm anchored her in place.

"Does this help?"

Her first thought was concern for his scarred shoulder, but when she glanced down, she found nothing but amusement in his eyes. If he wasn't troubled by her weight on his shoulder, she mused, then it wouldn't bother her, either. Her answer was flippant. "Yes, it helps. And if you hand up a cloth, I can dust the rafters, as well."

Jess heard the other women giggle, and several children made exclamations of delight as they entered the room to see her seated on Jake's shoulder. Then, Doyle was there, tilting his hat back from his face; he was joined by four or five other cattlemen, all making suggestions about the placement of the candleholder. When a position had been decided, Jake took the hammer Doyle handed him and passed it up to Jess.

Jake's eyes met hers again, and they shared a brief smile. Then, Jess leaned forward on her solid perch and lightly tapped the hammer to the outer edge of the wide, iron ring until the sconce was secured to the wall. Next, Doyle handed Jake a candle, which Jake handed up to Jess. She lowered it into the ring, and the base of the candle fit into the iron sconce perfectly.

And so it went. The men discussed the placement of each sconce while Jake walked her to the point they'd agreed upon. Then, Doyle alternately handed up slim, iron holders and candles to go in them.

"Where did you come up with the design?" Jake asked Doyle.

"It's what the miners use underground in the tunnels, maybe a little fancied up for Miss Jess," Doyle said. "I saw the miners' candleholders in a general store; I've never been in a mine, myself."

"They're going to look wonderful," Jess exclaimed from her perch. She looked back at the dozen or so sconces hanging almost perfectly level on three walls, and at the strings of colorful glass beads that Nettle, with Black-Eye's assistance, had draped between them. They had worked an hour or more, Jess figured—Jake setting her down once to lift her onto his other shoulder—and the cattlemen had dutifully stayed and eyed each one, their long-suffering patience commendable. "How many are left?" Jess asked.

Several male voices answered, "One!"

The Paiute children giggled.

Jess smiled, too, as Jake walked her over to the final place, and Doyle handed up the last iron bracket. Once everyone had agreed on its location, she pounded it in, set the candle, then passed the hammer down. Jake bent down, easily setting her on her feet beside Red Deer.

Jess linked arms with Red Deer and sighed. "What do you think?"

Her friend gazed happily around the room, three walls of which were now decorated with four sconces, evenly spaced and connected by colorful swags of beads. "They will be beautiful, Jessica."

The others had also paused to admire their collective handiwork. "I think we'll just leave them there from now on," Jake said. "It seems a shame to take them down."

"Good!" Jess exclaimed, relieved. At the curious looks, she

fanned herself and added, "I think the air's a might thin that high up."

There was a round of laughter, and Red Deer's nephew, Two Hands, burst in, excitedly sniffing the air and tugging on his aunt's hand as he spoke in rapid Paiute. The other children gathered around Red Deer, their black eyes dancing as they accompanied her toward the hearth and the bubbling pine nuts.

"It will be like ice cream," Red Deer explained to Jess over her shoulder. "Only it will not be cold."

"They'll love it," Jess assured her. Jess couldn't help sharing a last, warm smile with Jake before following Red Deer into the kitchen to help with the dessert.

The beads had been taken down after the celebration and returned to the Paiute women who had shared them, but the sconces remained, now wreathed in late-night shadows and in the memories of that day and of the people who had helped to place them there...many of them now gone, including Red Deer, who had become a sister of the heart to Jess.

Jake's arms slowly tightened around Jess, though he was still cautious not to press hard against her ribs. The Dutch oven, sitting between her floury hands, nudged her fully back to the present.

The image of the stillborn colt returned, but its vividness had begun to fade, no longer bringing with it the same intensity of ill feeling it had caused hours before.

Jake didn't probe her for answers. He didn't ply logic in a vain attempt to "reason" with her emotions. He also didn't throw up his hands and storm out in exasperation. He merely stood with her, being the connection to life and love and hope that she desperately needed.

Finally, Jess wiped her hands and indicated the long, curved handle that straddled the full width of the pot. "Does it need to hang above the fire? There are only the two hooks, and the apples aren't finished."

"No, it doesn't need to hang," Jake said, keeping his voice soft. "A Dutch oven sits right in the coals." He placed the lid on the pot and moved to the hearth. With a fire iron, he nudged the logs to one side, then set the oddly shaped pot into the glowing embers. Using the tin scoop from the kindling box, he piled more hot coals onto the lid. "The lid is made flat so there's heat above and beneath, just like in a real oven. Use the pot hook to lift the lid when you check the biscuits, and the coals will stay on top of it." He returned the scoop to the kindling box. "Shall I help you finish up so that you can get some rest?"

"There isn't much left to do," Jess answered. "The residual heat from the fire should finish cooking the soup, as well as the apples."

"Need anyone to taste the apples?" he offered, injecting a moderate amount of hope into the question.

Jess smiled, beginning to feel the lateness—earliness, rather—of the hour. She handed him a spoon. "Sure."

He sampled, and his closed-eyed response compelled her to get a spoonful for herself. It tasted like hot apple jam.

"It's delicious," Jake said, then leaned comfortably against the cooking table. "I suppose you made the biscuits and apples for Seth?"

"Diaz said that his gored leg is going to be fire, but Seth likes biscuits and apples, so I thought they'd make him feel better. The girls will enjoy them, too."

"So will everyone else," Jake agreed. "I'm sending Will and Charlie to Milford in the morning to get lumber so we can build another workshop. Do you need anything while they're in Milford?"

"We're less than a month away from the Fourth of July. They might as well pick up more flour so we can make pies and pastries. I've also written several letters to Ambrose that I'd like them to post."

"I'll let them know. The day after they come back, I'm going to take Will with me and sell thirty head of cattle up by Shaffer's Station north of Honey Lake. With all the immigrants going through there, the cattle should bring a good price."

Jess's tired mind came instantly alert. "Jake, I'd like to drive the cattle with Will. You have the fence to finish and the workshop to build, and you said you were going to try breeding the Thoroughbreds with the Morgan and mustang mares that haven't been bred yet. I'll have the laundry done by then, and Lily can prepare a day's meals on her own while I'm gone. Jake, I...I need to see that my efforts for the ranch are accomplishing more than tiny steps toward our goals. I need to collect the money that I've helped to earn. Jake, I *need* to go."

Jake rubbed his eyes, then his hands continued their restless upward movement through his dark hair. "I can't let you, Jess. I need you to stay where I know you're safe. Diaz can breed the horses; I would have put him in charge of it, anyway."

Jess gasped in frustration. "I wouldn't be going anywhere near Carson City. Shaffer's Station is in the other direction!"

"This isn't just about the arsonist, Jess," he said, as patient as ever. "We ran into that angry band of Paiutes—"

"That was near Smoke Creek."

"—and a gang of renegades who were willing to kill us just for a few bottles of whiskey."

"I can handle myself, Bennett, as well as the cattle and the transaction."

He briefly held her gaze when she called him Bennett, but

other than that, he gave no indication of losing his patience or of changing his mind. "I know that better than anyone, Jess."

Jess stared at him and noticed the tension, and the years, in the fine wrinkles at the corners of his eyes and around his mouth. He had lost his first wife and daughter on a "simple" trip like the one to Shaffer's Station; mother and infant both had been gunned down, and Jake had been the one who found them. *Jake has needs*, Jess reminded herself, *just as I do.* She recalled the words Nettle had spoken early that morning about the Paiute wedding vow a woman made to "be" her husband. What had happened to Olivia and little Sadie Bennett would always haunt Jake; that, and his fierce love for Jess, would always spur his determination never to let it happen again. Right now, Jake's concern for her seemed a little excessive—both of them knew that a trip up the eastern side of Honey Lake would be no more dangerous than crossing the ranch yard—and he had known when he married her that she possessed independent tendencies and a mind of her own. But, for now, she would back down to ease his concerns, and she would be patient with him, "be himself," and love him as he reacclimated to marriage. She would not, however, live out the next forty years of her life on a three-hundred-and-twenty-acre ranch.

"I'll stay, Bennett," she replied with none of the former bite in the way she said his name. "I know it's because you love me that you fear losing me like you lost Olivia."

In response, Jake swept her into his arms. For the moments he held her, the tightness of his embrace didn't fade.

Jake held Jess, his mind aching over her determination to leave the ranch. He knew she needed to ride, to work with the animals, to feel the wind in her face and a horse beneath her—he knew those needs himself—and he understood the passion that drove her to gain back the security she had lost when her family and home had been burned to ashes. Still, he was certain that another factor drove her, one she hadn't chosen to reveal to him, perhaps one she was not running toward, but running from.

When he had entered the cookhouse a short while ago, he'd figured she'd be grieving the loss of the colt, but instead he'd heard angry muttering and had seen white puffs of stray flour shooting out from beneath the table. The only part of her that had been visible had been a slim pair of Indian boots beneath tangled, white petticoats. He'd been glad to see her rage. For Jess, that particular emotion meant she was overcoming her challenge and fighting to fuel her determination to succeed.

Her only weakness was love—her love for her family, for her friends, and for him. Her strong emotions had carried her over great highs and greater lows, like waves of the ocean, since they had returned to the ranch—and before then, he realized. Her sporadic, seemingly unfounded frustrations had begun before they'd left Fort Laramie. This challenge of hers, then, clearly had to do with an aspect of their relationship.

He released her, and she looked up at him, her smile tired but sincere. She turned to check the progress of the biscuits, using the pot hook to lift the lid blanketed by coals.

When he'd asked her what was troubling her, she hadn't been ready to reveal it, and he'd decided he wouldn't press her. Sometimes, a body needed to figure something out on his— or her—own, and Jess had showed more than once that she needed occasional solitude just as much as the ranchmen did. She always told him what was burdening her...eventually. Until then, he'd give her the latitude she needed, and do his best to figure things out and help her through.

"I think the biscuits may be done," she said, some surprise in her voice.

Jake transferred the Dutch oven to the cooking table to provide her with a better view into the cooking vessel. Using the hook, Jess lifted off the lid and grinned with delight at the concentric rings of puffy, golden biscuits. She walked the few steps to the hearth and shook the lid's coals back into the fire, and then Jake helped her pile the biscuits, soft but hotter than spuds, onto a large platter.

As he looked down at the top of her head, something shifted inside his chest at the shining hair braided down her back and the loose strands that hovered around her face. Her sleeves were rolled up, baring her slender arms, and he knew that if she lifted her face to his, he would see soft, peach skin and eyes the color of summer sage. Suddenly, he felt uncomfortably warm, and had to wipe his face on his sleeve.

Since he revealed nothing, Jess remained unaware of the direction of his thoughts, and she began to place the remaining rounds of pastry into the oven, taking care to keep her hands away from the metal sides, which sizzled upon the addition of dough. When she had finished the task, she lifted the pot, her actions silently refusing any assistance he might have offered, and set the oven back into the coals. That done, she piled glowing, red coals onto the lid.

"The fire is getting low," Jake said. "If I bank the coals, the biscuits will finish baking on their own."

"While you do that, I'll wipe down the table," she said, and immediately began to do so, the back of her skirt swishing with her brisk movements.

"Now and then," he said, "I wish all the doors on the ranch buildings had locks."

Jess stepped out into the cool, late-night air with Jake, pausing to enjoy the view of a thousand stars above. Suddenly, she felt again the sensation of being watched—the acute, unsettling awareness, the sharp, prickling little claws.

She scanned the compound of dark, snoring mounds and the two men on watch, one of whom blew out a trail of cigarette smoke into the night, and then lifted her gaze to the foothills beyond the ranch house. Yes, whoever was watching them was positioned up there. Part of her trembled in terror, and, for a brief moment, part of her was almost angry enough to get a horse and gun and go settle the intruder's curiosity with a direct confrontation. But fear won out. She shivered.

"Almost two in the morning," Jake said, still eyeing the stars, not yet aware of her trepidation.

"How can you tell just by looking at the sky?" Jess asked. For once, her question was asked not because she wanted to appease her longstanding amazement with how cattlemen gathered precise information from their environments, but rather because she wanted to delay their walk to the ranch house so that she would have a chance to glimpse any movements in the foothills, aided by the meager sliver of rising moon.

"The Big Dipper rotates around the North Star once every twenty-four hours," Jake said, "like an hour hand moving backward around a clock. At midnight, the Dipper's at the nine o'clock position, and at six in the morning, it's at the six o'clock position, though the sun is up and you can't see it then. At six at night, the Big Dipper's swung around to the twelve o'clock position, though you can see it only on a clear winter night." He lowered his voice. "You haven't moved, Jess, so I know you sense something. Do you see anything?"

"No. Only shadows within shadows."

"Keep looking." He raised his voice. "Since the Dipper has dropped to about seven thirty on a regular clock, sort of to the left of the North Star and down a little, that means it's about two o'clock in the morning."

"Thank you, Jake," she said softly. "I'll be glad when the moon is full and we can see better."

"I see pretty well now, Jess," he said. "I've spent about half my life outdoors at night, four years of it here, and I can usually determine what belongs and what doesn't. Please trust me; I don't believe there is any danger for us waiting in those hills."

He seemed so certain that Jess nodded and continued with him to the porch. There, she hesitated, took one more look around, and stepped into the house.

A sudden, slight weight beside Jess awakened her. She pushed up on an elbow, peering blurrily into the darkness, her dream-bogged mind so groggy that the only clear thought she could form was that the night was as deep as it had been when she and Jake had come to bed. No more than an hour could have passed since then.

Where Jake had been lying, the covers now lay flat against the cotton mattress, and a small blur with four legs and a tail were curled in the vacated spot, purring softly. Jess touched the place, half thinking she'd find him there. The sheet and bedsack beneath it were cool.

She glanced around the room, seeing only the familiar furnishings and window. "Jake?"

The cat continued to purr, and the normal sounds of house settling came to her ears, but she heard no movements that could have been caused by the solid weight of her husband.

Pushing back the blanket, Jess swung her feet to the floor, then waited for her sleepiness to subside. Finally, she rose, tugging at her nightgown where it had twisted around her legs while she slept.

"Jake?"

Her hair hung around her shoulders, unbound, as she

stepped from the room and descended the stairs. She pushed the heavy tresses behind her, glancing about the main room with its empty furniture and cold fireplace. The front door was closed.

Jess peered into the kitchen and looked in the dining room, uncertain why Jake would be in either place at so early an hour, but knowing that he normally wouldn't be out, either, unless one of the cattlemen needed him for some reason. But, if that had been the case, there would have been a knock on the front door, and she would have heard it.

Aware of her state of dress, she moved toward the front window overlooking the ranch yard but kept to the side, leaning her head over to gaze out. Several ranchmen slept on, undisturbed; the barn door was shut, just as they had left it, and a few horses stood restfully in the corral.

Apparently, no emergency was forthcoming, but neither did Jess think it likely that Jake's absence could be explained as a simple trip to the outhouse, since his side of the bed held no trace of his body's heat. He must have left as soon as she'd fallen asleep.

Folding her arms across her chest in a hug of self-comfort, she climbed the stairs to the bedroom. At the big window that faced the Sierra foothills, she let her gaze wander over the places of light and shadow.

Was that a movement? Edging to one side to better see beyond the side of the house, she peered down to catch, for an instant, a silhouette that looked like a man jogging toward the rear of Hank's yard. It quickly disappeared from sight—if, in fact, it had been there at all.

Jess blinked sleepily and realized that she felt none of the awareness or concern that had gripped her when she and Jake had stood under the stars an hour before. Almost certainly,

Jake had gone to visit the grave of his wife and daughter, just as he had often done the year before.

With a yawn, Jess crawled back into bed beside the orange cat that little Sadie had loved, feeling oddly comforted to know how dearly Jake cared for the people who entered his life, and blessed that he now loved her with the same passion and strength that he had loved his Livvy.

Chapter Eleven

Rather than leave the day after Will and Charlie returned from Milford with a wagonload of lumber and flour, which would have been on a Sunday, Jake set aside the day as a time of rest and leisurely pursuits for the people of the ranch and instead left with Will and thirty head of cattle on Monday. That had been three days ago, but Jess didn't worry; Jake had told her they would be gone a few additional days if they weren't able to sell all the cattle at Shaffer's Station.

With the lively help of Lily and Nettle, bless them, Jess had boiled and scrubbed the laundry in the sizzling, mid-June heat—all the Paiutes and ranchmen's clothes, as well as the bedding and every bedsack from the bunkhouse. The women had made good use of the clothesline that hung between the back of the bunkhouse and the tall, rustling cottonwood tree behind it.

With her free hand, Jess unhooked the corral gate, backed into the corral, and then latched the gate. She lifted her armload of hay to the platform feeder Doyle had constructed of iron and wood to feed the horses at a comfortable level. Just now, only Luina occupied the corral, at Diaz's insistence, with the exception of Meg, her presence a comfort as Luina continued to recover from the difficult birthing.

Diaz had decided that Eli Payton was a fair man with a horse, and the two had worked together during the days of Jake's absence, breeding as many of the Thoroughbreds as they were able. At breakfast, Diaz had told Jess that he was pleased with their progress.

Jess gave Luina and Meg each a soothing pat, eyeing the progress the men had made with the fence. All the posts were in, the parallel wires had been strung the evening before, and the wide, northern gate leading out into the valley was already seeing use. The horses and cattle had spent their first night ensconced on their ranch, and Ho Chen seemed content to be preparing meals in the cookhouse once again. After the cattlemen completed the southern gate near the base of the Sierras, the fence would be secure.

Well, almost secure.

A few of the more skittish horses had startled at some simple provocation and snapped the fence wire. Twice. Since breakfast. After the second break, Doyle had sized up the situation while Taggart had grumbled and restrung the wires, then had gone to the smithy and heated up the forge.

A loud, metallic *tink, tink* had reverberated from Doyle's hammer and anvil for the rest of the morning—making barbs, he'd said, to prevent the animals from pushing against the wires—answered by the duller *crack, crack* of nails being pounded into the frame of the new workshop. The monotone blows back and forth had continued for so long that the sonorous pulses no longer stabbed her eardrums but merely thrummed them, causing her to think that part of her hearing had been temporarily deadened. Suddenly, she thought of the ongoing war, and Ambrose and the other men who lived amid the blasts of rifle and cannon fire. For those who survived the war, what level of hearing would they be left with?

Shaking off the grim thought, especially as it was something she could do nothing about, Jess went to the barn for another load of the dry, prickly hay and hand-fed several small bundles to each of the mares, then piled the rest in the grate atop the platform.

Behind the smithy and cookhouse across the stream, Lily and Nettle, along with Mattie and Grace in their new calico dresses and wide-brimmed, conical hats, diligently watered the garden they had planted this past spring, before the hostile, white ruffians had driven them off the ranch. With the dry, burning heat and arid soil, Jess didn't believe the vegetables would survive, no matter how determined their efforts; they'd had more water available the previous season, and it had been a struggle to keep every plant alive. Still, she had never been one to give up or to count losses, and, so far, Hank was keeping his young apple trees alive, so she latched the corral gate behind her with a decisive click and went to join the women.

To her surprise, when she rounded the cookhouse—she avoided the rear of the barn, where the black colt was buried— Hank was there, assisting the Paiute women. Jess lifted the hem of her dress, crossed the stream on exposed rocks, and stopped by the edge of the bank to fill two wooden pails that had been left there.

"Good day, Hank," she called out.

He smiled, his face pinker than usual and glistening in the heat. "Hello, Jess! I see the ladies out here watering every few hours—and you, whenever you aren't feeding horses or carrying water or nails to the men—and thought maybe another pair of hands would ease everybody's load just a little."

"It's appreciated," Jess told him, pouring a careful stream of water around the base of a potato plant.

"You should work more manure into the ground," Hank said. "It'll help keep moisture in the soil."

"I was just thinking the same," Jess said. She looked to the far end of the garden, half an acre away, where Lily and Nettle were chatting as they worked, pausing from time to time to compliment Mattie and Grace on their efforts. "Hank, I hope you don't mind my asking you a question."

His cheeks looked pleasantly like cherries as he grinned. "Not at all."

"You're a farmer; why do you keep so many cattle that you don't sell?"

Hank chuckled and pulled a folded handkerchief from his pocket to pat his face. "They were my wife's joy. She kept them so she could sell the milk, and she also made cream, butter, and cheese to sell. I'm grateful for your fence," he said as a side thought. "The cows have never wandered far from our homes—they know that's where the apples are—but the fence makes it easier for me to bring them round to milk them. I may need to put one up, myself.

"Since I was a young man, I've always had a way with fruit trees, and I've usually kept bees, as well, so the income from the apples, peaches, cherries, and honey has kept Mary and me comfortable through the years. Until this year," he added, standing upright with his bucket to cast a dubious glance at the cloudless sky. "Spruzy makes some of the cleanest butter I've seen, next to Mary's, and it keeps in the cellar under the house until I have a load to sell." He resumed watering, keeping up with Jess, plant for plant, in his row. "Now I may need the income, if the saplings fail. Anyway, I keep the cows and my wife's horses to remember her by. I don't pine for her, mind you—she's in a better place—but I like to keep her memory alive to remind others that, when they pass, their memories live on, too, much more than they might expect." He smiled broadly, unabashed before Jess and anyone else about his viewpoint. "It's my way of letting folks know that everyone is special."

Jess held her bucket still. Her reply was just as direct and forthcoming as Hank's answer had been. "I'm so glad you're our neighbor, Hank. I know Jake feels the same." She looked toward the place where Olivia and Sadie Bennett and Red Deer were buried, on the far side of what was now Hank's land, beyond the field where Bennett grains had always grown tall and strong. "The day we rode in after being away for the winter, we were astonished to see your cattle and your house on land that had been ours when we'd left. I think now that a hand of Someone wiser directed the events leading to that."

"Certainly One wiser than the money-grubbers at the land office," Hank said.

Jess scoffed. "Yes; it takes cleverness, though not wisdom, to dream up such a scheme and get away with it. Anyway, I'm glad you're here."

"So am I." Hank's round belly shook as he chuckled. "Not all neighbors return my apples in the form of cinnamon apple crisp. I confess, I licked the pan clean, but I did wash it before I gave it back to Ho Chen."

Jess nearly dropped her pail, laughing, and Hank joined her. His mirth subsided as he directed his gaze where Jess had moments ago—the far western border of his land.

"I've told Jake, and now I'll tell you—you're free to visit that grave site anytime you wish, day or night, and you never need ask. You're always welcome to come over. As Doyle has invited me to the cookhouse since the first day I arrived here, and as Jake has invited me since, I'll keep you supplied with butter and cheese as long as Spruzy tolerates me, and apples and honey when the trees and bees see fit to produce them. Doyle and Seth have shown me by their generosity that folks in this part of the country look after one another, and I'm glad of it, because it's the way I was raised."

What could Jess say to that but "Thank you"?

Hank gave her a bright smile in response, then continued watering down the row.

Jess bent down to water another plant, but the sight of a

tiny, ancient Indian man shuffling across their land and leading a cow was so unexpected that she was moving toward the man before she even realized it.

He headed in the direction of the hammering, hunched and leaning heavily on the worn, knobbly branch he used as a cane. He crossed the simple, wooden structure that bridged the two banks of the stream at its narrowest part, turning stiffly to be sure the docile cow followed him.

Jess rounded the cookhouse, fascinated by the leathery, wrinkled old man. He stopped in front of the barn, looking around him at the young, hearty men moving about, tending to their chores. He looked as rickety as a toothpick among so many oaks.

"May I help you, sir?" Jess asked, stopping a short distance from him, half afraid the breeze created by her approach would knock him over.

He continued to stare at Seth, who splashed his face with water from the horse trough, then showed a slight recognition that she had spoken to him. He turned on nearly petrified feet, the wizened face beneath rigid strands of white hair reflecting no awareness that he heard her...or even saw her. Then, he blinked once, his rheumy gaze fixed in her approximate direction.

"Trade. Cow." His voice sounded like it had long ago turned to dust.

Worse, Jess didn't understand what he meant.

"Trade," he said, and held out one feeble arm, the one grasping the rope, toward the cookhouse.

Apparently aware that she hadn't understood, he turned and pointed with the same hand to the cow, and Jess finally noticed the bold, Bennett Mountain Ranch brand on its hindquarters.

The cow was the same breed they raised, and the brand was clearly theirs. This red and white cow—it had a white patch on its red side that looked very much like one of Jake's socks—must have wandered far from the ranch, and this old man had brought it back.

He turned again like a rusted puppet to face her, and pressed the lead into her hand.

"Trade. Cow."

Jess finally realized he must be hungry, and nodded and smiled as she stepped aside to tie the cow to the stable door, where one of the ranchmen would feed and water it.

Then she and the venerable Indian began the painstaking, fifty-yard trek to the cookhouse, his bony hand seemingly a part of the gnarled branch that served as his cane as he lifted it, placed it, and then shuffled toward it every step of the way.

Inside, Jess led the man to a bench and helped him to sit, anxiously biting her lip when he nearly fell backward off of it, and called to Ho Chen to give the man a meal.

The ancient didn't acknowledge her further—not that he had to begin with—but rested his gaze on the planks of the table, like a wooden gnome that had been carved there.

Ho Chen brought him a plate heaped with cornbread, beans, and bacon, as well as a mug of coffee and a cup of water. Jess gave her friend an appreciative smile, then stepped out, leaving the old man in his good care.

At the barn, she found Seth already tending the cow. Her now-empty water bucket sat beside the animal, and Seth was feeding it handfuls of hay as it languidly chewed.

When he saw Jess, Seth bobbed his hat toward the cookhouse. "Who was that old man?"

"I don't know; I was hoping you or one of the Paiutes knew him."

"Lee and Natchez both said they've never seen him. Any idea where he got this cow?"

Jess shrugged, recalling all of the watering she still needed to do. "Perhaps it wandered off last summer. Jake's sold cows all over Nevada Territory; people know him and the brand. The cow could have come from anywhere."

As Seth bent to feed the cow, Jess noticed that his injured leg didn't seem to be troubling him—or, if it was, he gave nothing away to indicate it. Had it been infected, his actions wouldn't have been quite as nimble. Satisfied that he was going to be fine, Jess picked up her bucket and headed back to the garden, where Lily, Nettle, and Hank were still watering.

About an hour later, Jess finally set her bucket down for the last time and stretched her back as she surveyed the neatly dampened rows of vegetables. She lifted her gaze to look over the ranch. Far to the north, beyond the gate, a tiny form shuffled stiffly through the dry grasses of the valley, leading a docile cow on a rope behind him.

"Ho Chen?"

"In here, Miss Jessie."

Jess closed the cookhouse door behind her, still not seeing Ho Chen in the kitchen. She rounded the sideboard, then finally found him squatted behind the barrel of dried beans, gathering spilled lentils from the plank floor. He put the last few in the bowl he held and stood up.

"No worry. I wash them anyway."

"I'm not worried. Jake hired the best cook available." She smiled. "Did you learn anything about the Indian man?"

"He say nothing, and I not know what say to him." Ho Chen lowered his voice conspiratorially. "I think maybe he never visited China."

Surprised at the quiet man's sudden humor, Jess laughed, as delighted at his jest as she was at the blossoming romance that she suspected had inspired it.

"You are not always happy," Ho Chen noted in an unexpected, direct way as he sorted the good beans from the broken ones.

Since her family had moved west and hired Ho Chen as their cook, the small Chinaman had counseled her and had always been able to see straight through her with little more than a glance. He had always listened to her, but this was the first time he had initiated a discussion about one of her concerns; normally, she went to him. The fact that he'd done so now startled Jess. It also told her how concerned he was for her, and for Jake, and knowing that flooded her with happiness that he cared—and restrained relief that she could finally tell someone all about her troubles. She couldn't tell Jake; it would hurt him too much. Ho Chen was no more, and no less, than a dear friend.

"You remember that my mother had miscarriages…that she had great difficulty conceiving children?" A lump seemed to swell in her throat, but Jess spoke past the tightness.

"I remember." The beans measured and set aside, Ho Chen began to slice strips of bacon into squares.

With considerable effort, she forced the words out. "I believe I'm unable to have children."

Ho Chen's yellow-brown face lifted to hers, then lowered again to his task. "You have been married less than one year," he said. "Children not always come right away."

"My mother's difficulties…." This was so hard to say, even to Ho Chen. "What if…?"

"You want to give children to your Mr. Bennett."

Momentarily unable to speak at all, she nodded.

"You not have that ring on your hand when you left ranch," he said, drawing her gaze to her delicate, silver wedding band. "To some women, wedding ring is shackle. When your Mr. Bennett put wedding ring on your hand, it became shield. Before you marry him, you tell me that you fear he may not be good man. Then you see he is good man, and you marry. A good husband is shield for his wife, and a good wife is shield for her husband, but you must let your husband be your shield. Just as the ring protects part of your finger, you must let your Mr. Bennett protect your heart."

"But if I tell him that he will never again be a father...."

"You fear he will hurt?"

Jess sighed, briefly closing her eyes. "Yes."

"You not tell him why you sad, you hurt him already. Sooner or later, you must tell, Miss Jessie." His voice softened, and his dark brown eyes looked solemn, almost fatherly. "You cannot be happy until you move past the sad."

"Jake already protects me so much that I sometimes feel I need to go riding or else I'll go crazy. If I tell him, I fear he will smother me with trying to keep me from any harm."

"Then go riding, but go with Mr. Bennett," Ho Chen advised as he started peeling an onion. "His fear will pass in time, as will yours. What you each hold back is what hurts you both."

Jess breathed deeply and slowly, taking in his words, as well as the aromas of bacon and spice wafting around them. In a way, Ho Chen was right, but for the first time that she could recall, part of her disagreed with him. She *couldn't* tell Jake that he would never be a father—not while they had so many other trials to face. And not until she could accept the loss herself—the soft, warm bundle she would never hold, the love she would never pour out, the family they would never be. She would never see delighted faces on Christmas morning or cross the ranch yard to see Jake with a child seated before him in the saddle, patiently teaching their little one to ride. There would be no reason to bring in a Christmas tree to decorate, no one to ride horses with them. She and Jake would journey through life alone.

Ho Chen laid down his knife and faced her. "Think not of

what you do not have, Miss Jessie, but remember all you do have."

His gaze was calm yet penetrating; he knew she had finally heard, and understood.

"You're right," she said, and she silently promised herself to do exactly what he'd recommended from that minute forward. Relieved to have confessed her cares and to have received a wise answer, a path to follow, Jess broke a chili pepper from its stalk, sliced it open, and industriously began removing the seeds too hot for almost everyone except Diaz to eat.

A Bible verse appeared in her mind: *"Casting all your care upon him; for he careth for you."* At the thought, she recalled the many other times she'd prayed to the Lord, and how relieved she'd felt afterward, as if she'd been handing over all her troubles for her Father to fix. It was comforting to know that she could simply let her concerns for them go, knowing that God would take care of all her troubles—and her, as well.

Last summer, she'd experienced a miracle. She'd been out walking among the sage and praying. She had just lost her family, felt horribly alone, and believed that God had abandoned her. Then, she'd prayed, and a strong wind had stirred up out of the still air. As it had passed her, brushing the skin of her arms, streaming through her hair, she'd believed she had heard a quiet, soothing voice within it, whispering, *"I am with you."*

Jess neatly sliced the chili, barely aware of her actions, but very aware of her need to pray. *Lord, thank You for reminding me that You are my Father, and that just as my father repaired my toy carriage when I was a little girl, so You have remained beside me and are still here to help me. My cares are many, as You already know—the ranch, my Paiute friends, my family's killer, Jake, who deserves to love a child, and the grief in my own heart that You may not have meant for me to have a baby. I'm beginning to realize that I've been so concerned with my own worries that I haven't been as good a friend or wife as I should be. So, just as I gave my toy carriage to my father to fix, I'm giving You my troubles now to make right. I should have come to You to begin with; You are the only One who can fix anything. Also, please give me the words to help bring Ho Chen and Lily together, just as you gave Ho Chen the words that brought Jake and me together.* Absently, Jess turned the strips of chili and began to dice them. *And, Jake and I constantly have a great deal of work to do. Help me take the time to find ways to show Jake my love for him.*

"You are very quiet," Ho Chen observed.

Jess used the flat side of her knife to crush the mustard seeds he passed to her. "I was just thinking about what you said, about everything I *do* have, and I was trying to think of ways to show Jake..."—this felt rather personal, but Ho Chen always understood—"to show Jake that I love him."

"You will think of ways, Miss Jessie. How does he show you?"

She detected a hint of personal curiosity in his question, and she halted for a moment and smiled, realizing that God—the Almighty, as Jake called Him—was already answering her prayer about Ho Chen and Lily.

"Jake bought me fabric for a dress. He built me a jewelry box, and a washstand, late at night after working long days on the ranch. He listens." She paused, then asked calmly, "How do you show Lily?"

"I—"

Jess had never seen yellow skin blush pink before, nor seen a man focused so intently on his work. For long moments, he kept chopping in silence.

Having prayed, Jess felt relieved enough of heart to tease her friend. "Ho Chen, are we going to need that many onions?"

He glanced aside at her, and his face, now a mottle of crimson, managed a grin. "Eventually."

Jess said nothing, but busied herself cutting salt pork, letting him see by her manner that she would stay until he was as forthcoming as she had been.

"I marry once before," he finally said. "In China. My wife died in war soon after we marry."

A thousand questions flooded Jess's mind at this piece of news, but she forced herself to emulate Ho Chen's way of listening quietly and respectfully instead of peppering the speaker with questions.

"Lily is special," he said, "but she is also Paiute."

"I've seen other Chinamen marry Paiute women, Ho Chen."

"So have I, but I do not know how to ask. In China, a woman of forty or fifty, a matchmaker, arranges the marriage. A son's parents go to matchmaker and tell her their son's...what he does well."

"His skills?"

"Yes. Then they pay matchmaker to find a suitable wife for their son. When matchmaker finds a suitable wife, she meets with that woman's parents and tell them man's qualities. If woman's parents agree the man and their daughter would be good match, then woman's parents go to her and ask her if she agrees. Maybe five days later, woman's parents tell matchmaker if woman agrees. If so, man's parents send many gifts to woman's parents many times, and they decide date of marriage. After, man sends many gifts to woman."

Jess began to wash the lentils in a large bowl of water. "What kinds of gifts would he send her?"

"First gifts are two gold earrings, two gold bracelets, four chickens—two cocks and two hens—and often money, always in even amount, for woman to buy present for herself." He smiled, his face its normal shade of yellow-brown, though his black eyes remained animated. "You want to ask me why in twos. It is because a couple is always made up of husband and wife, so gifts are in even numbers.

"First gifts are important," he went on. "They show man's gratitude to girl's parents for raising so nice a girl. They also show their two families from now on will be close relatives. Second gifts may be gold ring, gold hairpin, gold necklace. Man may also prepare and send porks. With second gift, a bridegroom's man will discuss date of marriage with woman's parents. Third gifts are beautiful clothes of silk or of other precious cloth, as well as money for other expenses."

Jess drained the water from the pot of beans. "When do the man and woman meet?"

"They meet at wedding ceremony."

"I would not have made a good Chinawoman," Jess said. "Still, after so many beautiful gifts, the woman would already look forward to meeting the man." She thought of the Paiute traditions she'd learned from Nettle and Lily and, as casually as possible, told Ho Chen everything she knew of Paiute customs while he fried the bacon and salt pork in the bottom of a kettle over the fire. "It wouldn't be difficult to combine the customs of both your peoples," Jess finished gently.

Ho Chen stirred thoughtfully, then added in some of the onions and a sprinkle of seasoning. He was silent for so long that Jess began to realize how much she'd been missing Jake—being close at night, glimpsing him throughout the day, hearing the sound of his voice. She may not have a child, but she had Jake.

"Miss Jessie," Ho Chen said, his eyes meeting hers, almost formally, she thought. "Will you be matchmaker for Lily and me?"

Me, a matchmaker? Jess thought, and was glad she didn't speak it. "You said that matchmakers are middle-aged women. Wouldn't Nettle be a more logical choice? You could tell her all that you've told me. She knows her people's traditions far better than I do."

"You are friend to Lily and to me," he said simply.

How would she combine their traditions? Sure, she could take two bracelets or a hairpin to Lily and arrange a wedding date, but she couldn't help Lily stack wood for twenty-five days; they all had too much to do!

"In this country," Ho Chen said, "a man ask woman's father for permission to marry. Lily has no father, but I must ask your Mr. Bennett and her people for permission to marry her. Perhaps you will tell me your answer after," he said.

"I'll need to discuss it with Jake," Jess said, thankful for his gracious allowance of time for her to weigh her thoughts. "I'll tell you as soon as I have an answer."

Ho Chen eyed her. "You are sad once more?"

Jess sighed and smiled softly. "No, I just miss Jake."

"You do not need to miss any longer," he said, cocking his head to the side.

"Why not?"

Just then, the cookhouse door swung open, and Jake stepped through, his hat in his hand. He didn't slow when he saw her but came straight over and swept her up in his arms. Ho Chen slipped quietly out of the cookhouse, a grin lighting his face.

"Think not of what you do not have, Miss Jessie, but remember all you do have." The words came back to Jess as she clasped her hands behind Jake's neck and his brown eyes settled warmly on hers.

"I missed you, Jess," Jake murmured. "Three days is a long time to be away from you." He nuzzled the sensitive place beneath her ear, his lips fervent, taking. "I didn't hurt your ribs, did I?"

Jess met her husband's mouth for a long kiss filled with love. "What ribs?"

Chapter Twelve

Ho Chen had asked permission to marry Lily not only of Jake and the Paiutes, but also of Lily's daughters, Mattie and Grace. Jess and the two girls had been gathering sage leaves in the desert to make tea when Ho Chen had come and asked them.

Grace had run up to him and leaped into his arms, answering with a glowing smile and a tight hug. Mattie had remained at Jess's side, staring at him, as he'd set Grace back on the ground. "Will you promise to always be kind to Mother and to us?" Mattie had asked.

Ho Chen had removed his hat and bowed very low, so that his long, black braid fell forward over his shoulder. Then he'd stood upright again and met Mattie's eyes, gaze for gaze. "I promise you for always," he'd said.

The next day, Lily, the bride, and Jess and Nettle, her two bridesmaids, walked along the stream, gathering wood and chatting happily. They stacked the wood behind the cookhouse near the chicken coop and pigpen, then did the same several times throughout the day, until they had made fifteen piles. That evening, Lily bathed in the river away from her village, then walked back to her wigwam with Nettle and Jess.

"Will Mattie and Grace stay with Spruzy and Lee tonight?" Jess asked Lily, ducking inside the dwelling of carefully woven branches.

"Yes." Lily's coffee-with-cream skin flushed softly. "Spruzy told me this morning that she and Lee will keep Mattie and Grace until after the wedding."

Jess settled onto a mat of woven reeds near the open, arched doorway, comfortable in her calico dress and moccasins, and not missing her hat or gun belt. *Tonight is a night to celebrate Lily and Ho Chen, and the blessing of love,* she thought. It was Sunday, a day free of ranch duties, one that Ho Chen and Lily had decided was best for their "courtship."

Jess felt sad to be away from Jake less than two weeks after he'd come back; it was only for a night, but the focus on romance that day and evening made her think of him frequently.

Shortly before sunset, Diaz and Mattie brought the first gifts—a pair of gold earrings, which Ho Chen had travelled to Susanville the week before to purchase. As Lily's attendants, Nettle and Jess graciously accepted them on her behalf.

Jake and Grace arrived a short while later and presented two slim, gold bracelets. Rather than give them to Nettle or Jess, Grace stepped past them into the lodge and hugged her mother around the neck. "These are for you," she said. "They are from Ho Ch—they are from Father."

Jake and Jess shared a long, peaceful look, then Jake left, holding Grace's hand and twirling her like a dancer.

Soon after, Doyle, Taggart, Seth, and Will approached, each of them carrying a chicken tucked under his arm. There were two cocks and two hens.

"In China, gifts are given in even numbers," Jess explained to Lily, "because a couple is made up of a husband and a wife. The men will take the chickens back to the pen behind the cookhouse to keep them safe from predators, but they are yours."

After the men left, the sisters, Lily and Nettle, happily hugged a little and cried a little, and Jess saw memories and sadness and hope pass wordlessly between them.

As the sky grew dark and night sounds blended into the trickling of the stream behind the lodge and the faint wind soughing through the cottonwood leaves above, Jess lay contentedly on her bedroll between Lily and Nettle, who both fell silent but, she knew, were not sleeping. Jess had just begun to drift off to sleep when she heard a movement. She parted sleepy eyelids to see Ho Chen sitting quietly at Lily's feet.

Her dear, Chinese friend—the only person aside from her brother, Ambrose, who had known her family almost as well as she did—now felt, in a way, a part of her new family. One day, Ho Chen, Lily, and the girls might move away, but everyone at the ranch would always have this night, the memories of the lives and traditions they'd helped to join, finding peace in the lawless West while war raged in the civilized East.

After hours of trying to stay awake for her friends, Jess finally closed her eyes and fell asleep, leaving the remainder of the night to Lily, who, from tomorrow forward, would always have a good man at her side, and to Ho Chen, who had promised a little girl that he would be a good husband and father, and who continued to sit quietly at Lily's feet.

At dawn the next morning, the ranch people stood under the cottonwood trees, gilded by the rising sun as if brushed by gold. Ho Chen wore new buckskins and a blanket secured at his shoulder in traditional Paiute style, the fringes of his blanket and the eagle feathers tied in his braid swaying in the wind. Opposite him stood petite Lily, her light-brown skin and hair aglow, her hazel eyes glistening like amber against her midnight-blue silk dress, which Jess had sewn in traditional Chinese style from the silk ball gown she had worn on her last night in Carson City. The night when Jake had told his friend, Lone Wolf, to bring her to the ranch. Lily also wore the gold earrings and bracelets Ho Chen had given her, and the jewelry winked in the bright rays of sunlight.

Black-Eye, Lily's brother-in-law and the head of their clan, began to speak, reminding Ho Chen and Lily of their duties as a married couple, tailoring his words to Ho Chen and Lily's situation.

Jess stood with Jake; Nettle, Mattie, and Grace stood beside them; and Hank and the rest of the cattlemen and Paiutes formed the remainder of the circle around Black-Eye, Ho Chen, and Lily. To Jess, this was her family, and these were her people.

When Black-Eye finished speaking, he motioned for everyone to sit. Nettle, Spruzy, Mattie, Grace, and Jess distributed baskets of food—the wedding feast—then sat down with the others. Ho Chen and Lily sat alone in the middle now, and Lily lifted the basket of food she had prepared herself and held it out to him. Following the Paiute marriage custom, Ho Chen did not take the basket with his right hand but instead took hold of Lily's wrist and received the basket with his left hand.

They stared at each other for a moment, and then Lily leaned close and hugged him while the Paiutes broke out in applause and cheers. They were married.

Jess brushed away her tears, and Mattie and Grace ran to embrace their mother and their new father. Then, everyone was standing and talking, and Jess could no longer see the girls. Jake smiled down at her, and then the crowd parted. Mattie leaned down to hug Ho Chen.

Then, darkness.

An image flashed through Jess's mind—a moonless night, a pine forest, a clapboard house in a clearing, growing distant, the house no longer visible. Then, a flicker of orange through the trees. The thick, choking smell of smoke. Eerie dread filled her. It was a place she had never seen. Then, she realized that she could hear no wind, no movement, no sound at all.

There was a flash of daylight, then the sound of celebrating began to return, and, with it, the awareness of strong hands gripping her arms.

"Jess?"

Her vision cleared, and she saw Jake, his face tense, his eyes sharp.

"Jess, talk to me."

"Let's go back to the house," she whispered.

Jake quietly drew her away so as not to disturb the celebrants. When they had stepped inside the ranch house, he closed the door and then gently led her to the leather sofa. As she lowered herself onto the cool, pliable leather, he pulled off his hat and sat on the edge of the low table before her.

"Jake, I think something bad is going to happen."

"You had another premonition." He rested his forearms on the thighs of his trousers, and his eyes never left her face. He was listening.

"Yes. It wasn't here, or any place I've ever been. I saw a pine forest at night, then a house in a clearing. I think the house caught fire, because I smelled smoke. You know what was really odd? The fire didn't frighten me, but the house did." A shiver rippled through her, and she rubbed her arms in an attempt to calm herself.

"Do you remember anything else?"

Jess thought for a moment. "No, nothing."

"Did you see anyone there?"

"No."

"Any idea when it might happen?"

"No! All I know is what I saw. I didn't hear anything, and I didn't see anyone. I don't know if it will happen tomorrow, next year, or never!"

"All right, Jess," Jake said, taking her cold, clammy hands in the strong grip of his warm ones. "It's all right, love."

She wanted to argue with him that, no, it wasn't all right,

but with him sitting before her, so calm and so determined to keep her safe, even though nothing else made sense, she trusted him and let herself breathe.

Apparently satisfied that she was more collected, Jake patted her knee, then stood and went to the kitchen. A moment later, he emerged, wiping out a small pot with a towel. He filled the pot from the bucket of water they kept, hung it in the fireplace, then paused, his eyebrows lifted in a question. "Will a small fire trouble you, Jess?"

"That should be fine."

The vision swam in her mind as Jake lit the kindling and then, when it caught, added a few dry sticks. As the fire grew, he added a quarter log, sawed from a pine tree that had been split into fourths. The concurrent images began to feel as much nightmarish as real: pine trees, flickering, orange flames, the thick smell of smoke....

Jess pushed to her feet and began to circle the room, touching the tangible, knotty pine banister that had been sanded and worn smooth, breathing in the leather scent of the sofa and its wide, matching chair, to anchor her senses to the present. Behind the desk, the plank floor showed a hole that had been patched—the place where Jake had shot a rattlesnake the year before. Her moccasins whispered along the boards; her yellow, calico dress and the petticoat beneath it brushed airily against her legs as she moved. Her wide, braided leather belt felt warm and just a little snug around her waist. Her heavy braid of hair shifted against her back with her alternating steps, like a pendulum.

These were real. They were here. She could touch them.

The room began to smell pleasantly of sage tea.

Jake leaned a hand on the mantel. "How are you doing, Jess?"

"A little better." She pushed loose tresses back from her face, wishing she could brush away the images just as easily. "This vision carried a lot of emotion with it. I'm finding it difficult to let go."

"I understand." Jake laid the towel over his shoulder with a smile that matched his words, then went back into the kitchen, from which Jess could hear the clinking of coffee mugs.

Jess held that last, striking picture of him in her mind—the tall, imposing rancher in a blue cotton shirt and red bandana, a towel over his broad shoulder, and the air scented with desert sage. It was a far better vision than the last one she had beheld.

Jake returned, without the towel this time, and lowered the water dipper into the steaming brew. He filled two cups, then laid the dipper aside. Since Jess was standing behind the sofa, he reached across it to hand her a mug.

Jess took a sip and felt the fragrant heat of it in her mouth, her throat, her stomach. It soothed her, despite the heat suffusing the room from the baking sun outside and the susurration of minute flames warming it from within.

An energetic knock on the door added another welcome dose of realism to Jess's growing array of palpable stimuli. Sunlight flooded the room as Jake pulled the door open wide.

"Charlie," Jake said in greeting.

"Good morning, boss." Charlie touched his hat brim and tipped his head to Jess, his tan face charming a grin out of her from behind his thick, blond mustache. "Is there anything I can do? I saw you escorting Mrs. Bennett away, and you, ma'am, looking a little peaked. It's a beautiful morning. I'd hate to see you miss a minute of it."

Jess smiled helplessly at Charlie's lightheartedness. Whenever she saw him working, he was frequently talking—and receiving uncomplimentary glances from the others, most of whom preferred a good silence to the "noise" of conversation.

"I'm fine, thank you, Mr. Shane. We'll be out soon."

Charlie hesitated for a moment, as if trying to see past her assurance, then appeared to be convinced and pleased that she was, in fact, recovering from whatever had ailed her.

"I'll see you later, then," Charlie said, and genially lifted his hat. "Boss. Ma'am." With a sprightly bow, he stepped out and closed the door behind him.

Robbed of Charlie's lively chatter, the room felt hushed, placid.

Jake leaned against the mantel, sipping his tea, and watched her, his expression enigmatic and, she thought, still a bit concerned for her.

Not certain which of his reactions she should address, she seized upon Charlie Shane's propensity for discourse. "Well, Jake, do you think Mr. Shane is driving the other men daft?"

He considered her comment but answered with a question: "What are your thoughts about him?"

His voice remained impassive and his gaze steady, almost too steady, prompting another question of her own: "Do you find my behavior toward Mr. Shane in some way inappropriate?"

Jake blinked, as if thrown off the path of his contemplations. "No, Jess, not at all. You laugh at his antics, just like you laugh at Taggart's. You seem unusually perceptive, even for a woman," he said, the corner of his mouth quirking. "I only wondered what you thought about him and Payton."

Taking another sip of tea, Jess settled down on the sofa, reviewing her collected impressions of the two since they'd arrived at the ranch. "Unfortunately, I have no outstanding perceptions regarding either of them. Mr. Shane talks quite a lot, and I wouldn't want to lose any of the men who've worked here for far longer because of it, but he seems eager to please, if a little exuberant."

"If he shows too much starch, I trust the other men to

come to me before packing up and leaving," Jake said, easily dismissing her concern.

"As for Payton…." She hesitated, not wanting to injure a man's reputation unjustly. "He seems quiet, even for a cattleman." She didn't mention the looks she had felt from him more than once, his watchful, almost penetrating eyes, the mild discomfort she felt when she couldn't discern the expression behind his black mustache and beard. "Though, he's a fair enough hand with a horse." She decided to change the subject. "Have you met Pete?"

Surprise lit Jake's features. "Pete?"

Jess bit her lip against its urge to grin. "He's the old Indian man who shows up each morning with a cow to trade for a meal. The first time he came to the ranch was when you and Will were away selling cattle, and I walked over to meet him. All he said was 'trade' and 'cow.' The cow bore our brand, so I tied the cow to the barn door and asked Ho Chen to feed the man. The old fellow has been back every day since."

"Yes, I've seen him," Jake said. "Tried talking to him a couple of times, in English and in Paiute, but I've never heard him say a word." Jake set his mug on the mantel and bent to bank the fire, the curve of his mouth suggesting that he had already begun to see the humor in the ancient man's ploy. "He moves pretty slow for someone who catches a runaway cow every day."

"Well, you don't have to be fast to catch the same cow," Jess said with a giggle.

"What?" Jake shifted to face her.

"Every day, the cow has the same, white patch, shaped like a sock, on its left side. The man brings it here, as if he's found it only that morning, and leaves it by the barn for the men to feed and water. And each time I discover he's left for the night, the cow is gone, too."

"He brings the same cow?" Jake chuckled, then threw back his head and laughed, pressing a hand to his stomach.

"Seth started calling the man 'Pete'—short for 'Re-Peat,'" Jess said. "I never bothered to tell him that it isn't spelled the same."

Jake wiped his eyes. "So, all the men are calling him Pete?"

"I think a couple do. Most of them are too busy helping with the weak foals and calves and attaching Doyle's 'barbs' to the fence wires to pay him much notice." Jess paused a moment, the thought prompting her next comment. "Bennett, what do you think of Doyle's attaching those little spikes to the wires? I've always trusted him completely, but the barbs could hurt the horses. I'm not sure I condone the idea."

"Now, don't you be worrying about your horses, Mrs. Bennett," Jake said, rounding the sofa to squeeze her arm. "I reckon it's like sitting on a pin. Once they get too close to the fence and get stuck, they won't want to do it again. We still have hundreds of acres for them to run, and I'm guessing your pa's horse paddocks in Kentucky weren't nearly as big as that. Didn't horses in Lexington need to learn not to run into fences?"

"Yes, they did," Jess said, grinning up at his handsome, though unshaven, face.

His gaze warmed, then his face sobered, and he lowered his mouth to hers.

Jess grabbed hold of his bandana to keep him from backing away, and she pulled it down toward her, urging his lips to hers once more before she finally, reluctantly, released him.

"Only twelve hours until sundown," he murmured, the side of his face pressed tenderly against hers.

"Only twelve hours," she agreed. The image of the dark clearing and the clapboard house flashed through her mind once again. "It might be a long day, for more reasons than one."

Jake leaned his forehead against hers, and she felt the force of his love flow into her. "This is Ho Chen and Lily's day, as well as Mattie and Grace's. Let's help to make it the best day for them that we can, and we'll deal with the vision when we have to. Okay?"

She nodded as he folded his hand around hers and held tight. "Okay." She was a Hale. And a Bennett. She would endure.

Chapter Thirteen

Jess eased away from Jake and his deep, sonorous breathing, shifting the blanket over the place where she'd been lying so the cool air wouldn't awaken him. From a peg on the wall, she lifted one of his long, cotton shirts and put it on, instantly warmer clear down to her knees, where the shirttails hung. She slipped out the door and pulled it closed behind her, then simply stood for a moment on the landing, holding Jake's shirt collar to her face, trying to lose herself in the softness and the masculine, leathery scent of it, trying not to acknowledge what the pain in her lower back meant.

She felt her way through the darkness with her bare feet on the plank floor and her upper arm against the wall, half leaning against it, wishing it would hold her, comfort her. Heartsick, weighted down with the monthly betrayal of her own body, she opened the door of the middle bedroom and stepped inside, praying it would provide refuge.

Though she hadn't explored the room now used for storage, Jess had brought up an oil lamp and matches, since visions of the clapboard house in the clearing had haunted her for the past several nights while she'd slept. She had known she might encounter a night when she wouldn't be able to return to sleep and would perhaps organize the room.

She silently closed the door behind her, and her hand found the lamp and the matches. Jess squinted against the flare of the sudden flame, orange at first, then gold, lighting her hand, the white sleeve of her nightgown, and an orb of space around the match but leaving the rest of the room feeling cavernous.

As she moved the match, it laid a small circle of brightness on the dusty table, then on the brass base of the oil lamp, then on the wick inside its chimney. Oddly, the match was providing an intriguing distraction, as Jess saw only parts of objects, almost as if looking through field glasses. The flame neared and warmed her fingertips, so she lifted the chimney, lit the wick, and blew out the match.

The wick crackled and sputtered, then quieted as the flame steadied and glowed, illuming the room's clutter and walls. A small window divided the wall opposite the door, its panes dull with dust. Jess lifted her eyes to where the upper walls met the ceiling, low above the window and rising to the roofline high above the door, the uppermost timbers lost in shadow. Here and there, spider webs dangled between ceiling and wall in the corners. The room smelled of dust, of disuse, and of old papers and books.

Heading to the left, Jess waded past crates of various sizes and a bunk that stood on end against the wall, on the other side of which Jake was sleeping. She saw the tiny washtub that her Paiute friend, Red Deer, had brought into her room when she had first come to the ranch. There was also another, larger tub. She touched her fingers to it, leaving five clean lines in the layer of dust. Like the cattlemen, she had been washing from buckets or going for swims in the river to keep clean. A bath now and then would be welcome.

Aside from assorted crates and odd bits of furniture, there was the loom she'd once used to make a blanket, and beautiful Indian baskets piled with dozens of balls of yarn, which had undoubtedly been collected by Jake's first wife, Olivia. Jess bent, as much to relieve the expanding discomfort in her lower back as to sort through the colors of yarn, some in baskets atop crates, others on the floor. So much yarn, she decided, would not go to waste. There was plenty to make blankets for the Paiutes, perhaps as Christmas gifts. Jess lifted the lid of an unmarked crate and discovered stacks of neatly folded fabrics that had never been sewn into clothing. Her fingers brushed soft, lightweight cottons—one appeared to be burgundy, another dark green. They would make comfortable, serviceable petticoats to replace the stiff, heavy one she'd been wearing. Out of the corner of her eye she glimpsed, underneath a small table, a rocking bassinet.

"For Sadie," she murmured, her heart twisting with sadness that Jake had lost his daughter, with despair that she had come into this room to forget the hopeless condition of her body but was being reminded of it at every turn.

Setting aside the yarn she'd collected in her arms, Jess moved a broken chair and then nudged aside a trunk as quietly as she could. The table was just high enough that she could pull the bassinet out from under it.

It was made from a hard wood and sanded smooth, about two feet long and a foot wide, the curves at the head and foot strongly reminiscent of those Jake had cut into the table of the washstand he'd made for her. Jess knelt beside it, her hands moving over the curves, reaching down to run along the inside where Sadie Bennett had lain. Jake had made this with his own two hands, and with the tools that had been destroyed when the workshop had burned down along with the supply shed and stable.

Perhaps, she thought, Mattie and Grace would like to play with the bassinet, since they had so few toys. She would ask Jake and make each of the girls a doll to place in it.

Inspired by the distraction, Jess retrieved the sewing kit from its place on the table and settled onto the floor beside the crate of fabric.

Jake lay in bed with his hands folded behind his head, listening to Jess's soft movements in the adjoining room. She had been sleeping less and less during the past few months, and when she did sleep, it was often fitfully. Whatever had been troubling her in her waking hours was following her into her dreams.

Lifting a hand, he rubbed his forehead with his thumb and fingers. The images she saw—the premonitions, or whatever they were—were enough to haunt his sleep, as well; he couldn't begin to know what they were doing to her. But her sleeping trouble had begun before she'd started seeing visions, before they'd come back to the ranch. He briefly wondered if she had an illness of some kind that she hadn't mentioned, then immediately dismissed the idea. She looked as healthy and as beautiful as she had the day he'd married her.

That left only his previous notion that her difficulty wasn't physical but rather had to do with a matter between them. He had been patient with her, the way his pa had raised him to be with a woman, and he didn't want to intrude if she wasn't ready to talk to him. However, he couldn't bear to see many more of her occasional moments of deep sadness without being able to help make whatever was wrong right again.

Jake pulled on his trousers and padded in bare feet to the middle bedroom. He knocked softly on the door so as not to startle Jess, then eased the door open, letting a triangle of lamplight fall onto the hallway floor.

Jess sat with her back to him amid various crates and baskets of yarn, with cuttings from whatever she was sewing haphazardly littering the floor. Her thick, brown hair covered her back and pooled on the floor behind her, but he saw the sleeves of one of his shirts over her arms, and her nightgown covering her legs and ankles but not her bare feet. She'd heard him come in—the needle in her fingers had paused, and she had glanced aside—but she continued now, weaving the needle in and out of the material in tiny, careful stitches. She didn't seem angry or in any way put out with his presence; she merely seemed distant.

"Jess?" Rubbing his eyes, he entered the room and took a seat on the floor near her, leaning back against an old dresser that needed to be refinished.

She sent him an appraising look, starting at his bare chest and ending with his bare feet at the end of his trousers, then pulled the needle through the material, a long thread following after.

"Aren't you cold?" she asked without looking up.

"Are you coddling me, Mrs. Bennett?" he asked softly, teasing her with words she had spoken to him on their way back from Fort Laramie.

Rather than answer, she glanced at him again, her green eyes and the slender shoulder she lifted showing a trace of concession. Then, she returned to her project.

Jake searched his mind for words that would encourage her to share her burden but not push her further away. While he waited for his brain to accomplish that dubious task, her project began to draw his notice, and he deemed that topic safe ground to tread. "What are you working on?"

She hesitated, then turned over the small, oddly shaped bundle in her lap.

It was a doll for a little girl—for Mattie or Grace, he surmised—made of what looked to be one piece of ivory fabric—batiste, he thought it was called, cut square and larger than a bandana. Jess had tied two opposite corners to make knots that looked like tiny hands, and the other two opposite corners hung down, making up the front and back of the doll's skirt. Jess had added machined lace along the bottom edges, and stuffed the middle of the bandana, tied closed with a ribbon, to form the doll's head. She had added lace over its head to look like a bonnet, and a tiny string of seed pearls—probably left over from Olivia's wedding dress—just beneath the ribbon. The entire doll, material, lace, and pearls, were ivory, but the ribbon was pink.

"It's a war doll," Jess said. "My mother made one for me when I was a girl. She told me that during times of war and financial hardship, real dolls are difficult to find and even more difficult to afford, so many women sew dolls for their daughters from whatever bits of fabric and ribbons they have on hand. This one for Mattie is almost finished; I just have to attach the rest of the lace to the bottom. Then, I'll make another one for Grace."

"It's a pretty little thing," Jake said. "Mattie will love it."

Glimpsing a curve of dark wood, he nudged aside the cuttings of material that had fallen and pulled out the bassinet he'd made when Olivia had been expecting. He remembered the first time Livvy had set Sadie into it. He'd placed it in the middle of their bed so that while Livvy rested, the baby could sleep beside her. Livvy had wrapped Sadie in an Indian blanket that Red Deer had made for her and laid her on another, folded blanket in the cradle. She'd smiled up at him, her black hair and blue eyes shining in the afternoon sunlight, and Sadie had looked just like a miniature of her, with the same pale skin, the same brilliant blue eyes.

Beside him, Jess continued to work. Her peach-toned skin, red-brown hair, and sage-green eyes—and her lips, the blush-red tone of roses—were shades of the earth, and of the life that sprang from it. Livvy and Sadie had been the day and night sky—the white of the clouds, the blue of the expanse above, the satiny black of night. The two women were more similar in their personalities than their looks—intelligent, direct, having a love of horses—but Jess also possessed single-mindedness, independence, and the determination of about four men. He had loved Olivia dearly—it had nearly killed him when she'd died—but what he felt for Jess went even deeper, as if he were one of the lengths of cloth that lay folded by Jess's knee, and all that Jess was rained down on him but didn't stop at the surface; she drenched him, filled him, and ran through him. She had become an inseparable part of his very being.

And now, she had retreated into her solitude, and his heart and mind were drying up without her.

"Jess, I'm worried about you, love."

She knotted the thread, not responding. After a moment, she spoke. "The images I saw aren't going away, and neither is the horrible, sick feeling I get inside every time they come to mind. It's getting worse, stronger." She shook back her hair, the oil lamp revealing an unusual pallor in her face, then sighed and snipped the thread. "The house scares me badly, Jake, but I think there's even more to it than a house fire, as much as that thought alone troubles me."

By her avoidance of eye contact and her unwillingness to confide freely without being probed, he knew there was more to say than what she'd revealed, though, heaven knew, it was probably enough to disturb even the stoutest person. Besides, she had spoken openly to him about the visions.

"What else is bothering you?"

She gasped, and her green eyes shone with astonishment. "Isn't that enough?"

"You began having trouble sleeping months ago," he said, taking care to be gentle, "long before your first premonition about the ranch buildings."

"There's a medical condition—insomnia. Perhaps you've heard of it?"

"Jess."

At his tone of censure, she dropped her forehead wearily into the palms of her hands. "I'm sorry." For an instant, she appeared to be battling inner demons, then she abruptly dropped her hands and began rummaging through the crate of fabric for more material.

"Jess, I need to know what else is troubling you. Whatever it is, it's beginning to come between us."

Her head dropped back, her green eyes slashes of weariness. "I get tired sometimes, Bennett. I'm tired, and I worry about the ranch, the horses, the money, the Paiutes, the arsonist, the outlaws, the heat, the drought.... I try not to worry, but the challenges are there every time I turn around. And now, I have premonitions, and I don't know why. I'm not sure if they're real, and if they are, I can't do anything to stop the pictures from popping into my mind. I worry how you feel and what you think about this.... And sometimes I just get tired, but when I want to sleep, I can't!" Jess pulled out more of the batiste and began to measure its length using the floorboards to determine where to cut. She was still shutting him out of some deep, intimate part of her.

Jake sat forward and braced his elbows on his knees, willing to concede once more to give her the seclusion she apparently believed would help. "Are we basically all right, Jess, you and I?"

Jess glanced over her shoulder at him, her expression calmer, genuinely tender, though visibly relieved that he was letting the matter be. "Yes. I love you. I'm sorry that I'm not able to show that very well just now."

"We have time, Jess. And I love you, too."

"Would you mind if I let Mattie and Grace keep the bassinet with them and play with it? I'd like to give it to them with the dolls in the morning."

"Yes, that'll be fine, Jess." He gave her sleeve—actually, his sleeve—a light tug. "It'll be Sunday, and the day before the Fourth of July. Everyone should have a good time getting ready for the celebration." He leaned over to kiss her cheek. She turned her face to meet his lips with hers, then smiled. "I like my shirt on you," he added.

"I like it, too. If you were just a little taller, it would keep my feet warm."

"Yes, even while you're standing."

She laughed softly, and he smiled back.

"I'll see you when you come to bed," he said.

Jess nodded but didn't answer and went back to measuring material.

By late morning, preparations for the Fourth were in full swing. Jess entered the new workshop to get a hammer, and when she stepped outside again, she had to press herself against the wall, barely avoiding being run over by Nettle and Spruzy, who ran past, neck and neck, in what appeared to be an impromptu—and startlingly fast—footrace. The cattlemen paused from choosing their mounts for the yearly horse race to watch and cheer them on, and Ho Chen and Lily looked up from the two fire rings they were building before the smithy, their grins wide. Mattie and Grace trailed behind the two women, and even Mattie was laughing. Both girls clutched their new dolls, not having set them down since they'd received them from Jess.

Earlier that morning, before presenting the gifts, Jess had asked Lily for two feathers, which she'd quickly sewn to the dolls as head ornaments, and a handful of glass beads, adding a colorful necklace to each one. The bassinet looked at home in their wigwam, and the girls awoke to the gifts, clutching the dolls, thanking "Mother" Jess, and so in awe of the wooden bassinet that Jess had needed to coax them before they were willing to touch it. Soon, it had been lined with a blanket and filled with "babies" of pinecone, rock, and corncob.

Nettle and Spruzy were still racing each other, and Hank opened the gate that Jake had built into the fence between their houses, then stood back to let the women through. Chuckling, he walked through the open gate and then closed it behind him, balancing a crate of apples topped with a cloth-covered bowl against his belly.

Jess carried the hammer to Doyle, who dusted off the two sets of stout iron spits and crossbars he had fashioned, one to roast a pig, the other for a side of beef.

"Thank you, Jess," Doyle said. Then, when Ho Chen and Lily stepped back, he began pounding one of the Y-topped poles just outside a stone fire ring.

Beyond the garden, Mattie and Grace raced along the inside of the fence, trying to keep up with Spruzy and their aunt, who appeared determined to circle every last acre of the ranch without slowing.

Behind the two women, dust flew up from their feet, rising in small clouds, blending into a single cloud behind them, rising, expanding, and dissipating into a mere haze, rising.

Sudden dread overcame Jess, and dark spots blotted out everything she saw. Her head felt light, dizzy. *Lord, why does this keep happening?*

"Jess?"

She felt Doyle's big hand grip her arm and hold her steady. Gradually, spots of daylight began to return, and within moments she could see normally again.

"Come on, Jess," Doyle said. "Why don't you sit down?"

He led her to a bench at one of the tables the men had carried out of the cookhouse to make room for dancing. Doyle helped her to sit, and she looked up gratefully into his concerned face.

"What's the matter?" he asked.

"The cloud of dust," Jess said. It had looked menacing. Seeing Doyle's frown, she decided it best not to say so. "It's hot. I think I'd best get some water."

"Well, you stay put," Doyle instructed her. "I'll get it and come right back."

"Thank you."

Doyle ducked his head as he stepped under the lintel and entered the cookhouse. A moment later, he stepped out again, carrying a coffee mug. "Here. This'll help some," he said.

The water was cool; it had been drawn recently from the well. She nodded her thanks before he went back to his task of setting up the iron spit, then let her gaze slowly take in her more immediate, tangible surroundings. Lily crossed the small bridge over the stream to bring back the girls, Ho Chen smiled gently at her as he talked with Hank about apple recipes, and, at the far end of the table, the ancient Indian, Pete, bent over a plate heaped with beans, one skeletal arm lifting his spoon. In front of the barn, Will fed the cow with the white, sock-shaped patch on its side.

Her gaze shifted back to the elderly Indian, whose face was wrinkled like the bark of a pine tree, lined with the knowledge of many more years than she had seen, perhaps by a factor of four.

Jess had learned from the Paiutes that it wasn't uncommon for their people to see visions or to have dreams of events before they transpired. She had once pondered the possibility that people who lived close to the land, who were essentially part of the land, developed intuitions and instincts similar to those of animals that sensed danger, or a long, oncoming winter, or even an earthquake. Perhaps, by living close to the land, she was developing similar sensitivities. That possibility lent comfort, but only a little. She couldn't talk to the old man—he was, by all appearances, deaf—but perhaps Lily or Nettle would know more. She would ask them after the holiday, as soon as she had the chance.

The floor rumbled and the windowpanes shook, and Jess was awake and out of bed beside Jake, tugging on clothes. "What is it?" she yelled to be heard above the shaking.

"Stampede!"

Jake yanked on his boots, grabbed his Henry rifle, and ran down the stairs. Jess was less than a minute behind him.

She ran out the front door and onto the porch, the starlight almost bright compared to the inside of the ranch house. The horses and cattle were far beyond the fence, running northeast. A distant, high-pitched voice carried thinly on the air: "No ranch Indians!"

Outside his house, Hank stood in his nightshirt and held a lantern while Jake and two of the other cattlemen swung onto the bare backs of their horses, apparently using ropes for bridles. As Jake and the others kicked the horses into a run to pursue the herds, Jess leaped down the porch steps and ran to the barn. She grabbed Meg's bridle, then raced to the corral.

Whistling for Meg, she burst through the gate, latched it, and turned to find Meg immediately before her. "Good girl!"

Jess slid the bit over Meg's teeth and pulled the bridle over her ears, which pricked forward, alert. Her fingers rapidly buckled it, and then she grabbed a fistful of mane, preparing to mount.

"No, *Mariposa*." Diaz's hand clamped on her arm. "The boss said you are to wait here!"

Jess spun to face him and saw Charlie hurrying toward them from the direction of the bridge.

"He's right, Mrs. Bennett. It isn't safe. Everyone has already gone after the herds. They'll bring them back."

Jess pulled her arm free. "Only Jake and a few others have horses. The rest of the men are on foot. I have to help."

The Spaniard shook his head, looking wary.

Jess wasn't having any of it. "Diaz!"

"I'll take your horse and go, *señora*."

"Diaz, those are my horses and cattle, and I know what *this* horse is capable of!"

He muttered something in Spanish, then gave her a hand up.

Charlie held the corral gate shut, preparing to win the fight that Diaz had conceded, but Diaz pushed him aside and opened the gate himself.

"They broke through the eastern fence, *Mariposa*. Ride north along it and you'll find the break!"

Jess jabbed Meg with her heels and sped toward the narrowest point of the creek. Meg galloped over the bridge, her neck and legs stretched out as she gave chase.

Within a minute they'd cleared the fence, and less than two minutes later, Jess began to pass cattlemen who were on foot. She tasted particles of dust in the air, and the sagebrush seemed to fly past Meg like starlit rocks in a landslide as the mare lunged even faster, thrilling at the pursuit.

Like a boat's sails catching wind, Jess's unbound tresses and long skirts whipped out behind her. She feared for the herds, especially her Thoroughbreds, but the wind wending through her hair refueled her spirit, sating a need far greater than she'd known she had.

The thunder of the herds grew louder, and Jess began to see definitive shapes of mounted cattlemen ahead—and, between them, dividing the sky-on-desert horizon, the rolling, wavelike swarm of the herds.

As she watched, dust flew up from their feet, rising in small clouds, blending into a single cloud behind them, rising, expanding, and dissipating into a mere haze, rising.

A hot, cloying sickness choked Jess as she realized what she was seeing—dust, just like the dust Nettle and Spruzy had raised when they had raced, dust that had evoked a feeling of something ominous.

Just then, Meg raced past a small, flat shape lying on the earth among the sage, and then another, and then another, and Jess screamed in horror, though the sound was lost to the stampede.

Four foals had been trampled by the herds, as well as several calves.

Sensing a new urgency, Meg sped up as she approached the tail of the herd, and Jess, seeing that the few mounted men had begun to turn the mob, reined Meg toward the left flank.

A spot of orange flashed near the left point, followed by the report of a gun.

The animals veered hard right, away from the shot, and then another round of gunfire sounded, turning the herd in on itself and bringing them to a gradual standstill.

Jess slowed Meg but continued walking her around the drove, watching for restlessness which might signal another mass bolt. The animals chuffed and blew, their sides heaving, as the horses moved closer to one another for comfort. Lifting her gaze, Jess identified Doyle as the tall man mounted near the front of the herd. Jake rode opposite her, and Seth nudged his horse cautiously forward at the rear.

Without needing to communicate, as one, they began to walk the herds back to the ranch.

Minutes ago, Jess's flagging spirit had flared to life. Now, she acutely felt the deaths of the young foals and calves she had fed and cared for, which had not been fast enough or strong enough to keep up the frenzied pace with their mothers.

Jess glanced up to find the North Star and the position of the Big Dipper, recalling Jake's instructions about telling time by the stars. Only ten thirty at night. Still seven hours until the daylight would reveal how many of their horses and cattle they had lost.

The night Jake had told her about the North Star—about three weeks ago—had been the second time she'd had the sensation that someone was watching them.

Jess looked to the far side of the drove, to Jake, wishing she could tell him, wanting to ask if he'd seen anyone who might have stampeded the animals. Yet, just as she had no choice but to wait until sunrise to count their losses, so she would have to wait until they had reached the ranch and seen to the animals to piece together what had happened and why.

A wolf or coyote might have spooked the cattle, she reminded herself. A ranch hand's sneeze could have done it, though her gut told her otherwise. Whatever had prompted the stampede, all she could do right now was guide the cattle and horses, help keep them calm, and wait.

Chapter Fourteen

Jess, Jake, Doyle, and Seth wrangled the last of the animals through the opening in the fence, then continued driving them toward the stream. They had lost three additional adult cows to extreme thirst or exhaustion and one of the Thoroughbred stallions to a rabbit hole in the desert floor, which snapped the horse's leg. To cool the herds before they drank, and to watch for injuries, they had walked them slowly all the way back. Now, knowing they were home and near water, the animals lifted their heads and made for the stream.

Jess's mind felt raw from all that her eyes had seen, and her veins hummed with lightning-like liquid heat, yet Jake's voice seemed to float toward her from a distance, detached, and, at the same time, oddly loud.

"Doyle, Seth, you two stay with the herd. I'll—"

"They've taken them!" Lily shrieked, running toward them with Nettle and Ho Chen close behind.

Immediately, Doyle and Seth moved to calm the newly startled drove.

"What?" Jake spurred his horse to meet Lily, and Jess felt the thrumming in her veins turn to ice.

Lily's face streamed with tears as Jake and Jess dismounted beside her. "Three men took Mattie and Grace!"

"When you go after stampede," Ho Chen explained calmly yet urgently, "three men on horses come and take the girls."

Jake stared down at Jess, his face mirroring her thought: the stampede had been a diversion.

Jess recalled the distant, high-pitched yell, *"No ranch Indians!"* and the words spoken at the Pyramid Lake Reservation the day they'd brought the Paiutes home to the ranch: *"At times, they harm our women and steal our daughters." "So many girls are taken that soldiers cannot find them all or punish the men."*

Her knees began to tremble in soul-chilling dread; it swiftly spread throughout her body. Mattie. And Grace.

"We'll bring them back, Lily," Jake vowed, his voice that of a warrior. "I won't come back without them. Ho Chen?"

"I will come with."

Jess forced her legs to move, then hugged Lily firmly against her, silently making the same vow Jake had.

With rapid strides, Jake and Jess crossed the bridge, Jess pulling Meg close behind her. She continued toward the corral, where Diaz already had a bucket waiting near the water trough. Jess felt the water with her hand; it was warm, and Meg had completely cooled. She should be able to drink without developing colic. Meg pulled against the reins and lowered her lips to the water.

"Shouldn't she be sponged instead, *Mariposa?*"

"We walked them back," Jess answered Diaz, already heading back toward the gate. "She should be fine. I'll need her ready to leave again in a few minutes."

Jess strode to the front of the barn where Jake was issuing orders to the men, the liquid fear in her solidifying to steel.

"We'll take only the fastest horses and the ones that see best at night," Jake was saying. "Check their legs for heat, and be sure they're watered. I want them saddled and ready to leave in thirty minutes."

The men responded with rapid nods and ran to do as he'd said.

"Thirty minutes?" Jess said, not bothering to keep her voice low, since they were the only two standing there. "The men who took the girls already have three hours' lead time. They know where they're going. We'll have a slower time of it because we'll have to track them." She forced herself not to dwell on what might be happening to Mattie and Grace. "We have to leave now."

"I'm not leaving here unprepared, Jess. That gets people killed, and it won't help Mattie and Grace. We have to gather supplies, since there's no telling how long we'll be gone, and the horses need water, or we won't be able to outride anyone if we have to."

During his explanation, Jake remained calm. Jess didn't.

"The horses are watered, Bennett! I'll fetch the canteens, and we can leave!"

"Diaz!" Jake called.

"Yeah, boss, right here." The Spaniard jogged over, leaving the horse he'd been inspecting tied to the corral fence.

"I'll be leaving with the Paiute men and Ho Chen," Jake said. "Your job is to keep Jess here."

Diaz divided an uneasy look between them, but he nodded. "*Sí*, boss." As quickly as he'd come, he left to help ready the horses.

"I will not stay here, Bennett!" Jess declared. At his cool glare, she immediately shifted her headstrong, emotional appeal to a logical one. "You and I are the best shots on this ranch. What good will it do you to leave me here, where I can't assist or watch your back?"

"I can't deal with you now, Jess."

She stared at him, her mouth agape. *Deal with me?*

"Diaz!" Jake called again, and Diaz hurried back over. "Get your rope."

Diaz dashed into the barn and was back moments later. Jake grabbed Jess's arm and steered her to the ranch house, gesturing for Diaz to follow. Inside, Jake released her, lit an oil lamp, and retrieved his canteens from the kitchen while Jess and Diaz eyed each other in the main room like two cats determined to catch the same mouse.

Jake paused between Jess and the front door, a tall obstruction barring her way, his granite eyes on her. "Diaz? If she tries to leave, tie her." Without another word, he stepped out and definitively closed the door.

Rope in hand, Diaz positioned his brawn like an ironclad warship between Jess and the door as Jake, Ho Chen, and the five Paiute men rode out of the compound and into the night.

Jess's inner struggle to obey her husband was short-lived, and his order roundly ignored. Moving past Diaz into the kitchen, she filled the remaining canteen then ran upstairs to her room, where she retrieved her rifle and two blankets. These she stuffed into her bedroll, and then she swiftly plaited her hair.

Diaz stood where she'd left him, arms crossed, feet rooted to the floor. If she were to try forcing her way past him, he looked fully up to the task of preventing her.

Instead of launching a physical assault, she tucked several loose wisps of hair behind her ear and spoke softly. "Jake's a large target. Are you going to stand alongside me at his funeral, as well?"

Diaz stared at her, unflinching. Then he muttered something under his breath, and caved. "Do you know the situation you put me in, *señora*?"

"This is not between you and Jake, Diaz. It's between Jake and me, and he knows it. You're the best night tracker here, but I'll go without you, if I must."

Resolute, Diaz pulled open the door. "Le's go, *Mariposa*."

Jess left her bedroll and canteen at the corral gate and

sprinted into the barn for Meg's saddle. She hefted it onto her shoulder and strode back to the corral, entering the gate just as Diaz stepped from the bunkhouse with his gear.

Jess saddled Meg, and Diaz entered the barn to saddle Luina.

"Diaz, are you certain she's ready? She gave birth just three weeks ago."

"For three weeks, little Luina has rested, and she is one of the few horses who did not run with a stampede less than an hour ago. Also, she is a very good night horse." He patted Luina's neck firmly. "She'll be fine."

As Jess buckled the cinch and lowered the stirrups in place, she repeatedly glanced up to the other ranchmen who still lingered in the compound, openly watching her. Doyle hung back, flanked by Taggart, Seth, and Will, near the two fire pits, where a pig and a side of beef roasted over glowing coals, unattended. Charlie stood near the gate as he had earlier, his facial muscles taut and his white knuckles visible in the pale glow from the stars. Jess couldn't help but admire his staunch loyalty to Jake. On the opposite side of the corral, Lily and Nettle were huddled together, pale and tense, and Spruzy stood like a stone. Jess surmised that, had the rest of the horses been fit to go, the three women would not be standing there. As it was, the riders would risk each horse that they took. Jess tied on her bedroll, hung the canteen from the pommel, and slid her rifle into its sheath.

Just as Diaz mounted Luina, Jess stepped up into her own saddle and looked at the faces once more. From the doorway of the bunkhouse, Eli Payton gazed in her direction, his eyes glittering, evoking an unexpected tremor of fear.

During recent days, Jess mused, the cloudless sky had been

a curse—they'd had no shade from the blistering sun, nor a drop of the rain they desperately needed. Tonight, though, the lack of clouds was a great blessing, as the crystal sky shone, unimpeded, on the desert around them, lighting the tracks that, she prayed, would lead them to Mattie and Grace.

Diaz hadn't said a word since they'd left the ranch. He merely slowed on occasion to study the ground and rode on, his black hair lifting in the wind to the beat of Luina's lope. If Diaz had seen the icy glare Eli Payton had impressed on her, he made no comment.

Jake, Ho Chen, and the Paiute men had left only minutes ahead of them, yet Jess hadn't glimpsed them in the distance. For a moment, she feared that Diaz was intentionally leading her in another direction to keep her safe, but then she saw the fresh prints of horseshoes on the ground and reminded herself that Diaz was a man of honor, like most cattlemen, and had given his word.

Besides, he cared fiercely for Grace—little *Mariquita*, ladybug—and Mattie, whom he called *Valentía*. Courage.

Talons of fear tightened around Jess's heart, and she dug into a mother lode of Hale tenacity to fight it. She'd let herself cry, scream, and wail later; for now, she needed a clear head and iron-hard *valentía*.

Jess glanced at the Big Dipper's position relative to the North Star. One thirty in the morning. They'd run the horses full out along the base of the Sierra Nevadas, heading northwest for a solid hour and slowing only a few times to read signs. By her estimation, they were nearly twenty miles from the ranch, in a part of the northern Sierras that she had never seen.

Scattered pines began to dot the landscape, and Diaz held up a hand to slow her. Jess eased Meg's pace to match Luina's lope, following Diaz's gaze at the rocky soil. The horseshoe prints, previously spaced far apart as the horses ran, had grown closer together as they'd gradually slowed to a canter.

Luina and Meg walked now that the stands of fragrant pine grew denser. Diaz led them through narrow passages as dark as mine tunnels between smaller trees and beneath larger ones, the prickly, green branches brushing Jess's skirt and occasionally snagging her sleeves.

The unclouded starlight was a blessing, yes, but even a curl of moon in the sky would have enabled them to see between the boughs.

Abruptly, the branches thinned, and Jess saw a clearing ahead...and the corner of what appeared to be a timeworn, clapboard house.

"The boss and the others went right," Diaz murmured, indicating tracks that Jess couldn't see.

"Then let's circle around to the left," Jess whispered back. "Divide and conquer." And avoid Jake, who would try to stop her.

As they walked the horses around the edge of the clearing, Jess calculated the open space to be no more than an acre across. At one time, a garden had been planted, and an effort had been made to remove the stumps of trees that had been felled, but the unkempt plot held only the remains of skeletal sticks and vines, and the sizable pile of rotted stumps and gnarled roots had never been sawed into firewood or burned. A pair of wagon wheels with missing spokes leaned against a heap of broken barrels and crates, all of which glinted with shards of splintered glass.

The low-roofed, clapboard house itself, she now saw, was little more than a two- or three-room shack, probably abandoned long ago, and well enough concealed to make it an ideal escape for roughnecks who lived beyond the law. No smoke rose from the crumbling chimney stones, and only a faint, white glow—no more than a single lamp—shone from one of the front windows.

Diaz reined in Luina and helped Jess down. Dry pine needles crunched beneath her moccasins, as startlingly loud as her breathing in the stillness.

Diaz tied the horses to a branch several paces beyond the edge of the clearing, and then Jess crawled beside him to the edge of the wood. He pointed. "There's the boss."

Jess and Diaz lay almost directly behind the house. Along its front and two sides, brief bits of shifting shadows indicated that Jake and the other men had begun to spread out, keeping low, though Jess couldn't distinguish one man from another in the darkness.

At the muffled crackle of pine needles, Jess instantly honed her hearing to discern the origin. It came from beneath her hands; she was shaking. Warm sweat began to trickle down her spine and the sides of her neck, dampening her wool gown.

"I have to get them," she heard herself saying, and Diaz glanced at her. "I have to get the girls now. If I don't, Jake will, and they'll be afraid of him." She had hoped to find the kidnappers camped around a small fire or sleeping near their horses in the open, where she and Diaz could have looked out for Jake and the others while they closed in and fired three quick shots to end the nightmare. But this.... The house blocked their view of the men and where they were keeping Mattie and Grace. They couldn't open fire because they couldn't see their targets, and Mattie and Grace might be killed. One of them had to go in, and that person couldn't be one of the Paiutes; if a white man was shot by an Indian and word got out, it would be all the reason whites needed to declare war on the Indians. Ho Chen, as a Chinaman, wouldn't fare much better. It had to be Jake, and Jess was as desperate to prevent Jake from being shot as she was to get Grace and Mattie out.

"The girls might be so terrified that they'll scream at the sight of any man and alert the kidnappers. It has to be me."

"The girls...they may be dead, *Mariposa*," he warned her gently.

"No. The men who kidnapped them want their sick, insane 'entertainment' to last. No matter what else has happened, they're alive."

Diaz nodded at the logic of that. "I'll be right behind you."

Jess pushed herself to her feet, grateful that the dark-red shade of her dress would cloak her passing. She eyed the window nearest them. A crack split the lowest pane, and the upper corner of the glass was missing. Seeing no face beyond the window, she crouched low and ran.

Rather than pause at the woodpile with Diaz, Jess scurried all the way to the house and flattened herself against the boards beneath the sill, as anxious to escape Jake's notice as she was to escape that of the men inside. Again, not waiting for Diaz, she peered through the glass, cupping her hands around her eyes to block the reflected brightness of the stars. Nothing but blackness.

Once more, she flattened herself against the wall for an instant, breathing hard, summoning her grit. When she reached up to lift the window, a brawny hand gripped her wrist and yanked her back.

Jess was certain her ribs were all that kept her heart inside her chest. Lee stood over her, his gaze steady, his long, black hair unbound. Jess panted, glad it was Spruzy's husband rather than her own. Her next thought was that, if she were captured, she would be at the kidnapper's mercy. If Lee were seen, he'd be killed. At the realization, Jess shook her head in amazement. "You've got guts," she breathed.

For the space of a heartbeat, Lee stared into her face. "So

have you." Then, he pressed his bow and arrow into her hand and moved to raise the window. It was jammed.

He nudged her to the side. "Stand away." He reached over the broken part of the window, grabbed the glass, and, with a fierce tug and a grunt, yanked it out onto the grass.

The panes broke with a dull crunch, and Jess pressed herself against the house, waiting to see if one of the kidnappers had heard and was coming to investigate. No one came. With the glass gone from the window, Jess now heard muffled crying coming from inside the house.

"Lord above," she whispered.

Lee took back his bow and arrow from Jess and moved toward the window.

"No!" she hissed. "If the men see you, they'll kill you. They won't kill me!" *God willing.*

Before he could argue, she stepped in front of him and glanced expectantly over her shoulder. His mouth grim, Lee cupped his hands to receive her foot and lifted her into the window.

Jess felt her skirt tear on the remaining fragments of glass as she ducked inside. The room was empty—no Mattie, no Grace—with only a few pages of old newspaper scattered over the floor. Seeing the cell-like room took her thoughts back to the federal prison at Camp Douglas, and how terrified she'd been that Jake would be shot. Now, she was the one going in.

Lee stepped to the floor beside her, and Jess advanced toward the dim outline of the door.

Jake forced himself to relax his grip on the stock of his rifle before he broke it. He'd been mad at Jess before, but never had he been enraged. Their plan to draw one or more of the men out of the house had been rendered moot. No doubt, Jess had worked out some rationale for her actions in that stubborn head of hers, but that would be little comfort if he found himself burying another wife.

Lee was in. Jess may have thought that she, as a woman, would have some chance of surviving if she were caught. But she was wearing her gun, and if the kidnappers discovered her, they would see her as a threat. Hiding out in the woods, far away from the nearest settlers, they wouldn't be concerned about anyone hearing gunshots.

No longer confident about how this would pan out, Jake rose to a crouching position and signaled Black-Eye that Lee had gone in.

Jess hesitated at the door and unbuckled her gun belt. She handed it to Lee, then drew her revolver from its holster and slid the piece into the deep pocket of her skirt. Lee slipped the belt over his head and one shoulder, then readied the bow to fire.

Grasping the cold, metal knob of the door, Jess had to force herself to proceed slowly. She could hardly see past the cruel images of the kidnappers and the girls that her mind had conjured and her urgency to get to the girls *now*.

A horse screamed outside near the front of the house. A moment later, boots pounded the floor on the other side of the door, then hurried away.

"Now," Lee urged her.

Jess pulled open the door to a short hall but saw no one. Pale lamplight issued from the front room where the footfalls had led, and she heard the murmur of two agitated male voices. Another door to her immediate left stood closed. She twisted the knob, eased it ajar. She saw the night sky through a window, and a man with his back to her; she heard a child's voice gasping and crying.

Mere inches from Jess's ear, Lee's arrow hissed against his bow as he pulled the arrow back. Sensing his nod, she pushed the door wide.

All at once, the lamp in the front room went out, hammers of guns were cocked, the male shape in the room rose up, gasping, an arrow in his back, and, outside, there was the sound of a horse running away.

Lee darted past Jess and covered the man's mouth before he could cry out and alert the others. Jess saw the man reach for the chair where he'd left his gun. In the next instant, her revolver was in her hand, and the man was staring down the barrel. Mattie carefully stood up, pulled the gun from the chair, and gave it to Jess.

With a quick tilt of his head, Lee motioned for Jess to get out. Grace was hunched in the corner, crying softly, quaking. Jess knelt beside her and waited for the space of several endless heartbeats for the little girl to recognize her. The man Lee held grunted, and Jess knew it would be only moments before one of the men in the front room came and found them.

Mattie moved around Jess, sat down beside Grace, and gently took her hands in her own. Grace, still shaking, lifted her tear-streaked face to her sister, then cried harder when she saw Jess. Jess motioned for Grace to stay quiet and lifted her in one of her arms. Grace held on tight and buried her face between Jess's neck and shoulder. With her gun hand, Jess took hold of Mattie's hand and brought it against her skirt. Mattie grabbed hold of the fabric and held on.

Jess edged on silent feet toward the doorway, leading with her gun hand, Mattie close behind her. The agitated male voices in the front room had grown louder but were still too low for Jess to make out the words. Apparently, Jake and the others had them confused and distracted, but no shots had been fired.

Keeping her gun in position to shoot, Jess stepped out into the hallway and nodded for Mattie to enter the room next door. As Jess backed toward the room, she looked over Grace's head at Lee, who was silhouetted against the window glass, his face fierce, his long hair flowing, the muscles in his arms tense as he held the man with the arrow in his back immobile. The handle of a knife protruded menacingly from Lee's belt, and Jess didn't believe that it would be a comfortable end for the man who had hurt Mattie.

Jess backed into the room where Mattie waited, and she continued moving toward the window, with greater urgency now. A glance outside assured her that Diaz was waiting for them.

The voices in the front room grew louder, almost shouting.

"I have you, *Valentía*," Jess heard Diaz murmur from the window. "Stay here next to me."

Her gun arm steady, Jess laid her index finger along the trigger guard and slowly lowered Grace to the floor. As the little girl reached for Diaz, Jess stood up again, then moved to press her back against the wall beside the open window, becoming one of the shadows in the dark.

"*Mariposa*," Diaz whispered, "come!"

"I'll leave with Lee," she whispered back.

As she spoke his name, Lee appeared in the doorway, then started easing the door closed. In a few, rapid steps he was beside Jess, then helping her through the window, then joining her and Diaz and the girls behind the house.

"Go!" Lee said. "I'll join the others and see that you get away safe."

Diaz pushed Grace into Jess's arms and picked up Mattie himself. Lee swiftly handed back Jess's gun belt, then backed toward the mound of broken wagon wheels and debris so that he could keep an eye on two sides of the house.

With Grace clinging to her neck, Jess picked up her skirts and ran. Diaz followed a few steps behind her. She pushed through the branches at the edge of the clearing, ignoring the scratches to her face and hands, moving faster now, as if wild dogs were chasing her. Diaz told her to go left, and then she saw the horses. Jess handed Grace to Diaz, who untied the horses one-handed while Jess buckled on her gun belt—or tried to; the buckle pin wouldn't find a notch. She tried again, unable to see the holes in the dark, fumbling with her fingers as she felt for the notches.

"*Mariposa*! We must go!" Diaz hissed.

Suddenly, the pin found a notch, and Jess drew the leather tail through the buckle, then slid the gun into its holster. She took Meg's reins from Diaz and swung up into the saddle. Grace was in her lap, and Diaz was lifting Mattie onto Luina's back and climbing up behind her.

They turned the horses and circled the clearing the way they'd come. Diaz found the place where they had entered and led them through the mine-black tunnel of pine boughs.

Jess's blood hammered in her ears. She listened, waiting for the sound of gunfire, then looked back, trying to see the others. *Jake....* The clearing grew distant as she and Diaz rode away, until the clapboard house was no longer visible. Then Jess saw a flicker of orange through the trees, growing brighter. Eerie dread descended down her throat like bile, just as she had felt when she had first seen the vision. The clean scent in the air rapidly thickened with the acrid smell of smoke.

Still, Jake and the other men did not come.

As the woods behind Jess brightened with fire, she remembered what Lee had said at Pyramid Lake: *"Many of our daughters have been treated very bad and hurt as though their souls have been taken from them, and the guilty men are not punished."*

Jess realized she would never know who had lit the fire. It could have been Lee, Black-Eye, Ho Chen, or one of the others—even Jake—but she would never ask. Whether the method was right or wrong, the Paiutes were witnessing one kind of justice tonight.

The sound of riders coming up behind them startled Jess. She had been listening for Jake, Ho Chen, and the Paiute men for so long that she had feared they had been lost and that the kidnappers were coming after them. When she turned and saw the shape of Jake's sturdy build and Lee's long, unbound hair, she let out the breath she'd long been holding and called for Diaz to slow down.

Within a minute, Jake came up alongside her, his eyes blazing at her with a look as fierce as Lee's expression had been. He silently communicated that they would discuss this later; then he took over the lead, and the nine horses stretched out into a lope.

Jess kept her right arm secured around Grace. "Would you like a blanket?" She asked her softly. She didn't believe that Grace was cold—the night air was about eighty degrees—but she had asked so that the six-year-old would begin to see that she, and not some violent man, was now in control of her person.

Grace shook her head no but didn't speak.

When the horses began to chuff and stumble, Jake slowed the group to a walk and spoke to Black-Eye and Ho Chen. The three seemed to reach a consensus, and then Black-Eye dropped back with Lee and Natchez to watch the road behind them. Everyone rode in silence, keeping the horses at a slow walk, for more than an hour.

A farm appeared on the horizon. Jake spied it a moment before Jess did and led the group in that direction. Too tired to study the stars, Jess estimated that sunrise was still a few hours away, and figured no one at the farm would be awake.

They found two water troughs near the barn—thankfully, both were filled—and everyone stepped down and took turns leading the horses over for a drink.

Before Jess could dismount, Ho Chen was beside her, bowing in gratitude for what she'd done for him, Lily, and the girls. Then, he gently reached up for Grace, who went willingly into his arms and burrowed her face in his neck, as she had done when Jess had picked her up. Ho Chen lifted out an arm to Mattie, but she wouldn't let go of Diaz.

Ho Chen sat on a bench with Grace while Natchez watered his horse, and Jess pulled the two blankets from her bedroll, giving one to Diaz to wrap around Mattie. The other she draped around Grace.

Ho Chen worked his mouth, seeming reluctant to ask Grace what had happened, but both he and Jess knew he had to. He tucked the blanket around her and looked up at Jess, the plea in his pain-filled eyes asking her to stay. Jess sat down beside him on the bench.

"Grace," Ho Chen asked, his voice loving and calm, despite the tears gathering on his cheeks, "did those men hurt you?"

Grace shook her head, then nodded at Mattie, who remained in the saddle, leaning against Diaz. "A man reached for me, but she pushed him away and stood between us. She kept pushing him away from me. He laughed, then he hurt her, instead." She looked up at Ho Chen, pride for her sister in her voice. "She would not let them hurt me."

Jess strived to mimic Grace's prideful comportment as

Mattie looked absently over at her. For hours, Jess had held back screams and tears; she pressed her fingernails into her palms, not certain how much longer she could keep from crying out.

Diaz finally stepped down with Mattie so that one of the men could water Luina. By the grim regret and anger in his face, and in the faces of Jake, Lee, and the other men standing amid the horses, they had heard what Grace had said. Mattie stood beside Diaz, twin lines of tears streaming down her cheeks.

Grace eased away from Ho Chen and stood up, still holding her blanket around her. She walked several paces over to her older sister and stopped before her. "I love you, Mattie," she said, and reached up and embraced her with young, motherly gentleness.

Jess stood up from the bench and walked away to the far side of the barn, where no one could see her, and collapsed against the wall. Not wanting the girls to hear her, she pressed her sleeves against her mouth and sobbed.

Then, Jake was beside her, the lines around his eyes and mouth no longer fierce but pained, just as she felt. She pulled his head against her shoulder, and they both cried.

When they reined in beside the Bennett Mountain Ranch corral at dawn, a tearful Lily was there to receive her daughters, as were Nettle and Spruzy. Together, the women and several of the Paiute men began to walk the girls toward their dwellings.

Ho Chen, Lee, and Black-Eye held back to thank Jake, Jess, and Diaz, then turned to follow them.

"*Valentía*," Diaz called out.

The Paiutes stopped, and Mattie turned.

"I named you well when I called you Courage," he said.

As the Paiutes and Ho Chen continued their foot journey home, the rest of the cattlemen came to see to the horses.

Apparently, Will and Doyle had been tending the fires under the pig and roast beef. The two ducked into the cookhouse and emerged with plates, utensils, and carving tools, and Seth added a little water to a coffeepot that sat in the coals under the side of beef. He gave it a swish, then poured out steaming cups of the strong brew for Jake, Jess, and Diaz. Cowboy coffee. Jess gulped hers down, ignoring the sodden grounds that floated on the surface, trying not to taste it. It was better that way.

Taggart was telling Jake the grim news about the animals killed in the stampede. Like the other cattlemen, who had dressed rapidly in the dark when they'd felt the stampede, Taggart looked haggard and disheveled. His shirt was unbuttoned, revealing the red union suit beneath, and its tails had been jammed haphazardly into the waist of his trousers. One pant leg was caught around the top of his boot, just below the knee.

"In all, boss," Taggart said somberly, "we lost one Thoroughbred, four mares, five foals, three cows, and nine calves. Some were trampled; others were worn out from heat and dehydration."

"Anyone hurt?" Jake asked.

"Only Payton." Taggart lifted his hat and scratched his orange jumble of hair. "He was on watch when it started, said his horse bucked him off as it went to join the others. All the animals have been fed, watered, and seen to, and the fence has been repaired."

Jake tiredly slapped Taggart's shoulder. "Thank you."

Jess knew that "seen to" had been an understatement. The cattlemen accepted plates from Will as Doyle sliced meat from the roasts and Seth brewed more coffee. They all sat at the tables, exhausted, the long hours they'd spent awake showing beneath their eyes, their shoulders slumped. Pete sat down with a plate beside Charlie, who moved over to give the ancient enough room.

As Jake went to speak with the men, Jess leaned back against the corral fence, wishing absently for a refill of the repulsive coffee but unwilling to go any nearer to Payton to get it. Even as the thought crossed her mind, Payton looked up at her, expressionless, unblinking, then bent his head over his plate.

Will—spindly and tan, every inch of him, with the exception of the circles beneath his eyes—came to take her cup. His jaunty smile appeared to have taken some effort. "Are you wanting something to eat, Miss Jess?"

"No, thank you," she said, then lowered her voice. "Will, what do you know about Eli?"

"Payton?" Will's molasses-slow voice was just as quiet as hers. "Not much. He's one of them fellers keeps to himself. Knows his way around a horse."

When Jess realized that was all Will had to say, she murmured her thanks and started walking toward the house. It may have been the Fourth of July, but it was no longer a day of celebration. She intended to spend it communing with her pillow.

"Jess?"

Or perhaps not.

Jake's long, patient stride brought him in step with her. He glanced at her as if trying to gauge how much more she could take. "Doyle says that Hank helped with the animals all night. He turned in shortly before we arrived back here."

"He's a good neighbor," Jess said, sending up a heartfelt prayer of thanks for him as she climbed the two porch steps, crossed to the door, and pushed it open.

Jake closed the door behind them and clapped his hat onto a peg near Jess's. "Payton says he didn't see or hear the three men until they attacked. He was riding the east fence when the animals stampeded. He figures the men let themselves in through the north gate and stayed low in their saddles to blend in with the herds. He heard the crack of whips, and the next he knew, he was on the ground looking up."

Jess busied herself building a fire. She struck the match, reminded of the clapboard house fire, and wondered how long it would be before Bennett rattled the rafters over her decision to help with the rescue. He'd already started to pace the floor behind her. Apparently, not long. She decided to save him the bother.

"How were you and the others intending to get the girls out of that house before I came?" she asked.

"You and Diaz," he corrected her.

Jess blew steadily into the base of the flames until they caught the larger sticks. "Don't blame Diaz," she said. "It wasn't his fault."

"I don't blame Diaz at all. I blame you for forcing him to go against his loyalties. You owe that man a solemn apology."

"I know."

"To answer your question, I had planned to go in and get Mattie and Grace, and the others were to stir up the horses to distract and separate the kidnappers, maybe get one or two of them outside. We wanted to be careful not to be seen. If bullets started flying, we could have lost Mattie or Grace, or one or more of us." At the stairs, Jake spun around and paced behind her toward the door, his boot heels striking the plank floor as steady as drumbeats, his spur rowels matching the beats with their sharp, silvery *snick*. "We were taking position near the lean-to, where they'd left their horses. I saw Diaz near that heap of stumps, then Lee running across the clearing." Jake stopped behind her. "Seeing you disappear through that window was like—" His voice caught, but he spoke past it forcefully, his anger building. "It was like the day I saw Olivia covered with a coffin lid."

Jess stood and faced him, her own anger kindled. "And just how many chances do you think God will give *you*? Do you think I want to see a coffin lid nailed over you? Don't you think I'm afraid I'll lose you just as much as you're afraid to lose me? Don't you think I have those nightmares?"

The steel faded from his gaze, but only slightly. "Why didn't you tell me, Jess?"

"What would you have said?"

"I would have said no."

Jess flicked her hand. "There you have it. If I don't share my thoughts, then I'm not obligated to listen to yours." How could he believe she would *ever* stay behind if he was placing himself in danger?

"You think I'm self-serving?"

"I wouldn't have married you if you were self-serving; I've witnessed too much of that trait. I've also seen that for a marriage to bring joy, both have to give. If even one of the two makes demands, that person places his own needs above the needs of the other, and there can be no happiness. One knows selfishness, and the other knows only what it is to exist in an interminable, painful void where personal needs go unmet."

His leather-hued skin reddened. "You're saying I'm selfish."

Jess made an effort to gentle her voice. "You told me to stay behind because you wanted to protect me, because you didn't want to lose me. I'm thankful for your protection. I really am. But I don't want to lose you, either. Jake"—she pressed her fingers to her temples, imploring him to understand her—"do you have any idea what a large target you are? Don't you realize that if you, or any other man, had gone in to get Mattie and Grace, those girls might have feared you in the dark and screamed out, and you all could have been shot?"

A muscle twitched in his jaw. Evidently, he wasn't ready to see reason. Jess raised her chin, refusing to back down. His bent toward controlling her had gone on long enough.

"You've always been a good listener, Bennett. Don't refuse to listen to my viewpoint when I may have thought about possible consequences you might not have. You don't want me going off and getting killed. Fine. Do you think I want you to do the same?"

"There's a reason why the Bible instructs wives to listen to their husbands."

Jess drew back, briefly affronted, then regained her ground. "And God gave men the wisdom to listen to their wives. That isn't what this is about, Bennett, so face the truth: this is about pride. You're the man; I'm the woman. Since you're male, and since you've lost so much, you think that you're always supposed to protect me, that a wife never should need to protect her husband. Your pride was stung because you *did* need me, and without me, you'd probably be dead. Well, I have pride too, Bennett. I'm as proud to be able to defend you as I am to be called your wife. If you had died last night, I'd be the one defending my home and my family, like many widows in this harsh land. Who would protect me then?"

Jake pressed his warm hands to her cheeks, his brown eyes fervent. "I'll stand between you and a score of bullets if it means keeping you safe."

Jess laid her hands over his. "Don't you realize that I know that? And that knowing it terrifies me?" She closed her eyes and let herself feel Jake's touch, let herself feel his fingers, which were rough from building a ranch and working it tirelessly, rough from drilling fence posts and hammering together a new workshop. Yet his hands remained loving and tender when he touched her. "Now, I know you're still upset. I may have put myself in danger—"

"You did put yourself in danger, and not just today. I don't want you to risk yourself for me. Ever." His voice caught again, and he leaned his forehead to hers, curling his fingers into her hair. "What if I lost you, Jess? You're tearing me up inside."

Jess shifted her head and pressed her temple to his, loving the surprising softness of his skin there. "I had a better chance of getting the girls out of that house than you did," she said quietly, "and I did what was right. Don't fault me for that."

She felt Jake's reluctant smile. "You've got grit, Mrs. Bennett. I've never said otherwise."

Jess knew the conversation was reaching an end, and she wanted to remind him of just one fact. "I don't want to lose you, you big ox."

Jake's grip in her hair tightened in his need to hold her close, his temple still pressed to hers. "Jess, promise me you won't put yourself in danger again."

Jess lifted her mouth and kissed his cheek just above the unshaven bristles. "I'll pray that neither of us will have to make that decision again, but, Jake, you knew who I was when you married me. Please, don't try to control me, and don't try to change me. This is who I am. If you try to change who I am, then I'll no longer be the woman you fell in love with. Do I tell you to quit wearing flannel or to cut your hair? No." She smiled to soften her words, and he grinned a little with her. "Neither one of us can be happy in this marriage if we can't be ourselves. Now, I know this land is dangerous, and I'll strive to be more aware and more careful. But I can't plug my instincts with a stopper. And, if you ask me to, I fear I'll come to resent you for it. If you go to help someone, I'll want to help, too. If you go out to ride in the wind, I'll want to be with you."

"You'd ride without me, too."

"So would you." She patted his sides. "That's one of those passions we share that prove we're right for each other."

Chapter Fifteen

Jess paused at Hank's side door and lowered the hand that had been about to knock, feeling the prickly awareness of someone watching her. She shifted the heavy basket of apple tarts and stretched her lower back as if it pained her, turning as she did to scan the Sierra foothills, then the ranch yard, for an attentive pair of eyes.

With the folded bandana she always carried with her now, Jess patted the perspiration from her face and neck. During the three weeks since the stampede and kidnapping had happened, the temperature had reached more than a hundred degrees each day, and the land had been baked dryer than year-old breadcrumbs. The sagebrush was more brown than gray-green, and the horses and cattle had eaten the bunchgrass down to the rocky soil and were now surviving on hay and grains. In the ranch yard, several cattlemen pumped water from the well into buckets, which other men carried to the troughs, in a full-time effort to keep the horses and cattle watered. They were losing the battle; the animals had become weak.

Taggart currently worked the pump with Charlie, who set down two empty buckets and reached for two more. Catching Jess's eye, Charlie paused and lifted his hat to her, as spry as a palomino enjoying a lope on a cool autumn morning. Near the barn, Jake, Doyle, Diaz, and Lee led two painfully thin cows into the shade of the barn to care for them, with old Pete following them at a slow hobble. Farther to the north, the other Paiute men and Seth and Will rode among the herds, looking for the animals needing the most assistance, then roping them and leading them to the barn.

Behind the cookhouse, Ho Chen and Lily diligently watered the garden, in which most of the plants had miraculously survived—so far. Nearby, Mattie and Grace filled empty buckets in the remaining trickle of the stream, their dolls clutched tightly in one hand. The love of the Paiute people was helping the girls to recover from the trauma of kidnapping, though Jess knew they had permanent scars—and a greater distrust of white men. Still, the three Paiute women looked at peace as they worked with Ho Chen, a good, honorable man who would always be there for them with patience, a ready smile, and love.

Jess searched the ranch once more, feeling rather disconcertingly like a target. She didn't see Payton anywhere, nor did she see the source of her apprehension. Despite the sizzling heat, she shivered.

Shifting her basket once more, Jess knocked on the door. A moment later, Hank pulled it open, his pink face and bald scalp damp from the heat. He smiled broadly.

"Ah, there you are. Come in! I'm glad I finally have a visitor."

Hank closed the door behind her, and Jess took in the room as her eyes adjusted to the dark, which, she realized, made the space feel cooler than the blinding out-of-doors, though she knew the temperature was nearly the same.

The curtains Gusty had sewed hung in the windows, slightly parted to let in minimal sunlight, and added dark-blue charm to the bare floor and Spartan furnishings—a few chairs near the fireplace, a rectangular table and a few more chairs in the dining area. If ever a man's home needed a woman's touch, this, she decided, was such a place. Her eyes became accustomed to the low light, and then she saw the paintings on the walls. Actually, the paintings *filled* the walls.

Jess set her basket on the table and moved slowly around the room, studying each extraordinary, colorful painting. They were hung edge to edge like a puzzle of squares and rectangles, some small enough to set on a tabletop, and several larger than the door she had just walked through. Each of them displayed an image of people in dramatic, jewel-toned settings, unlike anything she had seen before, of the same style and apparently by the same artist. Suddenly, despite the heat, she wished for better light.

One painting depicted a blue-eyed little girl with long, chestnut hair picking an apple from a tree; clearly, the season was autumn, judging by the other apples that had fallen to the ground at her feet. Another picture had captured two brothers with matching overalls and grins alike, one boy blond, the other with brown hair the color of Jake's, nailing the door of an outhouse shut. Yet another one depicted a gentleman with gray hair and a beard guiding a plow behind two draft horses through a field of newly turned earth, encircled by pine trees. Beside that painting was one of a middle-aged man sitting outside a general store and smoking a pipe with a friend, a game of checkers on a barrel between them. Most of the remaining paintings were of a black-haired, brown-eyed lady at various ages—a young, happy woman in a lacy, white wedding dress; a few years older, picking a bundle of colorful wildflowers in the woods; older still, perhaps thirty now, sitting on a picnic blanket in the grass, smiling at a chipmunk that was cautiously inspecting the picnic basket. The paintings continued, nearly all of them of people and outdoor scenes, and most of them of the smiling brunette. The oldest she appeared in any of the paintings was about forty-five; she had a few silver hairs among the black and looked terribly thin, but none of the brightness had gone from her eyes.

Finally, curiosity drew her gaze to the signature on the bottom of this last painting: H. S. Beesley. She looked over at Hank, who had been following her at a distance, his expression one of sheer pleasure that she was enjoying the paintings.

"Hank, you're an artist? What are you doing in the middle of the desert, raising cows and apple trees?"

"It isn't always a desert," he replied, smiling as always.

"But you could be living in San Francisco in great comfort," she said, trying to understand why he was wasting his talent helping her to water onions in her garden, among other things.

"This is where I want to be," he said simply. "I could live in San Francisco in a large house with fireplaces of Italian marble and chandeliers and servants. In fact, I did at one time—see this painting of Nob Hill?—but I became restless and missed my life of working with my hands, tilling the soil, watching plants and trees grow from the efforts of my labors. I still paint now and then, but for the pleasure of it, sometimes to make gifts for special people who have touched me in some way. Here, people know what it is to have to work hard to survive, and I've learned that many of them are better people, honest people, because of it—like you and Jake and the cattlemen. Let me show you something."

Beside the window that faced the ranch yard and barn stood an easel with a half-finished painting. On the canvas, two girls stood on different rails of a corral, the older one wearing a dress of tan and blue calico, the younger in a dress of tan and green, petting the nose of a horse that Jess recognized as Luina.

"This is why I'm here. The large house in San Francisco didn't have children who played with horses, or apple orchards, or open places, or mountains. Do you see?"

"Yes," Jess said, patting away her sweat and smiling, "I do understand. I came here from Carson City, and I've never wanted to leave, even with the challenges we're facing. When I arrived, I discovered the same characteristics of this land that you have. It's a special place, as if expressly blessed by God to touch the hearts and lives of all who come here."

"I felt the same way when I first saw it," Hank said.

Jess circled the room once more to see the other paintings again. "This woman in many of your paintings...was she your wife?"

Hank rested his thumbs in his suspenders, smiling as his gaze caressed the woman's face. "Yes, that's Mary. Lovely as a rose on a spring morning."

"And these?" She indicated the girl picking an apple and the two boys and their outhouse shenanigans. "Are these your children?"

"No, Mary and I were never able to have children. These were children I saw at different times. I remembered details of them in my mind and completed the paintings later."

Jess felt humbled. Her great talent was balancing numbers in a ledger.

"Hank, may I ask you a personal question?"

He held out a hand to invite her to sit at the table, and then he poured them each a glass of milk.

"You completed several paintings of children. It's plain that they inspired you. How did you and your wife manage, not being able to have them?" Jess had ached to say these words, and Hank's kind nature allowed her to feel comfortable asking the question.

"God blesses different people in different ways. He blesses some to have children, others not to. Some He blesses with a spouse, and others He blesses to remain unmarried. Mary and I didn't have children, and for a long time that was difficult for us, especially Mary. I think God gives women the need to have a child, while He gives men the need to...well, to be close to their wives, if you understand my meaning. Because Mary and I had only each other, as well as a mutual sadness, we were very close all our lives. We both enjoyed working on our farm—I moved here from there; Sacramento City had become too noisy and crowded—and we learned to laugh together, and we loved each other. We also learned that if you pay too much attention to the bad, you fail to see the good."

That seemed to be a recurring lesson Jess was learning these days, and it was a wise one. She longed to probe Hank's years of wisdom on another matter, but it was so private; she hadn't spoken of it to anyone.

"What is it, Jess?" Hank asked kindly, his fatherly smile dotted with milk at the corners.

"Do you think it's possible to love someone too much?" she asked, startled that she had actually spoken the words, and startled even more when the words wouldn't stop. "I was so afraid to marry Jake. We both had lost people dear to us, and I loved him so much that I was terrified to lose him. I've tried to keep a tiny corner of my heart from Jake," she quietly confessed, "thinking that if I ever lose him, I'll have that corner that never got close to him, that could never be hurt. But he's gotten in there, too."

Hank patted her hand. "Worry is time wasted, and time is the stuff that makes up life. Good and bad will come, whether you worry or not, but when you look for the good, you'll find it. And if you look for the bad...."

"That's what I'll see," Jess said, completing the thought he'd intentionally left unfinished.

"It's a bit of an effort to look out at a dying desert and see the good," Hank admitted, "but you keep looking, and you may discover the joy and beauty of two little girls petting a horse, each creature sharing a moment of happiness with the next. That's what I've decided to fill my life with. Of course, sharing the good with someone else makes the experience twice as special."

"Well, since you mentioned sharing a good thing with someone else, I brought you apple tarts, like the ones my mother used to make." Jess pulled her basket over and lifted out the cloth-covered plate. Her heart dwelled on all Hank had said, and she was certain it would continue to do so for a long time to come. But now was a chance to focus on delight and overshadow the misery of the drought.

Hank brought over two plates, and, together, he and Jess savored the sweet pastries.

When they had finished the tarts, Hank sighing in bliss, Jess lifted her empty basket and followed him outside.

They walked northwest along the base of the Sierra Nevadas, Jess doing her utmost to leave behind her concerns for the ranch and worries whether someone was watching her.

"This is the first time I've gone to visit the grave since Jake and I returned from the States," Jess said, "though I believe Jake has visited it a time or two. It's peaceful here," she said, listening. "And quiet."

A hawk called as it glided overhead, the sound echoing over the land as if over a chasm. The sagebrush leaves rustled in the breeze, and the pebbles underfoot crunched under Jess and Hank's feet. To the north, the lone, red-earthed mountains stood peacefully, and the childlike part of Jess longed to walk around one, just to see it from every side.

"It's difficult to believe the States are at war," she said, "and that Union and Confederate conflicts could erupt here at any moment. It seems so isolated, so protected from the ravages of war."

"More immigrants come through every day," Hank said. "It won't be as isolated if more folks settle here."

"I hope any new neighbors we get will be as kind to the Paiutes as you are," Jess said, "though, away from the ranches, that quality is rare. Jake has heard news of ongoing attacks against ranches that employ Paiutes. They're people, just like anyone else, trying to provide for their families."

"Well, Captain Wells and his company are stationed at Smoke Creek now," Hank commented, "so perhaps there will be fewer disturbances between the Indians and the whites. I hear the commanders at Fort Churchill plan to set up another camp on the other side of Honey Lake, closer to Susanville. That should help ease the tensions between the Unionists and the Southerners living there, as well."

"Thank the Lord for that," Jess said with an edge to her voice. "Paiutes and Southerners have endured enough persecution."

Hank motioned to her basket with a teasing smile. "Since you mentioned the Paiutes, I see I'll have to remind you that you had intended to give me a lesson in their healing medicines."

"Of course!" Jess felt her cheeks pinken beyond what the heat had accomplished thus far. Her mind had been focused on the ranch, and she had completely forgotten why she had come. She stopped at a stand of sagebrush with leaves that had not dried as much as many of the others had and pulled a small knife from the sheath on her belt, cutting off a few branches with the greenest leaves.

"A tea made from sage leaves will help heal mouth sores and an aching throat, and will often calm a stomach ailment. A strong tea made from dried leaves can help heal a cut or abrasion—I learned that firsthand—and a compress made with fresh leaves can help even more." With her forefinger, she wiped a fine layer of dust from one of the leaves. "Be sure to wash the leaves first," she added with a grin.

Hank smiled with her. "Noted."

"While on roundup last year, I also saw a few cattlemen crumple fresh leaves to release their oils and press these to their faces after they'd shaved. Jake said that more than a few use them...well, under their arms, too, to help with the odor."

Hank's mouth twitched. "Considering how hard they work, it's a blessing sage grows here in abundance."

Jess laughed, certain she'd remember Hank's jest every time she saw the plant in the days ahead.

Hank borrowed her knife and stooped, grunting as he bent over his paunch. He cut a few more branches and dropped them in her basket, then returned her knife.

As they continued walking toward the grave site, Hank seemed to be pondering some thought or another. "The past few years have been very hard for you, haven't they?" he finally asked in a gentle voice.

"At times. Not always. I lost my parents, my baby sister, and a friend, and my brother, Ambrose, is fighting in the war, mostly because he intends to defend our family home in Lexington." A thought occurred to her. "In a letter he wrote me a few months ago, he said he'd send a painting of my mother when she was young. I'd like to show it to you when it comes. The jewel-toned colors in the paint remind me of your work."

"Of course, I'd like that," Hank said, and returned to his previous thought. "The reason I asked about the past few years is that I see determination in your eyes, your face, and the way you hold yourself and move. It's an aspect of you that indicates you will accomplish many things."

"Now you sound like an artist, the way you notice details," Jess said, feeling a little uncomfortable at being studied so closely, like a firefly in a jar. Still, she was intrigued to know what else Hank might see in her.

As if hearing her thoughts, he said, "I also see love in your face—love when you look at Jake, love when you talk with Mattie or Grace or walk among the horses. All varying kinds and degrees of love, some softer, like the love with which you observed that hawk a few minutes ago. It softens your face, makes your eyes look wide with wonder, lifts your cheeks just a little."

Now she definitely felt like an insect in a jar.

Hank studied her briefly, but with artistic interest, not making her feel self-conscious or defensive. "And there are also touches of humor, a little beneath the surface, in the muscles around your mouth and nose. You like to laugh, but laughter doesn't come often."

Jess looked away, letting the ever-present wisps of hair around her face cover her discomfort. Hank was nothing but kind and professionally complimentary, but he saw too much, and it unsettled her.

"I apologize, Jess. You are someone I would like to paint—"

"You paint people, too, and not just canvas?" she teased, eager to break the tension.

"Well, you know what I meant to say," he said affably. "I also meant to remind you that although you've been through quite a lot in your young life, you've grown from it. You haven't let sadness have the last say, nor will you ever. You're a person who will always overcome. If matters with the ranch get much worse, you may feel better to remind yourself of that."

Jess pushed her hair back and grinned wryly. "Jake says I remind him of a keg of gunpowder with a lit match hovering nearby. I believe he actually means it as a compliment."

"Coming from a cattleman, I'd say it's a certain compliment," Hank agreed.

The gravestone of Olivia and Sadie Bennett and that of Red Deer became visible about an eighth of a mile ahead. Jess stopped at a juniper tree, the first of several sprinkled at the bottom of the hillside, and she drew her knife to cut off a few of the outer branches. "The Paiutes eat the berries to help with dropsy," she said. "I've also seen them dry the branches and use them as smudge sticks to keep flies out of their wigwams."

"Smudge sticks?" Hank asked, his curious frown revealing his unfamiliarity with the phrase.

"Indians gather many plants and dry them, then burn them like incense. The smoke is fragrant; some plants are soothing, others medicinal, and some simply freshen the air or keep the insects away. I've smelled their juniper smudge sticks; they have a wonderful, piney scent, even long after they've been harvested."

Jess looked to the two slightly rounded mounds at the foot of the shared gravestone. The last time she had been here had been the day she'd left to go east to find Ambrose. She and Jake had not been married, and Jess felt oddly traitorous visiting the first Mrs. Bennett now that she had the same name. But she knew that Jake loved them both, and that, had Jess met Olivia as an acquaintance or neighbor, she would have become a dear friend.

"Shall I wait for you here?" Hank asked kindly.

"No," Jess said. "You carry on Mary's memory to remind others that each person is special and makes a difference. These people made a difference in Jake's life—and in mine. Come, I'd like to tell you about them."

Pleasant recollections of Jess's midday walk with Hank were rapidly pushed aside as the ranch yard came into view, and they saw Seth and Will riding toward the barn, each with a bony, limp calf over his lap. Jess pushed the basket of cuttings into Hank's arms with a glance of apology and rushed to the gate. On the other side, she lifted her skirts and ran past the bunkhouse, cookhouse, and smithy to the barn, where the two men had dismounted and were pulling the calves into their arms.

Jess slowed to avoid startling their horses, then took the reins to hold them. "How bad are they?"

Both young men looked out at her from beneath their tan hat brims, one as reluctant to answer as the other.

"It's hard to say, Miss Jess," Seth said, walking into the barn.

"Their mamas don't have enough water, and so the milk is drying up," Will explained apologetically, then followed Seth.

The moment they stepped out of the barn without the calves, Jess pressed their reins into their hands and hurried to join Jake, Doyle, and Lee inside. The far door had been opened to let light in, and the calves lay near the center, with the three men bending over them.

"Neither can stand," Jake said, lifting one's listless head. "They aren't going to be able to nurse."

Jess dropped onto the edge of the straw across from him. All three men looked frustrated yet resigned. "My father once used a pig's bladder to feed milk to a horse that wouldn't nurse," she said. "Could we do something like that here?"

The men exchanged glances, considering her idea.

"The pigs are still using their bladders," Taggart said from behind her with only a trace of his customary humor.

Doyle shook his head, his face dour. "We can't rightly kill a healthy pig to save a dying calf, Jess," he said.

"We could save several calves," she persisted, "at least those old enough to drink water."

"Yes, we could," Doyle agreed, "only the younger ones that need milk still won't make it."

Jess dug her hands into the ground in helpless anger. One

calf had closed its eyes, and the rise and fall of its sides slowed as its breathing became labored. The other calf nosed the straw, making sucking sounds, desperate to quench its thirst. Jess knew ranchers lost cattle to heat and drought, that it was an accepted part of their lives, but it wasn't part of hers. They needed these animals—all of them—if they were going to survive, and she wouldn't accept their deaths as inevitable. There had to be a way to save them.

She heard light shuffling in the dirt behind her, then saw the shadow of a hunched, scraggy body fall over the calves. From his narrow belt, Pete's gnarled fingers untied a large, flat leather pouch with a tiny bulge in the bottom of it. With molasses-slow movements, he unwound the leather cords that held it closed, then removed a half-eaten biscuit from the bottom. He handed the leather pouch to Jake with a faint wave of his hand, urging him to take it. When he did, Pete gestured with the back of the same hand at the knife on Jake's belt.

Understanding him, Jake widened the top of the pouch and laid the leather against the ground. With the tip of his knife, he pressed a small hole into the center, then returned the knife to his belt. He glanced up at Doyle, who was already on his feet with an empty bucket in hand. He jogged out of the barn and was gone for several minutes.

Pete took nearly that long to open a smaller pouch, this one of rabbit fur, place the remaining biscuit inside, and close it again.

Taggart chuckled. "Jess, ye should tell Dough Chen that someone thinks his biscuits are worthy of savin'."

"He's a good cook, and you know it," Jess said defensively, in no mood for a verbal duel with Taggart.

Doyle returned with the bucket, having put about a pint of milk in the bottom. "Let's give this a try."

Jake had already closed the leather pouch partway so that

it resembled a pliable, brown udder without teats, and he held the top open while Doyle poured the milk from the bucket. A few drops seeped through the tiny knife hole in the bottom and plopped onto the dirt by Jake's leg. So far, the bag was working.

When Doyle had emptied the bucket's contents into the pouch, Jake tightened the thongs at the top to avoid spillage, and a thin stream of milk spurted out the bottom. While Jake held the pouch, Lee pinched the rounded bottom so it would fit into the calf's mouth.

The instant the calf tasted the milk, it suckled eagerly, and rapidly drained the bag.

Though Jess's pulse pounded heavily as the breathing of the calf nearest her became terribly shallow, her heart lightened with hopeful expectancy that the other calf might still recover. She lifted a smile of gratitude to Pete, but he was already turning stiffly toward the open barn door, mumbling almost soundlessly, his rheumy eyes focused once more on the world where his mind dwelled, within.

As soon as the calf had started suckling, Doyle had left to refill the pail with milk. He settled near Jake now and refilled the pouch, but the calf nearest Jess wouldn't drink.

Jess looked to Jake, desperate, and he handed the pouch to Doyle and moved to kneel near the calf's head. With careful hands, Jake turned the calf's unresisting head, his fingers splayed on either side of its two half-moon ears, one red, one white, until its muzzle was lifted toward the bag. As before, Lee pinched the bottom of the pouch, and milk dribbled into the calf's mouth, but it didn't respond.

"Why won't it swallow?" Jess asked of nobody in particular, already knowing the answer: it was too weak.

She placed her hand over its throat and vigorously rubbed the neck, hoping to stimulate its muscles to swallow, while Lee squeezed the pouch. Finally, Jake laid its head down and let it be. Doyle fed the rest of the milk to the first calf.

Jess's exhalations came in deep, exasperated huffs as the calf beside her stopped breathing. She tipped her head back, looking to the rafters high above for answers. Why would no rain come? Why did owning a ranch have to be this hard? How did people survive this?

A cat-sized blur of orange raced by, chasing a mouse-sized blur of gray, to Jess a sign that life must go on, and that she must go on and lend a hand wherever it was needed.

"Jess?" Jake said in that tone of his that needed to know if she was all right.

"I'm fine, Bennett," she said, determined to be as strong as her tone conveyed. "I'll go see where I can be of use."

She stepped out into the sunlight, lifting away her hat to let the breeze cool the hot, damp hair beneath it. With her much-used, no-longer-folded bandana, considerably the worse for wear, she wiped the moisture trickling along the tops and backs of her ears, her gaze resting on Luina and Meg in the corral.

All at once, Meg's front legs buckled, and then the rear, and she abruptly lay down in the dust.

"Jake!" Jess screamed and ran headlong for the corral. Rather than bother with the gate latch, she hiked up her skirts, ducked between two rails, and slipped through.

Meg thrashed in agony. After an instant of panicked thought, Jess reached beneath her overskirt, tore off most of her petticoat, and dunked it in the shallow pool of water at the bottom of the trough. With the dripping cloth in hand, she dropped to the dirt behind Meg and smoothed the fabric over Meg's neck and side in an effort to cool her.

"Someone get water into this trough!" she heard Jake order. Then he was on the ground beside her, trying to hold Meg still so she wouldn't kick Luina or one of the other riding horses they had begun keeping in the corral since the night of the stampede.

The pump handle complained as someone worked it forcefully, and water finally came sloshing into a wooden bucket, but to Jess, every second felt like ten. Will hurried over with a bucket in each hand, and rather than dump them into the trough, he let himself in through the gate and brought the first bucket directly to Jake. Seth was on his way with two more buckets.

"Sorry, boss," Will said. "We filled the trough less than an hour ago. I wouldn't have thought twelve horses could drink it down so fast."

"The mare will be fine," Jake said, as much to reassure Will as Jess. "We'll have to keep a man on that pump the rest of the day and all night, or until the animals stop drinking."

"We'll do it, boss."

Already several buckets of water had been emptied into the trough, and Taggart and Charlie brought over more.

Jess stood, taking up one of the buckets, and poured the water slowly over Meg. Jake petted the mare, soothing her and rubbing the water into her coat. With effort, Meg rolled herself onto her stomach; then, Jake held the bucket low in front of her. Meg drank it down to the wooden bottom.

Seth handed Jake two more buckets, and Jake watered Meg as Jess cooled her with the cloth. Finally, when Meg was sated, she attempted to gain her feet. On her second try, she planted her feet beneath her and stood.

Jess stood up with her. Jake took the damp piece of petticoat from Jess, lifting an eyebrow at her as he recognized the lacy fabric. Jess managed a small grin and a shrug of her shoulders, and Jake placed the cloth over Meg's neck and partway down her back. It stopped just short of her rump.

"Let's take her into the barn and out of the sun," Jake said.

Jess took hold of Meg's harness and led her past Cielos, Luina, and Broom to the gate. As the trough began to fill, the other horses walked toward it and nudged one another aside to get the first sip. When Cielos, Luina, and Broom became aware of it, they lifted their heads and strolled away from the gate, Cielos, Jake's headstrong black stallion, in the lead.

Jake closed the gate behind them. Jess stroked Meg's nose as she walked her, offering what comfort she could. It was just too hot to speak.

In the barn, Jess pulled Meg into a stall, and Jake filled the small trough from the buckets he had brought. Pete brought over a handful of hay, and Taggart had grabbed an armful, no doubt aware that Meg would be ravenous by the time the elderly man returned with a second handful.

"She *will* be all right," Jake said to Jess as she left Meg in the stall and closed the gate behind her.

"For how long?" With a sigh, Jess ran her fingers through her hair, wondering where she had dropped her hat. Taggart handed it to her, along with her bandana, then picked up the empty buckets and left after she'd thanked him. "It's the end of July. As hot as the summer has been, it could be October before the temperature begins to cool, and if it's a dry winter, we may not get any snow at all, and no rain until next spring, if then. Most of the animals won't make it. Four of Hank's cows have died, and he said he heard that the drought is even worse west of the Sierras and to the south. The only place that saw snow last winter was far up in the mountains. Very little of it reached the low ground."

Jake leaned an elbow on the top slat of the stall, looking to Jess as if he were about to solve all their problems in one stroke.

"What?"

"That's what we'll do," Jake said. "We'll take the herds into the Sierra Nevadas. I've been considering the idea, and now I don't think that we have any other options."

Jess placed a hand along his face and patted his cheek, chuckling softly. "You're mad."

He grunted and pushed her hand away. "Just listen for a moment. Five years ago, when I first built the ranch, I rode up into these mountains. There's a stream a six-hour ride away, maybe eight or nine with moving the herds."

"Eight or nine hours?" Jess couldn't believe he was considering this. "Jake, many of the animals will die before we get there."

"After we've gone most of the way up on the first day, we'll send ahead every man who isn't needed to wrangle the herds, to look for broad-leaved trees, bushes, anything other than pine. Where we find those, we'll find water, at least a little, and, perhaps, a larger stream than the one I found."

"And then?"

"Charlie knows many of the roads up in those mountains; he may know of a place near a lake or a river where we can stay until rains or snows come, and the Paiutes may know even more. If not, then, when we come to a place that can sustain the animals for a day or two, we'll stay and scout the area for a better location. We'll keep doing that until we find a site where we can stay for a few weeks, or longer, maybe until autumn sets in."

Jess searched his face, worrying that the sun had gotten to him, but, despite his shirt clinging damply to him with sweat, he looked hearty enough. "Jake, we don't know when we might find water. This area has been battling drought for three years. You lost animals the summer before last. The heat and drought could have dried up the stream you found. It could be a lot longer than eight or nine hours until we find water. It could be two or three days. We could lose every last one of our animals just by attempting this." Jake began to speak, but she held up her hand to silence him. "And if, by some miracle, we do find water on the first day, and this idea of yours works, what will the animals eat? It's pine forest up there. They can't live on cones and pine nuts."

"Where there's water, there's forage, at least a little. If we stay here, love," Jake said softly, "all of them will die. It'll just take longer."

"Before we risk the herds, let's at least send a few riders to scout out the area," she suggested. "Then they'll be able to guide us to the water, and we'll know the best way to get there. If there is no water within a few days' ride, we'll lose only three or four horses. The men will have to walk back, but that will take only a week or so. We could hold out that long, couldn't we?"

Jake tipped his head toward Meg. "Do you think we can wait, Jess? The horses and cattle get a little weaker every day. How many of them will be left by then? How many will be strong enough to make the journey a week from now?"

Jess strode away from him, then back again, balking at Jake's proposal yet despairing equally about any other option. Plainly, there was no other choice. She looked up at him. In his face, she saw a look that said he'd already made the decision; he was just patiently waiting for her to accept it. "You want to leave tomorrow, don't you?" she asked.

"Yes. The midday heat weakens the horses, so we'll go at first light, when they're rested and fresh, and we'll go right up the foothills behind the house. By the time the sun is overhead, we should be higher up, which will mean a little less heat, and, maybe by afternoon, we'll have some shade."

"You're not going to ask me to stay behind, where I'll be safe?"

"No. I need you with me. You're about as good as any man here with the horses. Besides," he added, his whiskey-brown eyes teasing, "you don't seem familiar with the word *can't*."

Jess grinned a little, then thought of the dead calf, and of Meg thrashing in the dust of the corral. She looked through the stall slats at the mare, her dread of losing her beloved horse still pulsing within her. Reaching out a hand, Jess touched the still-damp flank, feeling the subtle shifting of muscles beneath as Meg lowered her head to get a mouthful of hay, then lifted her head again to chew. Meg definitely felt better, Jess thought as the stiff strands of hay in her mouth twitched and rustled and grew shorter as she munched. Her muscles had thinned but remained sound.

If they took the herds into the mountains, Jess wondered, would they save most of their animals or lose them? If they survived until fall, and if rains or snows came, would they have any animals to bring home? The last time she and Jake had been away from the ranch, it had been attacked twice and partially burned. Would they have any ranch to return to?

Yet, if they stayed, the animals would surely die unless the rains came. If they went into the mountains, many animals would probably die on the way, and the rest of them would die if they didn't find water on the first day. They would know within twenty-four hours whether or not they had a chance.

If they did find water in the mountains, most of the herds would live, provided they also found grazing land.

"Jess, either we take a chance and possibly succeed, or we do nothing and inevitably fail. There is no other option."

She pushed back her hair and smiled bleakly at him. "I just arrived at the same conclusion." *Lord, help us.* "So, we leave in the morning?"

"We leave in the morning."

Chapter Sixteen

Taggart, Ho Chen, Lily, and the girls looked like little more than early-morning shadows waving from the ranch yard as Jess helped wrangle the herds up into the foothills. Hank stood near them, his grin not visible in the meager light, though Jess knew he was wearing one, just the same. He had asked Jake to take his cows along with theirs, promising to help look after the garden and the ranch while they were gone. Jess took one last look around the ranch and the long shadows spilling to the west of the empty buildings, hoping the structures were still standing there when they returned.

Shifting her mind to the job at hand, Jess pulled the bandana knotted around her neck up over her nose and mouth, having already swallowed dust from riding drag at the rear of the horses, ahead of the herd of cattle. She had chosen to ride the roughest position, knowing she would keep a closer watch than anyone else on each animal. The success of their efforts was far more than a job to her. Success would mean that she hadn't ruined everything Jake had spent half a lifetime working toward and building. It would mean she had given him worthwhile assistance for all he had done for her.

If they failed today, they would lose the ranch, the cattlemen would lose their livelihoods, and they would have failed the Paiutes, to whom they had promised work and a place to live. Jess knew Jake would never blame her if they failed, but she would blame herself, and it was most unlikely she would ever be able to make up for everything he would have lost.

As the occasional horse fell behind or attempted to stray, Jess whistled and waved it back into the herd. The sun was barely up, and Jake, riding point far ahead, was moving slowly to avoid overworking the droves, as well as to prevent any broken legs or other injuries while they traversed the rocky soil in the low light. He had been right to start the ascent at five in the morning, Jess reflected. At about seventy-five degrees, the air felt relatively comfortable, but the sun would heat it an additional thirty degrees by midday, at which time, she prayed, they would be at a more temperate elevation, and near a water source large enough to sate one hundred and fifty animals.

Unable to resist, Jess cast one last glance toward the ranch, looking back over the heads of the cattle that followed a short distance behind her. Jake led them up the hill at an easy diagonal to limit the animals' exertions, and now they were high above and to the west of Hank's property. Only the northwest corner of their land was still visible, dotted with a few fence posts that appeared as small as slivers. Jess faced forward again, resolved to trust God with the people and belongings they had left behind.

After three-quarters of an hour, Jake turned them to the southwest. Though Jess had scanned the hillside as they were climbing it, she had glimpsed no remains of a small fire or any other indication of where someone might have been camping out those times she had felt eyes watching her. Jake had gone up there, looking for tracks or other evidence, and had said he'd found nothing at all to cause concern. It would seem that the two visions she had seen had unsettled her to the point of imagining danger where there was none. Relieved to be rid of her worry, she mentally set it aside in the category of unexplained events that had occurred but were no longer relevant, and concentrated on the task at hand.

As the sun rose above the edge of the earth, Jess looked

out over the Honey Lake Valley far below. Even the small, orange-red mountains that had always seemed to Jess to have been dropped onto the desert like blobs of biscuit dough onto a baking pan now sat hunched below her. The cattlemen didn't turn to take in the view. They merely whistled and waved their coiled ropes to urge the animals on and keep them in place.

Less than two hours into their journey, a cow stumbled, then fell at the base of a juniper tree. It lay on its side, panting, and didn't try to rise again. Jess's stomach clenched as if she'd been kicked. She'd known this would happen, and so had Jake, but she had to squelch her need to try to save the cow. Before they'd set out, Jake had given the order that if a calf or one of the four remaining foals collapsed, it was to be carried across a saddle for as long as the horse could bear the extra weight. If an adult horse or cow went down, it was to be left in hopes that it would rest and then follow after them. They had to care for the majority and simply could not risk two herds for the sake of a single animal.

Four more cows and two horses fell and were left behind before midday. Jess's heart sank with despair for each one, and her fear of losing all of them grew apace. They were in the midst of junipers now and infrequently passed a pine or two, but many of the needles had dried and fallen, and they saw no evidence that the previous winter's snows had fallen this far north.

Eight hours into their journey, the junipers had all but disappeared, and Jess no longer saw the valley, the lower mountains, or anything else past the thickening pine trees. They gave off a pleasant fragrance, one she would have delighted in if the animals had not begun to resist being driven onward. Meg had stumbled several times, and her forelegs had buckled once, but she had stood again and continued forward. None of the broad-leaved trees or bushes Jake was hoping for had appeared, and the air felt only marginally less like a furnace than it did at midday at the ranch. The animals had begun to tire hours ago, and Jess didn't know how much longer they could press on before larger numbers began to fall. The necks and chests of the horses and cows were damp with sweat, and several animals had begun to foam at the mouth.

She looked across at Diaz, riding drag a dozen or so paces from her, and saw Luina go down beneath him and roll onto her side, trapping his leg.

"Jake!" Jess screamed, the sound startling only one or two of the enfeebled animals, which scared her even more.

Doyle, riding ahead of her, called forward to Lee, who called up to Jake. Seeing that help was coming, Jess leaped to the ground and ran over to Diaz, who was pushing ineffectively against Luina's back. Jess fell to her knees beside him. The silent pain in his face told her his leg was likely broken. Not bothering to contemplate longer than an instant the odds of her being able to budge a twelve-hundred-pound horse, Jess braced her shoulder beneath Luina's withers, joined a moment later by Doyle, who did the same on the other side of her, near Luina's rump. Within seconds, Jake had positioned himself beside Doyle and taken hold of the saddle, and the four of them—Diaz pushing as much as he was able—lifted and shoved Luina far enough for Diaz to pull his leg out from beneath the palomino.

Jake drew his knife and eyed Diaz. "Is it broken?"

Diaz panted and squinted one eye against the sun. "If it is, boss, I'd rather you shoot me than stab me."

Jess rolled her eyes, in no frame of mind to analyze the cattleman's bent toward humor during dire circumstances.

However, the corner of Jake's mouth lifted in manly appreciation of the jest. "I don't intend to put you out of your misery, Diaz. If you tell me where the pain is, I'll cut away your trouser leg so you can have a look. Unless you'd rather I expose your leg to Jess and all creation, that is."

"Then don' bother with my *pantalones*. It's my ankle, but if you think to cut away my boot, then go ahead and shoot me."

"I'll see you get a new pair," Jake avowed.

Diaz considered this, one black eyebrow nearly disappearing into the brim of his hat. "New? Hand-tooled, with scrollwork like these have?"

"You can have your name engraved in them, if you'd like."

"That's worth breaking a bone for," Diaz said, tugging back his pant leg. "Cut the boot."

Jake cut the boot away, and Diaz slid down his sock. His shinbone was clearly broken; his foot hung off center, angled inward. Jess shuddered and petted Luina, as eager to soothe the horse as she was herself.

Jake lightly gripped Diaz's ankle, carefully pressing his thumbs into the leg alongside the bone. Diaz grunted in pain, then used his bandana to wipe the sweat popping out of the pores on his face.

"It's a clean break," Jake said, glancing at him. "If we wrap it tight, will you be able to ride?"

"No problem, boss."

Jess knew it *was* a problem. Diaz wouldn't be able to use the stirrup, which would be plenty uncomfortable for him, but he would also be placing more weight on the horse's back rather than on its withers, which would be an added burden to the animal.

"He can't ride Luina," Jess pointed out. "Jake, if we rest the animals here awhile, Luina may recover."

"Jess—"

"We might be able to save her, Jake," she pleaded. "We have plenty of daylight left, and it isn't going to get any hotter. Only an hour, Jake. Please."

Jake rubbed her cheek with the back of a gloved knuckle. "All right, Jess. We'll stay an hour. Doyle, tell everyone to loosen all the cinches so the horses can cool a little, and then they can get something to eat. And tell Black-Eye and Lee to ride ahead to see if they can find the stream. It should be no more than a forty-minute ride due south."

Doyle slapped Diaz on the back, then strode away.

Jess stood. "I've sewed three skirts over the past few weeks," she told Jake, "since I seem prone to ripping them. I'll fetch the blue one and tear it into strips to use as bandages." With effort, she gave Diaz a teasing grin. "The color is more masculine than the shades of green and burgundy of the other two."

"I'll be completely unmanned," Diaz announced with a mischievous smile. "Unless, of course, *la Mariposa* wishes to bandage my leg for me."

Jess looked to Jake for approval, and when he nodded with a grin, she went off to fetch the skirt.

"I'm beginning to think you let yourself get hurt just so women will flutter around you," she heard Jake say.

"It appears to work, no?" Diaz answered.

Unable to set aside her fears, Jess pulled the blue cotton skirt from her bedroll, looking over her saddle to where Luina lay, panting heavily. As she watched, Jake removed his hat and flipped it upside down. Diaz uncapped his canteen, took a long drink, and then emptied the rest of the water into Jake's hat. As soon as Diaz's canteen was empty, Charlie walked over with his canteen and did the same. Smelling the water, Luina raised her head to the hat Jake lowered in front of her, and drank.

Jess knew that all of them would share their remaining water with Diaz and Charlie, but that the two wanted to ease Jess's mind as much as they wanted to save Luina. Diaz patted Luina as she finished off what the men had poured. *Well,* Jess thought, adjusting her assumption, *Diaz probably did it more for his "leetle Luina" than for me.* He loved that horse, just as dearly as any man ever loved a creature. Luina stirred and rolled onto her stomach, daintily nosing Diaz, looking to be petted.

Hot tears of relief pricked Jess's eyes. They would rest for an hour, and then Luina would be able to go on.

Charlie smiled broadly at her and gave her a deep, gentlemanly bow. He looked as though he wanted to remain nearby, perhaps to assist wherever he could, but Jake's penetrating stare sent him back to his position alongside the resting herd of horses. *Now, what was that about?* Jess wondered.

Drawing her own knife as she walked over to where Jake sat on his heels beside Diaz, Jess made two cuts through the hem she had sewn, about six inches apart. She slid her knife back into the sheath on her belt, then tore the woven fabric along each of the cuts.

Doyle walked over, carrying a relatively straight section of juniper branch about a foot long, which he had cut down the center. He handed the pieces to Jake and slapped Diaz on the shoulder harder than before, causing the Spaniard to flinch, yet he merely grinned up at the black man. Cattlemen's humor again, Jess supposed.

While Jake pressed the two strips of juniper on either side of Diaz's sock to straighten the ankle, Jess wound the blue strips tightly around the sticks and leg to immobilize the fractured bone, tossing an apologetic glance at Diaz each time he hissed in pain.

"It's all right, *Mariposa*," he said. "The good that comes from this is that you'll have to change the bandage later, no?"

"There is that," Jess said, tightening the final knot. She looked around at the flaccid forms of the horses and cattle, most of them with their heads bowed, too weak to lift them. One of the cows shifted her head to the cow beside her and shamelessly began to drink from her udder.

"Another half hour," Jake said softly. "Then we'll have to move on. You might want to get something to eat, Jess."

"I'll have roast chicken and mashed potatoes," Diaz spoke up.

This drew Jess's attention. "And a cold beer to wash it down?"

Diaz waved a gloved hand, grinning. "If it would be no bother."

Jess let herself laugh a little, thankful for the Spaniard's attempts to lift her spirits. She retrieved a nearly full canteen from Meg's saddlebags, along with enough biscuits and dried jerky for three of them.

As they ate, Jess watched for Black-Eye and Lee to return. Any minute, they would come riding through the pine trees, their faces brimming with good news. They had to.

The hour passed, and then they waited another thirty minutes, but Black-Eye and Lee didn't return. If the stream was only forty minutes away, Jess reasoned, they should have been back by now. The only explanation for the delay must be that the stream had dried up, and that they had gone looking for another water source.

Jake told Diaz to ride Cielos, since the glossy, black stallion was the strongest horse and was therefore the one best able to support Diaz's weight on his back. Luina had regained her feet and appeared steady, at least for now. Since Jess was the lightest rider, Jake told her to take Luina but to watch for any wobbling, and to jump off if the horse started to go down. Jess watched while Diaz hobbled unassisted to a large rock, hopped up onto it, and, from there, dragged himself rather smoothly over Cielos's saddle. He eased his broken foot over the horse's back and rode with his right foot bare, the mutilated boot tied on behind the saddle like a cherished trophy. Once Diaz was mounted, Jess stepped cautiously into Luina's saddle, reluctant to add any burden to her. Luina didn't seem to be troubled by the extra weight and stood still while Jess adjusted herself in Diaz's unfamiliar, lavishly decorated saddle.

Jake gave her an encouraging wink, then reined Meg to the lead. The cattlemen whistled and slapped the animals' rumps to get them underway again.

A full hour passed before they met up with Black-Eye and Lee on their return. Jess looked between the bobbing heads of the horses, trying to see the men's expressions. Unable to, she called ahead to Doyle. "Can you tell what they're saying to Jake?" she asked him.

Doyle turned his head to face her. "Whatever it is, it doesn't look good," he said, then shifted in his saddle to face forward again.

They travelled on for another two arduous hours, frequently slowing to nudge animals back into the herds that wandered beyond eyesight through the thick pines.

Jess saw another horse collapse, then two more cows behind her. Natchez and Payton each carried a calf over his saddle, and even Nettle ably carried one over hers.

Abruptly, the forest tilted, and Luina fell to her knees. Before the mare could stand again, Jess leaped to the ground, and Luina heaved herself to all fours. Jess held her reins and led her, perfectly willing to walk if doing so meant Luina could continue on. Eli Payton flashed her a look that could have been one of disgust or of respect, but Jess was unable to tell due to his long beard. Luina stumbled again, then Payton returned his attention to working the cattle.

Another hour passed, and several more animals fell. A piece of Jess's heart fell with each one of them. *Aren't You there, Lord?* she prayed silently. *These are Your creatures. Don't You care that they're suffering, and that I'm suffering to have to leave them behind? Last winter, You sent snow to these mountains. Where is the snowmelt? Why are there no streams or even ponds from the runoff? You once showed me a miracle to remind me that You are with me, and even Jesus said, "Are not two sparrows sold for a farthing? and one of them shall not fall on the ground without your Father....Fear ye not therefore, ye are of more value than many sparrows." Please show us this is so. Please help us to find water soon!*

Jess's feet and legs ached, but she ignored the discomfort. Diaz's pain had to be worse, and he didn't complain, and Luina was sluggish and weak but managing. That was what mattered.

Besides, one tiny flame of hope flickered in her heart: the next of her monthlies was four days late, and no telling twinge had developed yet in her lower back.

The bottom curve of the sun touched the western edge of the mountaintop, and, as it did, the horses grew restless. Instantly alert, Jess laid her hand on the butt of her gun and lifted her head to scan the pine forest. Wolves could be waking to hunt, and bears, as well. Behind her, the cows' ears turned forward, and despite the men's efforts to keep them herded, they hastened their pace, as did the horses. Luina began to pull against the reins, using enough force that Jess felt comfortable to mount her. If Luina was going to bolt from a predator, Jess had no intention of being left behind.

The drove of horses topped a rise and began to hurry down the far side, beyond Jess's line of sight. Though Luina kept trying to step aside and foil her efforts, Jess finally managed to get a foot into the stirrup, and she hoisted herself into the saddle. Moments later, Doyle descended over the rise, several horses and cattle with him. Jess reined in and peered through the trees to the pine valley below, trees seeming to fall away from her like the green foam of the ocean seen from atop the crest of a wave. The view was unlike anything she had seen before, a pine valley dropped from the kingdom of God above.

Between the heady, fragrant trees, the rushing horses and cattle parted to reveal a wide stream wending through the middle of it all—a winding, golden street of heaven, shimmering in the bright, orange light of the setting sun.

"We still have sixty-one horses, seven of them Thoroughbreds, and all four foals that we started with this morning," Jake told Jess solemnly as he nudged a burning log with a stick, his face and upper body gilded in the circle of firelight, the rest of him lost to the dark evening shadows. "Sixty-eight cows made it, and nine calves."

The small campfires that flickered between the trees should have seemed cheery but didn't. "We lost more than one in four of the animals," Jess said, wishing she could be numb so as not to acutely feel the loss of each one. "Thirteen horses would have earned us nearly three thousand dollars if we'd sold them outright, and would have brought in far more than that for the foals they'll never have. And we lost at least that much in cattle. That's more than a ranch hand earns in twelve years." She shook her head, hardly able to conceive of it.

"We saved the rest, which otherwise would have died," Jake said, gazing steadily at her.

The flames danced along the crackling pine logs, their reflections resembling spears in Jake's brown eyes, which were flecked with amber, like honey poured over whiskey. Even exhausted, with a long day's worth of dust and dried sweat clinging to him, Jake was a handsome man.

"Tomorrow, after breakfast, I'll send out as many men as we can spare to scout for a place with more water and some grazing land. The animals can last another day, maybe two, before hunger gets the better of them. I don't expect we'll lose any more until then."

"It's cooler," Jess commented. "The air feels refreshing. That should afford the herds decent rest, perhaps better than they've had in weeks."

Jake patted her arm. "It should help you to sleep too, Jess. With all these dense pine trees, the horses and cattle will have plenty of places to wander. Each of the men and I will be up half the night keeping watch so that we don't lose any more. I'm taking first watch so some of the men can sleep."

"Wake me when your watch is over," Jess said. "I'll take Diaz's shift so he can rest his leg."

Jake's gaze held hers and conveyed love and admiration. "You're some woman, Jessica Bennett," he said, then stood and walked into the trees to keep watch.

Jess lay down and pulled a blanket up to her midriff, using her saddle as a pillow. High above, stars shone between the whispering tops of the pine trees, their clusters of needles nearly black against the star-spangled sky. She should have felt great relief at reaching water, but she didn't. They had lost fifty-three animals in a single day, and they would lose more if they didn't find grazing land by this time tomorrow. Where would she be lying down to sleep in twenty-four hours? And how many more wasted animals would she be counting then?

Late afternoon the following day, Jess stepped down from Meg for the last time in what she hoped would be several weeks and began to remove her saddle. Meg ignored her efforts as she ripped ravenously at the tall grasses.

As it turned out, Lee had found the grassy valley after recognizing landmarks that he had last seen as a child. The valley was narrow but void of pines that might otherwise have obscured the animals' movements, and the grass bordered the shallow river for nearly a mile. An old cabin of logs hunkered along the forest edge, quaint and charming with the exception of its broken windows and the large section of roof missing.

Jess walked around Meg, running one hand along the mare's hide. The other hand she braced against the unwelcome, swelling discomfort in her lower back as her heart plummeted. She lifted the right stirrup and hanging length of cinch, laid them over the saddle, and rounded Meg again to pull the saddle and blanket from the mare's back. When the saddle began to slip off, Jess shifted the weight and laid it in the grass. She then returned to Meg, who jogged a few steps, wanting to be left alone to feast. In a deft movement, Jess caught her reins, but she had to stoop to unbuckle and remove the bridle. That task accomplished, she left Meg to stuff herself contentedly.

Seeing no better location to set up camp than the flat land surrounding the log house, Jess folded the bridle over the saddle, then hefted all her gear and went to join Spruzy near the cabin. Nettle and the cattlemen did likewise, and soon the yard around the cabin took on the appearance of a battlefield strewn with worn-out soldiers. Jake ordered a minimal watch—two men stationed at the tree lines and one at each end of the valley. According to Charlie, they were less than five miles from an abandoned wagon road, and the nearest people were likely ten or more miles away. The valley, Jess reflected, would make a beautiful temporary home. However, as she placed her saddle on the ground near Jake's, she thought that she would have moved to a mosquito-infested swamp if it would have meant not losing two more cows and another Thoroughbred that afternoon.

She and Jake had left Iowa with twenty stallions. Now, only six remained.

Unable to match the uplifted spirits and lighthearted jokes of the others, Jess went to explore the arm of the valley behind the house, where she had glimpsed some debris that the previous owners must have abandoned.

Once the joviality of the others had been left behind and the camps were no longer visible, she braced both hands against the discomfort in her lower back and lifted her face as she searched the merciless, unclouded sky for answers. Nearly everything she had worked for or hoped for had failed or was failing. She had wanted to turn the cattle ranch—one in a region overflowing with cattle ranches and competition—into a much-needed horse ranch with superior-quality breeds, which would have ensured the future of the ranch. But the government land office had cut their property in half, and the heat and the drought, as well as a stampede, had greatly diminished the number of their horses and cattle. She had wanted safety for the Paiute people. Instead, the ranch had been attacked the previous winter and again in the spring; then, they had been nearly attacked again the day they'd brought the Paiutes home to the ranch, and Mattie and Grace had been kidnapped, with Mattie hurt before they could rescue her and her sister. And, she had desperately wanted to conceive a child with Jake. Jess moved her fingers from her back around to the narrow flatness of her stomach. The large, round buckle, with its leather belt of rawhide strips that Jake had braided, cinched in her tiny waist, and her gun belt, with its holstered Remington revolver, hung just below it, the leathers dark brown against her old, yellow calico dress.

She was a Hale. Never in her life had she given up hope. Until now. The land redistribution laws and climate were making their chances of saving the ranch next to impossible, the Paiutes would have to go on fighting just to survive, and she would never see Jake hold their child, would never hold their child herself. All she and Jake truly possessed were the remains of the ranch, their home, which they couldn't afford to keep much longer. After that was gone, all they would have would be each other, with the failed ranch she had cost him lying like its barbed wire fence between them. If they lost everything, would she and Jake still have each other?

Among the debris behind the house, Jess spied a basket woven from grapevines. One of its two handles was broken in the center, resulting in two ragged-ended strips that rendered the basket useless. Jess lowered herself onto a large rock and pulled the basket into her lap. It was as big around as her arms, fully outstretched to encircle it, and the grapevines were about the same diameter as her fingers, though now dry and no longer pliable. Still, if she found a way to mend the handle, the basket could again be of use.

Jess drew her knife and sawed a narrow branch from the pine tree standing immediately beside her. Disregarding the rough bark and sharp pine needles that sliced hot, red scratches into her hands, she stripped off the branch's smaller, outgrowing twigs and needles, then cut the bare branch to match the length of the intact basket handle. Almost desperately, she pushed aside her skirts and cut two lengths of leather strips from her moccasin laces, then returned the knife to its sheath. With one of the leather strips, she fitfully tied one end of the fresh branch alongside the broken handle, using her final ounce of determination and the strength in her hands to reinforce the break. She had to make something whole, had to make *something* succeed.

With painstaking care, and force that set her arms to trembling, Jess curved the unbound end of the new branch to meet the topmost grapevine she would fasten it to, her head bent low as she strained to hold the branch in place and began to fasten the second leather tie.

As she forced the branch to curve just a little farther, it suddenly split with an audible, woody *snap*. Jess shifted her eyes and opened her hand. The new branch lay in her palm, broken in the center, exactly like the previous handle.

Clutching the ruined basket against her chest as if it were the child she would never have, Jess slid down the rock into the grasses, wailing into her arm to quiet the sobs. "Oh, Lord, why?" she cried. "Why would You take away all my hopes for anything better than this? You promised to be with Your children always, and You gave me a miracle a year ago to prove it. But where are You now? Why have You made everything I've loved die or disappear, and everything I've wanted impossible? I didn't want wealth or a mansion or trips abroad. I didn't ask for an easy life. I wanted only Jake and a family and a ranch where we could work together. That's all. You tell us in Your Word that if we believe, we will receive whatever we ask for in prayer. I have nothing left to believe in."

Jess dropped the basket and crossed her arms over her face, sobbing so bitterly that she could hardly catch her breath. Then she sensed Jake's large presence beside her, and then he was holding her firmly against him. She wrapped her arms around his neck and cried into his shirt collar and bandana, torn between loving him and hating what her presence in his life was doing to him.

"I love you, Jess," he murmured and said nothing more.

Gradually, Jess's tears diminished, and she burrowed into him, needing the comfort of his body heat, despite the uncomfortably warm temperature of the air.

Jake pulled a spare bandana from his pocket and handed it to her, and Jess blew her nose, letting Jake rock her like a child, as thin trails of hot tears continued to run down her cheeks. She felt his head tilt as if he were looking down at her, but she didn't lift her gaze from the debris pile beyond the basket.

"I've put together that your silences come, and you withdraw from everyone around you, about every four weeks," he said softly. "The sadness you've been trying to keep from me is that you haven't been able to have a child, isn't it?"

Jess dug her fingers helplessly into the bandana. "It's one of the reasons, yes."

He briefly tightened his embrace, sending her strains of unfaltering love. "And the other reasons?"

With the stopper thus pulled, her words came out in a flood. "Mattie and Grace, the Paiutes, the horses and cattle, the ranch. You. I wanted to give you a child. I wanted to have a child. I have always survived, no matter what trials came my way. 'I'm a Hale,' I always reminded myself, and I always found the strength to endure, no matter how terrible the circumstances were. But this—the men who are determined to drive out the Paiutes, the drought that is determined to drive us out, my inability to have children—this is more than I can bear up under. It's just too much to stand against, too much to fight." Jess's shoulders shook, though the force of her tremors was subdued by Jake's oak-solid grip. She knew he wanted her to tell him what she felt, but she couldn't make herself utter the words that would make him fear for her more than he already did. He was so afraid she would one day give up and leave. Her promise before God and their witnesses that she would be Jake's wife until death was one her honor would not permit her to break, but for the first time, she wondered if it wouldn't be better for Jake if she did leave. She had brought him nothing but trouble.

Jake removed one arm from around her and lifted away his hat, then set it under the tree beside them. Jess's mind latched onto the fact that he had only once before purposefully removed his hat in a demonstration of respect to her—the day they were married.

"You once told me that you aren't with me to share the good times," he said, "but that you are with me to share the journey. I love you, Jess, but I'm hurt that you think I married you only for your knowledge of Thoroughbreds, or so I could have another child. Both of us have been scarred by loss, but you are causing another scar inside each of us by pulling away and not allowing me to love you."

Jess felt a jolt like lightning ripple through her at the rapier thrust of his words. He hugged her tighter, and she rested her head against him, listening to the steady beat of his heart.

"Without a doubt, we've had a hard year," Jake said, "and all of us have suffered from it, but we've also grown. Don't you recall that Bible verse in Romans, chapter five? We rejoice in sufferings, because we know that suffering produces perseverance; perseverance brings about character; and character brings about hope. I've seen you persevere these past months, and your character has grown stronger than ever because of it—strong enough to overcome even this."

Jess pulled back and stared at him with rising fury. "Are you mad? How can anyone facing hopelessness rejoice?"

Jake's gaze remained steady, undaunted. "It's easier than you think. Just remember the times God has been with you in the past and helped you get out of hard situations. If He helped you before, you know He is fully able to help you again, and always will be. That is why you can hold on to hope, even now."

Jess recalled hearing God's gentle whisper in the wind—a touch from God, the memory of which remained as strong now as the moment when it had happened—and her outrage subsided a bit.

"Jess, that pressure you feel isn't the stress or weight of your troubles, love. That pressure you feel is the Almighty's embrace."

With a last swipe of her face with the bandana, Jess contemplated his words, then stood. "I'll remember that."

Jake rose to his considerable height beside her and gestured to the grassy field in which they stood and the river that swirled in a hush beyond the pine trees bordering it. "Can't you see God's love for you, Jess? Can't you see my love for you?"

Jess closed her eyes and let herself feel Jake's heat and nearness, and feel God's nearness in the forest, grass, and water He provided. Yes, God had saved most of the horses and cattle, and for now—and for weeks to come—they would be well cared for. The animals would grow stronger, and, perhaps, she and Jake would, as well. But she didn't know what hope existed beyond that.

She met Jake's gaze. "I dearly wanted to give you a child, and I wanted the horse ranch to succeed." Her eyes filled again as the pain of regret and disappointment knifed through her. "I'm so sorry for being distant, but I was afraid that my nearness would remind you of your losses and the children you could have had if you'd married someone else. I'll always be a reminder of what you've lost and given up."

"Let me show you a reminder, Jess," he said, and pulled her against him.

Her arms automatically went around him, and her hands absently stroked his back as she tried to piece together what he meant. Then, through his sweat-dampened shirt, her fingertips brushed against the long, sickle-shaped scar down his back, a reminder of the scar he'd received after trying to save her father from her family's burning home. Jake was a man who gave, she recalled, and a man whom God had blessed with the ability to love—over all and through all.

She coughed to clear the web of emotions from her throat, then raised her face to reveal the extent of her own feelings for him. "I was wrong to doubt how you felt about me," she said.

Jake chuckled and gathered her even closer. "Yes, you were," he agreed, then kissed her soundly.

When he lifted his head, Jess suffered mild disappointment that their pleasurable interlude had been so very brief. Then, she saw his need for her in his face, and before she could form another thought, he bent, tightened his embrace, and lifted her, pulling her up along his body, causing their gun belts to momentarily catch on each other, which made her smile until he began pressing kisses to the sensitive place beneath her ear, down the side of her neck, and down. Through the leather of her moccasins, her toes could feel the tops of his boots, and she dug her toes into them, using the leverage to squeeze herself tighter against him, her need for his touch, his nearness, his love, and all that he freely gave her driving her to give back just as passionately, just as freely. Her lips found his, and she told him without words but with quick, fevered kisses that she would never stop wanting him, that she could never stop loving him. His heartbeat hammered almost directly against hers, and she dug her fingers into the thickness of his hair, loving how it tickled the webbing between her fingers, loving the light brush of his whiskers against her skin as his mouth left hers and ravished the soft underside of her jaw, forcing her head back and causing her arms to tighten around him. As she began to yearn for greater closeness, Jake softened his kisses and slowly loosened his embrace. Gradually, her awareness of the world beyond them returned—the scents of the pine trees, the sounds of the wind ruffling their needles like distant wind chimes, occasional banging or a fragment of voice as the cattlemen and Paiutes set up camp a quarter of a mile away. With a smile, Jake lowered her reluctantly, and her feet met the earth. Her acumen was the last faculty to return, but as it did, she realized that Jake had told her without words—just as she had communicated to him—all that he felt.

"Better now?"

Realistically, their situation was no better than it had been before she'd soaked his shirt with her tears, but he'd revealed how deeply he loved her, and that he would always be with her, even though they would not have children. She had persevered through what others might have deemed impossible, and that had given her strong self-reliance and confidence. For her next goal, she'd strive to recall God's hand in her life, and to look ahead with hope.

Jake retrieved his hat and pulled it over his head while Jess took in his handsome face and his brawny, sinewy shape as he moved.

"Now, what set you to crying in the first place?" he asked.

Jess pointed at the broken basket, lying in the grass nearby. "I tried to repair its handle, but the pine branch snapped."

At the same moment, they looked down at the branch she had added to reinforce the broken handle. Both the pine branch and the original handle of grapevine were lashed to the top curve of the basket with moccasin lacings, like two arches of a double rainbow.

Both handles were smooth and solid, as if they'd never been broken.

"Almighty God," Jake breathed, stunned amazement lighting his face.

Immediate certainty poured into Jess as solidly as a hundred pounds of grain poured into a burlap sack: the Lord was showing her that what she couldn't mend, He would.

Deep in her gut, Jess felt a spark of hope reignite.

Chapter Seventeen

For more than two months, the Bennett ranch had seemed to Jess to be a world away from the thickly forested land she had come to love in the high Sierra Nevada Mountains. Now, as they descended the dry, decreasingly forested northern slopes toward the ranch with their herds, Honey Lake Valley, with its gray-green dots of sagebrush, spread out below them, both foreign and familiar among the long, evening shadows.

Cooking over a campfire had become commonplace to her, as had eating the venison from the deer shot by the Paiutes with bows and arrows, the rabbits they had snared, the pine-needle-tip teas they had brewed, the salmonberries, wax currents, and few chokecherries they had gathered, the hazelnuts they had roasted, and whatever edible mushrooms and plant leaves they had been able to find. Jess had hunted and gathered side by side with the Paiutes, as had Jake and the cattlemen when they weren't looking after the herds or retraining the long-unridden horses. Almost constantly, she had used the grapevine basket with the miraculously restored handle, cherishing it whenever she used it, just as she cherished the hard work and resulting gains and successes of her efforts.

Beside her, the now plump, red and white cattle and calves she was wrangling plodded along, their spotted ears bobbing, as they picked their ways down the mountainside. The cows and horses, calves and foals had grown strong and healthy and, she thought with a flutter of hope, stood every chance of living out the winter. The temperature in the valley had dropped greatly, so that it felt to Jess like October in northern Illinois, and the chill in the air meant that the animals would no longer be beaten down by the relentless sun in the high desert. Every two weeks during the time they had spent in the Sierras, Jake had sent two of the men, usually Seth and Will, down to the ranch for foodstuffs and other necessities, which Taggart and Hank had kept in good supply. According to a report from Seth the previous week, Hank had harvested two hundred acres of hay. Due to the drought, this amount equaled far less than what he would have harvested during a good season, but to thank Jake for taking his cows to the Sierras, he was going to share it with Jake to get all of their animals through the next several months.

Ahead of Jess, two cows started to stray from the herd. Jess nudged Meg, and the mare shot spryly forward until a wave of Jess's lasso startled the pair back into place with the other cattle. When they had saddled their horses that morning, Jake had told her that, as generous as Hank's offer was, his hay wouldn't be enough to get the animals through the winter. So, Jake planned to take one of the men, and Hank, if he wanted to go, north toward Oregon to bring back as much hay as they could carry in the two wagons plus a third that Jake would purchase. The summer heat and lack of rain had undoubtedly been hard on every rancher and farmer in California and the Nevada Territory, Jake had said, and only a small supply of hay or grains would be available in the region to purchase. He had no choice but to go north, and Jess knew it, but she and Jake had grown closer than ever, and already she dreaded the time he would spend away.

Far ahead of the herd of mustangs, Morgans, and Thoroughbreds being wrangled by cattlemen and Paiutes, Jake's brown hat and blue-flannel-clad shoulders were just visible above the backs of the black, chestnut, paint, and

271

buckskin horses as he led them down a gentle slope. Jess had climbed this mountain nearly nine weeks ago with worry for their future and at an emotional distance from Jake, but she had reclaimed her determination, her love, and an unexpected peace in the mountains, as if living a simple life with Jake among God's creation and seeing the results of hard work had been all that she'd needed all along.

Jess pulled her feet from the stirrups and let her legs dangle at Meg's sides for a few moments to rest them. She rocked slightly in the saddle, the leather soughing as she shifted. The landscape may have seemed somewhat foreign, but the mingled scents of sage, horse, and leather, and the view of wide-open wilderness sprinkled with lone red-orange mountains shaped like the underbellies of ships, were smells and sights that would always bring her the calm assurance she was home.

As she slipped her moccasins back into the stirrups, the northeastern fence of the Bennett Mountain Ranch eased into view. Gradually, she saw more and more of the fence line, then the creek and clusters of cottonwoods that resembled green broccoli tops hovering above silver stalks. Then, she saw the Paiute village, the corral with a few horses, and the barn, smithy, cookhouse, and bunkhouse. She found herself standing in her stirrups as the high, peaked roof of the ranch house appeared over the final foothill, and then the tiny outhouse behind it. Like the animals, which had picked up their heads as well as their pace, she wanted to run all the way to the gate, but she wouldn't give in to the urge and risk causing an injury to Meg or to one of the other animals.

Hank's house appeared, and Jess noticed that he had enclosed the other three sides of his property with the same wire fencing Jake had used around the ranch, almost certainly with Taggart's help, minus the barbs. His orchard had been planted, and many of the leaves had already fallen from the trees, but those that remained were a healthy shade of green, and the earth around the trunks appeared to have been recently watered.

Just as she was thinking of him, Taggart stepped out of the cookhouse, followed closely by Hank, Ho Chen, Lily, Mattie, and Grace. And then came Pete, hobbling stiffly, his gaze fixed in front of him where his cane met the ground. Amid a flurry of wagging arms, Hank separated from the gaggle and jogged toward the gate southeast of the ranch house, his pink face alight with a smile and his beefy arms pumping amiably. Grace broke into a run after him, leaping toward the gate, her tan-and-green calico dress billowing around her.

Out of the corner of her eye, Jess saw Jake return the wave, but she kept her gaze on Mattie. Jess had hated to leave her after she had been hurt, and had wanted to be there for her, offering the presence of another person besides her mother and Ho Chen whom she could trust. But Jess had known that Mattie's family would help her to heal, and her own place was beside her husband and among the herds they all depended on. Physical pain knifed through Jess to see Mattie lingering warily behind Ho Chen and Lily.

But then, Mattie's tan-and-blue skirt appeared as she stepped out between her parents. She walked slowly past them, walked more quickly, and suddenly burst into a run, as if she needed to reach the gate before a horrible current carried her away. When Mattie's eyes found Jess, her mouth curved into a grin with a brightness to rival that of the setting sun. Jess didn't know why Mattie was as happy to see her as she was to see her and her sister, but as she guided the cattle behind the horses through the gate and finally jumped to the ground to pull the girls into her embrace, she knew Mattie would be all right, and she heartily, silently thanked God for it, and for the blessing of home.

Jake, Doyle, and Hank left early the next morning, Jake and Hank each driving a wagon pulled by two horses, Doyle riding a horse and pulling another one behind him. Jake and the cattlemen had strapped two large water barrels and several bales of hay into the bed of each wagon—enough, Jake said, to get them to their next water source and food stop between the ranch and the hay fields of Oregon.

That night, Jess wandered aimlessly through the empty house like the sole mouse in an ancient tomb, and her bed, when she finally slipped into it, felt sepulchral. Every night after that, she took the orange cat with green eyes to bed with her so she wouldn't feel Jake's extended absence so keenly.

One night, three weeks later, she paced the house, peering frequently through one window or another and watching the horizon for the shapes of approaching wagons. She held Jake's flannel shirt tightly around her sleeping gown as she bent to look through her old bedroom window again. For a moment, her breath fogged the chilly glass, and she felt its radiant cold against her face, and that of the plank floor against her feet, intentionally sockless to keep herself awake and alert. The last quarter moon spilled luminous, silver light over the ranch and the valley beyond. She scanned the land slowly, holding her breath to keep the window glass clear of condensation, but no wagons piled with hay took shape.

Jess returned to the loom and the half-finished blanket and turned up the wick on the oil lamp. She tugged the shuttle from the taut yarns into which she'd wedged it and continued passing it between the yarns of the warp. The tan and green yarns of this blanket would be a close match to Grace's dress, she reflected for the dozenth time, then rolled her eyes at the recurring thought she was using to distract her attention from the window. She leaned back in her chair and glanced at the tan and blue blanket she had already completed to match Mattie's dress. If Bennett was gone much longer, she thought with wry amusement, she'd weave enough blankets to pave the compound, provided the supply of yarn held out.

That thought led to a troubling remembrance of their other supplies, or the lack thereof. The previous week, she had sent Seth and Payton to Carson City to sell four more horses, as well as to post some mail—several letters she'd written to Ambrose, and one for Edmund Van Dorn, inquiring after her father's bank accounts and investments. Since Jake had needed to dip into their funds to purchase another wagon, she knew he would approve of her decision to sell the horses to make up the loss. In the morning, she would send two of the men with the balance of the earnings to purchase coffee, beans, and other foodstuffs they would soon need. The supplies would get them through till spring, but not beyond that.

Jess resumed her weaving with added force. Just as strongly as she longed for Jake to return safely to the ranch, she longed to hear from Edmund about the status of her father's accounts. If next summer was anything like this one had been, they would need the income to keep the workers and animals alike fed. Initially, Jess had believed that Ambrose should receive the earnings left by their father, but Edmund had said that her father had wanted to provide for her himself, and although Jake likely thought the money should go to Ambrose as the male heir, her father clearly had meant for the inheritance to go to Jess, and she intended to use it to support the ranch until it could solidly support them. It would be her way of repaying Jake for all he had risked for her. Her father had loved horses, and she felt certain he would have approved.

The wintry nip seeping into the room from around the windowpanes gave Jess hope that snows might yet come. It also compelled her to seek out a pair of wool socks and her moccasins before her teeth began to chatter.

As she pushed back from the loom, she looked out the window again out of habit, turning down the wick of the lamp so that no reflection dimmed her view of the valley to the north. The valley remained devoid of movement. It had been full dark for nearly an hour. The only circumstance in which Jake, Doyle, and Hank would push the horses past sunset would be if they were within a short distance of home.

Rather than fetch her socks and moccasins, Jess nestled the shuttle once more between the taut yarns and blew out the lamp for the night. Morning would come sooner if she slept, she rationalized, and, perhaps, before another day ended, Jake would return.

Jess wasn't sure what awakened her. She felt the cozy heat and weight of the blankets tucked around her body, and she turned her head on the pillow so she could listen with both ears. Beside her, the covers were lifted up, and the cat startled to her feet, the rigid arch in her back conveying her vexation at having been displaced. The large form that settled beneath the covers reached out a strong arm and drew Jess wonderfully close.

"Hello, Bennett," she murmured, and tossed the indignant cat onto the floor.

The underside of Cielos's big, black hoof clamped between Jess's knees seemed laughably out of place among her yellow calico skirt and her long, thick braid of hair, which dangled from behind her right ear to the ground.

"What's next, Doyle?" she asked with good-humored impatience. "The blood is rushing to my head."

Doyle's coffee-black hand entered her range of vision and

pointed to one of the tools on the ground before her. "Use the nippers and remove each nail."

Keeping her eyes on the hoof mere inches from her face, Jess adjusted her work glove, which had begun slipping off her hand, by pressing her hand to her hip to hold the gauntlet and wiggling her fingers deeper into the oversized, hollow, leather digits. With the glove once more in place, she lifted the heavy nippers and gingerly began to work the first nail loose, careful not to pull outward against the hoof wall and risk breaking it. Despite the cool of the air, droplets of sweat gathered at her temples.

"How often do you do this, Doyle? File down the hooves and replace the shoes, I mean."

"Oh, 'bout every six weeks. Their hooves grow like people's toenails. When horses are in the wild, all the runnin' they do keeps the hooves trim, but when they live on a ranch or work on a farm, the hooves need to be filed to keep them from breaking. If large pieces break off or a hoof grows uneven—"

"The horse can go lame, I know. I just didn't realize how often farriers did this." Jess tucked her bottom lip between her teeth and patiently pulled against a stubborn nail. "I'm grateful to you for showing me. Seems like a task a woman rancher should know." She glanced up over her shoulder at Cielos's enormous backside and long, twitching tail, both of which suddenly felt much closer than what she deemed safe. *I hope you went before we left the house*, she thought drolly.

Doyle drew a breath to answer but looked up; at the same time, Jess heard the far-off clop and clatter of a horse pulling a wagon.

Proudly removing the last nail, then taking off the weighty, iron shoe, Jess handed the nippers and horseshoe to Doyle before releasing the hoof and standing up. Gradually, the dizzying pressure in her head from being partly upside down eased, and she looked toward the wagon road that hugged the foothills just beyond the south-facing end of their fence. It wasn't a wagon that appeared but rather a regal-looking, two-seated, shiny black buggy, complete with a matching roof providing shade. A pair of grays pulled it as if out on a Sunday jaunt.

Rather than continue up the road in the direction of Milford and Susanville, the carriage slowed and finally rolled to a stop at the south gate. Taggart left Charlie filling buckets at the water pump and crossed the ranch yard to the gate, his orange mop of hair streaming out from beneath his hat in the cool wind.

"Folks probably lost," Doyle speculated.

Jess nodded her agreement and reached for the large hoof file. "I imagine so."

Taggart pushed the gate open wide as the driver turned the grays into the compound. Payton passed in front of Jess, pulling Luina, the next horse to be shod, and Jess looked around the palomino mare to catch a glimpse of the travelers. The forms in the front seat took shape, and when Jess recognized Edmund and Miriam Van Dorn, she glanced excitedly at Doyle. "They're friends of my parents."

"Go," he said with an understanding smile. "I'll teach you shoein' another time."

Seeing that Edmund was hesitantly guiding the grays toward the corral and water troughs, Jess hurried toward the buggy, gesturing for him to stop. In the corral, Jake resolutely rode out a cantankerous, thrashing mustang that had rejected the men's previous attempts to break it to the saddle. Edmund apparently had understood Jess's signal and the danger to Jake if the mustang were startled, because he reined in a safe distance beyond the water pump to wait.

But then, to Jess's horror, Miriam's round bulk rose from

the seat, and her pudgy arm flapped a white handkerchief in the air. "Halloo!" she sang out.

In the corral, the mustang spooked, and then, with a fierce leap, bucked Jake over the fence as if he were a hundred-and-ninety-pound tumbleweed.

Blissfully unaware of what she'd provoked, Miriam popped out of the conveyance like the cork out of a bottle and bustled toward Jess, leaving Edmund sitting stunned in his seat. Her matronly bulges were clad in white silk over an impossibly wide hoopskirt and topped with a broad-brimmed hat, and as Miriam stretched out her arms to embrace Jess, she flicked a frown at Jess's dust-covered, calico dress and, instead, stopped short and clapped her curiously tiny hands together. "Oh, Jessica, dear! It was so good to receive your letter; we just had to come see you! Why, we've gone all summer without a word...."

Edmund tied off the leather lines and stepped down, hurrying to help Jake to his feet. Before Edmund reached him, Jake, a veteran of being thrown, stood of his own accord, stretched his arms forward to ease a new stiffness from his back, and shook Edmund's hand with a hearty smile of welcome.

Miriam chattered on about society's seasonal parties as Jess attempted to draw her in the direction of the shady cottonwood trees that stretched over the creek beside the cookhouse. Jess paused to receive Jake's wink of assurance that he was unharmed, but Miriam continued her forward momentum with little, mincing steps, still gushing high-pitched prose and earning unappreciative glances from the cattlemen.

"Taggart," Jess heard Jake say, "get a couple of the boys and put one of the tables and a pair of benches under the cottonwoods, please."

"Can I call ye Jackson, then?"

Jess turned in surprise as Seth joined the men, combing

back his mud-brown hair with his dirt-crusted fingernails and peering at Taggart. "Jackson?" the youth asked.

Taggart's round belly shook like that of a man who had long savored a choice bit of news. Jess could not believe that the Irishman had been able to wait this long to torment Jake with his birth name.

"Ye don't think his pappy named him Jake, do ye?" Taggart gamely jabbed a plump elbow into Seth's ribs. "That's all his father—named Jack—called him while we stayed at his farm. Jackson—son of Jack, ye see?"

Seth whistled in amazement. "Is that so?"

Edmund grinned, clearly entertained by the antics.

Jake lifted a brow in Taggart's direction. "If you call me Jackson, I'll call you by the name your pa gave you...or was it your ma who thought up Rosemont?"

"Rosemont Taggart," Seth echoed, and his mouth fell open in a shameless grin as Taggart's pale cheeks flushed like turnips beneath his carrot-colored beard. "Did she call you Rosie?"

Taggart rubbed his nose with the back of his hand and coughed to cover his embarrassment. "So, ye want just one table moved, boss?"

"One will do," Jake replied.

Smothering a grin, Jess pulled off her gloves, tucked them into her belt, and, in a few steps, caught up to Miriam. The woman abruptly stopped, and her pinched lips clamped shut as she turned to gawk at old Pete, who steadied himself with his cane as he shakily lifted a brimming bucket from the water pump, and at Lee, whose unbound, black hair streamed over the Indian blanket knotted at his shoulder over his buckskin tunic. Lee's arm muscles contracted smoothly as he picked up two rope-handled buckets in each hand and strode toward the corral, where Will had already led the Van Dorns' carriage horses to drink.

"You employ savages?" Miriam asked in astonishment, neither lowering her voice nor caring whom she might offend. "Jessica, dear," she implored, her pretty, gray eyes wide as she pressed a hand to her bosom, "they'll steal your possessions, abuse your person, and scalp you—haven't you heard? And worse, scoundrels are going from ranch to ranch to rid them of these—these—"

"People," Jess finished in a brittle voice, struggling not to revert to despising her mother's dearest friend. Taking a deep breath, she steadied her voice. "They are people, and our friends. They saved us and the ranch from the drought by helping us to survive in the Sierras; they work as hard as anyone; they love and respect one another, and I've never heard of the Paiutes scalping anyone. That's more common among the Plains Indians, on the other side of the Rocky Mountains."

Miriam glanced doubtfully at Pete's dry, wrinkled face as he began his trek toward the water trough, then let her eyes linger on Lee in a way that began to make Jess feel uncomfortable.

"Well, Georgeanne, you'd best watch out for them."

"Jessica," Jess said.

Miriam blinked, her eyes on Jess once again. "Hmm?"

A small ache erupted in Jess's heart at the sound of her mother's name, even if spoken by mistake. "You called me Georgeanne," she said with a reflective smile.

Miriam braved the dust Jess's dress had gathered throughout the morning and linked arms with her as they continued walking, Miriam's face gentle again, and a little sad, as if she, too, was reliving old memories. Behind them, Jess heard Edmund quietly apologizing to the Paiute men for his wife's thoughtless comments.

"Edmund, Isaac, and I all went to grammar school together before Isaac met your mother, did you know that?" Miriam twittered, as if her concerns over the Paiutes had never existed.

"I excelled at English, which Edmund and Isaac both struggled with, but they knew mathematics, which I…well, let's just say I don't have your easy ability with numbers." Miriam's corpulent, silk-draped arm hugged Jess's arm tighter as she giggled. "So, what we did was…."

Jess nodded with all the social politeness her mother had bred into her but glanced longingly at Cielos, whose hoof was now being filed by Doyle's capable hands, as she and Miriam passed by. It seemed that learning to shoe the horses, as well as the other tasks she had planned to accomplish that day, would have to be put off until later. Edmund and Miriam's trip from Carson City was a day and a half's journey, and they would certainly stay for a few days and visit and rest before returning home.

With quips of "Rosieee" rendered by Seth in a feminine, singsong voice amid gruff, Irish-accented utterances of "sheep brain," Taggart and Seth jiggled a long plank table out the cookhouse door, Will stepping after them, trying to balance one bench inverted atop another in his spindly arms. As they rounded the cookhouse and headed for the shady spot beneath the cottonwoods, Ho Chen slipped out through the doorway carrying a baking pan-turned-serving tray with mugs and two coffeepots—the steaming one of coffee, and the other of lemonade, Jess surmised, sending him a smile of gratitude for preparing refreshments so quickly.

Suddenly, Miriam paused her childhood recollections. "Ho Chen!" she squealed, throwing out her motherly arms as she had when she'd greeted Jess.

Startled like the mustang had been, Luina jerked back from Payton's hold, almost colliding with her silk-wrapped tormenter, and bolted in a flurry of dust.

Miriam drummed Ho Chen's narrow back with her hands, her vivacious blows nearly felling him. "I didn't know Jess hired you to work here! Just like her mother hired you, hm?" In mild flirtation, she tossed her dyed head—thankfully, her hatpins held—giggling as she latched her free arm onto Ho Chen's and walked between him and Jess toward the table and benches. "Now, you really must tell me how you came to be here. It was after the fire at the Hale house, yes?" She clucked her tongue ruefully. "Dreadful thing, simply dreadful...."

Behind her, Jess heard Edmund murmur apologies to Payton and Jake. Always a man who calmed others, always a man of honor, Jake told Edmund there was no need for concern.

As Ho Chen set down the drinks, then tactfully withdrew to the cookhouse, Edmund, Miriam, Jake, and Jess seated themselves on the benches beneath the sprawling limbs of a cottonwood tree. Miriam's effusive prattle had shifted to compliments about how healthy Jess looked while the men talked about Hale Imports and the ranch.

"Really, my dear," Miriam burbled, subtly condescending, "not many women would expose their skin to the detriments of the sun, but yours looks so absolutely radiant that I don't know why women don't give up wearing hats altogether. And I love your charming print calico, and you don't need to fuss over a little dirt the way you would have to with silk. Oh, what a bother silk is. It really is."

Since Miriam had stepped off the buggy, Jess had been wondering why a woman of her age would travel in silk at all— white silk, especially. It was a color and fabric that Jess and her friends would wear to cotillions in Lexington when they were very young women, the gowns usually trimmed with ribbons and lace in summer colors.

Pondering the thought, Jess watched Miriam scoot a little closer to Edmund with a beatific smile—Edmund paused in his conversation to reciprocate with a doting one—and the final cinders of frustration Jess had been feeling toward Miriam dissolved. When he was alive, her father had always worked long hours, but as an employer and then a co-owner of the import store, he'd had the flexibility to stay home with her mother whenever she was ill or needed to feel his reassuring presence. Jake would do the same for her, Jess realized. Unfortunately, Edmund had rarely had that freedom. She'd just heard Edmund say that he'd recently hired a man to help with the store, but Jess doubted Edmund had taken off any day but Sunday since the night of the fire a year and a half ago.

Miriam had lost her best friend and was aging and lonely. That was probably why she dressed as she did, and why she showered those around her with her effervescence. She wasn't a person comfortable with silence or with being alone.

For several minutes, Miriam sipped her lemonade and seemed content to passively observe the cattlemen as they performed their tasks, chiming in now and then with a lighthearted comment on the tail of something Edmund had said. When a break occurred in the men's conversation, she let out an indolent sigh.

"Horses are gorgeous creatures, aren't they?" Miriam asked, smiling easily at Jake. "I've always loved horses, did you know that? Edmund and Isaac taught me to ride when I was too young to button my boots, just about the same age Ambrose taught you, Jessica, if I recall correctly." Her soft, gray eyes settled on Jess. "Love has made you more beautiful than ever," Miriam said a little wistfully. "Isaac would have been so proud. You look so much like your mother."

With another sigh, Miriam summoned a burst of energy and stood up from the bench more gracefully than Jess would have expected for a woman with her curves and waved to Payton, who looked a little ill at ease, just having returned from catching Luina.

"Young man?" she trilled and pranced toward him. "Since

you don't appear occupied at the present, would you be a dear and show me around this exceptional ranch?"

Aside from flattening his mouth dubiously at being called "young," Payton betrayed no emotion but tied Luina near where Doyle was working, tapping small nails into Cielos's new horseshoe, and walked sedately in the direction of the barn while Miriam's tiny hand patted his sinewy forearm.

Despite Payton's martyr-like bearing, Jess sensed an undercurrent of patient amusement in the man, like a still pond with a sole minnow darting beneath it. She wondered if the minnow had always been there and she simply hadn't noticed it because she hadn't looked beyond what was easily discernable on the surface.

As soon as Miriam disappeared around the far side of the barn, Edmund let his carefree demeanor fall to the side as he leaned his elbows on the table and rubbed his thumbs together. "I don't normally discuss business matters in front of ladies, Jess, but you and I worked together and have had discussions about the store for a long time. Besides, this concerns you."

"Have you heard news of Ambrose?" Jess asked, though somehow that possibility didn't fit Edmund's mood or Miriam's presence. If the worst had happened, the four of them would not have been sharing lemonade and coffee in a picnic setting, and Edmund would not have brought Miriam along, given her tendency to emote unpredictably.

"No, no, Ambrose is fine, as far as I know, though I haven't yet received the painting of your mother. I did read that his general, John Hunt Morgan, was killed in early September."

"War keeps a man busy," Jake said, using quiet logic to still Jess's worries, as he always did. "I'm sure Ambrose is fine."

"Thank you, Jake," she told him softly. "I'm certain Ambrose is, too. Few soldiers, even Morgan's men, are as audacious as the general was." She turned to her father's friend. "What's troubling you, Edmund?"

"I came here because of the recent letter you sent. I found the address of your father's lawyer in San Francisco and wrote to him shortly after you asked me to in June. He wrote back, saying that he'd found a paper revealing your father's personal banking information, but that the will itself, with the details of Isaac's investments, had been misplaced. He's reputable, so I'm certain this year's stock fiasco has most lawyers in San Francisco hopping and their offices in chaos, even now. He said he'll try to locate the will as soon as he is able. I sent him a polite reminder a little more than a month ago, but he hasn't replied. It may be a matter you wish to look into, Jake."

Jess studied the man she'd known since she was born. Edmund's gray hair hadn't thinned noticeably in the five months since she'd seen him last, and he looked as dapper as ever in his modestly distinguished suit, but his clean-shaven, fatherly face revealed that he was holding something back.

"What is so difficult to say, Edmund?" Jess asked.

"According to your father's last written communiqué to his lawyer, he wished to invest ten thousand dollars from his personal account to set up another business—perhaps a second imports store, as Isaac and I often spoke of that—and he had asked his lawyer to scout around for available property that he could purchase."

With a spurt of excitement, Jess leaned forward, gripping the edge of the table to keep from falling off the bench. "Jake, ten thousand is how much he wanted to invest. He would have left much more than that in the account to take care of Mother and me, in the event that something happened to him. Such an amount would be enough to buy ranch land in Oregon, where we could drive the cattle and horses during difficult years, with a great deal to spare."

Jake turned his coffee cup in his hands, his eyes on Edmund.

Across from Jake, Edmund opened his thumbs as if silently asking her to understand. "Jess, I went to the bank to close your father's account and bring you the money. It's gone, all of it."

Silence fell as solidly as the hush after an avalanche.

Edmund pulled an envelope from his pocket and placed it on the table. "All the information is there. I'll help you in any way I can."

When Jess remained as rigid as a stone, Jake picked up the envelope and tucked it into his vest. "Thank you, Edmund."

"Thank you, Edmund," Jess echoed after a moment, letting the stiffness leave her shoulders. She and Jake had each other, and between Bennett patience and Hale tenacity, they could accomplish anything. Somehow, sometime, they would find her father's money.

"You see that, Jake? That's her Hale stubbornness, just like her father's."

The three traded grins, then Jake described for Edmund with a storyteller's savvy the highs and lows of his trip to Oregon with Hank and Doyle to purchase hay.

Miriam followed Payton from the barn to the paddock to the corral, then, as if a fire bell had sounded, parted company with him and hied as purposefully as an entire hook and ladder company for the outhouse—the "necessary," Jess recalled Miriam's referring to it in the past—oblivious to the bemused looks the cattlemen sent her way.

"Doyle is taller than Hank," Jake was telling Edmund with a chuckle, "and has the build of an ox. He couldn't see Hank on the other side of the two bales they were carrying, and when they reached the back of the wagon, Doyle pushed the hay in, and Hank was dragged along with it."

Edmund wiped moisture from his eyes as he laughed at the comical situation but stopped short as Miriam stormed up to them.

"That does it! I refuse to stay away from civilization a moment longer!" Miriam glared at Jake. "You think that foul privy of yours is a suitable arrangement for a lady?" She jerked her chin at Jess. "I don't know how she can abide living in this place, or how she can abide living with you!"

Edmund and Jake both rose, plainly as shocked as Jess at Miriam's outburst.

"Miriam…" Edmund said.

Without a word of good-bye, Miriam stalked past several stunned ranchmen, who backed away as she headed for the carriage. She plunked herself inside and stared straight ahead.

Edmund uttered another sincere apology, said proper good-byes to both of them, and then left to help Diaz hitch up the horses.

As the Van Dorns pulled out through the gate, Jess looked up at Jake, refusing to let the morning die on a sour note. "When *are* you going to get those tapestries hung?" she asked in mock exasperation.

The corner of Jake's mouth twitched, and he gazed down at Jess's twinkling, green eyes and the rosy pink that bloomed on her cheeks. A breeze lifted the wisps of chestnut hair that danced around her face, and he couldn't contain his love for her or his laughter any longer.

Jake lifted Jess in his arms and swung her around and around beneath the cottonwood tree, thanking the Almighty yet again for the blessing of his wife, and mesmerized by the way her "charming print calico" flowed away from her slender waist like a wind-ruffled field of flowers.

Chapter Eighteen

W hy are you bringing the Henry rifles?" Jess asked. She paused near the middle of the stairs as Jake descended toward her with both repeating rifles slung over his left shoulder, their barrels nearly lost in the deep shadows of the early morning hour.

Jake halted a step above her, his brawny hand casually resting on the pinewood railing he'd built with the same saw, lathe, and patient sanding he'd used to build the house she loved.

"I thought we might go shooting tin cans after breakfast," he said with a smile. "We haven't gone all summer, and it's best to stay in practice."

"Just as long as I get to shoot the empty radish tin," Jess said with a theatrical shiver. "Those radishes were awful."

Then, darkness.

An image flashed through Jess's mind—a hand gripping a gleaming Derringer, rising from a field of blue. Beside Jess, Jake's face contorted in alarm and rage, and his mouth formed a single word: *No.* The Derringer bucked as it fired. Jake's eyes registered pain; then, he twisted and began to fall. Eerie dread swam feverishly through her with hot, stinging tendrils. Jess realized that she had heard no gunshot, no movement, no sound at all.

There was a flash of early-morning daylight; then, the sound of Jake's voice began to return and, with it, awareness of the handrail, the stairs…and the intuition that a fatal threat was imminent.

"...and Hank told me he'd gladly paint your portrait. Your new blue dress is beautiful on you. Would you wear it?"

"What?" Jess struggled to distinguish the dreamlike images from reality. Jake wanted a painting of her. Desperately, she grabbed hold of his arm. "No, not of just me. I want one of you, too—one of us together."

"But—"

Angrily, fearfully, she stomped her foot on the step. "Jake, promise me!"

What if they didn't get the chance to have a portrait made, and then she lost him?

Jake eyed her with concern. "I promise.... Jess, what just happened?"

In the space of seconds, she told him about her vision, the sense of an approaching threat driving the speed of her words. "I don't know when this will happen, but...." Her breathing quickened, and she suddenly felt like she was a fox being hunted, that they all were.

She met Jake's sharp gaze. "It's here."

"Injun lovers!"

They both raced down the stairs and out onto the porch, Jess snatching a rifle from Jake's hand before she found the presence of mind to decipher from which direction the shout had come.

Half-dressed cattlemen armed to the teeth poured from the bunkhouse and sped across the ranch yard like vengeful hornets from a shaken nest. Concussive blasts of rifle fire sounded all over the ranch and on Hank's property.

Jake's chest swelled as he drew a breath, no doubt preparing to issue orders for her to stay put.

Jess held firmly to her rifle, trembling in dread but poised to join the fight. "I am not going to stay safe inside while you or anyone else dies, Bennett! This is my ranch, too, and these are my people!"

Jake's eyes bored into hers as he rapidly, mentally debated, then he gave a crisp nod. "You stay right beside me. The fear you saw in my eyes during your vision could have been fear for you."

Jess nodded. "I'm with you."

They paused for only an instant to take in the situation, then ran into the compound to join the cattlemen.

Blinding sunlight flashed intermittently from steel barrels, and horses and cattle darted and careened amid the chaos.

"Injun lovers!" a man screamed again, and turned with his revolver and shot Seth in the leg.

Seth staggered against a corral post and fell into the rails.

Before the gunman could take aim and squeeze off a second shot, Diaz leveled his own revolver and fired. Not stopping to watch the man fall, Diaz swung up onto Luina's bare back and galloped her out of the corral gate he'd left open, then kicked her into a dead run for the Paiute village.

Jake pulled Seth to his feet. Jess added her strength to Jake's, and, together, they helped him hop-run to the front door of the barn, where Pete's anxious cow was tethered.

Jess squinted against the rising sun. "Pete's already here?" she yelled to Jake over the cacophony of gunfire and frightened, running animals.

"He may have stayed the night," Jake yelled back.

Seth balanced himself against the front of the barn, his back protected, his gun in hand. "There must be a dozen of them, or more!" he shouted to Jake. "Should I ride to Smoke Creek and bring the soldiers?"

"This'll be over before they could get here," Jake answered and grabbed Jess's hand with what seemed like the strength of an iron clamp.

Jess held in a voluminous breath, the only means she had of raising the length of her skirts, as they ran back to the corral, Jake occupying one hand, the Henry rifle the other. Driven on by her love and her fear for her Paiute friends, Jess stretched out her legs, determined to keep pace with Jake.

At Jake's shrill whistle, Cielos came at a brisk trot, stopping just inches from them. Jake bent to lift Jess, but she saw a movement at the water trough—the icy eyes, thin, hollow cheeks, and long, black beard of Eli Payton as he stood up from behind the trough, his rifle stock to his shoulder, the barrel pointed at her. She shook free of Jake's grip and lifted the Henry to the ready. She curled her index finger over the trigger....

Payton fired.

"Jess, no!" Jake roared, his voice raw with warning.

A pocket-sized revolver struck the ground beside her, followed by a man with the chest and stomach of an ox, his lifeless eyes reflecting the sky, blood matting his filthy hair and pooling into the dirt around his head.

Payton sprinted over, his rifle pointed safely skyward.

"Thank you," Jake said.

Jess stared at Payton, trying to find words. All this time, she had thought the worst about him.

A cattleman who spoke even less than the other ranchmen did, Payton simply answered, "Yup," then hurried toward the Paiute camp.

Another shot rang out, and Cielos bolted from the corral. Jess saw Jake's jaw twitch in anger. His gaze rapidly flitted to the cattlemen running and riding toward the Paiute village, then to the ranch buildings, and finally to Charlie and Hank, who ran around behind the bunkhouse and leaned out to exchange fire with two or more men hunkered behind the barn.

"Come on!" Jake ordered her.

Their eyes alert to sunlight on rifle barrels and unexpected movements, Jess and Jake crouched and ran to join Seth at the front of the barn, where the young man aimed his gun around the corner, helping Charlie and Hank to keep their attackers at a disadvantage.

Jess pressed her back to the barn door, scanning eastward, to where the Paiutes were fighting, then to the northwest, watching for oncoming gunmen. Across from her, the wooden planks of the bunkhouse wall splintered as bullet after bullet punched holes into them. Abruptly, the shooting in the space between the barn and the smithy stopped.

Hank cupped his hands to his mouth to be heard above the other commotion. "They're heading for the cookhouse," he called.

Beyond the smithy, Ho Chen stepped out of the open cookhouse doorway, a wickedly honed kitchen knife in his fist, and hustled after Hank around the far side of the cookhouse.

"Seth, you stay here," Jake directed him. "Watch for the gunmen to come out between the smithy and the cookhouse. Jess and I will round the smithy from this side and send them your way."

Seth braced his shoulders against the barn, his trembling legs sprawled for balance. "S-sounds good, boss."

At Seth's pallor, Jess eyed his blood-soaked pant leg. The red dampness caused the fabric to cling to his thigh, the same thigh a cow had gored months before.

"Jess!" Jake called.

Hating the fact that any delay would risk more lives and that Seth's wound would have to wait, Jess gripped her rifle like a drowning woman clinging to a life raft and, when Jake broke for the smithy, scurried immediately after him.

At the smithy, Jess pressed her back to the building and her left shoulder against Jake, using her arm to feel him as he eased sideways along the wall and to guide her as she kept apace with his steps. From the front corner of the barn, Seth kept a steady eye on the smithy and the cookhouse beyond it. To the south, the ranch house stood as solid as a rock, with a tide of panicked bays, chestnuts, and blacks swirling around it, their white ankles rising and churning like foam. Behind the house, cloud shadows rolled over the Sierra foothills, distorting the already wavering, skeletal fingers of sage, making the mountain itself seem alive. Jake advanced several more steps, and Jess could no longer see Charlie or the bunkhouse except for the front.

A scrabbling noise grated along the smithy roof above her head. Seth shouted, but Jess was already lowering her rifle and reaching for her revolver. Jake, his Remington already in hand, backed purposefully into her, pushing her protectively against the plank wall.

Seth pointed his rifle barrel to the rooftop over their heads and fired.

Two big men jumped down, unharmed, on top of Jake, knocking him and his Remington to the ground. The impact sent Jess reeling and spilled her rifle. She steadied herself against the smithy, drew her revolver, cocked it, and waited for a clear shot at the men, who wielded lethally sharp knives.

Jake shook one of the men off him like a bear throwing off a hound. The man instantly got to his feet again. Knives swung evilly at Jake's body, winking lightning-fast, as Jake dodged them and snapped out punches that sent one man after the other staggering back, but both rapidly recovered and slashed at Jake, their intent to kill locked in their faces.

Jess had never seen Jake so furious, so deadly of purpose, nor had she ever watched him fight so hard to stay between her and a threat.

A strong arm clamped around Jess's waist and yanked her away from Jake, around the corner of the smithy. She saw Seth's eyes look at her, then back at Jake, and he kept his rifle aimed at the fray, waiting, as she had, for a safe opening to shoot. One of the ranchmen must have grabbed her, then, if Seth hadn't showed alarm. An arm with golden hairs was pressed to her ribs—Charlie had pulled her out of harm's way.

"Charlie, don't!" she yelled, wriggling to break free. "I'm a fair shot; I can help Jake!"

"Jake would want you safe," Charlie said, and lifted her against his hip as he half carried, half dragged her to the rear of the bunkhouse and the shelter it provided.

"Let go of me!" she screeched, enraged, and thrust a hard elbow into his gut.

Charlie grunted and his arm loosened, but his hand caught her wrist. His thick, blond mustache curved up as he spoke. "Jake's all right, Jess. He's strong and Seth is watching out for him. Calm down," he said. "I'll keep you safe."

Unable to see Jake or anyone else, Jess jerked her wrist free, her eyes searching for the outlaws. Gradually she lowered her Remington, panting to catch her breath.

Charlie strode a short pace away, likewise surveying the open places and the desert, and then he drew his handgun, cocked it, and took aim. At her.

An odd whistling rent the air, then Charlie twitched as a feathered arrow impaled his chest. He brandished his gun, struggling to focus his aim.

Frozen and witless, Jess stared at the hole welling with red around the arrow, like raspberry jam seeping from a fresh pastry, feeling detached, as if the top of her head had risen off and taken her mind with it. Somewhere miles beneath her, her feet felt ponderously heavy, as if welded to the earth.

Two more whistles, and two more rippling arrows pierced his chest. Charlie's gun dropped, and he groaned, then fell graceful as a leaf to the ground, his body weight snapping the shafts of the arrows with audible cracks.

From the direction of the foothills, a tall Indian in buckskins ran toward her, a bow in hand, his dark eyes hard, his face concerned.

"Lone Wolf?" Jess gasped as the man and the mountains seemed to tilt.

Lone Wolf caught her before she slumped against the bunkhouse wall.

"Breathe slowly, Jessica," he said, easing her to the ground with his available arm.

Jess listed against the bunkhouse and blinked rapidly to clear her visual and mental haze. Lone Wolf was kneeling beside her. "You have to help Jake," she said, still breathless.

"No," Lone Wolf said softly. "I would no longer be of help to him."

"What?" Jess's eyes suddenly brimmed with scalding tears. *No!* "W-why can't you?"

Two big hands that smelled of leather turned her head to meet a pair of whiskey-brown eyes and a ruggedly handsome face in need of a shave.

"Jake," she whispered, then scrambled onto her knees and leaned heavily into his solid embrace.

"Because he is here," Lone Wolf answered, a smile in his voice.

For several moments, Jess merely breathed and held her husband as her heart threatened to burst through her chest. Jake, she realized, was quaking nearly as forcefully as she was.

Jake pulled back, his hands on her cheeks again. "Are you hurt?"

"No. You?" Jess pushed his hands aside and began checking him for injuries. From her quick assessment, he had a nasty cut on his shoulder that he'd already stemmed with his bandana, and a few lesser cuts on his arms.

"I'm all right. Lone Wolf?" His expression that of a man

beholden, Jake clasped wrists with his closest friend, who returned his look with a nod to acknowledge a debt repaid.

Jess also realized that, though she hadn't seen Lone Wolf in a year, Jake didn't appear surprised to see him.

Just then, her mind fully cleared. "Jake! Seth and the Paiutes!" She listened. The gunfire from the Paiute village had faded to infrequent shots.

Jake's attention snapped to Lone Wolf.

"None of the Paiutes was killed," said a strained voice Jess had never heard before.

She staggered to her feet and spun around. The formerly rickety Indian man she had known as Pete approached, no longer hunched over or shuffling but moving at a steady walk, carrying the cane.

"Seth will need minor stitching," Pete told Jake, "but he should be fine. Stalwart boy, Seth is."

"Minor stitching"? Jess thought. "Stalwart"? Pete speaks English…educated English?

Jake nodded. "I smelled alcohol on the one Payton shot at the corral. If more of those men had been drinking, too, we'll have a lot of burial holes to dig."

Hank hurried toward them from the cookhouse, patting his flushed face with a handkerchief. "Everyone all right?"

"We're fine here," Jake said, then tipped his dusty hat in the direction of the barn. "Seth could use a couple of stitches."

"I just saw him hobble into the bunkhouse, probably for that very purpose, and I saw Ho Chen and Lily going to tend to everyone's injuries." Hank's face, as red as one of his apples, creased into a confident grin for Jess. "And from where I'm standing, Mattie and Grace look just fine."

"The horses and the cattle?" Jake asked.

Using both hands to shield his eyes from the sun, the fingers of one hand pressed to the backs of the others, Hank squinted to the east, north, and west. "Only a few got out, and if that's orange hair I see under that hat, Taggart's already bringing them back." He lowered his hands, and his grin widened. "Most of the animals broke through your western fence and onto my property. We'll let them crop the hay stubble left behind from harvest and bring them in later, when they've had their fill."

Jake shook his hand firmly. "Thank you for all you've done. Hank, this is Lone Wolf, a friend of ours who helped us work the horses and cattle until last winter."

"Hank, Lone Wolf is also the man who pulled me away from my family's burning house last year," Jess added, sending Jake's Paiute friend a look of renewed thankfulness. "A few moments later, the house would have fallen on me. Lone Wolf, you just saved my life again." She shifted her gaze to include Jake and Pete, and sought to keep new-sprung sparks of ire from her voice. "Please know that I'm grateful to each of you, but I'd like to know what has been happening here. Now."

Jake looked down his slightly hooked nose at her, as if inwardly bolstering himself for battle. Lone Wolf stared down at her with an exact replica of the expression. *Joining ranks*, Jess surmised.

"Jessica," Lone Wolf began, "the day you and my white brother returned from the States, it was I who shot your horse. Because of me, you suffered injury to your ribs and arm."

"You were wearing britches," Jake gently reminded her.

"I did not see my brother through the horses," Lone Wolf said stiffly, like a man who rarely spoke, "but I realized who you were when I saw your hair come loose when you fell. Because I caused harm to come to you, I stayed in these hills until I spoke to my brother and told him I would watch out for you until the injuries I caused you had healed."

Events from the past months flooded her mind, and happenings that she had dismissed or explained away at the time started making sense. "Because of my hair, you realized it was me. That's why you stopped shooting." She lifted a hand when both men attempted to speak. "I understand, Lone Wolf. White settlers forced your people out, and some bad ones have harmed the Paiutes. You and those with you were simply trying to keep the immigrants away by staging attacks. In your place, I would have defended my people, as well." That said, she crossed her arms and looked at Jake, letting him see her irritation. "Lone Wolf is the reason I kept feeling that I was being watched. But you searched the hills. You said no one was there. No"—she tried to recall his words—"you said that there were no *strangers*, no reason to fear. You had to have found Lone Wolf that morning, and you didn't lie but still managed to keep the truth from me."

"If you knew Lone Wolf was planning to spend weeks hiding out on the mountainside until he knew you were safe," Jake patiently countered, "would you have permitted it?"

Jess pushed her hat back on its strings and swiped several loose hairs from her face. She was already annoyed that Lone Wolf had done so much for her without her knowledge, more still that Jake had known but had kept it from her. Most of all, she was annoyed that Jake's reason for not telling her about it was sound. "You're right. I wouldn't have permitted it. I just don't understand how you could let me go on being concerned when you knew I could feel someone's eyes on me."

"Lone Wolf planned to leave once you were completely well again," Jake said. "Then, after our visit with Tom at Fort Churchill, I wanted to be sure someone was looking out for you at all times, and I asked him to stay on until winter, when he would need to go back to his family and I would have more time to look after you."

Jess propped her hands on her hips to keep them from curling into angry fists. She badly wanted to remind Jake that she was fully capable of looking after herself, but she supposed that Charlie's dead body at her feet proved otherwise.

"You were the friend of Red Deer," Lone Wolf said, gesturing to the clothesline, water barrels, and pair of fire rings behind the bunkhouse where, the year before, Jess and Lone Wolf's wife, Red Deer, had washed laundry together and cultivated an enduring friendship. "You brought her happiness while she lived, and helped her to die in peace. I protected you because of these things you did for her."

Thinking of her friend brought the press of tears to Jess's eyes. She missed Red Deer's laughter and her generous heart, and she also felt sorrow for the honorable man Red Deer had left behind, the man who still loved her. With effort, Jess set the thoughts aside for a later time, knowing she needed answers now for her own peace of mind now.

"On the night of the stampede," Lone Wolf began, "I did not know Lily's daughters had been taken. Had I known, I would have gone in your place. I see now it is good I did not go. You would have been here with only one man to protect you from this man who now lies dead."

The reminder that she should be grateful instead of annoyed further vexed her. Though Lone Wolf and Jake were forthcoming at present, they *had* kept secrets from her, as if she were a mere child.

Keenly perceptive of her thoughts, as he almost always was, Jake arched an eyebrow. "Lone Wolf watched out for the Paiutes here while we were in the Sierras. I was the only one keeping an eye on you then."

A few flies had landed on Charlie. Jess turned away, shivering in revulsion. "Why did Charlie try to kill me?" she demanded. "And who is Pete?"

To answer her first question, Pete bent to search Charlie's pockets, scattering the buzzing flies when he rolled the dead man onto his side. From Charlie's vest pockets, Pete pulled out two thick stacks of greenbacks and handed them to Jake.

Hank edged a shoulder in as Jake thumbed through the bills. "There must be nearly a thousand dollars there," he said quietly. "Extraordinary."

"Lone Wolf kept an eye on *you*," Jake told Jess. "I hired 'Pete' to look and to listen all over the ranch." He turned to the wrinkled old man. "Jess, this is Stone Bird."

Jess managed a polite smile in Stone Bird's direction, then shook her head in burgeoning confusion. "Jake, when did you hire Stone Bird?" She looked at the ancient again, unable to believe how completely he had convinced her that he was feeble, how completely he had convinced them all. Even Seth had found humor in his simplistic, doddering ways.

"I contacted Stone Bird shortly after Charlie and Payton hired on," Jake answered, "when Will and I drove the thirty head of cattle to Shaffer's Station. Charlie was fair with a horse, but he concerned me from the beginning."

Again, Jess shoved loose strands of hair back and held her hands against her head, willing everything to make sense. "How did you know? Charlie was a little talkative for a ranch hand, but the man was charm itself."

"There's a lot of wisdom in the Bible," Jake commented. "Years ago, I was paging through it and found a passage in Proverbs that stuck with me, which basically says that charm is deceitful. That verse has served me well. I've found that people who find favor by charming others nearly always have something to hide."

Another cognition took root and budded within Jess. "Lone Wolf and Stone Bird are the reasons why you kept wanting me to stay at the ranch, or at least two of the reasons—so they could watch out for me."

"They are two of the reasons, yes," Jake affirmed. He

glanced down at Charlie's still form. "I'm fairly certain now that Charlie planned the stampede and kidnapping, as well, to get most of the men away from the ranch and to get you alone. He would have known I wouldn't let you go after kidnappers who might also be murderers. Charlie could have arranged the stampede when he and Will went to Milford and maybe offered the men Mattie and Grace as some form of payment. When Will and Charlie reached Milford, they had different errands to attend to." Jake looked to Lone Wolf and Stone Bird for confirmation.

"He tried to get Jessica alone at other times," Stone Bird said in his strained voice, which hinted at just how old he might truly be, "though his actions may have been interpreted as something else." He paused and looked at Jess with profound sorrow in his eyes. "Yesterday when the round woman and her husband came, I heard her speak to one of the ranchmen behind the outhouse, and I saw her take the money from her skirt, though I saw little else because I was walking in a direction away from them."

Miriam?! Jess felt the color drain from her face and her mind became muddled. She leaned weakly against a water barrel for support. "Stone Bird, did you hear what Miriam—the round woman—said?"

"Yes, I did." Stone Bird's voice sounded more strained than ever. "She said, 'Stop delaying and kill Jessica.'"

"Stop delaying?" Jess glanced anxiously at Jake, struggling to sort out the implications. "That means Miriam likely hired Charlie to come here and ki— to put an end to me. She paid him to kill me," she repeated, the words falling numbly on her own ears. "Jake, when we were at the import store, Miriam heard you tell Edmund that you planned to post a notice for hire before we left town. She must have decided to hire Charlie then."

"Yesterday, Stone Bird couldn't find a way to speak to me unobserved," Jake said, "so he told Lone Wolf last night, and Lone Wolf told me. Each of us was prepared for the worst"—he nodded to the Henry rifles leaning against the bunkhouse— "though I didn't expect trouble to come so soon. When those men attacked this morning, I think Charlie saw it as his chance to do what he came here to do."

"Because of Stone Bird's information, Lone Wolf was keeping very close watch," Jess said, feeling more thankful than she ever had in her life...her life, which she still possessed.

Hank stepped fully into the circle, his protective nature not permitting him to remain on the outskirts of the conversation any longer. "How would Miriam find a man such as Charlie? And why would she want Jess dead in the first place?"

Jake reached down and seized the Henry rifles. "That's what I'm going to Carson City to find out."

"*We're* going," Jess corrected him.

Jake glanced at the men. "Will you excuse us?"

Lone Wolf and Hank nodded, then hoisted Charlie's body by the arms, Hank grunting at the ungainly weight as they thrust their shoulders under the dead man's armpits. Together, they carried the blond corpse out of Jess's sight, the toes of his boots drawing two wavering lines in the dust. Jess recalled the man Payton had shot near the corral, the man whose chest and stomach had put her in mind of an ox—he had been carrying a pocket-sized revolver, similar to a Derringer, and had worn a field of blue: his shirt. Because of Payton, Jake hadn't been shot, and the terror that had shaken Jess since the premonition struck had been resolved. Unfortunately, the cattlemen would face a day of transporting bodies and explaining matters to the federal cavalry at Stone Creek. There was no help for it.

With Charlie's body out of the way, Stone Bird retrieved

the dead man's gun and followed Lone Wolf and Hank out of hearing and sight.

Jess met Jake's hardened stare with a flinty glare of her own. Neither of them said a word. Neither of them needed to. She knew he would try to force her to stay at the ranch, and he had to know that nothing would stop her from finding out why Miriam wanted her dead.

Jess drew in her breath and softly murmured the single piece of logic that would convince Jake to allow her to go with him: "Miriam thinks I'm dead, so she won't be expecting us. She won't have the chance to cause me harm." Jess thought for a moment, then went on. "If we ride hard, we should arrive at their home only an hour or two behind them. Edmund would not have risked injury to the horses by driving all night."

Jake's hard stare hadn't flickered a mite. "Doyle, Diaz, and Taggart come with us," he said flatly, "as well as the sheriff."

The sheriff? Jess thought in utter disbelief. *Are we actually traveling to Carson City to have Miriam arrested?* "How could it have come to this?" she asked, though she knew there would be no answer until they arrived and heard an explanation from Miriam.

Jake didn't respond. He looked fully capable of tying her to the ranch house if she so much as fluttered an eyelid in objection.

Jess wet her suddenly dry lips. "Doyle, Diaz, and Taggart will be good company," she said, loving Jake desperately yet feeling furious with him, all in the same moment.

The tension left Jake's stance, and he pulled her roughly into his arms, like a man whose wife had just looked death in the face. "Jess, I was so afraid that I'd lost you," he said into her hair. "When I saw Charlie pulling you away, and those two with the knives were between us...." Jake drew back just enough to gaze at her, a fiercely protective expression on his

304

face. "You've been attacked because of horses you own, because you care about a race of people some men hate, and because this is a hard land that has a hard effect on some folks."

"So have you," Jess said stiffly. "So has everyone else here. If you dare suggest we leave this ranch and live some other life—"

"The ranch can go to blazes!" Jake roared. "How many more times do you think I can stand here and watch this place threaten your life?"

"You could *not* leave this ranch."

"You *could*," Jake said quietly, putting a small space between them, giving her the choice.

Jess jerked rather than tilted her head to the side. "You think so?"

In the next instant, Jess spun, strode past the bullet-pitted wall, and stormed through the ranks of wide-eyed cattlemen, who scrambled out of her way as she crossed the compound.

In the workshop, she snatched up a spade and the grapevine basket she had brought back from the Sierras, the basket with the mended handle that would always remind her that what she and Jake couldn't mend, God would.

Her jaw set, she marched out the doorway past Jake and scanned the ground. A trio of brown, dried weeds snagged her gaze—weeds that, in hospitable weather, would flower magnificently. She dropped to her knees, dug up all three along with their roots and thrust them into the basket. Still ignoring Jake, she carried basket and spade to the house, briefly eyed the vacant ground in front of the porch beside the steps, then planted the weeds in a row.

Jess pushed herself to her feet, tramped to the water pump, grabbed a full bucket, and returned to water the sun-baked plants. Finally, she threw the empty bucket to the ground and faced Jake. "I'm not going anywhere," she said.

Jake put his hands on his hips, and his mouth slowly formed a sheepish grin. "Perhaps I could build a few rocking chairs for the porch this winter," he said.

Jess smiled back. "Perhaps you could."

Jake sat on the table outside the cookhouse, his good arm resting on his knee, as Ho Chen stitched the knife wound in his upper arm. Across the compound, near the ranch house porch and the weeds Jess had planted—he surely loved her grit— Jess presented Lone Wolf with two blankets she'd woven. One would be for Lone Wolf's adopted son, Two Hands, and the other for the son whose birth had coincided with Red Deer's death, both of whom were being looked after by Lone Wolf's family in Idaho Territory. Jess had made the blankets with Mattie and Grace in mind, Jake recalled, and he knew that if he wanted to locate Jess in the days ahead, he'd find her at the loom, producing blankets quicker than Sam Colt's company could produce a six-shooter.

After a final pat to Lone Wolf's arm, Jess hurried over to a table where Lily was seated. Taggart supported Diaz as they made their ways toward it, trading insults amid eye rolls and energetic hand waves. When they reached the table, Lily frowned at Diaz's foot, then uncorked a new bottle of whiskey and pulled a folded towel from a stack. Jake chuckled. It looked like he owed Diaz another pair of boots.

"Please do not shake, Mr. Bennett," Ho Chen said. His needle pierced Jake's arm, then pierced it again, and he tugged the thread through—the friction burned—to pull the split skin together.

Lone Wolf secured the blankets Jess had given him in the bedroll tied to his horse. Jake nearly chuckled again, but out of respect for Ho Chen—and his needle—he held in his laughter.

The first night Lone Wolf had ridden in months before, he had turned his horse out with the ranch horses. With all the other horses they owned—again, Jess's doing—nobody had noticed the addition.

Jake raised his hand to wave farewell to Lone Wolf, who did the same in return, then leaped up onto his horse and rode out, heading toward the west gate. He would visit Red Deer's grave before he rode north for the winter, Jake was certain. After Olivia and Sadie had died, he'd visited their grave nearly every day for more than a year.

At the table with Lily, Taggart lifted an orange eyebrow and made some comment to Diaz that set Jess to laughing. Then Taggart drew his knife and gleefully sliced Diaz's new boot away, and Jake had a good notion of the target of Taggart's joke.

Jake saw Jess lift her gaze as Stone Bird strolled across the valley far to the north, barely visible above the sagebrush. She then smiled to see the cow he pulled behind him, and Jake suspected she was going to miss the old Paiute.

Jake sipped his coffee, unable to take his eyes off Jess. When Livvy and Sadie had died, all he'd done had been to work mindlessly, killing his pain with productivity from long before sunup till hours after sundown, when he'd ride to their grave. He'd slept little and spoken rarely. Then, Jess had come to the ranch, a green-eyed spitfire with a passionate love for the people, the animals, and the land, and he had come alive again, like a desert after a healing, summer rain. More than once, he had saved Jess's life, but she had shown him what it means to live.

As Lily poured more whiskey over Diaz's foot, Jess looked on with towel in hand. She smiled a little as Taggart continued to give Diaz grief, but she looked distracted, likely preoccupied with thoughts about all that Miriam had done and about what would happen to the woman next.

Of greater concern to Jake was how Jess would react when a woman she had known all her life was put into prison, or worse. After Jess had lost her family, the ranch had been her refuge. When they returned from Carson City, the ranch would be her refuge again. He would see to it.

"Finished, boss," Ho Chen said, and snipped the thread.

"Thank you," Jake said. He motioned to Taggart that it was time to go, then went to saddle their horses.

Chapter Nineteen

W hat a surprise!" Edmund's greeting was warm, though his eyes looked tired. "Miriam and I arrived home only a few hours ago. Come in, come in."

"Is Miriam here?" Jake asked in a low voice, his face alert as he eyed the doorways leading off the entrance hall.

Not a single porcelain vase had been moved from its place in all the years they'd lived here, Jess realized. The dark wood furnishings held exactly the same crystal figurines and silver candlesticks, set in precisely the same positions, every item meticulously spotless, thanks to the tireless efforts of the maids. Until now, Jess had admired Miriam's penchant for neatness and consistency. Now, she supposed it to be a strange obsession.

"Miriam is out shopping. She'll be sorry she missed seeing you." He started to close the door behind Jake, then noticed the sheriff standing close behind him. "Sheriff?" With a look of befuddlement, Edmund admitted the russet-haired sheriff, stepping aside to let the burly man through, then noticed Doyle and Taggart pacing the street like sentries on guard duty, their eyes alternately scanning the house and road.

Jess regretted that Diaz had been injured yet again, doubly so because, in Miriam's house, having four men with her—five, including Edmund—just didn't seem like enough.

Edmund closed the door and looked at Jake and Jess with his darkly circled eyes, his upturned mouth turning grim when he noticed their dismal expressions. "What is going on, Jake?"

"Edmund...." Jess hesitated briefly, but Jake gave her a nod to continue. Edmund had been her father's dearest friend and at times had been as much a father to her as her own. He would receive the difficult news about his wife a trifle better if it came from her. "Edmund," she began again, "Miriam hired a man to pose as a cattleman and to get a job at Jake's ranch," she said as gently as she was able. "When Jake and I came to see you several months ago at the store, she overheard Jake telling you that he intended to post a notice for hire at the livery stable in town."

"I remember when Jake said that," Edmund responded, his face paling as he gazed at each of them in turn.

"Two days ago, while you and Miriam were at the ranch, she gave the man, Charlie Shane, one thousand dollars in greenbacks. She was seen handing him the money."

"Actually, his name was Shane Lucius Porter," the sheriff put in. "He was wanted for several murders. Killer for hire, some lawmen believed."

"A thousand dollars?" Edmund repeated. "That can't be."

"Why can't it?" the sheriff asked. He pulled a notebook and pencil from his coat pocket and flipped the notebook open.

"We use gold and silver coin for currency, like most people in town—never greenbacks. And besides, I'd notice if that amount was missing. I'm an accountant," Edmund explained, though everyone present already knew that. "A businessman."

"Edmund...." Jess pulled off her hat and set it on one of the hall tables. How could she do this to Edmund? She took his hands in hers, said a brief, silent prayer, and forced out the words. "One of the men at the ranch heard Miriam order the man to kill me."

Jake's voice drew Edmund's attention. "Miriam's exact words were, 'Stop delaying and kill Jessica.'"

"Because of Miriam, two Paiute girls were kidnapped, and

one was violated." Compared to all that Mattie and Grace had suffered, she thought, the animals they'd lost in the stampede mattered very little.

Edmund turned back to Jake and stared at him disbelievingly, his face ashen.

Both Jake's and the sheriff's stances reminded Jess of matching brick walls, yet her skin crawled with apprehension, as if it had chilled and come loose and was scurrying to grasp its original place.

The sheriff moved to stand beside Edmund. "Any idea why your wife would want to have Mrs. Bennett killed?"

Almost imperceptibly, Edmund shook his head, his mouth slack. His pupils had shrunken to the size of pinpoints.

Jess began to fear for him.

Jake spoke quietly to the sheriff. "At the ranch, Miriam seemed emotionally volatile, perhaps mentally unstable."

"She was," Edmund murmured like a man coming out of an opium-induced stupor. "She always has been. Always. Though she's gotten worse in recent years."

"How long has she been this bad?" the sheriff asked.

"I don't know. Months? She went into a rage like I've never seen the night after—" He stopped himself and gazed apologetically at Jess. "The night after she saw you and Jake at the store."

Scribbling a note, the sheriff glanced at Jess. "What has been your relationship with Mrs. Van Dorn, Mrs. Bennett?"

Jess lifted a shoulder. "She was my mother's closest friend. She never cared much for my brother or me, but she seemed to adore my little sister, Emma."

"The girl who died in the fire," the sheriff said, his voice gruff yet his tone gentle. "I remember the investigation."

"Miriam, Jess's father, and I attended school together when we were young," Edmund said. "We've known each other all

311

our lives. Miriam's emotions were sometimes a little erratic, even as a child," he went on, trying to puzzle the matter out himself, "but I've been...concerned about her since Jake and Jess visited in June."

The sheriff's pencil scratched another note, and then he looked up from under his eyebrows at each of them. "Anything else unusual?"

Jess moved closer to Jake, wishing she could hold on to him and calm her quickening heartbeat. Something terrible was about to happen. She could feel it, like an immense hand steadily closing around her.

Edmund, pale yet dapper in his neatly pressed waistcoat and trousers, had dearly loved and lived for his wife all his days, yet he was an honorable man. "Jake and Jess asked me to contact Isaac Hale's attorney, since his assets and the income from his investments now legally belong to Jess and have for more than a year," he said helpfully. "I went to close his personal bank account to give the money to Jake and Jess, but the account had been emptied."

"At least ten thousand dollars," Jess said.

This piece of news kept the sheriff penciling notes until a few minutes had passed, and Edmund looked in want of something to do to occupy his thoughts until the sheriff finished.

For a moment, his face brightened a little, and he moved toward a closet. "Jess, when we returned home, I found that Ambrose's shipment had finally arrived from Kentucky. The man I hired to assist me at Hale Imports brought it over while we were visiting you," he said as he opened a closet door and pulled out a narrow crate that stood higher than his waist and was nearly as wide across as Edmund's arm span. "The front of the crate is a single piece nailed on. Jake, your knife should be able to pry off the front."

Jess moved nearer as the front was lifted away and the

brown paper-wrapped parcel was removed. Edmund set the empty crate beside the closet door, and Jake carefully propped the painting against the wall. Tiny birds fluttered joyously through Jess's insides. She understood fully now why Jake wanted a portrait painted of her. Though she had lost her mother, she had this picture of her, and it felt like she had received a part of her mother back to keep.

With trembling fingers, Jess tore the paper back from the gilt frame, then swept it over the top and to the sides, exposing the painting. Of all the treasures they had left behind in their Lexington home, this was one of the few that truly mattered to her. The portrait of her mother, Georgeanne McKinney Hale, was one of Jess's earliest memories, though she had no memories of her mother being as young as she appeared on the canvas. It had been painted, her mother had told her, as a wedding gift for Jess's father. In it, her mother looked to be a year or so younger than Jess was now. She wore a peach-hued gown a shade lighter than the blushing of her oval face, and her lush, curling, chestnut hair was draped over a shoulder as emerald eyes gazed tenderly toward the beholder.

"You look so much like her," Jake said huskily, and hugged her tightly to his side.

Edmund was still gazing at the painting when the sheriff glanced through his notes, then looked up with another question.

"Mr. Bennett, you said that the man Miriam hired was killed two days ago?"

"The ranch was attacked by men who intended to drive away the Paiutes who work for me," Jake explained. "Charlie—Shane Porter, rather—used the distraction to pull Jess out of sight. He drew his gun and aimed it at her, but one of my men saw and shot him first."

Jess noticed that Jake hadn't specified that an Indian had

shot Shane, a white man, and that the sheriff didn't ask, bless him. The Paiutes would not be troubled by an investigation.

A shrill screech pierced the air. Miriam braced her hands against the wall as she stumbled toward them, wearing a slate hoopskirt with a gaudy, low-cut bodice, her eyes wild as she gawked at the painting and then at Jess.

Immediately, Jake thrust Jess behind him. Jess stepped partway back. She needed to see Miriam, needed to hear firsthand from her why she'd tried to have her killed.

Miriam folded her tiny hands in front of her bosom and inched tentatively toward Jake, her gray eyes flooding with tears, as if she saw no one else in the room.

"Isaac, I hired a man to make Georgeanne go away, to make them all go away," she said softly, pleading.

Jess started forward, but Jake's arm held her back.

"Do you mean you hired Charlie to burn the Hales' house?" he asked her calmly.

Miriam's wrinkled mouth curved up hopefully. "Now it's just the two of us. We can be together." She reached for Jake's hands, but he avoided her touch. As if she'd been stung, Miriam pulled hers back and pressed them to her bosom. "I've seen the way you look at me. Georgeanne is gone. She was burned," Miriam said, growing angrier. "They all burned to death. You could have married me, but Charlie said you went into the house to save her. Why? You loved *me*! You loved me, and you wanted to be with me!"

Suddenly, her face snapped to Jess's, though Jess perceived that Miriam was seeing her mother, just as she'd seen Isaac in Jake.

"You don't know what it is to lose the man you love to another woman, to lose him forever. He was mine first." She lifted her tear-stained face to Jake and softened her expression. "I married Edmund only to make you jealous. And now, Rafael loves me, and I love him, and he's important, and he's going to give me everything I ever wanted, and we're going to be happy!"

From the edge of her vision, Jess saw Edmund staring at his wife in horror.

The feeling of imminent danger burned inside her like a sack of flaming gunpowder. In the hallway behind Miriam, Jess saw Doyle and Taggart creeping soundlessly forward.

Miriam backed away toward the hallway, reaching into her pocket, her demented stare fixed on Jess. "I knew Isaac for years before you moved next door and stole him from me. Now you'll know what it is to lose the man you love."

Time stopped as Jess watched her third premonition come to life.

Miriam's tiny hand gripping a gleaming Derringer arose from a field of blue—her slate-blue skirt. Beside Jess, Jake's face contorted in alarm and rage.

"No!" he shouted.

Edmund and Jake both moved—Edmund to trap Miriam's arms, and Jake to block Jess.

Jess screamed and pushed Jake aside.

The Derringer bucked as it fired a deafening round. Above her, Jake's eyes registered pain; then, he twisted and began to fall. To catch her.

Burning pain ripped through Jess's lower back and thigh. Jake's arms eased her to the floor, where she felt the prickle of the Turkish carpet's fibers against her cheek and palms; but then the prickling faded, and her face felt sweaty and cold. She heard a rush like champagne bubbles.

Somewhere, there was a vague, dragging sound and men's shouts, though Jess couldn't make out their words. Above it all rose Miriam's voice, sounding as if she were shrieking from far down the road. "You love me, Isaac Hale! Me! *Meeee!* Why would you try to save her again?"

Far closer, Jess heard Jake's gentle voice beside her ear, and felt the warmth of his hand on her wrist. "Because I love her," he murmured.

Then, darkness.

Jess leaned on Jake's arm as she paced the parlor floor, becoming accustomed to the tight wrapping around her hips and the sizzling pain through her right hip, which felt like she'd been speared through with a white-hot bayonet. The more she walked, the more aware she became, and her head continued to clear.

"Go slow, love," Jake cautioned her. "You fainted, and it'll take a bit to get your land legs back."

Jess smiled softly at his subtle humor, knowing he was trying to help her focus on something other than the horror of the evening, but still she was unable to let the events go. "Where did the sheriff take Miriam?"

Carefully, Jake turned her, and they started back to the other side of the small room. "To the jail beneath the courthouse. Edmund went with them."

"And Doyle and Taggart?"

"They're both fine. I'm sure that, by now, Taggart is reliving the encounter for the maids and enjoying their attentions. I got the feeling they didn't care too much for Miriam."

Poor Edmund, Jess mused. Miriam would almost certainly end up in an asylum for the insane, and Edmund would be left alone with a lifetime of his wife's fits of tempers and lies to ponder.

Jess felt some relief to finally know who had killed her parents and Emma, and why, though the reason was not like anything she had imagined or conjectured, and she was still in shock at the knowledge that her mother's most cherished friend had been responsible for her death. It was a small wonder Miriam had spent years as a dedicated presence at her mother's side—that's where her father had always been.

"At least now I have news to tell Ambrose," she said aloud. "That may be of some comfort to him."

"Ambrose sent you something else that you didn't see when you unwrapped the portrait." Jake stopped, supporting her with one hand, and pulled from his vest a cluster of tiny dried flowers of a faint purple hue.

Lilac blossoms from Mother's hedge at Greenbriar! They swam before her eyes due to the hot tears distorting her gaze, but she raised the flowers to her nose and inhaled their fragrance.

"The sheriff said he'll search for the man Miriam called Rafael," Jake said, and started walking her again.

To Jess, Jake's broad, cattleman's shoulders, flannel shirt, and brown hat atop his handsome head seemed completely incongruous with Miriam's formal parlor of dainty tea tables and lace doilies. But it was the tiny furnishings rather than Jake that seemed out of place to her. Jess wiped her eyes, already looking forward to being home.

"Given the circumstances," Jake continued, "the sheriff thinks it's possible that either Miriam or this Rafael knows something about what happened to your father's accounts."

"You mean that Miriam or Rafael, whoever he is, may have stashed away my father's savings, that we may still be able to locate the money and use it for the ranch?"

High above her, his hat dipped. "It surely won't be easy to find, but it may be possible."

They turned and started walking the other way, the pain in Jess's hip fierce. "When Payton shot that man at the corral," she said, "I thought we had circumvented the premonition. I'm so frustrated, Jake! I see these visions for only an instant—a flash of images—and I can't control them, or see more, or who, or tell when the events might take place. And I don't have these insights prior to every threat." Jess shoved loose hairs back from her face in vexation. "Why is this happening?"

Jake pressed her hand to the back of a settee, waited for her nod to be certain she had her balance, then crossed to the far corner, where a Bible was resting on a table. He flipped through the pages, frowning in concentration, then flipped a few more. "I've been giving that some thought, Jess," he said. "This is Romans twelve, verses six through eight: *'Having then gifts differing according to the grace that is given to us, whether prophecy, let us prophesy according to the proportion of faith; or ministry, let us wait on our ministering: or he that teacheth, on teaching; or he that exhorteth, on exhortation: he that giveth, let him do it with simplicity; he that ruleth, with diligence; he that showeth mercy, with cheerfulness.'"*

"You think my gift is prophecy?" she asked, incredulous. "Do you have any idea what this 'gift' feel like? It feels like a curse."

Jake set the Bible back on the table and rubbed his hands together. "Maybe not prophecy, exactly. The Almighty gave animals instincts—the instinct to gather extra food or build a thicker lodge or den when a long winter is coming, the instinct to fly south, and to sense danger. Occasionally, people have strong instincts, too. Perhaps the Almighty gave you something like that. He lets you know what's coming so that you can help someone else. Your premonition about the burned buildings at the ranch made seeing the destruction a little easier for both of us to bear. Your knowing about the clapboard house kept us alert, and we were able to get to Mattie and Grace before they were sold to a house of prostitution or underwent whatever ill those men had in mind. And, last year, your intuitions about Ambrose probably saved his life."

Jake stepped closer and cupped Jess's face in his big, warm hands. She smiled to see Jake's love for her in his face, and because she loved the rich, husky sound of his voice when he called God "the Almighty."

As if he'd heard her thoughts, he said the words again: "The Almighty helps everyone through tough times. Maybe this gift is His way of reminding you that He's with you, just like He reminded you with the basket you found and He repaired. When the Almighty gives you these insights, He's reminding you that He's helped you through tough times before, and that another tough time may be coming, but that He'll help you through that one, too. He doesn't have to reveal every trouble that's coming your way. Instead, He's chosen to give you occasional reminders that He's with you always. It's His promise, His way of giving you hope."

Jake paused with a contemplative look, then continued. "Like the Bible verses said, the Almighty gives every person a special gift, but He certainly didn't have room in that book to name them all." Jake brushed a kiss over her lips. "Whatever gift we each have, we've just got to do the most good with it that we can."

Jess stood up on her toes and met Jake's lips again. In her opinion, his mouth was one of the special gifts the good Lord had given Jake.

Jake smoothed a thumb over the soft skin beneath her ear. "Why are you smiling?"

She tilted her face coquettishly. "I was just thinking about what gift the Almighty might have given you."

"Horses."

She hadn't expected that response. "What?"

"My pa saw it in me when I was a boy. I come from five

generations of farmers—farmers and not ranchers—but Pa knew that I had a special touch with animals, and with horses in particular. He told me I had my own road to follow, and that I wouldn't be happy doing anything else. That's the gift the Almighty gave me, and I discovered it early on. You didn't discover yours until this past year, but now you know the gift He's given you, and I suspect that once you use it to help some folks, you'll never want to cast it aside again. Of course, the other gift He gave me is *you*."

Her heart was too full to say anything else, so she said simply, "I love you."

"I know. And I love you, too." Suddenly, a pained expression deepened the creases at the corners of his eyes as they dropped to her skirt, where it covered the bandage encircling her. "Jess…."

Whatever he wanted to say stuck in his throat, but she knew he must have spent several moments in the hallway believing she might have been shot through, and that he would have to bury another wife. "Jake, it burns fiercely, but you said yourself the bullet passed through just under the surface. *And* that I couldn't have gotten shot in a better place." She let her forehead fall against his chest and groaned. "If Taggart ever finds out I was shot in the rump, I'll never hear the end of it."

She felt Jake's shoulders twitch, but he was good enough not to chuckle out loud. "Shall we say it was your hip, then?" he asked, sounding at ease once again.

"That would be fine with me." Her own shoulders jerked, and she couldn't suppress reluctant laughter at her predicament. "Bennett, how am I going to ride home like this?"

After a moment's thought, he led her toward the door and pulled it open. "It's been a long time since you last rode with me."

Jess tossed him a sarcastically scathing glare at the reminder.

"Yes—that particular time, you bound me hand and foot like a yearling calf."

He braced his hands on the doorframes beside her and leaned in close, his whiskey-brown eyes fervent as he murmured a confession. "I was tempted to kiss you all the way home."

Jess lifted her arms and settled them around his neck. "If that's the way of things," she said with a smile, "then I believe I'll ride home with you."

Heavy rain danced atop the peaked ranch house roof, sounding like the applause of an audience, a sensation that filled Jess's heart as Jake hung the hammer over the back of the sofa and dusted his hands.

On the wall opposite the bright, whirling flames in the fireplace, Hank's painting of them now hung to the right of her mother's portrait.

Jake leaned against the sofa back and drew Jess into the sheltering circle of his arms. She smoothed her hands over his sleeves, marveling at the striking difference between the soft, flannel fabric and the hard curves of his muscles beneath it, and at the extremes in the man who loved her so tenderly, so completely, yet possessed the cunning and foresight to arrange for two Indian men to guard her and suffered cuts from lethal knives risking his life to protect hers, and not for the first time. Now her husband bore new scars. Jess had seen some women look delicately away from men's scars, fanning themselves and viewing the lines of ruined skin with abhorrence. To Jess, Jake's scars would always be physical reminders of his great love for her.

"What do you think of the painting?" Jake asked, nuzzling the soft place beneath her ear.

Jess tried to look at the portrait objectively but couldn't.

Beyond her blue calico dress that Jake liked and Jake's red flannel shirt, which she'd insisted he wear, Hank, with his artist's eyes, had seen each of them with perfect clarity. The painting pulsed with the love between them, their mutual commitment, and their hope for all the years to come. Jake's eyes were the same brown as the solid, enduring earth; Jess's were as green as the life that stems from it.

"It's perfect," she said.

Chapter Twenty

As a cold, November wind buffeted the Sierra Nevada Mountains, Jess nestled her tingling cheeks and nose into the cozy warmth of her sheepskin coat, and Jake pulled her closer against him, adding his heat to her own. Beneath the hillside where they stood, the ranch was abuzz with ranch hands tending horses and cattle or chopping and stacking the firewood they'd carted down from the mountains. Behind the cookhouse, Ho Chen and Lily fed the chickens, and in front of the barn, little Grace and Mattie, dressed in frocks made from Gusty's fabric remnants and draped with the long blankets Jess had woven for them, giggled and spun in circles. In the recently completed stable, simple but sufficient, round-bellied mares rested and feasted on hay—the beginning of the ranch's future.

Beyond the ranch, a dense, wintry fog, the likes of which Jess had never seen, enclosed the mountains and obscured all view of Honey Lake Valley, stirring like ocean foam and lifting in the pull of the fresh wind.

"The Paiutes and Shoshone call this fog *pogonip*," Jake said. "It means 'white death.' They believe the *pogonip* causes pneumonia."

"The deer hides we brought back from the Sierras will go a long way in keeping everyone warm," Jess said.

"That they will," Jake agreed, "and we've put by plenty of wood. No one knows better than Paiutes and cattlemen how to get through a long winter."

The thick fog, like snowflakes suspended in the air, looked

beautiful to Jess. After summers of drought, it brought the promise of snow that, come spring, would melt to fill the rivers and grow so much grass across Honey Lake Valley that the animals would grow fat from it.

Jess thought of her mother's portrait in the ranch house below and, for the first time since she'd lost her family, felt peace like a silent door closing on the unknowns that had tormented her for so long.

Still, she worried for the ranch, since her father's savings, which she and Jake would need to keep things going in the coming year, was mysteriously gone. If snows came, the animals would have grass, yes, but not enough acreage of it to feed them all for an entire year, and she and Jake would have to pay and feed the cattlemen and other workers. She also worried that they had not learned anything more about who was continuing to target transplanted Southerners, or who else was trying to drive out the Paiutes. But she felt hope that, with the Lord by their sides, and with the assistance of good people like Hank and the cattlemen, they would stop these wrongs and bring peace to their homes.

Hugging Jake's arms more tightly around her, Jess smiled softly. Perhaps the Lord would even help her to know more details through occasional premonitions or instincts. As Jake had said, He'd helped them through each of their past troubles, and she was certain He would always help them through troubles to come.

Jess's heart swelled with hope for another reason, and she moved Jake's hand beneath her coat to rest against her stomach.

"Jake," she murmured, "we're going to have a baby."

Those who hope in the Lord *will renew their strength.*
They will soar on wings like eagles;
they will run and not grow weary,
they will walk and not be faint.
—Isaiah 40:31 (NIV)

Coming Soon:
FAITH'S REWARD
Book Three in The Sierra Chronicles
By Tammy Barley

Chapter One

January 1865
Honey Lake Valley, Northern California

J ake?"
Jessica Bennett jolted upright in bed, her hand trembling as it searched the cold sheets in the darkness beside her. Her fingers brushed Jake's equally cold pillow, then the soft fur of the cat that huddled on it, the only trace of warmth in the place where her husband had gone to sleep beside her. *"Jake?"*

Wind rattled the windowpane with nearly enough force to crack it. The wintry cold had seeped through the glass and turned the bedroom to ice. Jess hugged her flannel nightgown firmly to her and sat still and alert, straining to hear over the storm for any indication of movement in the house, either upstairs or downstairs. She heard no thud of boot heels on the plank floor, no jingle of spurs, to suggest any presence inside the house but hers.

Judging by the thick darkness, dawn was still hours away. Though she and Jake had worked until sometime after midnight, until they were both exhausted, he must have rested in bed until she had fallen asleep, but no longer than that. Once he had been certain she and the baby within her were at rest, he must have gone back to work and joined the next shift of cattlemen who fought to keep their horses and cattle alive, digging them out of the snow and providing hay to stimulate their bodies' heat.

The misty darkness abruptly grew darker, closing in around her.

Then, blackness.

An image flashed through her mind—she stood in boot-deep snow under a gray sky, a Henry rifle gripped in her hands. At her sides stood two of the cattlemen. More than a dozen Paiute Indian men stepped forward to stand alongside them. She recognized one Paiute who worked at the ranch. The others were strangers. Their faces revealed fear, and resolve. In front of her, perhaps five paces away, stood thirty or more renegade white men who, as one, reached their hands to their holsters, drew their guns, then took aim at Jess and the Indians. Jess cocked the Henry rifle, pressed the butt to her shoulder, and sighted down the barrel at the cold, glittering blue eyes of the man who aimed the bore of his revolver at her. Though fear burned like liquid fire beneath her skin, she firmed her grip, shifted her index finger from the rifle's trigger guard to the curve of the metal trigger. And pulled.

An explosion rocked Jess, tearing her back to the present. Shaken, she waited for the effects of the premonition to ebb, and focused on palpable images as they came to her: her pulse, pounding like rapid drumbeats just beneath her ears. Her breath, passing though her parted lips in deep gasps, drying her throat. She swallowed. A chill permeated her flannel nightgown. The scent of forest that clung to the pine log walls filled the bedroom. The storm…. A second explosion!—no, not an explosion. It was the windowpane, pounded by the wind. Something trickled down her temples, rolled onto her cheeks. Startled, she swiped at it with her fingers. Dampness. Sweat. Nothing more. Sweat misted her forehead as well. She dried it with her sleeve and forced her breathing to calm.

Jess felt beside her, then remembered. Jake wasn't here. He hadn't gone to sleep the night before.

In one movement, she flung the covers aside and reached

toward the end of the bed for the union suit she had purchased two months before, shortly after she'd realized she was expecting a child. Leaving her flannel nightgown and stockings on, she stuffed her feet into the woolen legs of the union suit then stood and buttoned it up to her neck, using her thumbs and fingertips to feel the buttonholes and shove the buttons through. Jess hurried to the pegs on the wall near the window and felt for one of Jake's flannel shirts. Her hand brushed one, then a pair of his trousers. Frustrated with not being able to see, she grabbed both garments and flung them onto the bed then rounded it to Jake's side, where she felt along the surface of the tall chest of drawers until her hands connected with the oil lantern they kept there and the matchbox. After three strikes, a flame flared to life, and she lit the lantern then replaced the chimney with a glass-on-metal *clink*.

Winter buffeted the window once again. Jess ignored it. Moments later, dressed and belted, she slid her feet into her cowboy boots, then stuffed the extra fourteen or fifteen inches of Jake's pant legs into the boot tops. Just as rapidly, she plaited her hip-length brown hair and secured the bottom with a leather thong.

She grabbed up the lantern, threw open the bedroom door—the place where she first saw her tall, handsome Jake standing when she was brought to the ranch, she recalled with a sudden lightness in her heart—then hurried out onto the landing and down the stairs, her boots and the steps gilded by a wide ring of golden lantern light.

The fire in the hearth had burned down and gave off little heat. Jess set the lantern on the mantel and pulled her weighty sheepskin coat from its peg near the front door, then tugged it on, followed by her woolen hat, scarf, and gloves.

The premonition had shaken her more than the other few she'd experienced before it, but what truly unnerved her was the certainty that had woken her—something had happened to Jake.

Jess lifted the iron latch that served as a door handle. The front door blew in and struck her in the chest. Resisting the wind, she held tightly to the door as she stepped out onto the covered porch and pulled the door closed, straining against the force of the gales.

On the porch she huddled deeper into her coat, thankful it hung to her knees. Squinting against the wind, she scanned the ranch yard and glimpsed dots of orange that flickered ahead of her and to both sides, lit torches that were barely visible through the snowflakes being driven through the night and against her cheeks and chin. Most of the torches appeared to congregate near the smithy, ahead of her and to the left.

Jess descended the two porch steps and moved toward the smithy, leaning into the wind. Her nostrils stuck closed, and she was forced to breathe through her mouth. If Jake had walked in this direction and broken a path through the drifts, she was unable to distinguish his tracks in the blackness. Already her toes and fingers tingled in sharp pain as if rubbed by frost.

One of the orange torches blew out. A moment later, another torch relit it. The man who held the relit torch shifted the flame away from the others, toward the ground. Its fire burst to nearly thrice its size, then gradually settled back to its original mass. The men must be using kerosene to keep them lit. On the wind, the faint smell of smoke drifted to her.

She pushed on and lifted one booted foot after the other over the snow as she forced her straining muscles to move as quickly as she could make them go, feeling oddly off-balance due to her inability to see.

A torch broke away from the others and wended its way in her direction, no doubt carried by someone bringing hay for animals to eat so they could produce their own warmth. She and Jake had done the same, beginning late the previous afternoon when the storm had given its first whispers of the violence to come, and continuing until midnight, scattering hay about the ranch's main compound. But now the snows made foraging impossible. The men who gathered near the smithy must have found another way to protect the animals.

The light of the single torch grew brighter and nearer, and she altered her path to move toward it. Orange light revealed Taggart's surprised, round face as his eyes met hers, his hairy eyebrows, mustache, and beard frozen white with ice and snow.

Jess leaned close to his ear and shouted over the storm. "Have you seen Jake?"

"He's tendin' the fireplaces in the buildings!" he yelled back and jerked a wool-clad thumb over his beefy shoulder. His fingers held a coiled lasso. "He told the men to string a rope corral from the smithy to the cookhouse to the bunkhouse, and back to the smithy. We're searchin' for the beasts and bringin' them over, hopin' the heat from the buildings will keep the critters from freezing."

"By 'beasts' do you mean the horses?"

Taggart shifted the torch, apparently in mild impatience to be under way. "No, the cattle."

Jess's eyes searched the darkness and found a distant square of light emanating from the cookhouse window. Jake must be warm near the fires, or at least he remained so while inside, between jaunts from one building to the next in the deathly cold. Still, she couldn't throw off the conviction that something was horribly wrong. "What about the horses? Without them, we'll lose the ranch!"

"Jess, there's no time for explainin', though the boss knows about the horses," he assured her above the scream of the wind. "He ordered us to wrangle the horses to the barn and stable."

Jess nodded and held a glove over her nose, wishing she had a way to warm her face.

"Ye should be sleepin'," Taggart chastised her, "but since ye're here, we need ye." He took her arm and turned her to face the outskirts of the ranch. "We're able to drive the horses—a couple of the boys are on horseback doin' just that—but the cows are the problem. They turned their backsides to the wind and lowered their heads to stay warm, but the snow is coverin' them, and their breath and body heat have turned the snow into a casing of ice around them. They're suffocatin'. Come on!"

Within her, Jess's stomach sank in dread. She kept up with Taggart, step for step. They wended their way east past the ranch house and toward the Paiute village in the same manner he had approached her, occasionally changing direction from left to right as they continued forward, searching for cattle trapped in ice.

"Ye see? There!" Taggart held out the torch and headed toward a large mound half buried in a drift. The beast moaned, a pathetic plea that was nearly swallowed by the howl of the storm.

Jess thought the cow was merely covered in snow, but as she neared and touched its side, her glove stuck to ice.

Taggart kicked low to break the ice, again, then again, until it gave way with a dull crunch. The cow, with its first full breath, gave a loud bawl.

Desperate to help, Jess rounded the animal and kicked from the other side. Her toes stung unbearably with each blow, so she turned her boot and kicked with her heel. The frozen casing gave way.

Taggart secured the lasso around the cow's neck and rapidly pushed off the rest of the snow. "Can ye take her to the rope corral, Jess, then come find me again? With two of us working together, one can break the cows free and the other can lead them to the buildings."

Immediately, Jess took the end of the lasso from him. "If you wander too far, I won't be able to see your torch."

"Ye will. The wind's still a fury, but the snows are dyin' down. See?"

Jess realized he was right, though she was still forced to squint. *Thank You, God, that the snows are dying.* "I'll hurry back."

She had to pull to encourage the cow to move, and had to keep pulling against its wont to stop and hunker down. At the rope corral, she exchanged brief nods with the ranchmen there, and lifted the looped end of a rope from an iron post to lead the cow through to join the others. Jake's idea was working. The cow nosed its way into the warm press of livestock and lowered its head to eat from one of the bales of hay. Though she paused to scan the open spaces between the buildings for Jake, she didn't see him.

For the next several hours until sunrise, Jess helped the men rescue cows mired belly-deep in the snow, pausing only to gulp hot coffee kept in constant supply by the Chinese ranch cook and her longtime friend, Ho Chen.

Gradually, the snow had slowed until it resembled falling dust, but it wasn't until dawn, while she led yet another cow into the corral, that she finally saw Jake. He was making his way toward the ranch house, hunched over, coughing uncontrollably, and was supported by two of the cattlemen, Seth and Lee.

The last of Jess's strength bled from her. Jake had passed between extreme heat and cold, into hot buildings and out into the frigid storm, all night. She knew what such extremes did to miners who descended shafts to work in the hot steam more than two thousand feet beneath the surface of the Comstock, then later emerged up into arctic gales. Countless numbers of the miners died. From pneumonia.

"Lord Almighty," she breathed, and ran toward the house. *Never again,* she promised God, *never again will I doubt the instincts You gave me, if only You will let Jake live.*

About the Author

Tammy Barley's roots run deep and wide across the United States. With Cherokee heritage and such ancestors as James Butler "Wild Bill" Hickok, Ralph Waldo Emerson, and Henry David Thoreau, she essentially inherited her literary vocation and her preferred setting: the Wild West. An avid equestrian, Tammy has ridden horseback over Western mountains and rugged trails in Arizona. Tammy excelled in her writing studies at a local college, where she explored prose, novel writing, and nonverbal communication. She even enrolled in acting classes to master character development.

In 2006, she published two series of devotionals in *Beautiful Feet: Meditations for Missionary Women* for the Lutheran Women's Missionary Society. She won second place in the Golden Rose Contest in the category of inspiration romance, and she serves as a judge for various fiction contests. In addition to writing, Tammy makes a career of editing manuscripts, ghostwriting, and mentoring other writers. She also homeschools three children. Tammy has lived in twenty-eight towns in eight different states, but the family currently makes its home in Crystal Lake, Illinois.

Lassos-N-Lace Newsletter

Enjoy the latest from author Tammy Barley,
delivered right to your e-mail inbox! In addition
to receiving special giveaways and surprise
goodies available *only* to newsletter
subscribers, be the first to be notified of
new releases, book giveaways, contest news,
appearances, media events, and more!

Lassos-N-Lace Newsletter
Always something new.
Always inspiring.
Always great with chocolate.

To subscribe, simply visit
http://www.tammybarley.com
and look for the yellow Subscribe box.

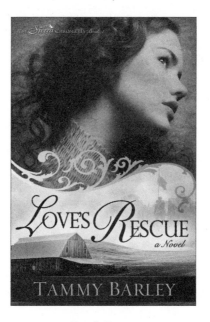

Love's Rescue
Tammy Barley

To escape the Civil War, Jessica Hale flees Kentucky with her family and heads to the Nevada Territory, only to lose them in a fire set by Unionists resentful of their Southern roots. The sole survivor, Jess is "kidnapped" by cattleman Jake Bennett and taken to his ranch in the Sierra Nevada wilderness. Angry at Jake for not saving her family, she makes numerous attempts to escape and return to Carson City, but she is apprehended each time. Why are Jake and his ranch hands determined to keep her there? She ponders this, wondering what God will bring out of her pain and loss.

ISBN: 978-1-60374-108-8 • Trade • 368 pages

WHITAKER
HOUSE